SANDMAN

Also by Richard Martins

THE CINCH

SANDMAN

Richard Martins

Atheneum • New York • 1990

Atheneum
Macmillan Publishing Company
866 Third Avenue, New York, NY 10022
Collier Macmillan Canada, Inc.

Library of Congress Cataloging-in-Publication Data
Martins, Richard.
Sandman / Richard Martins.
p.   cm.
ISBN 0-689-12095-8
I. Title.
PS3563.A7345S26 1990
813'.54—dc20   89-38127   CIP

10 9 8 7 6 5 4 3 2 1

Printed in the United States of America

For ANNA GUIDA MARTINS,
my mother

SANDMAN

. . . a building finally creeps into view at the end of the motor-way. It is flat, gray, graceless; even in the rare March sunlight it seems to ingest light, to consume it so that not one pane of soot-streaked glass gives off a glimmer of reflection or warmth. To anyone but the boy, it would appear forbidding, even hostile. But he is too excited to sense its grimness. He leans over Harry's shoulder to peer through the windshield at the yellow vans swarming the terminal, to ask about the flagpoles stuck like birthday candles into its stark facade. Harry begins a quick identification for him: the white Swiss cross, Canada's maple leaf, the French and Dutch tricolors—one up and down, the other sideways. The boy edges forward, anxious to get there and soon to be flying home.

Harry pulls the Rolls-Royce saloon car into an empty slip alongside the terminal. Two large, dark men come outside and stand by the trunk; Harry gives them directions for the luggage in a soft voice. Even in the loose-fitting chauffeur's suit, his thick arms and shoulders are clearly defined as they press against the black cloth; he is taller and stronger than the baggage handlers, than the boy's father, than most men the boy knows—perhaps the reason Harry never has to speak loudly to be heard and obeyed. But he is gentle, too, always ready for a game, and in this place where everyone insists on calling the boy Miles, Harry still calls him Mickey, which is what his grandfather does too, and which the boy likes much, much more.

Mickey grabs his carry-bag and beats Harry's huge hand to the door handle. He is impatient now, eager to get on board, anxious to hear the roar of the engines and feel the seat-pinning thrust of takeoff—then the liberal ration of sodas and peanuts and snacks that his mother and Harry permit him whenever, like today, his father is delayed at the last minute and has to settle for a later plane.

There is a queue even for the first-class passengers, Harry tells his mother impatiently. He will tend to the baggage and deposit the Rolls at the car park while they wait to check in. Mickey sings a wordless nonsense song as he follows his mother inside the terminal, dragging his carry-bag along the floor, trying to envision the face of the woman with the singsong voice who is calling out places like Bombay and Bahrain and Abu Dhabi, all millions of miles away.

Their line moves forward a few feet at a time. His mother grips Mickey's shoulder softly, reminding him to move his bag. He lifts it by a single handle, tipping it sideways. A Kit-Kat bar and some pencils fall out, and the thin wrapping paper tears apart. Before he can gather his things together, a blue-uniformed policeman is standing over him, examining the stock of fine English walnut.

His mother laughs softly, then tells the policeman her name and the name of their company, which is what Father always does when meeting someone important or bothersome. It's only a souvenir, she says, purchased at Windsor or Warwick or one of those castles. It's a toy.

The policeman holds the muzzle of his own weapon snugly against his hip as he takes Mickey's newest most-prized possession from the bag and plucks hard at the bowstring, testing its tension and strength, speaking over Mickey's head as if the bag wasn't even his, saying sternly that it appears to be in fine working order and therefore is a problem. The boy can hear the impatience in his mother's reply. It is a *toy* crossbow, for heaven's sake. Besides, they're fresh out of arrows.

A man behind them mutters that the policeman is being bloody ridiculous, but his intrusion only seems to harden the officer's resolve. The airline classifies crossbows as weapons, he says, so this one will have to go as baggage or be stowed in the crew's locker, even if the thought of a seven-year-old's souvenir being used to hijack an airplane seems ridiculous to some.

The muttering man behind them volunteers to keep an eye on things as Mickey's mother agrees to follow the policeman to the baggage service counter. She'll be right back, she assures her son, no doubt with his souvenir in hand. Seeing the policeman striding off with a machine pistol in one hand and the crossbow in the other, the man mumbles "bloody ridiculous" again and pats the crown of Mickey's head. Had Harry been there, the boy is sure, no one would ever think of taking his crossbow away.

He watches his mother disappear inside an office. Then, at the far end of the concourse, two men come running through the glass doors that lead to the departure gates. Running fast, as if racing to a plane seconds before it locks its doors. Both of them wear loose white pants and white shirts; they look like baseball players who have lost their caps rounding second. That's it, Mickey decides. Crazy guys playing bases tag in an airport. They have bats and balls in their hands, too. But even at a far distance, Mickey sees that the bats look funny, with dark handles shaped like his crossbow's. And the balls have been used so much they are stained as dark green as grass.

Suddenly, from the opposite end of the terminal, he hears explosions as loud as fireworks. The man behind him lets out a terrible cry and tries to grab his shoulder, but Mickey steps away quickly as he sees a baseball thrown toward him. He leaps forward to field it on the short hop, body squarely in front of the ball, just as Harry had shown him.

Curses of rage and cries of agony pierce the horrific rattle of automatic weapons fire, too late to warn him. As Mickey stretches to catch it, the grenade explodes in a flash of searing orange light . . .

God has never made any man
with two hearts inside him.
The Koran
(Surah 33, Al-Ahzab)

Chapter 1

Hallet spotted the black sedan as he swerved off a traffic-snarled Lake Shore Drive and sped westward toward the Midway Plaisance. A Ford, maybe a Chevy, gaining on him steadily; inside it, two men wearing suits and ties, dressed as Westerners instead of Arabs, trying to fool him to protect their identities and their mission—to stop him before he could get to Sandman.

A drenching sweat soaked Hallet's once-white shirt, fogged his sunglasses. He tossed the glasses aside and squinted into the glaring sunset that streamed over the treeless plain of the Midway. Sun blind, sinking, the shaking came again; fear fighting resolve inside him, winning. He tried to focus on the task he'd sworn to complete, to will his mind free of its demons, its ghosts.

The sedan pulled closer. Hallet braked into a left-hand skid that pointed his nose toward the entrance to Jackson Park— with its sharp curves and sudden cutoffs, a good place to shake his pursuers. That's what they'd think, anyway, Hallet guessed. So, inches before the dividing island took away his option, he veered hard right and began careening down the Midway toward the university campus. Seeing the sedan had missed the turn, he let out a roaring victory cry that was premature, for the car chasing him spun straight into the teeth of oncoming traffic and again began climbing his tail.

Heart banging, stomach muscles clenching, Hallet swallowed a sour breath and fought back the bubbling sickness that rose in his throat. With what seemed like the last of his strength, he pulled the steering wheel hard right again, bounced over the curb and across the newly mown esplanade grass, lopping sixty degrees off the ninety that formed the intersection with Woodlawn Avenue. That gave him an edge, put a good fifty yards between his car and the sedan—enough time to get back to the mansion and, before they could capture him, to stop the killing by destroying Sandman.

Finally, the Institute. Hallet skidded down the driveway that curved behind the mansion. The sedan held course behind him, flashers glimmering like orange sunspots in his mirror. He smashed through the wooden barrier at the card gate that Bryce Vreeland had installed to block students and locals from using the private lot, then tried to push his way into what looked like an open space between two parked cars. Instead, he shaved off large slivers of chrome trim and a pair of side mirrors. Realizing he was trapped, Hallet gunned the engine again, tore a front fender from the body, and slammed into the back of the mansion just inches from the rear entrance he was desperately trying to reach.

Stunned, bleeding from a gash above his right eyebrow, Hallet ran past the gaping faces of the startled programmers and technicians who worked the evening shift. He would get to the mainframe somehow, and somehow purge every shred of data that, openly or secretly, he had ever programmed into it. Damn it, they could have him then. Or what was left of him. Which, after Sandman, would be nothing at all.

Without the current day's access code, Hallet pounded on the locked steel door of the computer room until his hands went numb and his fingers swelled. As he slumped to the floor, exhausted, resigned to defeat and surrender, he heard someone screaming, then laughing outrageously until the laughter broke down into a wail of sobs and tears.

Hallet mercifully blacked out when he realized he was hearing himself.

"At least we're the ones who found him for you," one agent said as Macdonald Clelland covered Hallet with a wool plaid game blanket and helped Bryce Vreeland lift him onto a makeshift cot in the EDP lounge. "Only it didn't work out quite the way we thought."

"Yeah, good thing the locals didn't get their hands on him," said his partner. "Looks like he's on a right mighty bender. Three days at least."

"Five, actually," said Vreeland. His voice was flat, but the ring of contempt crept through it nonetheless.

Clelland, the Institute's executive director, shook his head in distress as he stood over his colleague. "I want to thank you both sincerely. For all your efforts and, I'm certain, your discretion. Agents . . . ?"

"Rourke."

"I'm Williams," said his partner.

"At least you chased him home," Vreeland conceded.

"More like he led us," said Williams.

"One helluva chase it was, too," said Rourke. "If he could drive that way sober, we'd hire him to teach pursuit tactics at Quantico."

"Well, thank you again," Clelland said curtly.

"For whatever," said Rourke, looking at Williams and realizing no further explanation would be forthcoming. "Hope he'll be okay."

"I'm sure he will." Clelland shook both their hands and watched them away before turning back to Vreeland. "You'd best place that phone call now," he told his deputy. "And make sure everyone who saw this is instructed to keep quiet. Get them together and administer a large dose of milk of amnesia."

"Straightaway." Vreeland motioned the staff into the conference room and dialed his call as they filed inside it. "We've found our missing man. Hallet, Philip James. That's right, you pronounce the t. Age forty-two," Vreeland said, losing patience with the admitting clerk's questions about the state of Hallet's health and his need for isolation and detox. "Madam, I'm his employer, not his physician. But I'd certainly call it acute intoxication. Yes, as soon as possible."

Clelland knelt over Hallet on both knees, like a priest, and tucked the blanket snugly under his chin. Hallet made a moaning, gurgling sound and lapsed back into unfocused semiconsciousness.

"Damn son-of-a-bitch," Clelland swore. "Do you really hate it that much?"

The first days of Hallet's confinement at the Methodist-sponsored clinic in Oak Park went smoothly enough. His initial sense of outrage and the deep depression that alternated with it had passed. Within a week, his body began to rebound and, even if recent events were sketchy (a diagnosis of incipient Korsakoff Syndrome was considered and rejected as Hallet's all too capacious memory began to reassert itself), his thoughts seemed to flow in a sane, gentle motion.

He slipped easily into the clinic's impersonal, first-name-only regimen: daily blood workups and urine samples on demand; stinging, milky white injections of thiamine-rich vitamin B-complex; then, after group therapy sessions with a dozen sad and sobbing substance abusers, long, body-stiffening hours in the gym and on the sweat-stained running track until, gratefully, he received the evening's ration of chlordiazepoxide, which made his mattress feel softer and gave his sterile beige cell a larger, more salutary look.

Time grew soft. Macdonald Clelland, Bryce Vreeland, even

Isabel Ortega and her compulsion for forgiveness began to fade from his dreams. He no longer could remember the faces of the two boys hanged just short months earlier in a public square in Baghdad. He was no longer a man torn in two.

There were no Prophets.

There was no Sandman.

If only the forlorn apostles had not tried to save him with psalms, the abandon-ship klaxon might never have sounded inside Hallet's head. No, he decided after their visit, it wasn't their message, not the call to the Cross that drove him to escape. It was just the simple squalid sadness of the pair who tried to deliver it.

The evening had been tough enough on all counts: Hallet's appetite had suddenly vanished, his ration of tranquilizers had grown steadily ineffectual as the dosage was decreased, the gin-smells of juniper and rosewater again filled his nostrils like the phantom pain of an amputee's missing limb. Even the tape of Mozart's Divertimentos that Stan Bach, dear friend, had smuggled into him with his clothing and a cassette player sounded dull and dissonant when Hallet allowed Pam and Jerry to enter his room.

Jerry was a tall, gangly lay preacher with an acne-scarred complexion and a head of loose, oily curls. Pam wasn't nearly as plain as she presented herself in an oversized brown cardigan, her fine auburn hair pulled back into a matronly bun severe enough to give her watery blue eyes a painful squint.

Jerry produced his Bible and began to speak of the curative powers of faith. Turning the pages, his hands looked as soft and white as poached eggs.

"Without alcohol, you'll face a tremendous void in your life," Jerry said. "To stay sober, you'll have to fill that void with something positive, something constructive. With God's love, if you'll open your heart to Him."

Pam fixed her exhausted eyes on Hallet and began to nod slowly, as if mesmerized by a distant, subliminal chant. Hallet spoke only to her.

"You were on my side of the bed once," Hallet said.

Jerry paused, bouncing his eyes off both of them. Then he said, "She has suffered too, as have all of us who come here. As Jesus did to cleanse away our sins."

Pam silently hiked the cardigan sleeve up her meager arm. Hallet saw the mutilation of the needle tracks and the jagged, still-pink scar that traversed her left wrist.

"We send you no apostles who have not walked in the market-place," Hallet said.

Jerry threw him a quizzical look.

"It's from the Koran," Hallet explained automatically. "A prayer from an ancient Aramaic text that also appears in the Hebrew Kaddish."

"Amen," Pam mumbled, barely audibly.

Hallet saw that Jerry still looked puzzled. "It's how I make my living," he said.

"You're a Christian?" Jerry asked, as if he had misread Hallet's dossier and needed to verify it.

Hallet replied with a vague nod.

Jerry reflexively opened his Bible to the ribbon-marked passages from Jeremiah. Hallet was about to veto the reading summarily when Pam, sensing his withdrawal, reached out to him, her skeletal fingers almost fondling his patient's bracelet.

"The Lord is my strength and my song," she whispered. "He is also my salvation."

Hallet shut up and allowed them their thirty minutes. Jerry seemed to exude a sense of accomplishment when his reading was over. He left Hallet the Bible, said they would visit him again. Pam tried to manage a smile but failed to bring it off. Hallet knew the look all too well, from the thousand souks and kasbahs he had visited as a traveling salesman of dreams, and a thousand avenues which led the addict nowhere.

Hallet fell back on his bed, taking stock of the situation. After his first shaky days in the clinic, he'd begun to relish his sudden solitude, so much so that he now dreaded the approaching weekend, when visitors would be permitted. In fact, for the first time since his return and reassimilation to the West, he felt a degree of peace. But a lingering voice he could not silence inside him called out like a muezzin chanting the azan from a nearby minaret.

So he flushed the night's Dalmane capsule down the commode, found the blue jogging suit that had come with the mandatory physical therapy program, and put it on over his street clothes. The floor nurse seemed pleased when Hallet told her that a good run would be far more therapeutic than a sleeping pill. Twice around the grounds before lights-out should do it, he said, except that when he reached the darkened delivery gate, Hallet climbed it easily and turned eastward, running toward the city as if running for his life.

It was eleven o'clock by the time Hallet arrived at Fairweather's saloon on Rush Street. He'd flagged a Chicago taxi at the Oak Park border, ditched the sweaty running clothes in the rear seat. Val, the night bar manager, advanced Hallet his cab fare and an extra hundred in cash. He also noted his damp shirt and rumpled trousers.

"What the hell you been up to?" Val asked. "Somebody's boyfriend get home early and chase you down a fire escape?"

Hallet loved the simplicity, the naiveté of the question. Fairweather's, for him, was a wonderful bit of cultural apartheid— a place where he could escape the professionally inquisitive sherry-sippers from the Institute and its university neighbors, where the regulars didn't watch public television or belong to the Council on Foreign Relations and, consequently, weren't interested in Hallet's views on Middle East crises or infrastructure construction, let alone what he was currently writing or most recently had published. Fast money and good times were the operative interests on Fairweather's strip of Rush Street. As was big bucks sports gambling, until an FBI undercover operation had closed the place for thirty days after snagging Sonny

Greco, its resident bookmaker, and a half-dozen regular players. Luckily, neither Val nor Maurice, the dapper South Side hustler who alone among the patrons had recognized Hallet from his television appearances and enlisted his help in trying to learn some fundamental Arabic, had made the FBI's arrest list. For which Hallet and all of Fairweather's patrons were especially grateful.

"That it? Girl trouble?" Val asked again, a tinge of concern coming through his Back-of-the-Yards accent. "Or you got yourself a real problem?"

Hallet forced a smile. "As you guessed. A hasty exit after an auspicious beginning."

"Yeah, broads," Val shrugged as he began to pour Hallet's usual bucket of gin.

"Just club soda."

Val, the true professional, showed no overt reaction. "You got it," he said, drawing a circled "X" on the back of Hallet's bar check, marking it on the house.

Hallet sipped the vapid liquid, squeezed a lime wedge hard into it to lend a hint of taste. He would do what had to be done to survive, but, as always, he'd do it on his own schedule. And if Macdonald Clelland didn't like it, Hallet would tell him and Bryce Vreeland and the whole damn bunch of them that they could try putting Humpty Dumpty back together without him when pieces of the eggshell were spread over two dozen cities and campuses, not to mention an entire, hostile subcontinent.

It was just after midnight when Hallet, still drinking soda water and trembling openly, realized he had nothing left to do but call Isabel Ortega. Val, who had kept a close eye on him as the late-night thrashers and revelers began to assemble, seemed relieved when Hallet asked for the bar phone.

"Philip! Damn it! What's next with you?" Isabel Ortega's voice showed concern, anger, both inside an instant.

It hadn't taken them long to discover he was missing and alert the troops, Hallet figured. He could see Isabel's wild Castilian eyes firing up their emerald glower.

"You've heard from Clelland?"

"Mac's in Washington. But Bryce Vreeland called, wondering if I knew where you were. I barely catch my breath when Stan Bach comes on the other line, saying you disappeared from the clinic. Why? Would you tell me why?"

"Just because Clelland thinks I'm a drunk doesn't make it so."

"Philip, you've been drinking almost constantly for weeks. We're all of us worried about you. It's dangerous."

If she only knew, thought Hallet. If any of them did.

"It wasn't working for me," he said.

"What wasn't?"

"The clinic, is what."

"You wouldn't let it work. That's the problem."

"Let what? Group therapy sessions with a bunch of kids who blame Mommy and Daddy for all their problems? And a shrink who wants to hug you when the hour's over? How about throwing in two ex-junkies who think faith healing is the surest way to recovery? No, thank you, darling. I'm not ready to climb AA's twelve magic steps to recovery, which together take religion more seriously than a cloister full of Carmelites. I've seen enough religious fanaticism to last a lifetime. And compared to the patients on Clelland's magic mountain in Oak Park, I'd be better off staying drunk."

"That's what you're doing now, isn't it? Having one or two just to take the edge off?"

"I'm not drinking," Hallet protested.

"Then where are you?"

"At a place no one knows about. Someplace where they leave me alone."

Hallet figured Isabel couldn't keep up the pressure much longer. He knew he was right when she spoke again.

"I'm just glad you're all right," she said. "I'll let Stan know too, tell him he can go home. He's been out scouring the taverns around the Institute since Vreeland called."

"Stan? Our leading Talmudic scholar running around South

Side saloons, probably wearing tallith and tefilin while he sips blended margaritas? Maybe you should call out the militia to rescue *him*."

"Stop wisecracking!" Isabel railed. "Stan's your best friend and he's trying to help you. Help him, and me too, will you? Call Vreeland, tell him you're going back to the clinic."

"I'm not ready for Mac Clelland yet, least of all for Bryce Vreeland," Hallet said. At least Mac was a rational and caring being, while Vreeland was nothing more than Jason Kellaigh's toady and a general prick in the process.

"I need some time to shape things up on my own. I need to disappear."

"Please, Philip," Isabel implored him. "Go home now. Or wait where you are and I'll come collect you. We'll talk it through, and I'll deal with Mac for the time being. I can reach him at the Hay-Adams, tell him you're reconsidering your treatment."

"No way," Hallet insisted. "You can tell Mac that you've heard from me, that I'm fine. But not where I am. I'm not going home, and I'm certainly not going back to Oak Park."

"Then where?"

"I'm not sure yet."

"Stay here," Isabel volunteered, as Hallet had guessed she would. "You can stay with me. Consider it the perfect compromise, politically and otherwise."

"I'll think it over," Hallet said, knowing his options were limited.

"Philip . . ."

"Half an hour. I'll call you back."

Hallet saw his hand shaking as he handed Val the receiver.

"Another club soda?"

"No, I've about had it with kidney dialysis. Make it a Beefeater rocks," Hallet said. "Skip the twist."

Again, no reaction from Val. He poured the drink without bothering Hallet's circled check and muttered something about "broads" and what they could do to a man.

One and one only, Hallet told himself, as he raised the glass. A man's right, especially before facing prison.

He finished that one but took another with Maurice, who was working a trio of out-of-town conventioneers—probably setting them up for a card game, some women, anything but drugs, which Maurice disavowed passionately.

"I was ten years old before I knew they had more than horses at a zoo," Maurice was regaling them.

Hallet loved to watch Maurice do his street shtik. The short, impeccably and expensively dressed black man probably had more raw brainpower than anyone Hallet had encountered at the Institute or the faculty club. And even though Maurice was known to be backed by an investment portfolio that was long on triple-A and absent of junk bonds, he still couldn't forgo the hustle, the joy of playing the con.

"See, Saturday afternoons my old man tells mama he's taking me over to Lincoln Park Zoo. Only we're off to the race track every damn time. I thought the real name of the zoo was Win, Place, and Show."

Hallet joined the conventioneers in laughter, thinking to himself that Maurice was a subject worthy of a dissertation in cultural anthropology. He could speak perfect Boston Brahmin, up-market English, or lilting West Indian—all like his natural tongue and with an inspiring vocabulary. His ear for and sense of the complexities of Arabic was no less amazing than his easy use of Yiddish.

Hallet checked his watch, got the telephone back from Val along with a short topper.

"I'm glad," Isabel said when Hallet gave her the news. "We'll work it out together."

"Leave your service door unlocked," Hallet said. "I'll come up the rear stairs. Chances are, Vreeland has people watching your place already."

Chapter 2

Lieutenant Jack Corrigan tallied the years remaining before he could take early retirement as he walked wearily back to his office in the Eleventh and State headquarters of the Chicago Police Department. The main reason he played with the numbers was not age, but Jerry De Lorenzo.

For the past hour Corrigan had sat through Jerry De's weekly staff meeting, all the time fighting to keep his mouth shut and his head from shaking openly in disgust. To Corrigan and all the cops who had made rank working the streets, Jerry De, deputy chief in charge of special investigations, was an arrogant, imperious, contentious SOB who had made his mark in the department by ass-kissing the brass, playing palsy-walsy with select aldermen, and being especially solicitous to a source-hungry press. After being assigned to Jerry De's intelligence unit and seeing him in action firsthand, Corrigan had announced over a pitcher of draught Old Style in the local watering hole that, far as he was concerned, De suffered from severe delusions of adequacy—that he knew as much about Chicago streets as a visiting farmer from Nebraska—that his fawning over the press was turning Eleventh and State into One Bullshit Plaza, and worse. De Lorenzo had his ass on the carpet at nine the next morning, warning Corrigan that nothing was ever said about him, inside or outside the department, that didn't come back across his desk within hours, usually minutes.

But today, for the first time since he'd come off Vice and been assigned to headquarters, Corrigan's attention wasn't focused on how he could be transferred out again. His main worry was how long he could keep the murder reports in his operations file out of Jerry De's reach so he wouldn't call some goddamn press conference and blow things wide open. Corrigan prayed that the markers he'd called in from the heads of the city's six Violent Crimes sections would be enough to cover his bet.

He flopped back in his chair and pushed the cold, brown-stained coffee cup off his blotter. Nancy Morgan, a college-grad cop who assisted the department's civilian psychologist, walked by and drew an arrow-pierced heart in the smog that clung to the glass partition. Corrigan waved back, took in Nancy's bright, toothy smile. She was a class lady, mid-thirties and presently single; if Jack weren't as much in love with Margie as the day he'd proposed to her eighteen years ago, Nancy Morgan would be the first woman he'd try to tumble. As it was, they flirted openly, kidding around more than anything—which was just the way Corrigan wanted to keep it and, he assured himself, the way Nancy preferred it too.

"You looked steamed," Nancy said. She strode into the office and sat on the edge of Jack's desk, rocking her well-turned calves in a rhythm more girlish than sultry. "Five bucks I know why."

"I used to arrest bookmakers," Corrigan said. "But you're on for a fin."

"Jerry De's meeting. I walked by as it was breaking up. Lots of grumbling and muttering."

Corrigan grimaced and reached for his wallet.

"I'll take my payoff in martinis the night you ever leave this place on time," Nancy said. "What was it this morning? He hasn't made Page One or been on the evening news lately?"

"Joey O'Brien got his share of flak," Corrigan said. O'Brien was the press relations officer for the special ops sections Jerry De had created to command. "I got a large ration of grief myself. De's still reeling over how the FBI nailed the El Rukns for trying to sell Qadhafi on becoming his Chicago shock troops. Jerry thinks we should have got that one ourselves. Reason we never came close to it, says he, is that I'm still thinking like a street cop and not an intelligence officer. All of that."

"A South Side street gang that used to collect federal funds for feeding the elderly while it hooked two generations of kids on drugs wants to open up Murder Incorporated on behalf of the Libyans," Nancy said, eyeing the newspaper on Corrigan's desk. "They get busted. The trial makes the national news, but it's the Feds, not our De-man, on camera."

"Thing is," Corrigan said, "I kinda agree with him. Only Jerry's paranoid about us playing ball with the FBI. They're competition, right? Except we don't get national security reports from Washington mailed to our precincts. And thanks to the mob lobby in Springfield, we can't even get a phone tap working unless one side agrees to it. So, until we get the bad guys to go on tape voluntarily, or we're allowed to buy the feds a cup of coffee without Jerry De getting paranoid, I'd call it chickenshit to blame us for missing out on that kind of bust."

"This, too, shall pass." Nancy shrugged. "Maybe you can settle your debt tonight, say a drink at six o'clock?"

"Sure, Nance," Corrigan said reflexively. "I'll stop by your office, pick you up."

Nancy got the message that Jack was preoccupied and left to counsel some rookie cop who couldn't tolerate patrolling high school corridors as a career in law enforcement. Corrigan didn't realize for minutes that she had gone. He was just feeling his usual frustration over getting stuck on Jerry De's roster after all his years in Vice and Organized Crime. That was the department's usual means of rewarding a job well done: No promotion or recognition, just a transfer to broaden the resumé, provide experience as a means toward advancement. But, sufferin' Jesus, getting assigned to De's latest public relations venture—Hostage and Terrorism? The only terrorist ventures in recent Chicago history that would fit De Lorenzo's demented definitions were some local émigrés dumping chicken blood on the Polish Consulate to protest the silencing of Solidarity. And, of course, the famous trio of Croatian separatists who hijacked a plane to O'Hare and wanted to drop propaganda leaflets all over the city until they learned the hard way that the windows of a Boeing 727 don't open.

Not a beat for a street cop, Corrigan had realized from day one. Most of his time was spent writing policy and procedure manuals, and lecturing uninterested watch commanders on how to respond in the unlikely eventuality of a terrorist assault or a major hostage situation with touchy political implications—all of which had about as much chance of happening in Chicago as a subway World Series. Nothing akin to police work. No way.

Unless, of course, the reports he was concealing from Jerry De's hot sheet did indeed form a definite and deadly pattern.

Corrigan was on his way to refill his coffee mug when Cal Bostic phoned from the Austin District on the West Side. He knew from the instant he heard Cal's voice that it wasn't shoot-the-shit time.

"I think we've got Number Four," Cal said, trying not to reveal too much on a line into headquarters, especially to anyone on Jerry De's staff. "Leastwise, so it sounds from the overnights."

"When?"

"About one in the morning. The guy was cruising out here and never got to make it home. Looks like everything you put out fits the picture."

"We'd better talk face-to-face," Corrigan said. "I want to take a look."

"The coroner's chop shop," Bostic said. "Meet me there in twenty minutes. You remember where it is?"

"I haven't been behind a desk that long, pal. I'll be there in fifteen," Corrigan said. "And Cal, sit your pretty ass right on top of this one, will you?"

"You think I'd call you direct if I wasn't? Later, Jack."

Corrigan grabbed his worn plaid sports coat and hurried out of the office, stopping just long enough to check his incoming basket and with the clerks in the mailroom. Things like this, sometimes you get a letter, he thought. Some crazy writing to explain his twisted, death-dealing logic.

There was nothing.

Corrigan parked in a loading zone alongside the Fishbein Institute of Forensic Medicine, the morgue that sat just behind Cook County Hospital on the Near West Side. Cal Bostic was waiting in the lobby and led him to the coolers. A ragged, unshaven little man in an attendant's gray tunic grudgingly answered Bostic's summons and opened the locker door. He rolled out the slab and, in the same motion, pulled back the sheet.

"Here's your dead cabby," the attendant said, reading the preliminary report. "Hack license says he was one Ahmad Ramal. Sounds like some spook wide receiver for the Packers. Oh, hey, sorry."

Cal Bostic, who'd inured himself to the system's institutionalized racism from the day he'd joined the force, let it slide. But Jack Corrigan's glowering eyes told the attendant he'd better shut up and get lost. Fast.

"Close it back up when you're done," the attendant said as he scurried out into the hallway. "Anything's evidence they got locked up anyway."

"Yup, another one of my Muslim brothers," Bostic said as he studied the corpse.

"Only this one's not Iranian," Corrigan guessed from the name. "The three others were."

"Then maybe some Iranian decided to extract a little revenge?"

"No, shooter's the same," Corrigan said. He pointed to the exit wound that had ripped open the victim's mastoid just behind his left ear. "Another pair of twenty-two longs. I'd say an automatic, target model maybe. One exit wound, so the second round's probably buried in gray matter."

"That'll give us a clean slug for ballistics when they carve him," Bostic figured.

"He's been using hollow points," Corrigan said. "We got nothing but a lot of fragments. Still, there could be enough for a match."

"Back seat shot at close range. Inside the cab. Yeah, it looks like the same shooter," Bostic agreed.

"Sufferin' Jesus." Corrigan's eyes fixed on the dead man's face: expressionless, revealing neither fear nor repose; youthful eyes already sunken; skin the color of mocha ice cream. "We got ourselves a crazy loose on the streets."

He walked out of the viewing room while Cal Bostic scribbled the appropriate notes in his daybook. Corrigan wondered why people thought morgues reeked of formaldehyde or alcohol or some other flesh-preserving chemicals when, in fact, the prevalent odor was one of sweetness, like a hint of household Lysol or, more precisely, like those paper Christmas trees people hang off dashboards to make old cars smell new. But whatever described the smell most accurately, Corrigan hated every molecule of it he was forced to breathe.

The attendant was lazily smoking a cigarette and drinking a cup of vending machine coffee.

"You through, Lieutenant?"

"Done," Corrigan replied.

"Hey, maybe somebody gave him a two-dollar tip and he forgot to say thank-you. Now me, the driver don't say thanks, I leave the door open, make him walk around the cab to close it."

Corrigan fought his Mick temper back in check. "I want you to tell the examining pathologist we need everything we can get off him. What and when the driver ate or drank, where his clothes came from, right down to the ear wax. A quality job, no shortcuts."

The attendant shrugged incredulously. "You want to tell him that, you tell him yourself. We got more important things to worry about around here than some dune coon getting offed."

In one swift, strong motion, Corrigan grabbed the attendant's lapels, lifted him six inches off the floor, and slammed him hard enough against the coffee machine to rattle the coins and slosh the liquid inside it.

"The man on that slab may be a victim of some asshole thinks like you do," Corrigan fumed as he glared into the attendant's frightened eyes. "So you see the autopsy gets done right and that his family gets treated with respect when they i.d. him. You got that, pal?"

"Hey, Lieutenant, I didn't mean noth—"

"And I ever hear you use the word *spook* around Sergeant Bostic again, I'm personally gonna twist off your tongue."

"What in hell's going on here?" Cal Bostic asked as he saw the attendant cowering in Jack Corrigan's grasp.

The attendant looked sheepishly at Corrigan, then at the black detective. "Nothing, Sergeant. Hey, nothing at all."

Corrigan let him slide back to the floor and decided he'd buy Cal Bostic his coffee in a less depressing environment.

"Don't lose it on my account, Jack," Bostic said as they hit the parking lot. "Guy's not worth it."

"Me? No chance." Corrigan grinned. "I was just thinking about using my new clout with terrorists to buy that little bastard a vacation in Beirut."

MaryAgnes McCaskey had not heard from Jack Corrigan for more than six months. The phone call surprised her, but not where he suggested they meet: Bernie's Luncheonette in the South Loop was Jack's favorite, with the leanest, best corned beef in town, or so Jack swore, and tinted glasses filled with cold Heineken unlawfully earmarked for special customers. Bernie's also was where Corrigan used to meet Frank Thorne, a safe house away from the curious eyes at Eleventh and State and the FBI's offices in the Dirksen Federal Building—all of this back when the three of them had teamed up in Operation Clothesline, back before Thorne walked out on the Bureau, and on McCaskey too, for God only knew what or why.

She spotted the stress in Corrigan's face the moment she entered the restaurant: A deep furrow cut hard across his brow, and his close-cropped gray hair, normally brushed and shining, looked limp and shaggy.

"Good to see you, Lieutenant."

"You too, kiddo. And how about we skip rank and station?"

"Fine, Jack." McCaskey folded her Burberry raincoat neatly over the chair back, smoothed her charcoal skirt straight. "You're looking good," she fibbed. "And letting that crew cut grow out."

"Jerry De keeps reminding me I'm not a Marine anymore. Says I should look more like staff."

"So much he knows. Crew cuts are back in style."

"Too bad cops aren't."

McCaskey took a breath, ordered a grilled cheese sandwich and iced tea. "Other than the transfer, how are you doing?"

"Tell you the truth, I'm scared shitless."

"I doubt that. I've seen you in action, remember."

"You take a pretty good shiner yourself," Corrigan said, recalling how McCaskey had worked the final Clothesline setup and gotten herself punched around by a very nasty crooked cop just to keep the cameras rolling long enough to nail him. "Which is why I called you."

"Why, ex-Detective Massey getting paroled already?"

"No chance. He's still got a decade playing dodge ball and stamping out vanity plates down in Stateville."

"So much for the good news," McCaskey said. "Better let me have the bad."

"Hear me out, you'll have more than you want," Corrigan

said. "One thing up front. What I tell you goes no farther than here, least until I say different. None of your damned contact reports, no telling Doc Hermann or any of the briefcase brigade at the Bureau. The way I used to do business with Thorne."

"Now *I'm* getting frightened," McCaskey said. "But, okay. Deal. What've you got?"

"I've got four dead Arab cabdrivers. Three Iranians, one Palestinian. All in their hacks and down in the last three weeks. All head shots from the back seat, and apparently done by the same shooter. How's that for openers?"

"Nasty," she said. "But Iranians aren't Arabs, you know. They're Persians and they speak Farsi, not Arabic. So, for my openers, maybe you shouldn't try tying things up ethnically."

"Jesus, I'm glad you FBI people are college graduates," Corrigan said. "Except that maybe our shooter doesn't know the subtle differences between Persians and Bedouins and Berbers and all the Semitic tribes. You figure that?"

"Sorry," McCaskey apologized. "I didn't mean to sound like a prig."

"And I didn't call you to bark, either," Corrigan apologized back. From the night she'd stood up to Detective Tom Massey, the night she'd grown up and become a cop instead of an investigator, Corrigan had considered McCaskey first rate, and thought Frank Thorne was a dumb ass for taking off on her.

"So," she got back to business, "are you really talking the same shooter, or maybe just the same m.o.?"

"Everything says one man, but I rule out nothing. Why? Something come across your desk about anti-Arab crazies working the streets? Some guys who might go passing a twenty-two automatic around?"

McCaskey shook her head. "Not that I've seen, Jack. But I'll check it out for you. Quietly."

"I was hoping you'd say that, kiddo."

"It could be coincidental. Taxi drivers get robbed all the time."

"But not executed, which is what's happening out there.

Which is also why I've been pulling twenty years' worth of strings inside the department to keep it quiet until we know what we're facing. Otherwise, we'll have nothing but hysteria to work with."

"I see the problem," McCaskey said, "if you think the shooter's some avenging angel with psycho religious or political hang-ups. Which, I take it, is why you're treating me to Bernie's lunchtime special."

"Hey, you people operate from ocean to ocean. Me, I have to stop at the lakefront."

"So, what do you see on the beach?"

"Not a whole helluva lot," Corrigan said. "The drug angle went south right away. The Iranians were all straight family men, no police records of any kind, no associations to tie them to drugs. Politics, who knows? The Palestinian who went down night before last was a grad student at Roosevelt driving his uncle's cab part-time. He belonged to the usual pro-Palestinian groups, but so do hundreds like him. Everything else checks out legit. A few protests against Israeli policies, American warships in the Gulf, like that. Nothing worth a pair of hollow points in the medulla oblongata."

McCaskey sipped her tea and thought for a minute. "We monitor all the hard-line Zionist activists," she volunteered. "But I doubt there's anything to work on. It's not their style, at least none we know about. Besides," she added, "they like the idea that Iranians are killing Iraqis and Syrians and keeping the Arab world at each other's throats. That only helps Israel."

"So you think it's just some nut case? Some guy with a hard-on—hey, excuse me . . ."

"Go on, Jack," McCaskey said impatiently.

"Some guy who hates Arabs trying to start his own war? Or some crazy flag-waver who's fed up seeing Americans killed and taken hostage and wants a little revenge for himself?" Corrigan paused long enough to ensure he had McCaskey's full attention. "How about some black extremists who think they're helping out their Libyan brothers by bumping off a few Iranians to humiliate the U.S. and give Uncle Sam a world-class black eye?"

"Now I know what you're after," McCaskey realized. "The El Rukn files."

"Not just them," Corrigan replied, a thin craggy smile crossing his lips for the first time. "Because I know your people got a lot more than one gang of punks who thought it was hip to work for Qadhafi. You got wires into every far-out radical group in this town, stuff I can't get without warrants and writs and half the city council bitching about it. That's the kind of intelligence I'm going to need on this—all the lunatics who hate for a living."

"I had nothing to do with the El Rukn case, Jack. I'm too busy shadowing a handful of aging mobsters that probably commit fewer felonies than the National Security Council. But," McCaskey wondered aloud as Corrigan's request circuited through her head, "how does this fit in your new beat? You calling it terrorism?"

Corrigan paused reflectively, his eyes tightening. "Look, you want to talk about *real* terrorism? We got more terrorists per capita in Chicago than any place I care to think about. We got neo-Nazis who trash synagogues in Skokie, skinheads who smash Jewish storefronts on Kristallnacht. We got street gangs swearing allegiance to Islam while they murder their brothers for wearing the wrong color sweater, and a white working class thinks every black person in town should be sent back to Kenya. For good measure, throw in Puerto Ricans from the FALN running bomb factories in Humboldt Park, and lace-curtain Irish Catholics who think they're doing God's work by sending the IRA guns to kill Protestants in Belfast. I may not be the pipe-sucking intelligence officer my boss is looking for, but I know the streets and what's going on out there. Used to be, I went head to head against the mob. Now all I do is watch a hateful city hating itself. So damn right I'm calling this terrorism—the terror we live with day in and day out, not what makes headlines for Jerry De. And I'm asking you to help me nail at least one demented bastard who's responsible for it."

McCaskey now understood the stress that she'd seen in Jack Corrigan's face from the instant they'd met. His town, his streets, and he didn't like having to sit back and watch them being torn apart.

"Another thought," she volunteered. "Maybe there's some falling out *inside* the Arab community. There doesn't have to be a maniac who's trying to eliminate it singlehandedly. Some power play, some kind of Muslim-style tong war, a jihad."

"Good possibility," Corrigan agreed. "All I know, this old street dick's hunches tell me that it's got to be more than some nutso with a pistol who thinks taxi meters are fixed. The hits were precision work. The shooter uses an assassin's weapon. It looks too well calculated for a pure crazy."

"The cabdrivers did have their civil rights violated. That's federal," McCaskey said. "So tell me what you need by this morning?"

"I need anything you have in the victims' federal packages. Maybe we can turn up a link, something that will tie them together. More important, I need to see what you people have on the Arabs here—groups, sects, affiliations, whatever. Likewise all the radical fringe, the kind of people who want to settle foreign policy with pistols. You know the drill."

"Jack, you're talking major legwork here, not a few reports I can pull together in my spare time. Especially without telling my bosses what I'm doing."

"You send up the balloon, and this leaks to City Hall or the media, we'll get all the fanatics choosing up sides and trying to settle scores. Believe me, kiddo."

"I got the picture. And I don't like it either."

"Then do what you can for me." Corrigan slid the envelope under McCaskey's plate. "Everything I got's in there. Do whatever you do with it, and see what turns up."

"You sure you're not confusing me with Frank Thorne?"

"Lady, with legs like yours, it's the only thing I'm sure won't ever happen."

McCaskey slipped the envelope in her bag, breathed a sigh of consent. "Soon as I can, Jack. Promise."

"I hope so. Something's telling me that Number Five isn't too far away, and I don't know how long I can keep the lid on and Jerry De from going bonkers with the press."

McCaskey pushed her plate away, wanting to believe that the shiver running through her was caused by the sight of Bernie's greasy sandwich.

"You sure know how to show a lady a good time," she said, grabbing her trench coat and heading out into the mayhem of noontime traffic.

Chapter 3

Hallet awoke trembling and clammy, with distant voices and gray images lingering on the threshold of his awareness. He knew he had dreamt, but forced himself not to recollect any of it.

Isabel Ortega was already up and dressed for her long day of verifying the cultural, economic, and political output of the Arbor Institute for Middle East Studies. Hallet knew at any moment she'd deliver him a rich, healthful breakfast: whole grain bread, fresh fruit, a boiled egg. Nutrition was the key to recovery, Isabel insisted, the holistic way for Hallet to overcome his dark cravings. Fine, except for the coffee—a thin, decaffeinated brew far inferior to the rich Arabian variety Hallet liked to boil in his battered brass *ibrik*. But when he tried opting instead for tea, Hallet got only an herbal variety that smelled like compost mixed with raspberries, for Isabel argued vehemently that caffeine in any form would only intensify his withdrawal symptoms and return him to the tremorous state he had been in when he arrived at her tidy apartment in an old high-rise co-op on Hyde Park Boulevard.

Isabel came into the bedroom, sat at Hallet's foot. She was

tall, stately, with rich chestnut hair and glowing green eyes, their oval shape the only hint of a Moorish intruder somewhere long ago in her family's rich pre-Cuban heritage.

"You slept much better last night, save for some sunrise squirming," she said. "And you look better for it."

"I'm doing fine." Hallet pushed the vestiges of his dreams away with his breakfast of melon, mango, and muesli.

"Then I think it's time you call Mac Clelland. Tell him how well you're progressing, that you'll be back to work soon."

"I'm not ready yet."

"For work, or for calling Mac?"

"Neither one. Mac will no doubt want to pay me a sick call. Or he'll send the AA goons from the clinic to chat me through the day. Neither option is appealing."

"You're putting me between a rock and a hard place, you know. Mac's been exceptionally patient with my evasive answers, but I can't keep him at bay forever. He's my boss, too."

"A little more time," Hallet said.

Isabel, as usual, strove for compromise. "At least let me bring some things home for you," she offered. "Stan Bach has been doing some fine work on the Israeli occupation forces—what stress does to the personality of the occupiers as well as to the occupied. And you should get back to your paper on Islamic architecture. It will be excellent with some polishing."

"Like hell it will," Hallet said contentiously, aware of how flat and dissonant his recent work had become, how even the pure geometric logic of Islamic thought—the perfect dissection of circles to form arches and arabesques . . . the balance of line that is Kufic script . . . the classic purity of Hassan Fahti's new towns—had become suddenly complex and unfathomable to him.

Isabel managed to control her temper. "Some books, perhaps? To ease the transition back?"

"I'll let you know."

She let out a sigh of surrender, kissed him lightly on the cheek, and left for the Institute without another word. Hallet knew they could not carry this on much longer without clashing off each other like cymbals. But, as he tried to tell, even implore her, what he needed for the present was solitude, emptiness, peace.

He slipped back beneath the covers, closed his eyes to the intrusive sunlight.

From day one of Hallet's self-imposed exile in Isabel Ortega's apartment, the hours after her departure for the Institute had been a mixed bag. Some days, he would fall immediately back to sleep, exhaustion taking the place of his inexorable longings. Then, in the afternoon, he would relocate himself to the sofa and stare thoughtlessly at television reruns of Quincy and Rockford, or the pathos of the Cubs at Wrigley Field, anything except the news broadcasts and panel discussions—programs on which Bobby Inman and Stansfield Turner and other ex-intelligence managers would miscalculate Arab motivations so grossly—that Hallet feared would shake him from his semisomnolent state and force the world back on him.

Other days, he would scour through the kitchen cabinets and pantry, ravenously hungry no matter how much of Isabel's therapeutic breakfast he'd consumed. All alcohol, of course, from cooking sherry to bitters, had been dutifully removed from the apartment. So Hallet would whip up strange concoctions to satisfy his gin-anesthetized palate. To Isabel Ortega's dismay, canned chili con carne and black beans drenched with hot pepper salsa were staples: Hallet would heat the mixtures in one of the brown earthenware bowls that Isabel normally reserved for guacamole or refritos when she was called upon to forsake her proud Cuban heritage and prepare Mexican dinners for ignorant faculty and Fellows who thought that everyone with a Hispanic surname existed mostly on tacos and enchiladas con mole.

Then, with a certain suddenness, just two days earlier and about a week into his stay, Hallet had begun to feel more alive and, almost regrettably, more alert. Yesterday morning, to Isabel's surprise, he had dragged her back into bed and undressed her greedily. They made love for the first time in months, a little too quickly and roughly on Hallet's part, he'd decided afterward. But Isabel seemed satisfied and almost victorious when Hallet breathlessly emptied himself, as if it were the long-awaited signal that he was healing in both body and spirit. Last night, when she'd returned, was the only evening they had spent together that Isabel did not press him about contacting Macdonald Clelland and making arrangements for his return to the Institute. Too bad she couldn't hold out through the morning.

Hallet recalled the first time he'd met Isabel Ortega. It was at some university-sponsored function he could never quite re-call, back when she was wasting her considerable talents with a bunch of model-making economists searching for miracle systems that would turn the suffering nations of the Third World into prosperous growth markets. Hallet had just returned from a supposed lecture program in Riyadh, a program concocted by Mac Clelland whose real purpose was to send Hallet again into the back alleys of Baghdad and Tripoli and, in the process, unknowingly deliver two of his sad, innocent Prophets to the hangman's scaffold.

Isabel had joined a circle of people who were badgering Hallet for his views on the Iran-Iraq war. Kissinger had said it was unfortunate that only one side could lose, someone noted. Non-sense, Hallet countered. Both sides were losing with magnificent efficiency. And with the carnage went any hope for an end to the stalemates in Lebanon and the occupied territories.

Isabel, sensing that he was growing tired of the questions, interrupted to offer Hallet a ritual glass of sherry. He recalled the easy grace about her, the quiet elegance that belied her hard-line, computer-directed research skills. She laughed heartily when Hallet defined economists as men who knew forty differ-ent positions for sex, but no girls. As they refilled their glasses, she told Hallet she would like to hear more about his travels, his ideas. They began to see each other casually, over din-ner most times. Later, when Macdonald Clelland and Bryce

Vreeland announced at a meeting of Institute Fellows that a new research director was being sought (one with great discretion and a certain amount of naiveté, Mac told Hallet in private), he was only too happy to recommend Isabel Ortega.

They became lovers in an easy, undemanding way. Isabel, Hallet surmised by putting together fragments of conversation and some off-guard allusions, had recently concluded a painful affair with a dreary academic who was either married or bisexual, probably both. For his part, Hallet's years in the Mideast had been essentially celibate ones: The women that his hosts and benefactors offered him were unappealing in their dutiful compliance, which Hallet considered no better than slavery. Unlike old Lawrence, the paradoxical idol Hallet both loathed and loved, the wretched boys of the region held no appeal for him. So, until he started seeing Isabel regularly, brief encounters with a random Western visitor or a French tart on tour were all the passions Hallet had let creep into his life.

Hallet stopped himself from falling back asleep, allowing his mind to wander but not letting his memory exert itself. He would go so far, and no farther. Not yet.

He rolled over and buried his head in Isabel's pillow. It held a faint residual aroma of her perfume. It reminded him of gin.

Back in the clinic, after a group therapy session when the shrink had Hallet lie on the floor and the other members re-arrange his posture as if he were a Raggedy Andy doll ("You were eloquent in your submission," the shrink said afterward. "However they moved you, you stayed. Basically, you told them all to go screw themselves."), he had come to the conclusion that it was his selection of the powerful and unwieldy gin as his beverage of choice that had contributed to his sudden and shocking decline. Yes, it had to be a biochemical reaction to the particular formula of juniper and rosewater and other exotic botanicals that had stricken him. Only later, alone in his cell with no other company than Stan Bach's smuggled Mozart tapes, did Hallet decide it wasn't merely the gin, but all the years he'd spent sneaking it in juice cans and cosmetic bottles into hell holes like San'a and Najaf and Muharraq and all the rest of parched, fundamentalist, abstaining Islam.

Back then, Hallet had dismissed his omnipresent thirst as part of a game he liked playing with the officious Pakistani *douniers* the Arabs hired to perform the petty task of customs inspection. Later he realized that for a dozen years he had been denied the right to consume alcohol normally. Given where and how he had to live, it was inevitable that liquor grew to occupy an exaggerated position in his ethos. And, of course, the stress of his reentry and reassimilation to the West made it almost inevitable that a minor dependency would occur.

But in the end, when darkness brought back the nightmare that wasn't a dream, he knew the truth. It was fear. It was betrayal. It was Sandman.

Isabel Ortega returned home to find Hallet sprawled out on her white jacquard chesterfield and Jill St. John cooking al dente pasta on the flickering, ill-focused television screen. She woke him roughly. Hallet looked up, saw her eyes flashing and her patrician jaw jutting out at him like a lance.

"Look, Philip, I know it's been rough for you. I really do," she said, a slight tremor in her voice. "But you're not helping yourself by swapping dipsomania for clinomania. Maybe that's the reason you ran away from the hospital. They wouldn't let you stay on your back all day."

"Stop flexing your lexical muscles. Say what you mean."

"Clinomania. A psychological condition when a person becomes too dysfunctional to get out of bed. A couch potato, Philip. Which is you, day after day. And it's wearing me down."

"So get down here with me," Hallet said. Isabel's eyes only hardened. No smile whatsoever.

"I'm trying to understand that you need private time to get to the root of whatever been's eating away at you. But I can't come home each evening wondering if I'm going to find you lapsed into a state of catatonia."

"One of the Arab Emirates, isn't it? Next door to Qatar?"

"Your sarcasm is getting as boring as your self-pity, of which I've had a bellyful. So no more cutting slack or covering for you with Mac Clelland. Tomorrow, you come to the Institute with me, or I'll tell Mac you've been staying here and you can confront him yourself."

"You gave me your word."

"I know. But you're letting all of us down. We have important work to do, and we need you to help us do it."

"Now you sound like Bryce Vreeland at funding time," Hallet shot back, wondering how Isabel would respond if Hallet ran his machine for her, introduced her to his Prophets. "That I don't need."

"And I don't need to see you wind down to entropy like an old watch. Or to keep your true feelings hidden under a cloak of anger and insolence. Whatever you need to get better, you're not going to find it hiding here. Please, stop brooding and get back to work."

Hallet stood up, got his land legs pinned firmly under him. "Let me tell you something," he fumed. "The only thing I really need is for you and Mac Clelland and Bryce Vreeland to leave me alone for a while. That, and now that I think about it, a good stiff drink with people who respect my wishes."

He slammed out of Isabel Ortega's apartment as she weakly pleaded with him to stop. As he paused in the corridor, reconsidering for an instant, he heard her walk with uncommonly heavy footsteps to the bedroom telephone. He kept going.

Hallet climbed out of the Illinois Central station on Randolph Street, then walked north toward Rush Street and Fairweather's. His mind was made up: a drink, maybe two, with Val and

Maurice and his true friends, then a cab to his town house. He'd write the letter of resignation first thing in the morning, have a messenger service deliver it to the Institute. The few thousand dollars he had in savings would be enough to get him to—where? he wondered. Perhaps Toronto, where any of his Arab friends would be happy to take him in and where Mac would be bound by international law and treaty to leave him at peace? Or back to London, where he could teach again without all the secret baggage that had been his burden at the Institute?

He saw the woman in the oversized cardigan leaning against the alley wall of a Mexican restaurant that filled the north end of Rush Street with greasy, corn-oil frying fumes. Three men, two white, one black, stood beside her talking and swaying as if caught in a stiff wind. Hallet quickly saw the thousand-yard stares in their eyes. But his fixed on the girl: The sweater looked the same, the hair was auburn but, far from being wrapped in a tight Joan Fontaine bun, it hung halfway down her back in long, unkempt snarls. The men stared hard but harmlessly at Hallet as he walked up to her.

"Pam?"

The girl's head made a slow quarter turn, but she seemed not to see him.

"Who's that?"

"Pam, what are you doing here?"

"She's with us," one of the men said.

"Yeah, what's it to you?" another tried snarling.

Hallet told them to shut up, stay cool. "Pam?" he asked again, trying to focus her blown mind. "What happened at the clinic?"

"I know you?" she asked, squinting hard against the bright amber light of the sodium lamps that hung over Rush Street like mutant fireflies. "Yeah, you look familiar. I scored from you once, right?"

"Maybe he busted you once," the black man suggested, sneering at the prospect.

"The clinic," Hallet said. "You came to see me. With your friend Jerry. You wanted to help me. Remember?"

"Clinic? Oh, yeah. I was thoroughly bummed out, man. I remember Jerry, though. He wanted to fuck me, but I wouldn't let him."

"Come on, Pam. This time you can use a little help. Let's get out of here."

Pam's face crumbled into a pointless smile, the kind she couldn't manage back in Hallet's room. "Bummed out," she repeated, draping her arm limply over Hallet's shoulder.

"Let's take a walk," Hallet said. He grabbed the thumb of the skinny white kid who tried to interfere and twisted it expertly until the boy dropped whimpering to his knees. "Come on."

"Can't now," Pam insisted. "But if you could spare me ten bucks? I got some things to do. Maybe later I could meet you, you know. We could party then. Okay?"

Hallet, who thought he'd hardened himself against all the world's addicts and alms-seekers, reached into his pocket without thinking and pulled out his only pair of twenty dollar bills. He put them into Pam's sweating palm, closed her numb fingers around them.

"Take care of yourself."

"You're beautiful," Pam said, grinning. "The Lord is my strength and my song. Beautiful."

Hallet stepped back from the alley in a military motion, as if leaving a tribunal. He saw the three men hovering around Pam and laughing at her sudden prosperity. By the time he got to Fairweather's, he'd reached the decision he knew all along he would make. The only thing he asked of Val as he climbed onto a stool was the bar phone and permission to make a call.

41

Chapter 4

It was a perfect day for golf, and for everything else Usher had to do.

The sun was thirty degrees from its searing apogee. It hung at the best possible angle in the northern sky, just above the Windward Passage that separates Cuba and Hispaniola, putting it at Usher's back, giving him a clear view inland and blinding anyone who might hook a ball right of the fairway and out into the softly rolling surf where his stern-drive runabout bobbed lazily off a three-fathom anchor line.

The southwest wind from the Bartlett Deep was stiff and swirling. It would make his play more complicated than Usher had hoped, but he'd compensate for it with a good English-made ball, smaller and more tightly dimpled than the American version, and thereby better able to hold true in the wind. For the rest, he had rehearsed it over and over again, and knew that the tools buried in his golf bag would be up to the challenge.

It was the fourth consecutive day that Usher had arrived at the course thirty minutes ahead of the first scheduled starting time. The clubhouse smelled of stale grass and after-shave lotion; the manager, a big-bellied native with enough space between his two front teeth to run a bowline, greeted Usher like an old and dear friend.

Usher dropped the expensive new set of pro-model Ping clubs that would last him only one more round. "I'll work on the back nine today," he said. That would bring him in along the beach, positioning him perfectly between the sun and the runabout. He handed the black man a U.S. fifty-dollar bill, folded into quarters with discretion that was unnecessary in the empty clubhouse.

"No need to hurry at all," the manager said as he pocketed the cash and went about stacking boxes of golf balls on the counter. "Only one foursome going out before ten o'clock. A very private game, they tell me from the hotel. Probably with much money at stake."

Usher looked up from lacing his spikes. "After all this, I'd better make some money back myself when my match comes due."

"You are on top of the game, I can see from your swing. And you know every inch of our course. That is for sure."

Usher matched the black man's smile, but he felt nothing more than contempt. There was a code in every profession, even his, Usher believed, and he despised anyone who walked around with his hand out, ready to throw away the rules for a few extra dollars' worth of graft.

The first day Usher had arrived at the course, things had not gone quite so smoothly with the manager. When he'd asked to go off early and alone for a practice round, the club rules were laid out for him firmly—he had to wait for at least a twosome with which to team, no matter the starting time; a foursome was preferred, but a threesome would be allowed until he had the opportunity to make proper reservations in advance; and, of course, hiring a caddie was mandatory at all times—all of golfdom's inflexible, middle-class crap.

Usher had his argument ready: He had scheduled a big wager game for the following Saturday, and he needed time to learn the intimacies and intricacies of a strange course—to get his club selection down, play an occasional double shot, take some practice swings from the bunkers—all without anyone, especially a curious caddie, sticking the rules book in his face.

His argument made sense, but it cost Usher fifty dollars off the books to get to play one side each morning, going out alone before any of the club's overweight duffers arrived. Another twenty dollars went to keep the half-witted caddie sipping a cool Red Stripe in the clubhouse instead of humping Usher's bag around the empty course.

The first day, he concentrated on gauging the time it would take a slow-playing foursome to reach the green he'd selected. He checked and double-checked his computations carefully, measuring distances and wind tendencies and angles of approach. In the process, he even got his short irons working well and accurately, though, in truth, he vehemently despised the game of golf in all its aspects. Still, in a service business . . .

Usher finished lacing his spikes, slung the richly tooled leather golf bag over his right shoulder.

"Watch your greens carefully this morning," the black man said. "Most times, the roll is away from the salt air. But the winds have been unusual, rain and spray coming from all directions, confusing the grass. It will be like petting a dog from the tail frontward."

Usher thanked him for the advice. He was almost out of the clubhouse when he remembered it would be smart to buy himself even a few extra minutes. With the manager's hand always stuck out, he knew precisely what it would take.

"Two more days till my game," he said, pointing in the appointment book to the bogus reservation made by telephone weeks earlier. "You understand that if my opponents knew I'd been playing this course for a week, they might want me to handicap a stroke or two."

"At least one a side," the manager agreed.

"That's what I'd want."

"And so?"

"There'll be an extra hundred in it for you if you've never

seen me before. You don't recognize me if anyone asks. No matter who it is."

"You're a stranger to these eyes."

Usher strode casually to the tenth tee.

He was just under six feet tall with medium-length black hair that curled at the nape of his neck. In linen golf slacks and a knit shirt, his body exuded the graceful strength of a former athlete who had worked to stay in shape. Only Usher's cobalt blue eyes revealed that he had broken training in a major way: They had an icy glare, a reflection of pain and inner wrath, that made people who looked into them feel afraid.

He hit a true and easy three-wood that laid up on the fairway just at the break of the left dogleg. He checked the sun again as he walked out to his ball, then hit a full seven-iron to the front edge of the green. But instead of attempting the birdie putt, Usher picked up his ball and broke yet another club rule by veering out of bounds to his left, cutting through a thick clump of dwarf eucalyptus trees and rough island pines. He followed the tree line as it ran along the length of the par-three fourth hole until he found his chosen spot some fifty yards behind the small, well-bunkered, shrub-backed green.

The gully running behind the hole was deep enough to keep Usher in defilade when he kneeled. He threw his golf bag into it, and gauged his light one more time before climbing down, relaxing against the moist earth, lighting a Craven A cigarette. He took four long, deep drags; satisfied, he field-stripped the cigarette carefully, ripping the butt into microscopic shreds of paper, tobacco, and cellulose.

Fifty minutes later, Usher heard the dull thud of a golf ball landing in the sand trap to his left front. It was followed by a whistling rush of air and a hard slap as a second ball bit into the green. Usher waited patiently, but no other shots came in on him. That meant two players only. Two players, and probably two bodyguards. Nothing was ever as easy as they said it would be.

The second man to approach the green was the one Usher

recognized immediately. He was large, bald, and, even from fifty yards' distance, was visibly sweating. Usher studied his every move and mannerism as he walked to the green. The man carried himself with the brazen toughness a union boss has to exhibit to prove to his membership that, should he ever be voted out of office, he could again and without slacking assume the rigorous duties of the assembly line, the mine, the loading dock, or wherever it was he had worked back before all the college-boy labor relations specialists starting waving computer print-outs in his face.

The big man laughed uproariously as his opponent's ball flew out of the sand trap and, as if preordained for failure, rolled past the pin and off the far side of the elevated green. Usher listened to the big man's echo linger over the quiet course. Maybe that was his fatal flaw, Usher wondered. Maybe the big man talks too loudly and too openly, in a way that would cause the family to doubt his discretion. But Usher quickly put such speculations out of his mind. His concerns were never with why, only about how.

A second chip from his opponent, and the big man was now away. He lined up his ball carefully for a putt that, Usher reckoned, would break hard to the right and probably run past the cup since it would head uphill first, then roll down the undulating green. A tough shot—to strike it with enough force to push it over the rise meant stroking it too hard to hold the downhill break. But the big man putted masterfully, with surprising grace and finesse. The ball came within inches of dropping. His opponent and the two bodyguards who stood by their cart in the background all cheered him.

Usher, too, appreciated the craftsmanship of the big man's stroke. So he let him putt out for a nifty, well-earned, and final par before nailing him with a perfectly placed head shot from the scope-sighted and silenced Ruger Mini-Thirty rifle that had replaced the number four wood beneath the leather cover in his bag.

The Ruger ejected and rechambered smoothly as Usher

watched a chunk of the big man's jawbone fly past the pin flag. Two insurance rounds of 7.62 by 39 mm Power Lokt ammunition went into the sagging torso as it collapsed onto the already blood-stained green.

The other golfer, a small, meek-looking man with wire-rimmed eyeglasses and short white hair, was crawling like a crazed infant into the shrubs and azaleas that lined the back of the green. The two bodyguards had their worthless revolvers drawn and were scanning the horizon in slow, deliberate patterns. Like they expect me to walk out and inspect the damage, Usher laughed to himself. Like I'd just bagged a damn deer in the Adirondacks.

He stuffed the rifle back into his golf bag. With the tree cover still working for him, he headed to the ten-foot sand berm which ran along the seaward side of the seventeenth fairway. The biting golf spikes helped him move down the berm and wade out to the runabout without stumbling. He slipped the nylon line from the bow, leaving the leaden mass of anchor buried in the spongy Caribbean sand.

He swung the boat first north, away from the shoreline, then westward toward the town. His golf bag with the wonderful little Ruger still inside it went over the side and slipped down into the blue water. Usher followed it with his spikes and, inside them, the golf gloves he had worn every moment he was in the clubhouse or on the course.

Twenty minutes later, he ran his boat aground in a sandy cove that was protected enough to conceal the Ford Cortina he had stolen the night before from a car rental lot. In another twenty minutes, Usher was walking through passport control at the Montego Bay airport with sufficient time remaining before his flight to stop at the Duty Free shop and, as would any sensible tourist, pick up some quality rum and cigars at bargain prices.

Back in Miami, he cleared Immigration easily with an expired passport—valid enough for travel in the Caribbean, but not worth the INS going through the verification process that would show it was forged. Once inside the terminal and on his way to another departure gate, Usher picked up his new identification and a second set of airline tickets from a storage locker. In a men's room stall he shredded the passport that had gotten him home, flushing the shreds down the toilet along with the dark wig he'd been wearing with considerable discomfort since the day he'd departed for the islands.

Usher was back in Chicago an hour before sunset.

He sipped a glass of grapefruit juice as he unpacked his suitcase, throwing the hideous tourist's clothing in a corner of the closet, knowing he would never wear any of the garments again. That done, he went out to the living room, a large rectangle of barren plaster walls without any intrusion of art or color. Usher had rented the place from a Northwestern University anthropology professor who was off to Manitoba for a year to live among the Cree and master their language. He was, Usher decided when he'd first surveyed the spartan interior of the apartment, a man of modest means who could not turn down an offer of ten months' full mortgage expenses, including taxes and insurance, plus a twenty-percent profit on the total—all paid in advance so that Usher would not have to worry about providing references, or writing checks monthly, or seeing any of his available identities displayed on a notarized lease.

At six o'clock, he turned on the television set and added a decent measure of duty-free rum to the grapefruit juice that remained in his glass. The female newscaster was an Oriental with smooth, perfect skin and piercing black eyes. Definitely Chinese, Usher thought. Though he normally preferred the more sensual and alluring looks of Vietnamese and Thai women, this one had a taunting air about her, something like a bar girl who dared you to satisfy her.

Usher turned away, his mind wandering back to the war as the newscaster went through her story in a flat, emotionless monotone: the murder of a prominent labor union official on a Jamaican golf course, details to follow. What bothered Usher most when the full report aired were the repeated references to an assassin in hiding, firing from ambush, bushwhacking—all reasons why he preferred to work from closer range, in more imaginative ways. Still, the time frame he'd gotten from Ben, and the amount of so-called protection that was supposed to accompany the big man, obviated a more creative scenario. Had he the time and discretion to honor his contract in the States . . . ?

By nine o'clock, Usher was ravenously hungry. He dressed in polished cotton trousers and a striped oxford shirt with button-down collar; on the way out the door, he wrapped a blue cashmere sweater loosely around his shoulders. It was canon for Usher to dress in tune with his surroundings, take on protective coloration, speak when spoken to. His favorite book and movie were *Serpico,* neither for the writing nor the performance but for the way the cop blended in so perfectly with the hostile surroundings in which he was forced to operate. In his current neighborhood, this meant Usher had to look as much like executive material as possible, dressing out of Brooks Brothers or in Eddie Bauer's brand of outdoor chic. With his tall frame and fair good looks, Usher fit the Near North Side perfectly. Until one looked hard into his eyes.

He stepped into the corridor. Before he could press the call button, the elevator door slid open.

"Well, stranger, long time no see."

It was one of the two women who shared the corner apartment. Usher couldn't remember which one she was until he read the name tag on her flight attendant's uniform.

"Need a hand, Colleen?"

"Anytime. Thanks."

Usher took her suitcase and flight bag, leaving Colleen to search through her purse for the latchkey.

Colleen was tall and well-built in a way that Usher figured would soon turn soft and flabby. Her large eyes were warm, smiling, but her best feature was a head of rich blond curls that hadn't been developed at Revlon. By the mileage log that most stewardesses wear on their faces, Usher placed Colleen on the sunny side of thirty-five. Barely.

"Don't you look terrific," Colleen said. "Somebody's been to the islands, right?"

"Puerto Rico for a week. Business mostly."

"Must have been a lifeguard's convention, judging by your tan." She laughed. "Not fair. I fly to Miami a dozen times a month and I still look like a ghost. Sharon, too."

"Where is she?" Usher asked. "I thought you two traveled as a team."

"Most times. But not when she's playing good Samaritan by keeping a new co-pilot company during his layover. The bitch."

Usher stood by quietly as Colleen fiddled with the dead bolt.

"Lookit, I'd ask you in for a drink," she said, "but we've been flying so damn much, the cupboard's Mother Hubbard bare."

"I was heading out for one myself. You can join me," Usher said, surprising himself with his easy manner.

"Love to. But some other time, okay? Tonight I'm just too beat. Anybody asks you about airline deregulation, tell them about my flying thirteen legs in two days."

Usher carried her bags across the threshold. For some reason, the soft Oriental sensuality of the TV newscaster flashed across his memory.

"I've got something that'll help fix you up," he said. "Kind of a souvenir."

He went back to his place, grabbed the grapefruit juice and one of the two bottles of Appleton over-proof rum he'd purchased at the Duty Free store. "Souvenir of sunny San Juan," he said when he got back to the corner apartment.

Colleen read the label and made a shrugging gesture before going into the dish- and glass-strewn kitchen to fix their drinks.

"Here you go. Bobby, right?"

"To you." Usher saw the smear of lipstick around the rim of his glass and wiped it clean when Colleen turned her eyes away.

"Lookit," she said again, her Midwestern twang more evident as she began to relax, "give me a few minutes to freshen up and get out of this damned uniform. Then I'll enjoy my drink with you."

"Sure," Usher agreed, his eyes darting around the distressed apartment.

"Sit down anywhere, and forgive the mess," Colleen said as she caught him at it. "We had a party the night before we left and, with all the extra flights they're laying on us, nobody's had time to repair the damage."

Usher sat on the sofa and surveyed the mayhem: ashtrays overflowing with cigarette butts and marijuana roaches, cans and glasses everywhere. The pair of panty hose he saw stuck behind a cushion in the armchair disgusted him. Some party, he thought, wondering why he'd bothered speaking to Colleen in the first place, imagining her hiking her skirts for some leering pilot. Suddenly, the glass he held began to tremble in his hand.

When Colleen returned from her bedroom to join him, Usher was gone.

Chapter 5

At sunset, the stark right angles of the Mies van der Rohe apartment building threw a bleak, tombstone-shaped shadow across the shoreline of a glistening Lake Michigan. Hallet turned his face into it and walked slowly toward the entrance.

The doorman was a bulbous-nosed, sallow-skinned Irishman who looked as if he himself had lost more than one round in a championship bout with the bottle, and he seemed to recognize the same struggle raging inside Hallet. He eyed the dingy, rumpled shirt carefully, tilted his head sideways as if to catch a telltale whiff of Hallet's breath.

"Feeling all right, sir? . . . That's good, then," he answered Hallet's nod. "Mister Clelland is expecting you." He swung open the interior door without the requisite verification on the intercom.

Hallet walked through the lobby, pushed the elevator call, waited. Perhaps it was his unsteadiness and the lingering sense of disorientation that made him recollect the time he'd first met Macdonald Clelland, the day it all began.

Hallet had been dispatched by his eastern college employers—it was optional, they had said, though he learned later that was nothing more than false courtesy—to Fort Meade, Maryland, for a National Security Agency–sponsored briefing on signals intelligence, which Hallet understood even then meant the Agency's all-pervading and unmitigated eavesdropping. Things were heating up again, Hallet had heard from an old friend who ran the Middle East research and analysis section at Meade: NSA microwave dishes were virtually steaming with stuff coming in from Teheran and Beirut and Baghdad, the latter where the Kurdish People's Mujahideen was mobilizing to take on both Khomeini and Hussein by pressing its own ends in the war that Iraq had started along the thousand-mile border that ran from the desert banks of Shaat-al-Arab on the Persian Gulf to the wild Zagros Mountains of Azerbaijan.

Hallet's supposed task was to help evaluate the quality of combined intelligence sources and clarify the interpretations that desk-bound research analysts lent to the subtle complexities of Arabic, Kurdish, and Farsi. Of course, anything he could add to make their networks better and, as they said in Langley, more "relevant" would be appreciated greatly. That was it, his dean had told him: nothing that would compromise the university or its precious academic independence. Except Hallet knew from the instant his credentials arrived that would not be it at all.

Perhaps sensing the inevitability of his impending involvement with Macdonald Clelland was why he'd drunk so much the night before the meeting: cocktails in his room while dressing, a couple more at the hotel bar; several stiff martinis at the Occidental restaurant on Pennsylvania Avenue before picking numbly at what was probably a fine dinner; finally closing some pickup joint over on L Street before wandering back to the Madison to drain the few ounces that remained in his travel flask.

So, the next morning, catching the aroma of residual gin that hung over him like a mist, Hallet stopped in the Agency's commissary to purchase an effective but inoffensive bottle of cologne, then roamed the long, color-coded corridors under the watchful eye of the armed Marine guards (the metal badge Hallet wore on a chain around his neck was red and denied him unescorted access to areas denoted green and yellow) until he found an out-of-the-way lavatory where he could freely remove his suit coat and open his shirt halfway to the waist. He was rubbing his clammy chest and armpits with cologne, trying to stem the trickle that ran down his rib cage, when Macdonald Clelland walked in—the first time Hallet ever saw the man who was soon to control his life so thoroughly.

Clelland nodded passively at the compromised Philip James Hallet and had the good grace never once to mention the incident, though he surely recognized Hallet a mere quarter hour later when they were formally introduced at a conference that, Hallet recalled, accomplished little more than to resurrect reams of old security dossiers concerning the political postures of some 26,000-odd Iranian students then living in the United States—which among them had sold out their dissident countrymen to Savak, the Shah's still-active secret police, or had embraced Khomeini's fundamentalist fanaticism, or continued to lean toward Paris and Bani-Sadr and the other dead or exiled moderates who had tried to save Iran from its disastrous Islamic revolution.

But it was only after he had left Clelland and the NSA complex and was sipping genteel gin and tonics with his new control in a narrow Federalist safe house in Georgetown that Hallet got down to business and saw his life turn upside down. For that was when he again came face to face with Sandman.

Soon after, Hallet broke his promise to himself and the slowly dying Oxford don who had first recruited him—or, as Mac said, corrupted him—two decades earlier. He accepted the proposition that Clelland argued so forcibly, just as he had accepted the old don's mission as they strolled, speaking classic Egyptian Arabic, across Christ Church Meadow toward Merton College tower. Hallet would resign from his comfortable Massachusetts classroom and relocate to the colony of liberal academia that existed on the South Side of Chicago; he would become a Fellow of the Arbor Institute, and, with all the sad and secret people from his past, he would take on Mac's Prophets and, known to him alone, he would also take on Sandman.

Macdonald Clelland opened his door slowly, as if to make certain it indeed was Hallet ringing.

"I thought we'd lost you again," he said, his face clouded by the winter's worth of pipe smoke that hung like a fog in the apartment.

"Fact is, Mac, you'd never lost me at all. Not with Isabel Ortega's daily and, I'm sure, detailed reports on my condition."

Clelland merely shook his head. "Come inside, will you?"

Hallet followed him into the square, spacious living room, a testament to the confusion brought about by mixing too much new chrome and glass with old wood and leather. A crystal decanter sat alone on the table that hugged Clelland's reading chair; it was half filled with a pale amber liquid: quite unappetizing.

"I'm having sherry," Clelland said, noticing him. "I don't suppose you . . ."

"Nothing, thanks. I thought you knew from Isabel that I'm not drinking."

"As far as *she* knows, you aren't. But, seeing how you left her apartment as you did, the question has arisen. That, and where the hell you've been since."

"I've been not drinking. Let's leave it at that," Hallet said. Besides, the transient hotel where he'd sweated through the last three shivering nights was nothing he cared to discuss, least of all with the tweedy Mac Clelland, who thought anything less than the monastic accommodations at the University Club were beneath civilized man. "The same goes for any conversation about Isabel Ortega, my caring confidante."

"Damn it, Hallet! What's so untoward about our wanting to help you, about wanting you back at the Institute? There's work to be done, work that matters."

"It sure as hell mattered to those two kids in Baghdad.

Hussein's secret police hanged them with *wire,* Mac. You recall that?"

"Quite horrible," Clelland agreed sadly. "I know how you feel."

"Do you?"

Clelland leaned forward, picked up an unvarnished briar pipe from the table, rolled it gently between his palms. He was far from a tall man, and twenty pounds of recently acquired paunch made him appear shorter; he wore a head of fine-denier white hair cut short, and he accented its dignity with a neatly trimmed Vandyke. But today, Mac's complexion looked more hypertensively flushed than normally ruddy and florid. His voice, when he spoke again, had an edge to it that underscored Hallet's observation: Clelland was not playing the classically unflappable scholar-diplomat. He was back in the trenches of his real stock-in-trade, back before the sinecure at the Arbor Institute and his network of schoolboys and academic idealists. And that was using anyone and everyone around him to gather intelligence.

"Of course, I blame myself," Clelland said. "We took it too far. Those boys shouldn't have been there, and we shouldn't have allowed them to go. It's what happens when we go beyond our charter."

"So it's 'we' at last," Hallet said.

"It was always meant to be 'we,' " Clelland said. "If you'll only believe it and, for once in your life, trust someone."

"Like they trusted us," Hallet said, kicking himself an instant afterward for trying to spread whatever blame there was to Clelland's side of the equation. Not when the two Prophets were actually doing his private business.

"You want to mourn, Philip? I can understand that. But that doesn't give you license to go on another extended drunk and walk away from everyone who depends on you, everyone you owe. And you'd better face it—you owe me plenty. I'm the one who has tolerated your drinking, your arrogance, even your contempt for me and for what the Institute is trying to accomplish. I've tolerated them not just because of your talents—your genius, if you prefer. But because I, like Stan Bach and Isabel Ortega and other friends you probably don't deserve, care about your welfare."

"Not to mention my friends in Washington," Hallet swiped back.

"You have bargains to keep, Philip. And, perhaps now more than ever, I'm going to hold you to them. I want you back to work, and I want you back both sober and at once."

Hallet again studied Clelland as Mac drained his sherry in an uncommonly large gulp. He was pushing sixty, Hallet guessed, and had been considered an expert in their common field of Middle East affairs since the mid-1960s when, while ostensibly lecturing at the American University in Beirut, Clelland's fledgling, ragtag network of informers became a key in alerting both the United States and Israel to an imminent infiltration campaign directed by an unknown, diminutive Palestinian of dubious sexuality named Yasser Arafat. Later to become *the* Arafat, who was adopting the very same terror tactics the Israelis had used to great success against the British for his own newly formed arm of the PLO—the al Harakat Tahir Filastin, which became better known under its jumbled, punning acronym for "the conqueror," Al Fatah.

"Since I signed on with you in person," Hallet said, "I figure I'd be honoring my so-called bargain by telling you face to face that I'm going to resign. Effective immediately."

"The hell you are," Clelland fumed. "I've let you grieve in your own self-destructive way, but I sure as hell won't let you quit over two lives. Not when hundreds die each week."

"Not on my orders," Hallet shot back, then waited to calm himself before going on. "If you want it formal, Mac, I'll write the prescribed letter. That'll make it perfectly acceptable to Bryce Vreeland, and to Jason Kellaigh too, I suppose."

"Then what? Run back to your bucolic country classroom? Teach the literature of the Koran and the Sunna to graduate students who are only studying Arabic so they can get jobs with Standard Oil? You could go back to England, I suppose, except your welcome from those you walked out on the last time would be less than warm. Then, again, if you stay here, any good teaching position would require references."

"You bastard, Mac! Are you threatening me?"

"No, of course not," Clelland apologized. He took a slow drag on his pipe, let the smoke curl slowly through his tense lips. "Look, Philip, we're both under some stress here. So let's calm down and forget threats which we know would be idle at best. Besides, you understand more than anyone that what I'm doing is part of the job."

"And Albert Speer was merely an architect." The look that fell over Clelland's face made Hallet retract his words with a wave of his arm. "Damn you, Mac," he went on. "Damn the both of us. We used to do good work, you know. Before we started trading in people's lives. Before people became personnel."

"Back in the halcyon days when scholarship was an end in itself," Clelland sneered. "Do our research, write our books and monographs, pretend the history and culture we treasure isn't touched by the real world outside. Nonsense, Hallet, and you know it. Scholarship and intelligence have always suckled the same breast. Which is why I suspect you let your old maestro sign you up with the Brits."

Hallet was almost ready to tell Clelland about it, but caught himself. How could Mac understand when he himself was never certain why he'd ever agreed to make that first deadly trip to Damascus? "I was finished with it, Mac. The dirty work was done. Why I ever agreed to come here . . ."

"You came because you knew you could help save lives. Theirs and ours. And if you can see through the curtains of alcohol you've pulled over your brain, you still can."

Hallet found himself staring at Clelland's empty glass. "I'm tired of people dying in God's name," he said reflexively.

"It's a land war, Hallet. Not a holy crusade. It's territory and resources, and it has always been thus."

"But the land *itself* is sacred. That's something we've all forgotten in our self-serving smugness. This whole damned country, Mac. We no longer comprehend that things can be sacred."

Clelland's voice rattled in frustration. "This whole damn sacred country is what I'm concerned about," he said. "That's why I need you to pull yourself together, get back to it without the booze and without collapsing again should something turn sour. I need you to do it and, goddamn it, Philip, I'm ready to do anything I have to do to bring it off."

"You're telling me I have no choice in the matter?"

"I'm *asking* you to hear me out." Clelland lowered his voice as if suddenly aware of a third person in the room who might be trying to overhear them. "Word has come from our sponsors that we should expect visitors soon. Very nasty visitors with nasty plans. What we've read about as Project Export. At least the first stages of it."

"That's nonsense," Hallet said, which was exactly how he felt about the Export dossier from the instant he'd laid eyes on it and studied its doomsday appeal—an opinion which led many of the Institute's secret sponsors to consider him excessively pro-Arab and blinded to the viciousness for which the rest of the civilized world knew them capable.

"Terrorist attacks in the States, destroying nuclear reactors and hydroelectric plants? Nothing but rumors of war. Let's barricade the White House, prepare for invasion. Sheer nonsense. That's the last thing any Arab nation is going to try, Qadhafi's Libya included. Especially with half our fleet in the Gulf and an arsenal of Cruise missiles aimed over the desert. Panic peddling, Mac. Propaganda and nothing more."

"The airport massacre, last month. You consider that propaganda?"

"I was locked up in that detox resort in Oak Park, you'll remember."

"My point exactly. Perhaps if you were on the job, not drinking?"

"Better raise your sights if we're going any further with this," Hallet protested.

Clelland went to his desk, unlocked the center drawer, and produced a file jacket which Hallet could tell on sight came from Langley. "A repeat of the assault at da Vinci airport in Rome. Only this time in your beloved England, for God's sake. And soon to head our way."

Hallet went through the report quickly: six terrorists, all of them killed in the carnage, along with fourteen Americans about to return home.

Hallet tossed the report onto the glass table between them. "I think they have it wrong. The Revolutionary Guards that hit Rome have been pretty well dismembered. The Israelis got a bunch of them, the in-fighting after Khomeini's death took care of the rest. The Iranian Two-Ten Bureau that backed them is barely functioning, what with their Hezbollah units battling the Syrian Shiite militia in Lebanon. And with Arafat's own special operations group bringing the PLO hard-liners under control, even the Fatah Revolutionary Council is pretty much finished as a tactical entity."

"Which means other groups will rise to take their place, to pick up the standard and perhaps plant it on American soil."

"I still say the Export file is humbug," Hallet went on, knowing he was being duplicitous but having little other choice. "Look at what's been happening over there. The Iranians and Iraqis finally get a peace plan underway, Arafat denounces terrorism before the United Nations, even Qadhafi wants to talk with Washington. Believe it, Mac, the moderates are winning out. Sure, there will always be splinter groups of crazies like Abu Nidal and Islamic Jihad who want to avenge Iran Air Six-fifty-five by hitting Pan Am, but none of that signals all the commando-attack baloney that the boys behind the Export file have dreamt up."

"You used to think more like an Arab, Philip. If you'd focus again, you would realize what's really going on is not a process of moderation but a reaction to it. The Iran-Iraq war may be over, but the people who fought have nothing to show for it but eight years of hell and a million dead. Arafat's peace talks are only hardening Ahmed Jibril's extremists in the PLO-General Command, and much the same squabbling is occurring between Teheran and the Jihad. Everyone's ready to renew the war against the Great Satan, and everything the Export people learned says that we're going to see it here. Which means we'll have to keep turning to our Prophets for whatever they can tell us. That's why I allowed those boys into the field, that's what makes your coming back to work vital, Philip. I pray to God you're able to do it."

"We're not an intelligence service, damn it," Hallet argued. "We have a network of Islamic faculty and students who don't believe in terrorism as a means for justice. They're not working for us to betray their people or their governments."

"You really believe that's all there is? That's all they're willing to do for us?" Clelland asked.

Hallet shook his head, allowing Mac to see that he indeed knew better. He picked up the Export dossier, held it as if it were a boomerang. "Anarchy is loosed upon the world," he said. "And everywhere the ceremony of innocence is drowned."

" 'The Second Coming,' " Clelland knew. "You've always been too much the poet, Philip, and most times more a Brit than a Yank. But enough of two potty professors spouting poetry at each other. What I need to know is whether you have the courage left to help us stem Yeats's blood-dimmed tide. Can you stop denying what you choose not to believe and get things running one more time?"

Hallet picked up Clelland's decanter, poured himself a full glass of sherry, drank it down in a single swallow. "Doctor at the clinic says you have to hit bottom before you can resurface. Maybe I've already landed. If not, it can't be much farther down."

"Which I take to mean . . ."

"Which means I need a little more time to find out. When I do, I'll see you at the mansion."

"Until then?" Clelland asked.

Hallet rose and left without answering, though he knew at once that the only place left for him was home.

Usher stripped off his shorts and sweatshirt, rubbed his aching leg muscles briskly. He'd met Ben as soon as he'd finished a two-mile jog around the lagoon in Lincoln Park, and hadn't had time to cool down properly. Not when Ben had business to conclude. Usher never considered himself one of the fitness freaks who wanted to live forever and thought that exercise, oat bran, and Vichy water would get it done for them. He did only what was necessary to keep himself in shape. He had to. But he trained on his own regimen, without running marathon distances or spending hours in a weight room. The result was that his muscles were elongated and pliable, like a swimmer's— more with the potential energy of a coiled snake than the hardness of steel.

He decided on some stretching exercises, bending deeply at the waist, forward and side to side, then going into a squat on his tiptoes. He felt the tension ease in his calves and thighs. He unlaced his shoes, pulled down his long sweat socks, and removed the razor-sharp gravity knife that he'd taped to his right ankle as a self-defense weapon much preferable to firearms in a crowded city park.

The meeting with Ben had gone well: The receipt for the money deposited into his bank account was passed over, everyone was pleased with the outcome. More important, as they walked past the Conservatory and looked at the dazzling array of flowers caught in a perfect sunset, Ben said he had another out-of-town assignment ready, this time in New York. It sounded peculiar at first—what the hell did the outfit have to do with Arabs?—but as usual Usher knew better than to ask for reasons. Why should he? One more assignment would conclude the business he had contracted with Ben and the Chicago family, a profitable run begun one year earlier when he'd happily collected a local greaseball hood named Chuckie Franco, whom Usher told he was driving to a high stakes poker game but instead left waiting out an eternal flight delay in the trunk of his car at O'Hare airport.

Usher ran a hot bath and soaked in the tub for almost an hour, adding hot water at intervals to keep the temperature as high as he could bear. He seemed finally to relax, his mind wandering to no place in particular. Throughout his life Usher had loved flowers, and bright colors filled whatever dreams he had that weren't nightmares. So, as the scalding water forced drops of sweat to form on his forehead, he thought back to his work on the Jamaican golf course, recalling more the physical beauty of the location—the manicured shrubs that marked each fairway, the beds of sedum and tropical ground cover that gave even the sandy oceanside banks a lush look—than of bringing down the fat man with his .30-caliber ranch rifle. He thought, too, about his upcoming trip to New York, and how he might go about fulfilling the strange task he'd accepted from Ben. And, despite trying not to, he kept recalling the Oriental sensuality of the television newscaster who'd greeted his return home by reporting his story.

Usher took the clear plastic bottle of scented massage oil from the shelf beside the tub, dribbled long lines of it down his biceps and forearms, rubbed the satiny substance roughly at first with the palms of his hands, then softly with his fingertips. He allowed his head to fall back so the nape of his neck was completely underwater, then continued rubbing downward, squirting oil across his pectorals and the ripples of his abdomen. He closed his eyes as his hands eventually found his penis. But the woman he fantasized was neither the Asian beauty from the television screen nor the full-bodied blond stewardess who lived down the hall. It was the same nameless, faceless, loving woman he'd known with onanistic intimacy since his early childhood, the one woman who had never hurt him.

*   *   *

The doorman had a taxi waiting. Hallet took it north, up Clark Street. Heeding old instincts about never riding all the way to one's final destination, he climbed out in the middle of a long commercial block lined with renovated storefronts that offered the trendy Lincoln Park crowd overpriced antiques, custom jewelry, and desserts made with frozen yogurt—all just a few yards from the site of the great Valentine's Day massacre, now built over with a bland and depressing apartment building for senior citizens.

Hallet's town house was a quarter mile west: a two-story block of grayish brick and casement windows that sat behind a six-foot privacy wall. Of all the dozens, perhaps hundreds of places Hallet had lived, this was the first he'd ever owned or, in fact, inhabited to the end of a lease. He both loved its security and, like the nomad he'd once learned to become, hated its permanence.

He cut between a pair of late Victorian two-flats and followed the alley that paralleled his street. Alleys rivaled the lakefront as one of Chicago's greatest gifts to its citizens: They kept trash off the avenues and eased its collection; they provided room for garages and small gardens; most important, they gave people easy and private traffic paths that reminded Hallet of the maze of Arabian back streets where he had done so much of his study and his frightful business.

The night was clear, the alley well lighted by vapor lamps. Several people walking dogs passed by silently, fecal scoops at the ready. Hallet decided to use the rear door so that he could dash quickly upstairs without confronting the empty bottles and dirty glasses he'd left strewn across the bar.

He walked softly across the paving bricks of his back patio, unlocked the sliding door and its burglar bar, moved slowly toward the rear staircase in the throw of the street lights. He was six steps inside his kitchen when he saw the outlines—first the shape of a human form, definitely male; then the extended arm and the hand that held a pistol.

He felt no panic. In fact, since he'd been carried off to the clinic, nothing, including Clelland's hypotheses, seemed in any way real to him. Then an ancient Bedouin maxim flashed across his memory: It is better to stare straight into the eyes of one's attacker, for the threatening glare of eternal revenge might be sufficient to make him slow his sword for the instant needed to deflect it.

Hallet planted his feet for a kick thrust and parry as he turned on an overhead track of spotlights. Before his eyes could focus, he heard Stan Bach's heavy sigh of relief.

"You *putz*," Bach said, exhaling. "What the hell are you doing breaking into your own house?"

Hallet finally felt the icy shiver of fear run through him, too late to have been of any help or salvation. Stan Bach, well over six feet tall, bone thin, black-haired but fast balding, pulled the tortoise shell eyeglasses from his narrow face.

"You scared me half to death, damn it."

"I think that's my line," Hallet said. "And the way you're pointing that pistol, I'm *still* scared."

Stan Bach looked down at the compact Sauer automatic with disgust, as if his hand held a bleeding heart.

"God, yes. Sorry." He placed the gun carefully on an end table and stared at it intently. "What are you doing with this thing in the house, anyway?"

"My line again, Stan. What are *you* doing in my house, with my pistol?"

"Trying to remain your friend, I suppose, even though it's not me you reach out to when you need help. So I thought I'd clean up a little, sort out the real mail from the circulars. Maybe even find you," Bach added as he fell into an armchair. "See if I could help lead you back across the Styx."

"That's all?"

"Certainly," Bach said. "Just trying to help, old boy. Isabel called me after you walked out on her. She's worried, you know. So's Mac, I imagine."

"I've already seen Mac," Hallet said.

"That's a relief," Bach said, his eyes again focusing on the pistol. "Anyway, I found that ugly little thing up in your bedroom when I came to gather your clothes for the hospital. We assumed back then, of course, that your stay would be longer. When I came tonight, I figured I'd better stash it someplace out of the way."

"You thought I might use it on myself?"

"I thought that if I could find it, so could anyone else who might be afoot. That's all, Hallet. Until I heard someone sneaking into the house, maybe a burglar . . ."

"I say we both could use a drink."

"You're not serious?"

"I'm going to have some real coffee for a change," Hallet said, enjoying the look of embarrassment that crossed Stan Bach's face. "There's liquor in the sideboard if you want it."

"No, I'd prefer that sweetened mud you brew. Ruth has me on decaf exclusively. Rotten stuff, even when she grinds the beans fresh."

Bach followed Hallet into the kitchen, watched him fill the brass *ibrik* with water. When it began to boil, Hallet took it off the flame, added heaping spoonfuls of finely ground Arabian coffee and half as much sugar, placed it back on the stove until foam spilled over the brim of the uncovered pot.

"Ahwah mazbhut," Hallet said. "Coffee neither too sweet nor bitter. Just right. Better hospitality than you deserve for breaking in here."

"At my place, Ruthie makes you a nice glass tea," Bach said in a feigned Yiddish accent. "And I didn't break in, thank you. You'll remember I had your keys."

"And orders from Clelland?"

"Sure. If I found you, I was to keep you sober until Mac came around and got you back to the clinic. Or, I drag you back to Ortega's place if you didn't have your snout buried in a gin bottle. Admit it, Hallet. You're a *shikker*. That makes all of us worry a bit."

Hallet filled the demitasse cups carefully, handed one to Bach, sipped his with great relish.

"To relieve your anxiety," Hallet said, "Mac is satisfied I'm back on the straight and narrow."

"Are you?"

"Believe it. I'm coming back to work."

"Then I think you'd at least better call Isabel," Bach said. "I sense more than a dent in her formidable mask of composure."

"Later," Hallet said.

"Mind if I let her know you're okay, that you're not sneaking back into the desert like some wounded goatherd?"

"Go ahead. Tell Bryce Vreeland too, if you wish."

"Screw him," Bach snapped. "I do nothing that involves Bryce Vreeland other than cash paychecks over his signature." Bach finished his coffee in quick swallows. "Damn, this is good stuff. Fix me another, will you?"

"Don't squeal to Ruth and I will. My position on her list of family friends is low enough as it is."

"Nonsense," Bach insisted. "But she wasn't at all surprised when you ran out of the clinic. She said from the day you went in that you'd never stay."

"Why's that? Character flaws too deep?"

"Well, you could never suffer fools at all, Hallet, let alone gladly. So, reasons Ruth correctly, you'd never let the medics look inside your head, or seek support from other patients who may share your disease but not your intellect. That's Ruthie's scenario, at any rate."

"Ruth's, or yours? Somehow I can't hear the consummate sabra citing Saint Paul's epistle to the Galatians," Hallet said.

"The quotation was mine alone," Bach grinned. "I love you dearly, you see. But even I know you're an arrogant snob. I can say it because of the bond that unites us."

"Which is?"

"That we've both spent our lives in the mainstream of recondite minutia. And we're both foreigners preaching among the disingenuous gentiles."

Hallet threw up his arms and returned to the kitchen. He saw the bottle of clear, fiery Syrian arak when he opened the cupboard. His hand shook slightly as he bypassed it for the tin of coffee.

"Ruthie was only partly right," Hallet said as he handed Bach a fresh cup. "Sometime soon, when things are approaching normal, I'll tell you about my experience at the clinic."

"Can't wait."

"By the way, thanks."

"For?"

"For all you've done, and tried to do."

"All I did was deliver your clothes and sneak you a pocket cassette player and some Mozart," Bach said. "Incredible wardrobe, incidentally. Your damn closets look like some natty fagadashery on Savile Row. If I didn't know you were giving the old *shtup* to Isabel Ortega, I'd be sure your English schooldays had caused worse perversions than making you drink warm gin."

"My wardrobe," Hallet countered in mock indignation, "is a direct product of all my years wearing cheap white linen suits, like the poor academic I was. Nothing you'd understand, of course, as a member of the Zionist mercantile class."

"Such crap," Bach laughed. "You with the big-money television appearances and lecture fees, not to mention enough Islamic art to fill a wing at the Mayer Institute. So don't try to make me feel guilty because I wasn't born on a kibbutz."

"Never too late to repatriate," Hallet gibed. "Next year in Jerusalem."

"Don't laugh," Bach said, his tone no longer taunting. "Ruthie keeps talking about it. Seriously. If it weren't for the kids . . ."

"You're kidding."

Stan Bach rose, walked to the open patio doors, and stared out at Hallet's small plot of garden. Hallet couldn't make out precisely what he was mumbling to himself in Hebrew. Something about seeing orange trees bloom in the desert.

69

Chapter 6

Usher came above ground at the One hundred-sixteenth Street IRT station, nostrils ablaze from the lingering stench of the crowded subway, muscles tense from the assault on all his senses that characterized the ride north from Times Square. Only the absolute anonymity for which New Yorkers paid so dearly had made the journey halfway tolerable.

He walked south on Broadway until he stood directly across the street from the M'rabet, a dingy Middle Eastern restaurant with a streaked neon sign dangling precariously from its unwashed facade. In position, he calmly waited for Mohammed Saami to appear.

If nothing else, the Arab's movements so far had been regular, predictable, in line with the data Ben had provided. After classes on Tuesday and Thursday afternoons, Saami would attend regular meetings of the Islamic Student Association and, afterward, stroll across the Columbia University campus to exchange books at Butler Library, finally depositing them and his overstuffed briefcase at his office in Hamilton. Most times, he met his woman there, and the two of them would stroll to the storefront restaurant where Usher now awaited him. Absolutely predict-

71

able, which, for Mohammed Saami today, meant absolutely perilous.

Usher leaned back into the doorway that separated a used-book store from the butcher's shop where people were rushing to collect last-minute orders. He wore a mottled sports coat of thick Donegal tweed, striped shirt and calculatedly crumpled necktie, corduroy trousers—perfectly undistinguished and compatible with the university neighborhood. With his auburn-tinted hair and the thick Guardsman's mustache fixed firmly above his upper lip, Usher gave the sure appearance of someone who taught English literature at Columbia, probably eighteenth-century.

He checked his watch another time. Saami was uncharacteristically late. Just when Usher succumbed to the urge to light a cigarette, he saw the Arab approaching from the south, a rare departure from form. The reason why was instantly apparent—a new woman, her face not in any of the photographs Usher had been given. She was short, in her early twenties and already tending toward fat, though the long black dress she wore camouflaged her hips while accenting her melon breasts. Around her shoulders and high up the nape of her neck was a black scarf. A funereal bit of crepe, Usher thought, until he realized that it was a chador, the black veil of Muslim womanhood that was supposed to cover all but the eyes, but which Saami's companion wore as a fashion statement—a concurrent symbol of tradition and liberation.

Usher watched Saami and the woman enter the restaurant, decided to enjoy the rest of his cigarette before following them inside to face another platter of greasy lamb garnished with eggplant and a dollop of garlic-laden hummus. He went through his plan a final time. Easy is as easy does, he assured himself. Ben and his people will love it.

Usher field-stripped the cigarette butt as he walked to the corner, crossed Broadway with the light, came back down the west side of the street, and entered the M'rabet. After the subway and the exhaust fumes he'd breathed, the air inside the restaurant smelled cloyingly sweet, a mixture of cinnamon and clove suspended in a heavy aerosol of olive oil.

A passing waiter grunted at him and pointed to a small table against the left wall. Saami was directly across the room, seated with his newest lady at a large round table in the restaurant's front corner. The wog's equivalent of Booth One at the Pump Room, Usher thought as he eyed them discreetly. The woman's chador was fully down around her neck, her hair pulled back by a silver barrette. She was neither a beauty nor an Arab, Usher saw clearly. Her cheekbones were hidden by a healthy layer of flesh, her eyes were greenish that shaded toward hazel, her complexion eggshell pale. Probably some kind of Muslim groupie, Usher figured, deciding finally that the reason he had been dispatched to New York probably concerned Mohammed Saami's mistreatment of some local don's daughter. Still, Saami was such a patsy, any old numb nuts could handle it, make it look like a street crime any night of the week. So why did Ben have all the photos made, the timetable drawn? There had to be more. Usher stopped wondering as he watched Saami place his order in jabbering Arabic.

The restaurant served no alcohol, and allowed none to be carried in. Usher ordered Moroccan tea, which came in a tall clear glass loaded with sugar and mint leaves. He watched carefully to make sure the waiter followed his routine exactly as Usher recalled it. The glass was carried in from the kitchen; the waiter added the mint leaves and allowed the brew to steep for several minutes on a sideboard as he disappeared to pick up Usher's platter of rice and meatballs. His plate delivered, Usher watched the waiter return for the steeping tea, add a mound of sugar, and deliver it to the table.

"*Shukran*," Usher replied, mouthing his recently learned Arabic "thank you" well enough that the waiter muttered something back before retreating to the chaos of the kitchen.

Saami was busily disjointing a half chicken with his fingers while his girlfriend looked on transfixed, as if he were doing a grand and noble deed. Usher suddenly felt an intense dislike for the man, or at least allowed the emotion to surface as he watched Saami's doe-eyed admirer nod appreciatively at whatever Saami was saying to her with his mouth full of pita and chicken flesh. Just a little longer, Usher calculated, as he picked lazily at his own food and sipped the sweet, scalding tea.

Saami had finished his plate and drunk two glasses of water when Usher paid his bill and prepared to leave. Any minute now, Usher guessed. Yes, there he goes—Saami calling the waiter, ordering his own tea, as always after the meal, with a thick square of honey-and-nut cake that the waiter had to retrieve from a grimy plastic tray.

The waiter fixed Saami's tea, adding the mint leaves, allowing it to steep as he delivered the sweets. Usher rose and walked past the sideboard to the rest room. He didn't even have to pause as he slipped the water-soluble packet into the mint leaves that floated atop the tea glass.

Usher washed his hands carefully in the stained sink, dried them on a handkerchief he would dispose of within minutes. The waiter was carrying the tea to Saami as Usher came out of the washroom and started for the door. Saami's eyes caught his as he passed the table. Usher threw him a broad and final smile.

Hallet stretched across the sofa, feeling tired, anxious, both at once. He discarded the idea of taking any more Librium, or of tapping into the one unopened bottle of gin that remained in the cupboard. Still, he needed something to help him relax, for Monday morning would mark his less than triumphal return to the Arbor Institute for Middle East Studies, to Macdonald Clelland and Bryce Vreeland, and to what he had dreaded from the moment he decided that he hadn't the courage to resign— which was Sandman.

He checked the time. Another forty minutes before he could pick up BBC's Arabic Service on the shortwave radio in his bedroom. Probably just as well. He lifted himself from the sofa, turned on the record player. Solti conducting Mahler, he decided, but none of the depressing Nachtmusik of the Eighth Symphony. Maybe the rich French horns of the scherzo in the Fifth would elevate his spirits, something vital and brilliant and celebrating life.

As the music soared in his ears, Hallet poured himself a modest shot of arak and watched the clear liquid turn white as milk as he added a triple measure of water. He sipped the drink slowly; its licorice taste seemed harmless when so well diluted. It soothed and relaxed him as surely as the two hours he'd spent dining with Isabel Ortega had left him feeling pained and empty.

They had met at an Italian restaurant on Taylor Street, in what once was the heart of Chicago's Little Italy; neutral territory, Isabel tried joking when Hallet had phoned her, but with a distinct edge in her voice.

They were barely seated, a bottle of Isabel's favorite Pinot Grigio chilling in the ice bucket beside her chair, a glass of lime-laced club soda in Hallet's hand, when she attempted to clear the air by filling it with storm clouds. Why had he left her apartment as he had? What had he done in the days since then, and why did he neither call her nor take any calls when, according to both Stan Bach and Macdonald Clelland, he'd finally returned home and was soon to return to work? All she wanted was to help him, not to interfere. Why wouldn't he let her?

"You have this irrepressible desire to do everything alone," she said. "It's the way you've always operated at the Institute. Keeping to yourself, never sharing your work or your ideas. You run your damn programs like they're some kind of state secrets, no help from me or anyone else. I'm sure you were exactly the same at the clinic. You couldn't tolerate anything you considered interference, just as you couldn't stand being with me."

Hallet tried to apologize, saying her observations weren't true, wondering if after all this time, Isabel still had no idea about the Prophets.

"It wasn't being with you," he said. "I just needed to be by myself."

"You've had a lifetime full, I should think."

"It's worked out that way," Hallet admitted.

"I should have realized earlier," she went on, as if Hallet hadn't said a word. "Should have known all along you couldn't get close to anyone."

"People who drink *can't* get close to anyone, at least while they're drinking," Hallet said, an image of Pam and her junkie companions darting unexpectedly across his memory. "All I was doing was purging the booze, exorcising the demons so I could function again. Normally, both at work and with you. I'm asking you to understand."

Isabel seemed to calm down as she allowed Hallet to pour her another glass of wine.

"You're sticking to it, then? No alcohol?"

Hallet poked the green wedges in his glass. "Not a drop. But I think I've consumed more limes than the entire crew of H.M.S. *Bounty* on its voyage to Pitcairn."

"I'm glad for that much," Isabel said. "And that you're finally coming back to work. Even if I had to hear about it from Clelland and Stan Bach."

"Stan's upset I never called him either," Hallet said. "Maybe it's too many years among the Bedouin. We go alone into the desert wilderness to solve our problems. But we're great lovers when we get back to the tent."

"Sure, because your women are no more than chattel," Isabel said. "It's easy to think one's a great lover when you're dangling a sword over the lady's head. I thought Latin macho was bad enough, but compared to Arab culture, it's child's play."

Their evening ended with coffee. Hallet made no offer to extend it. Neither did Isabel as she kissed him lightly on the cheek and climbed into a taxi.

"I'll call you soon," Hallet said.

Isabel merely shrugged her designer-padded shoulders. And that was that.

Hallet changed records to a Mozart piano concerto, listened to it dreamily while studying the collection of Persian and Turkish prayer rugs in impossibly tight weaves and rich deep colors that hung on the walls. He tried to tell himself honestly that this was home. And probably it was. More than all the places he had lived, or better yet inhabited: the perpetually damp bedsit in Oxford; the stuffy flat in South Ken when he was completing his research in London; the apartments in the Middle East that were supposedly geared to Western preferences but which invariably missed the mark by miles, such as the one in Cairo with the sink *over* the toilet.

The only thing they had in common, Hallet realized, was that, save for one brief interlude, he'd lived in all of them alone.

With Isabel Ortega's words ringing in his ears, he thought back for the first time in fifteen years to the freckled young Welsh schoolteacher he'd known in London. She was studying French in hope of fleeing grimy Cardiff for a position on the Continent. Hallet, who'd mastered the language as a boy, slid from tutor to lover in the same casual manner he had found his way into Isabel Ortega's bed. Her name was Caroline. And Hallet would spend patient hours listening to her endless recitations of irregular French verbs (*devoir* and *recevoir* gave her inordinate difficulty) as she tried to compensate for her harsh Celtic inflections by softening her French until she had a lilt not far from the *pied noir* dialect of Algerians. Caroline Wade, who one day went off with nothing more than a kiss on the cheek, much like Isabel's just hours earlier, to teach British military brats at a naval base in Malta.

Hallet decided to top off his drink with a second splash of arak. Its medicinal purpose had combined with the music to relieve his stress, to make his morning reappearance at the Institute seem not nearly so ominous and foreboding. He would go upstairs, perhaps blue-pencil a no longer interesting monograph on Kufic scrollwork in Islamic architectural motifs, and listen to the BBC if the local horde of squirrels hadn't again eaten through the antenna wire he had run up the outside wall.

The knock on his front door was soft at first; then louder, more brazen, finally urgent. Hallet tucked his shirt back inside his trousers, made certain his hair was parted and combed.

"Doctor Hallet."

The face was familiar: wide-set eyes the color of cured olives, skin like polished honey pine. She wore blue jeans and a loose cotton sweater, which kept Hallet from recognizing her right away. Finally he remembered—one of the members of the Islamic students' group for which he acted as honorary advisor: an Egyptian premed major, an innocent.

"Nahid. From the Union."

"You remember. Thank you."

Hallet reflexively lapsed into Arabic and asked how she was. *"Izzayik inti, ya nahid?"*

"Ana kwayisa, il Hamdu lillaah," she replied, saying she was well and automatically praising God for it. But as Hallet welcomed her into the light, he saw fear gleaming in her eyes.

He led her to his study. Nahid looked surprised at the mass of papers and unopened mail strewn haphazardly over his desk.

"Will you take tea?" Hallet asked, suddenly conscious of the glass in his hand.

Nahid shook her head nervously. "Yousef said you have been gone for weeks, and has asked me to try and find you. He could not come himself. Not here."

"Yousef can come here whenever he wishes," Hallet said. "We are old friends."

"It is about your . . . friends," she hesitated, as if searching for the right word. "In New York, one of your friends . . . Yousef said to tell you. Something has happened."

"My friends?"

"I'm telling you only what Yousef said. He was Mohammed Saami."

"What do you mean he *was?*" Hallet asked, trying to mask

his surprise. Arab men rarely share their secrets with women, and for Yousef to even hint of the Prophets?

"Mohammed Saami is dead now. Murdered. Yousef wanted you to know this at once. He also tells you some others are likewise in danger, that their enemies are searching for them. He is trying to learn more, but is afraid to come here. That is why he sent me."

"I still don't understand. I vaguely know a Mohammed Saami, a doctoral Fellow at Columbia University. And Yousef said this is my friend?"

"Yes," she replied. "A friend, and also of al-Anbiya. The Prophets. He said you would understand this."

Hallet steeled himself against showing a response. But if Yousef would entrust Nahid with even the name . . .

"Are you certain it is our friend Saami who is dead?"

"He was poisoned. It happened in a restaurant. Saami and the women he was dining with. Both dead. And now," she went on as Hallet began recalling the warning Mac Clelland had given him, "Yousef says that he too is in great danger."

"Give me his exact words," Hallet demanded.

Nahid didn't hesitate. "He said, 'Tell Doctor Hallet they know of the Prophets, and they are coming to destroy them.' "

"Coming from where?"

"Yousef is not certain. That is what he is trying to learn now. It is why he cannot be seen here, for he believes that you too may be known. I'm afraid for him," Nahid said, "for Yousef says that what Saami knew, he knows as well."

"Yousef will be fine," Hallet assured her.

"*Inshallah,*" she whispered. God willing.

Hallet told her he would be back at the Institute the next day, and that she or Yousef could contact him there anytime, that it was safe.

"I have been ill," he said. "But no longer."

"Yousef will be glad," Nahid said, looking up at Hallet as if awaiting orders.

"Now, tell me all you know about Saami."

"We know nothing more. Someone gave them poison. Both died there, together."

"An accident, perhaps," Hallet wondered aloud. "It is not the way of our people to do such a thing. Never like that."

"That is what frightens Yousef so much about those who are coming here. It is because they are sent to do things our people would not."

Sergeant Cal Bostic was grateful for the slow night. One more week, and his twenty-eight-day rotation on the midwatch shift would be complete: no more greasy chicken dinners from Waldo's Birdland; no more arriving home in the middle of the night to nothing more than his wife's groggy welcome and missing breakfast with his kids before they went off to school; at last being able to enjoy the few rare days of a Chicago spring.

He relighted the stub of an A&C Grenadier that had smoldered out in its ashtray and decided he'd kill the final hour of his tour going through a stack of long-neglected fugitive warrants. For a change, everything pointed toward his being able to leave on time, even after a federal DEA crew had requested local assistance in grabbing a coke-crazed Colombian drug dealer inside a Latino nightclub—a plan which would no doubt have caught some civilians in a cross fire or a hostage situation of the primo class. Instead, Bostic had given the head of his tactical unit a well-earned bust: The tac cops took the dealer quietly in the parking lot, demonstrating to him graphically that he was sighted in enough cross hairs to get turned into a crowd should he or his bodyguards even think of reaching for a weapon.

The instant the voice yelled at him across the squad room, Bostic knew his plans for an on-time departure were history.

"Bostic, pick up on three!"

"Got it."

The voice coming across the receiver was cool and emotionless. Yellow Cab out by Douglas Park. Driver shot in apparent robbery. DOA at Cook County.

"Where was he hit?" Bostic asked, hoping against hope.

"Let's see . . . yeah, head shots. Looks like he caught a pair."

"Now you're going to tell me the guy's an Arab."

"Hey, you know him?"

"What I know is that you're going to sit tight until you hear otherwise. Nothing goes on paper until I get there, and keep the goddamn radio quiet. Any reporter calls, you're still unsure of what's happening."

"You got to be kiddin', Sarge."

"Officer, the only thing I'm not is kidding."

Bostic slammed down the receiver and compulsively bit off the soggy end of his cigar. He hated to wake up Margie and the kids, but if he didn't, Jack Corrigan would ream him a new asshole in the morning. Besides, Corrigan was the best white cop there was at Eleventh and State, and probably on the whole damn force.

Chapter 7

The Arbor Institute for Middle East Studies sits on the east flank of the University of Chicago campus in a grand Victorian mansion of deep russet stonework whose crescendo of gables and porticos make as eloquent a statement of architectural integrity as the famous Frank Lloyd Wright prairie house which lies a few corners south.

The Arbor Institute's curriculum vitae, however, is tied neither to its architecture nor to its university neighbors, but directly to the wealth and power of the Kellaigh family. Jason Kellaigh II and his son, Jason III, were both men of a certain vision. They had, in series, overseen the growth of their family's regional grain storage and shipping company into that of the giant Arbor Corporation, a billion-dollar agribusiness conglomerate that specialized in applying the skills and the will of the American heartland to backward, unproductive agricultures in every part of the world—most recently and profitably, to that of still-feudal China.

The Arbor Corporation's stated goals, Hallet recalled as he heard the rich melody of the Rockefeller Chapel's carillon tower for the first time in weeks, were global opportunity, prosperity, and security. They came to bear, wrote Jason II shortly before his death, in the corporate logo he himself had designed—an arbor of olive branches formed into an abstracted letter "A" and centered in a global ellipse of hemispheric meridians.

But the Arbor Institute that Philip Hallet watched come into view through the window of a rattling Yellow taxicab was the particular brainchild of Jason III, who, upon taking over from his father in the late 1960s, redeployed the assets of the family's charitable foundation into the formation of a scholarly think tank that would promote cultural, political, and sociological understanding among the diverse peoples of a shrinking world. In the younger Kellaigh's eyes, it was the responsibility of his enterprise, even if some saw it merely as enlightened profiteering, to make his corporation's olive branch more than a visual metaphor.

Jason Kellaigh II had developed a considerable interest in the region he called Arabia ever since the British folly in Egypt, when their ludicrous seizure of the Suez Canal had caused the Arbor Corporation serious distribution problems. But it was Jason III, barely in his thirties then and full of even grander world visions, who insisted after his father's demise and the two Israeli-Arab wars of the sixties that his newly formed Arbor Institute would thereafter concentrate its activities in the Middle East. Kellaigh argued vehemently and successfully with government agencies and private benefactors that only peaceful solutions to the region's frightful political problems could open its vast, oil-funded markets. But how could there be peace without understanding? he challenged them. How could Americans be effective either as diplomats or as marketers when we knew so little about the complexities and exigencies of the region, about the cultural and religious bonds that unite Arab and Jew, Bedouin and Berber?

Jason III's well-communicated visions produced the financing that, when combined with his personal resources, brought the Arbor Institute to the forefront as America's leading center of

Islamic and Hebraic studies—funding its cadre of world-recognized scholars and enabling its printing presses to churn out their eclectic analyses of cultural and political reality for more than two decades.

But that was history, Hallet thought as he climbed the mansion's limestone steps and buzzed himself through the well-secured entrance door. The Institute's present, even though only he and Macdonald Clelland knew the details, was being controlled by much tighter reins.

Someone had carefully cleaned and tidied Hallet's office. The books and manuscripts that perpetually cluttered his desk were now two neat piles at either end of his blotter, their bindings facing inward for easy reference and turned left or right depending upon whether they were in Arabic, Hebrew, or any of the six other languages that Hallet read. A fresh stack of note-paper sat next to the telephone, the desk drawers had been emptied of old pencil stubs and rusted paper clips, all liquor had been removed from the credenza. Only the safe—whose purchase he'd won despite Bryce Vreeland's carping when Mac Clelland interceded by noting that Hallet often stored rare artifacts for study—had remained untouched, unopened, apparently secure.

Hallet pushed aside the bundled stacks of mail and, without his usual ration of coffee, tried to settle in, to concentrate. It had been a difficult night: The more he fought for sleep, the faster his mind raced. He tried to slow it down by working up what would be his best-case scenario—that Mohammed Saami had betrayed one of the many cause-conscious, radical graduate students, a large number of them Jewish, with whom he copulated. In turn, perhaps Saami's spurned lover had dumped something into his hummus in an act of consummate revenge. Poison was, after all, the most feminine of murder weapons, with a history far beyond that of the Borgias. And Hallet had always warned Saami that his priapismic behavior would one day lead him to serious trouble.

But it was equally possible, Hallet knew as he rolled back and forth on the damp bed linen, that Yousef's cryptic but frightening message might be valid, that is wasn't merely another of his attempts to exchange exotic but generally worthless information for additional funds. Could Saami have been uncovered? Even worse, if any part of the Prophet network had been blown, not only would the Arab governments it touched be alerted but, sure as sunrise, the file would already be at Mossad headquarters in Tel Aviv. Which could only put Hallet's deep-cover operatives in a cross fire that even Sandman couldn't suppress.

It was four in the morning when Hallet abandoned all attempts to sleep. He would get to the mansion early, before the staff and the Fellows settled in and began their daily assemblage of data for the Institute's prestigious roster of corporate and academic subscribers, and prepare for the meeting he'd arranged with Macdonald Clelland when Hallet phoned him on their safe line and relayed what he'd learned from the girl Nahid about the death of Mohammed Saami.

Hallet checked his watch. There was still time. He could get a message to the Prophets that he was back on the job; he could run a printout of Saami's dossier in anticipation of his meeting with Clelland. He could even go to Sandman. But Isabel Ortega's light knock and quietly rustling entrance prevented any of it.

She wished him a quick good morning and deposited a steaming mug of dark liquid on his blotter. "To welcome you back," she said. "Since you won't drink our coffee and we damned well won't touch yours, I've tried some tea. Black tea, I think. I found it buried among the grape leaves in a Syrian market on Ashland Avenue."

"Let's call it a peace pot," Hallet suggested.

"Do we need it?"

Hallet replied with a shrug. "Anyway, thanks for getting my office into shape."

"Not I," Isabel said. "You don't think Bryce Vreeland would

stand to see your mess unattended for all those weeks, do you? He was in here himself, scurrying around like an obsessed charlady. Jason Kellaigh was paying us a rare state visit. That's the reason, probably."

The thought of Bryce Vreeland going through his papers made Hallet as angry as Jason Kellaigh's visit made him curious.

"Addressing the troops, was he?" asked Hallet.

"None of that. Spent the entire morning with Vreeland and never even saw Mac. Money matters, I'd guess."

"Probably Stan Bach's expense account."

"Stan's out of town, by the way. We're publishing his study of the Israeli occupation psychosis in book form. He's out getting some blurbs for the jacket. But he did ask me to pass along his welcome home greetings with the tea. Which is . . . ?"

Hallet sipped the brew carefully. Since weaning himself from gin, his palate had become acutely sensitive to hot and cold, as if awakening from a decade of anesthesia. "Delicious," he said, despite its scalding effect on his tongue.

Isabel smiled her satisfaction, pulled up a side chair and crossed her slim legs gracefully, without the slightest hint of nylon abrading against itself.

"You have one pressing commitment," she said. "Giving your basic overview on Islam to a group of graduate students. Someone over there is hiring MBAs for a king's ransom, and they'd like a backgrounding."

"I'm not in the job placement department," Hallet sneered. "They want an Islam One-oh-one course, complete with slides and travelogue, they can damn well enroll in it. Besides, since when is our research director playing appointments secretary?"

"Since Vreeland himself set the date and asked me to pass it on to you," Isabel replied. "Which again suggests that Jason Three is involved. And Bryce did point out that you've been lax in your cooperative efforts with the university."

"Enough," Hallet signaled with a raised hand. "Tell Vreeland to rest assured I'll be charming and enlightening."

"I think he'll be satisfied with prompt and sober."

Hallet pushed back from the desk and checked his watch as he stood. "I have a meeting with Mac," he said coolly.

"Philip, I'm sorry if . . ."

"Forget it."

Hallet's frustration disappeared as he closed the door behind him. To hell with Bryce Vreeland and anyone else who tried to stand in his way.

Agent MaryAgnes McCaskey snagged her forty-sixth pair of panty hose on the sharp inside edge of the gray metal desk in her office in the Everett McKinley Dirksen Federal Building. She took a bottle of clear nail polish from the bottom drawer and painted a circle around the tear, hoping to keep it from crawling up her leg like a spider. Though she'd sworn she would never demand a single thing from the Bureau that was considered specially feminine, McCaskey knew she'd have to ask one of Doc Hermann's bean counters to appropriate some furnishings that took less of a toll on the wardrobe which cost such a large percentage of her salary to maintain.

After half an hour, she gave up trying to concentrate on the ream of surveillance reports that covered her desk—reports only verifying that things remained peaceful inside the Chicago crime family, probably because the old man himself had come out of his illness-induced retirement and personally reapportioned businesses and territories among the nephews in ways that apparently obviated the use of silenced automatic pistols. For the present anyway, or at least until the old man's long-forecast demise came to pass.

The Bureau's current thrust—actually a weak series of probing jabs—was trying to link a handful of suburban real-estate developers to the Chicago syndicate. Doc Hermann posited that the mob was using its financial muscle as the mortar for a slew of shopping center developments where, he hoped to prove, labor union bosses were padding crews and skimming millions. But, despite months of coverage, the reports put no one from one side in bed with anyone from the other, at least not in ways that a federal grand jury might find conspiratorial. The only way to get at it, McCaskey had learned from her ex-partner Frank Thorne, was to get inside the organization and follow the money trails. It would take a good undercover cop to do it. So unless their surveillance yielded something positive soon, McCaskey would propose just such a move to Doc Hermann. And why not a female agent? One with good financial and technical skills? She'd done it once and could do it again. She had to. As with Thorne and Jack Corrigan, working the streets had become an addiction.

The paperwork she was forced to wade through daily seemed to summarize the past year of MaryAgnes McCaskey's life—the year after she'd transferred to Chicago from her outpost in sleepy old Rockford to work on the now infamous Operation Clothesline, the gambling sting which had netted the Justice Department a few less Mafia kingpins than it had anticipated.

McCaskey thought, too, that even though Clothesline came up short of its mob-busting mark—three captains were doing short time in Terre Haute and ex-nephew Sid Paris was barely earning his bacon in the witness protection program—little else had happened to her to commend either her decision to become a cop or to remain a single woman.

The job delivered none of the satisfaction she'd hoped for when she persuaded Doc Hermann to approve her transfer out of financial investigations and into fieldwork, though Doc had, in fact, cautioned her from the onset that being a street agent wasn't much more dynamic or free of paperwork than her past specialties of reviewing IRS records and stock transfer reports in the bowels of the Exchange Building on La Salle Street.

Socially, things were no better. Since the Sunday afternoon Frank Thorne walked out of her apartment (save for a short, stilted phone call en route to a sailboat in Grenada), McCaskey's emotions had been on hold. There was one brief and partially satisfying fling with a corporate attorney she'd met at a party, but McCaskey surmised that he was more interested in finding a stepmother for his two kids than in developing a relationship with a woman he viewed as headstrong and self-centered ("creatively self-involved" was the euphemism he'd used). And, after Thorne, there was never any thought of becoming involved with someone else from the Bureau, even though the offers were considerable no matter how icily and, said one rejected swain, "dyke-ily" she fielded them. So, the occasional weekend with the toothy blond instructor from her tennis camp was all MaryAgnes McCaskey had going. And it gnawed at her more this morning than any time in recent memory.

She lighted one of her seldom-smoked, extra-light slim cigarettes and stared out the window, across Dearborn Street, into the Federal Center Plaza and at the giant orange flamingo designed by Alexander Calder and executed by teams of perplexed ironworkers. For some inexplicable and surely masochistic reason, her former husband slithered into her thoughts. She wondered how he was surviving now that his short-lived career as a professional baseball player was over, and he could no longer brutalize some new woman when he lost a close one or was sent down to yet another minor league club. Whatever he was doing, she concluded, it could easily have her life-style beat— she was thirty-three, bored, and despite her good looks and appealing figure, she had no romantic prospects and had realized finally that she could have none as long as that rat bastard Frank Thorne continued to haunt her memory.

The ringing telephone brought McCaskey back to the moment. Lieutenant Jack Corrigan sounded tense, so she didn't waste time with pleasantries.

"We got ourselves another one. Number Five," Corrigan said. "Some uniforms in a squadrol were cooping for a few hours and found him when they came out of their alley. Guy was driving a private hack. Lucky break there. If he was driving for a fleet, the operators would be raising hell already."

"Small favor," McCaskey said.

"Not for the driver. But it may be the only one we get. You ready for the bad news?"

"That's not it?" McCaskey asked back.

"We may have more players in the game," Corrigan said. "Number Five was our second Palestinian. But it wasn't a twenty-two auto that got him. Thirty-two revolver is what it looks like."

McCaskey gave Corrigan a knee-jerk guess. "A payback for the other shoots," she said. "Some gang war between local Iranians and Palestinians. Over money, territory, drugs—something nonpolitical. Like the mob, maybe."

"Or we still have a single crazy who's changed pieces," Corrigan said. "Though I'm doubting that more every day. Still, we've had a watch out for people stocking up on twenty-two long hollow-points. Maybe our boy figured that and took out his backup gun."

"You're making him sound like a cop," said McCaskey, surprised.

"I don't care who, or how, or how many. I just want it over."

"You have anything worthwhile on the driver?"

"Don't know. Guy's so new on the job, the Hack Bureau hasn't got his papers in the drawer yet. Somewhere in transit, which means buried in somebody's in-box."

"You want me to check him out?" McCaskey volunteered.

"Only if you get more than you did on the others. Which was nothin'."

"Jack, I can't get more without going higher up. There's no one magic file drawer here that anybody can pull. Something called 'need to know,' which I don't have."

"Then we'll have to go to Doc Hermann. You get him to open up all those domestic security files, and we see what fits with what. I have to know if there's a connection, something that'll tell us what's going on in the Arab communities. Conspiracy's your turf, kiddo. So let's do it."

McCaskey checked her calendar as she almost gleefully pushed the pile of surveillance reports out of the way. "I'll see

91

Doc now, and start the tapes running this afternoon. Let's say we meet tomorrow and go over a game plan. Anywhere but Bernie's."

"Thorne liked it."

"Thorne's sailing rich tourists around the Grenadines. He's not interested in being a cop anymore," McCaskey shot back. "I'll meet you at The Chambers on Plymouth Court."

"With all them damn lawyers hanging around?"

"Jack, we sit on this any longer, we may need those lawyers ourselves."

McCaskey rode up to the administrative floor and wove her way between the potted plants. A disdainful nod from Doc Hermann's secretary, and she entered his office. Ernest R. Hermann, known by the acronym "Doc" since he had been Director of the Organized Crime strike force, was a thick, massive figure behind his mahogany desk. He looked up at McCaskey, smoothed the long, sparse gray hairs on his nearly bald pate, and reconfigured his jowls into a smile.

"Promise you'll take it easy on me, and I'll promise to get you the next field investigation that comes up. Okay?"

"That's not why I'm here," McCaskey said. "This time I've got something for *you*."

Hermann saw more than the usual intensity in McCaskey's face and rolled his chair back from the desk. "I hope I'm up to it," he said, clasping his hands on his neck as he leaned back. "Maybe I should have retired when I had the chance, when that little creep assistant attorney general had me halfway out the door after Clothesline. Right now, I feel like old George Smiley, out chasing demons long after his time, still playing the game when he should be writing his memoirs in the Cotswolds."

"Somehow, I never pictured you as a literary man," McCaskey kidded back. "More the *Sporting News* than memoirs and monographs."

"That's how little you know. Besides the similarities in body type, I am a very well read and studious person. The main differences between me and le Carré's creation is that my wife is disastrously faithful and I don't have a Karla to keep me going. My demons were exorcised long ago."

"As I said, I may have one for you."

"Oh, dear," Hermann sighed. "I guess you'd better tell me about it."

McCaskey went through the details succinctly. Doc Hermann pulled himself out of his slouch, and began making notes on a small tablet.

"Always the chance that it's some crazies on the loose," McCaskey said. "But Corrigan and I think we may have some kind of war going on inside the Middle Eastern community. Iranians versus Palestinians versus God knows who else tomorrow. With a quarter million-plus Arabs in the city, that could be major trouble."

"So you've already ruled out our cadre of Zionist fanatics," Doc wondered aloud.

"Doesn't make sense, but we've ruled out nothing. Which is why I'm here. You can get the domestic security and intelligence files open. Let's run everything we have on the dead drivers, and the whole Arab population if we have to. If we come up with a definite link, Jack Corrigan will step aside and let us work it."

"You think so? Corrigan's too hard-nosed to step aside, no matter what he says. And every time we cooperate with the locals, it backfires and my ass ends up in a sling."

"I owe Corrigan on this one," McCaskey persisted. "Besides, like Judy Holliday said in *Born Yesterday,* 'He don't come across, I don't come across.' "

"All right," Hermann surrendered. "I've always liked Corrigan. In a bent world, he's as straight as they come. As for the DSI files, I'll do more than run interference. I'll have you cleared for access, since you'll only be hanging over my shoulders anyway."

"I would indeed," McCaskey conceded.

"I know it. Your level of self-assurance is apparent to me and everyone else around here. No longer Miss Go-Along, are you?"

"It's a big city, and a girl has to survive."

"Clear your desk and push everything back to me for reassignment. Drop off whatever you have from Corrigan, and I'll get the tapes turning in the basement. Anything else?"

"No, except there are a couple people I thought about talking to for background. There's one professor at the university who's a specialist in Middle East politics. And of course, there's the Arbor Institute. There's an Arabist there I'm trying to remember. Always on the TV news and talk shows, knows a lot about the local community. Maybe, if we find out he's cleared, he could look at some dossiers with an unclouded eye."

Doc Hermann's fleshy grin returned. "You really light up when you smell a good case. God, if I were twenty years younger."

"Better make it thirty," McCaskey said, as she suddenly remembered the name she wanted. "And Doc, that name of the fellow from the Arbor Institute. It's Philip Hallet."

Macdonald Clelland's office was somber and vague, an insight into the man himself. While the Institute's other Fellows filled their workplaces with plaques, diplomas, and mementos of famous persons, the walnut panels that surrounded Clelland seemed to encase him in shadows; only a small fragment of a Roman mosaic (Hallet guessed Turkish or Syrian in origin) and two out-of-place ink drawings by a lesser German expressionist with a deep sense of violence broke the barren surface of Mac's office walls.

Hallet was about to speak when the clinking of a spoon inside a china cup came dancing over his shoulder. He turned and saw Bryce Vreeland, cup and saucer balanced in his left hand, a spoon held daintily in his right.

"I came to bid you welcome home," Vreeland said. "All's well with you, I hope."

"Feeling fine, thanks," Hallet replied.

"Good, then. We're all delighted to have you back, even if your method of recovery was slightly unorthodox."

"I've been through all that with Mac," Hallet said. "I'm sure he's briefed you, so I'd rather not waste your valuable time repeating myself."

"Yes, we have a full agenda to cover," Clelland said.

"Just wanted to see for myself how fit you look," Vreeland said. He took a sip at his cup and gave Clelland a glowing compliment on the Darjeeling blend. "I'll leave you both to business." Vreeland started for the door that connected Clelland's office with his, then turned to face Hallet again.

"I suppose you've heard of what happened to that poor fellow in New York City."

"No, I've barely cleared my desk," Hallet lied.

"Oh. A chap named Mohammed Saami. You do know him."

"Vaguely. He was at Columbia, if I remember. A friend of yours?"

"He was not unknown to me, in a manner of speaking. It seems he was on the payroll here. Small stipend recently. I thought you were his mentor." Vreeland waited for Hallet's response, got none, and continued. "Anyway, someone slipped him and his girlfriend enough potassium cyanide to kill a dozen camels. Product tampering, say the police. But I'd suspect one of his bloodthirsty brethren had a score to settle."

"An Arab wouldn't kill like that," Hallet said impatiently. "It's considered cowardly, and it's against Islamic law."

"So are kidnappings and car bombs, I'd imagine," Vreeland said. "But, then, Philip, you've always had a surprisingly romantic notion about Arab morality."

"That's what we strive to study and comprehend," Clelland interceded.

"I daresay," Vreeland uttered as he turned the doorknob. "Which is why I'm only the organization man around here, someone trapped in the maelstrom that is management while you thinkers and intellectuals plumb deeper waters. So, I shall now go uncover what, if any, responsibilities we have to Mister

Saami's heirs. And, of course, complete our payment for Philip's uncompleted treatment."

Hallet lashed out at Clelland as soon as the door was sealed. "What the devil was that all about? And how does Vreeland know anything about Saami?"

"Slow down," Clelland said. "I certainly didn't bring it up. No doubt Saami's name came across Bryce's desk somewhere along the way. For expenses, travel, whatever. His mind's like a steel trap when it comes to cash. So, when the poisoning made the news, Vreeland must have remembered him. He's an accountant, for Christ's sake."

"Yeah, they come in after the battle and shoot the wounded. But the Prophets are supposed to be paid from special funds," Hallet insisted.

"Only as regards that activity," Clelland countered. "Who knows what Saami was asking for? Could have been library or research materials, anything like that. And don't let your dislike for Bryce get in the way of things. He's genuine in his concern about you, as is Jason Kellaigh. I think that's why Bryce dropped by, so he could report to Kellaigh firsthand that you are well and back at it."

"He caught with me my guard down about Saami. I didn't stop to think it had made the news."

"With a little help from our sponsors and the local authorities, we did get out the message that it was a random case of product tampering—a one-shot deal, perhaps by a disgruntled former kitchen worker. But that's nonsense, of course. It was assassination pure and simple."

"And you think that Saami's people in Damascus may have found out he was facing Washington instead of Mecca and decided to take action?" Hallet asked. "I say not. Saami was as well covered as anyone could be. His people share roast goat in Hafez Assad's palace."

"He also may have found out something too important to let ride, something that relates to the Export file. That's what I'm concerned about. That's what the both of us had better track down."

"By us, you mean my people."

Clelland rubbed his gray beard in a motion that looked more sinister than pensive.

"You know what you have to do," he said.

Hallet locked his office door and instructed the switchboard that he would accept no calls, standard operating procedure when he was writing or translating. He pushed aside his half-finished monograph on Islamic architecture and the materials that Isabel Ortega had left to background him for the talk to graduate students, then swung his chair in a quick about-face to the computer terminal behind his desk. He ran automatically through the sequence of accessing procedures and waited as the machine cleared and the screen flickered on.

Hallet entered his first code. As the names began to scroll slowly down the screen, he again thought back to that first meeting in Washington, when his life abruptly turned upside down.

Despite what his sponsors had told the university, what actually had prompted Hallet's summons to that conference at NSA headquarters was the continuing failure of U.S. intelligence services to anticipate and forestall the blatant terrorist assaults on civilian and military targets in the Middle East. Of equal concern, once the damage had occurred, was that no American intelligence sources knew enough to identify exactly who was responsible, let alone format a proper response. As Macdonald Clelland had stated succinctly, unless the Hezbollah or Islamic Jihad or a kindred organization went on Radio Beirut and identified itself, the United States was incapable of even locating the haystack, let alone beginning its search for the needle.

With these overseas failures in mind, those responsible for

domestic intelligence and security, namely the FBI but including others whose lines of communication ran straight into the White House, decided to take the initiative and begin operations to safeguard against the likelihood, as outlined in the National Security Council's secret file, code-named Export, that terrorist activities would soon commence on U.S. shores. And this was where Clelland and Hallet and their Prophets came to bear.

The program decided upon was an infiltration of the country's Arab and Iranian communities, within which more than one million aliens at that time resided, a few of them certainly involved in espionage and possibly planning terrorist activities. The goal of this infiltration was to create an early warning system that would, if managed properly, alert the authorities to hostile plans and identify potential foreign agents who were ready to execute them.

Hallet, partly because his hangover and general clamminess left him feeling contentious, but more because he felt the plan was absurd, had objected immediately. There is no such thing as an "Arab community" in the United States, any more than there is a European one. The differences between nationalities are just as great, Hallet contended, and the warring sects of Islam made Muslims no more homogeneous than Christians. Moreover, he held fast as he saw Macdonald Clelland studying him silently, such a plan was blatantly racist—it would treat loyal Arab-Americans as potential subversives, just as we'd viewed Japanese-Americans as potential saboteurs during World War II. Merely because one is of an Arab heritage and a Muslim does not obviate loyalty to the United States, Hallet concluded, just as being a Jew does not mandate allegiance to Israel, or being a Catholic place papal dictates above one's citizenship.

The responses to Hallet's criticisms by the FBI delegation were unanimous: The government was merely pursuing intelligence, not persecuting either its citizens or legitimate foreign nationals. Loyal Arab-Americans had nothing to fear, added the representative from the National Security Council: Potential terrorists were the only targets. The more militaristic attendees from Defense Department agencies, namely National Security and Defense Intelligence, beat Hallet with the stick he'd grown accustomed to enduring—that he'd spent so much time living among Arabs, he tended to see their viewpoint in every issue ("Exactly why he is here," Mac Clelland had interrupted pointedly). More pertinent, said an NSC representative who was not introduced, the FBI had precedents for administering such a program, and it was not at all racist. "If you want to use World War Two metaphors," he said to Hallet, "witness what was accomplished in combatting Nazi sabotage and infiltration by knocking out the heart of the German-American Bunde."

It was at that juncture that Macdonald Clelland came fully to life, telling Hallet of their appointed roles in the plan, reminding him that their sponsors would proceed with or without his assistance, selling him on the fact that, with their special expertise and contacts, he and Hallet together could do the job well and fairly.

A quarter-million alien Arabs and Iranians are residing in the States either as university students or graduate faculty, Clelland said in a voice that told Hallet he wasn't estimating. Some, obviously, are intelligence operatives for their home countries; others, we have to believe, are sleeper agents who someday may receive directives to put down their books and pick up bombs. The United States must know about both, and the way to do this is not only to monitor these groups, but also to recruit people inside them to act as a distant early warning network. That was it, simply stated: The Arbor Institute would move from the scholarly to the strategic and Philip Hallet, as the Arab's perfect American, would be the control point.

The network Hallet was to recruit—Macdonald Clelland had already given them the designation *Prophets*—would be run from inside the Arbor Institute. It would include professors, students, and political activists located at major campuses and inside Arabic-speaking communities in the United States and Canada (though the Canadians would not, of course, be advised of this). What better "prophets" than Arabs loyal to their cause but sharing the enlightened beliefs that international terrorism was no answer for Arab suffering or a proper weapon against imperialism and injustice, and that fanaticism—whether Arab, Iranian, or Israeli—posed the biggest obstacle to peace in their hapless homelands?

All well and good, Hallet finally agreed. He would take Clelland's offer and leave his faculty position in Massachusetts for the Arbor Institute and Chicago. He had been sold.

But it was only later, in the pine-paneled basement of that squeaking row house in Georgetown, that Hallet's true control told him about the deep-cover network that he and his secret friends really wanted, about the plot within a lie inside a delusion.

"Only one man we can think of is capable of running *that* operation," Hallet's control said. "Someone we've known all along by the code name given him when he wielded his double-edged sword as an agent for the British."

Hallet brought his attention back to the computer screen. The linkage with the Institute's mainframe was established, the names of his university contacts had scrolled by. To go any farther into its classified depths, his secret program demanded identification.

Hallet's hands trembled unexpectedly as he typed in the cryptonym he'd used since that day on the Oxford lawn when he'd accepted the old don's ticket to Damascus.

This is Sandman.

Chapter 8

Hallet waited at the Institute until long after dark. No responses to Sandman's urgent directive came across the secured telephone lines that fed his secret modem. When he finally went home, he spent another night without enjoying any measurable amount of sleep, but this time without even a dash of arak to sweeten the excessive coffees he'd consumed while hoping for some further contact from either Yousef or his messenger, Nahid.

Again nothing. He toyed briefly with the idea of calling Isabel Ortega, but knew it was time for him to remain alone, remain sober, prepare for the worst. The only sounds he permitted to slice into the silence of his library came from memory: the final words he'd spoken with the two doomed Prophets who were off to do his secret bidding in war-torn Baghdad, and the startlingly candid conversation he'd had with Mohammed Saami when Hallet first moved to recruit him.

He had met Saami while visiting Damascus, supposedly to research a paper on some late Roman artifacts recently unearthed in the nearby hills by soldiers excavating an antiaircraft gun emplacement. Saami was part of the cultural delegation assigned to assist (and, Hallet knew of course, to keep track of) the visiting American scholar. While no art historian, Saami had amazing insights into the confusing cultural history of his nation, and knew what even Hallet considered to be minute details about the Roman legions who had spearheaded their empire from the Egyptian desert into the Aleppo hills. Three things about Saami became immediately apparent: that he longed to continue his education in the United States and earn his doctorate at an Ivy League university; that he held surprisingly negative views of Hafez Assad's monomania in making his homeland the military center of the Arab world and the main training camp for Shiite paramilitary fanatics; and, despite his easy recitation of views certain to be considered treasonous by his leaders, that Saami had direct lines into the highest levels of the Syrian military and Assad's six secret intelligence services.

"An absurdity," Saami said to Hallet as they openly sipped gin fizzes in one of Damascus's many French-style sidewalk cafés. Saami, constantly eyeing the Western-clad women who sauntered past, admitted between statements of greater political concern that if he had to be an Arab, beautiful and pleasure-bent Damascus was the only place to live as one. None of that hard-line austerity that had turned Baghdad into a replica of depressing East Berlin, or Riyadh into an imam's cave.

"Truly an absurdity," he continued when the small talk of women and whiskey and life-style seemed no longer appropriate. "Instead of assuming our rightful role of leadership and leading the Arab world forward, Syria is playing at radical theocracy by training martyrs to drive trucks filled with explosives into your embassies and your garrisons. And, perhaps some day soon, Doctor Hallet, to the very gates of the White House."

"You're suggesting this may actually happen?" Hallet asked.

"Who knows?" Saami shrugged before he leaned over to whisper and begin negotiations for a perfectly sensible bargain. "But I know the people who know such things, people who select targets for such activities, who decide when the chosen path must be assassination. More interesting to you, I should think, than carbon-dating the amphorae of ancient Roman legionnaires."

"My God, Saami. Who do you think I am?"

"I know exactly who you are, Doctor Hallet. And for considerations I believe will be acceptable, I'm willing to come to work for you."

Finally, Hallet slept. In the morning, he dressed quickly, skipped coffee, and was the first of its Fellows to arrive at the Arbor Institute's mansion. Again, in case he'd missed any shred of data that might point to a reason for murder, he began with Mohammed Saami's dossier. And again he found nothing.

Nor had Yousef left a message. Not surprising, Hallet decided, for the tough-minded Libyan math instructor was never one to play by anyone else's rules, not even Sandman's. Still, Yousef did possess the contacts to know if something was taking shape in the field, and despite Hallet's doubts, Yousef had always maintained that terrorist attacks in the U.S. were as certain to occur as another California earthquake. Not a matter of if, only when. Perhaps if he contacted Nahid through the League of Islamic Students, Hallet wondered for an instant. No, he decided. If there was any time to start at the top, to call in his markers, this was it. And that top was Mahmoud Dahran.

Dahran operated out of Dearborn, Michigan, a city which boasts of having more Arabic-speaking Muslims, mainly Iraqi Shiites and Lebanese, in its population than any other city in the Western hemisphere. Dahran was an eminently successful businessman along the Detroit-Dearborn axis—an importer of Middle Eastern food products and, Hallet suspected, questionable pharmaceuticals. He also was a well-known restaurateur and an astute art collector, the latter interest helping Dahran maintain ties with Arab students and faculty at the nearby University of Michigan and as far away as the moneyed Muslim circles in Toronto—which was critical to monitoring the Arabs who found Canadian visas easy to obtain and the narrow river between Windsor and Detroit a perfect way to enter the States illegally and clandestinely.

Hallet, locked in his office, transmitted an emergency contact message directly to Dahran's business phone, the only method by which he could be certain the busy and peripatetic Iraqi would respond. The message was an inquiry from an art collector eager to sell a certain Bedouin vase. Dahran would, in turn, contact Hallet at any of their preappointed hours on the secured telephone lines that ran to his home and his office.

Whatever there was to know about the murder of Mohammed Saami, and if Yousef truly might have stumbled onto something worthwhile, Mahmoud Dahran was the one to contact. For beyond his many business and cultural ventures, Dahran was a senior officer in Iraq's foreign intelligence service and a personal confidant of Saddam Hussein himself.

The call to Dahran completed, Hallet was considering other contacts, with his Yemeni operative at Arizona State University in Tempe and an Iranian professor at Georgetown who was being funded by both the university and the Islamic Jihad, when the intercom buzzed him with jarring alarm. It was urgent, the receptionist said, countering Hallet's objections to being disturbed: A government representative needed to speak to him at once. It could be regarding Saami's death, Hallet thought, or perhaps something had happened to Yousef after all. He asked that the visitor be escorted to his office and wound down the computer immediately.

Hallet had to mask his surprise when the visitor arrived—a striking, raven-haired woman dressed in a business suit of light gray pinstripes over a pale blue blouse with a gently ruffled collar. When Hallet stood to greet her, he realized she stood as tall as he did, about five foot ten, and that, as she scanned his office in darting glances as if trying to memorize the location of every item in it, her complexion was a soft Wedgwood white and her eyes were as dark as pea coal. It was the perfect face of Ireland, all right, as if adoringly rendered by Rossetti or another Pre-Raphaelite painter. So Hallet wasn't surprised when she gave her name, MaryAgnes McCaskey, only that she introduced herself as a special agent of the FBI.

"Thank you for seeing me without an appointment, Professor Hallet," she said.

"Not professor," Hallet replied. "The Arbor Institute is a close cousin of the university's, but completely independent. We often lecture there, of course, but none of our Fellows is on faculty."

"Doctor Hallet, then. And I am pleased to meet you in person. I've read many of your articles and seen you often on television."

"I'm flattered."

Hallet wondered how he could buy time to excuse himself and check out Agent McCaskey's visit with Mac Clelland, who kept up whatever contact was required with the Bureau. But her easy manner swayed him against it. For the moment, anyway. He offered her one of the Queen Anne chairs that formed a small conversation area in a corner of the office, in front of what were among the mansion's richest walnut bookshelves.

"How may I help you?" he asked.

"Well, Doctor—"

"Philip would work just as well," Hallet interrupted softly. "Unless you're taping this and want everything formalized."

"Not at all," McCaskey replied, her face giving off a hint of a smile which Hallet found quite fetching. "Our conversation will be completely confidential," she went on. "I'm interested in learning about the Arab community here in Chicago. You're quite active in it, I understand, and are certainly considered an expert."

"I keep in touch," Hallet nodded. "I'm sort of an honorary advisor to Arab student groups at our universities, and I take a hand with civic and cultural organizations like the Arab-American Union, the Lebanon Association, several others. Basically, I get to keep up on my Arabic and, in exchange for some wonderful meals, they get an after-dinner speaker without having to pay an honorarium."

"So, given all these contacts, you'd certainly be qualified to assess the current mood of Arabs here in Chicago. You'd know the positions they would take on social and political matters. And, if there were serious divisions among Arab groups, you'd be aware of them also."

"You're conducting an investigation of some kind," Hallet realized.

"In a way," said McCaskey. She sat back in her chair and gave her black hair an easy tussle. Body language: relaxed, confident. "Doctor Hallet, are you aware of any serious discord in the Arab community? Not just the normal ethnic bickering, but differences serious enough to lead perhaps to violence?"

"Disharmony is a way of life in the Arab world," Hallet said. "It's only the Westerner who believes all Arabs are brothers, and that's because he hasn't taken time to learn the vast difference among them."

"But Islam unites them certainly?"

Hallet knew how he had to go about it, the game he had to play, and wondered if Agent McCaskey would be able to pick up on it in time. "No more than Christianity unites the Irish in Ulster," he said. "To begin with, though Islam reaches all around the world, only ten percent of all Muslims are Arabs at all. There are a hundred million Muslims in Russia and India *each*. Twenty million more in China. In all, Islam represents a quarter of the world's population. As for Arab unity, the Druse fight the Shiites, who've waged a thousand-year war against the Sunnis for grievances that trace back to deciding which leader should have succeeded Mohammed as the messenger of God. No, Agent McCaskey, the only thing Muslims have in common are the pillars of Islam—that they pray five times daily, fast during the ninth month of Ramadan, pay their tithe or *zakah*, and make the sacred hajj to Mecca so they can walk seven times around the Kaba. After that, and especially among the Arabs, how to practice religion becomes as contentious an issue as it was during the Christian Reformation."

McCaskey waited patiently through Hallet's lecture and decided to try to zero him onto the target with his own words. "I recall your once saying that, to an Arab, religion is not a fact of life. It is life itself."

"The word Islam means submission. To God's law. At any cost," Hallet said.

"Which makes it important enough to kill for."

"That's the easy view. Islam is important enough to *die* for. In fact, the creation of martyrs is a fundamental goal of the Shiite sect. It represents instant sainthood, and rewards the martyr with the keys to heaven itself. But," Hallet said as he looked straight into McCaskey's hardening eyes, "I suspect you're here to discuss the killing part."

"I'm afraid so."

"Then you'll have to tell me exactly who it is you're investigating before we can go any further."

Hallet studied McCaskey's face for a reaction. Her eyes didn't flinch, her face stayed soft and composed. Whatever else she was, Agent McCaskey was well trained.

"I really don't know," she said after a moment. "Right now, I'm looking for reasons. And hoping they may lead me to the person we want."

"I don't understand," Hallet said.

"I'll explain it to you, but on the condition I stated earlier—that everything we discuss here is confidential on both our parts. Absolutely and unequivocally. Agreed?"

Hallet nodded, relieved at the answer, realizing that he'd gotten what he wanted from the unwitting Agent McCaskey—that she didn't know about his covenant with Macdonald Clelland and had not come about his Prophets.

"In the past several weeks," she began, "five taxi drivers have been murdered in Chicago. Executed is a better word. They were all shot in the head while behind the wheel. All at night, none of them robbed."

"Sounds like a gangster movie from the Roaring Twenties. Pay your protection or die."

"Nowhere near. You see, all the murdered drivers were Arabs. Three Iranians, two Palestinians."

"But Iranians aren't Arabs," Hallet began.

"I understand that, Doctor Hallet," McCaskey interrupted, realizing how pompous she must have sounded with Jack Corrigan. "But I don't know if our killer has the anthropological background to make the distinction. In his eye, we believe, they were Arabs. Or Middle Eastern Muslims, enemies of the United States, or however else he's chosen to categorize them. Nevertheless, in some ways, it appears that Iranians may be the killer's principal target."

"An Iraqi, perhaps? Someone who wants to keep the war alive? Or why not a Lebanese Christian?"

"We're considering all those possibilities," McCaskey said. "We are also considering that some kind of Iranian and Palestinian gang feud may be going on that we don't know about."

"And from me you want?"

"From you I want intelligence and insights. I want your wisdom and experience, and your access inside the Arab community. I want to know if you've heard any whisper of a blood feud, or some other plot which would account for the shootings. I want to know if the Mideast mayhem is about to manifest itself in Chicago, and if you think from the evidence we have to date that the killer is himself an Arab, or some psychotic trying to extract revenge from innocent people simply because of their ethnic background. I want all of that, and perhaps more. I want you to be my eyes and ears with every Arab group you know."

"You want me to spy on friends," Hallet said.

"God no! I want to find out why your friends, as you define them, are being murdered. I want the killing stopped, Doctor Hallet. I should think you would *want* to help."

Hallet liked the way McCaskey came to life as she stated her dilemma, was sorry he had to treat her so poorly, but knew he'd have to continue doing so. He had no choice.

"I've learned long ago," Hallet began, "that it is quite improper for scholars to involve themselves with intelligence matters, with police work if you will. Ours is a world of arts and letters, not of criminology. But I can tell you this—I've heard nothing whatsoever of any political or familial discord among our Arab citizens that would prompt such insane violence. I should also tell you that, of late, I haven't maintained my local contacts as diligently as you suspect. There's a book I'm working on, which takes up all my time. And some recent health problems. However, should I hear of anything that may help your investigation, I'll pass that information back to you in the manner I choose—such as omitting whatever names or specifics may embarrass my friends and not advance your case. Simply stated, I'm not going to begin snooping on your behest, nor will I take any active role in your search beyond our conversation today. But should something that regards the matter cross my desk . . ."

"I simply don't understand why you won't help me," McCaskey argued, an icy chill now in her voice. "Lives are at stake here. Innocent lives, from all we can see. Would you like to hear about those men who were murdered?"

"Not in the least," Hallet said. He couldn't stand to. Nor could he risk his assets by helping the FBI chase some nut off the streets when there was Sandman's work to be done. "As I've said, I am an Arabist, a Fellow at the most prestigious Middle East institute in the United States. I study the Arabic language, and the culture and history of the region. I'm not paid to get involved in petty Chicago street crimes, even if the participants happen to Arabs and Iranians."

"You mean the victims," McCaskey said through clenched teeth.

"I'm sorry if you think me heartless."

MaryAgnes McCaskey stood, smoothed her skirt, and stared hard into Hallet's eyes. God, she thought, if there were a way to hit this son-of-a-bitch with a subpoena and drag his pedantic ass into court.

"Thank you for your time," she said. "And for the free lecture on the reaches of Islam."

Hallet refused to blink. "I'll tell you one more thing," he said.

"I doubt sincerely that your killer is an Arab at all. We certainly have our share of assassins, but not serial killers who shoot only from behind. I'd look elsewhere."

"You're sure of that?"

"With the Arab personality, one is sure of little. But blind-sided execution isn't in a general profile. I hope that helps you, though I'm wondering why the FBI is involved and not the Chicago police."

"The Bureau is responsible for domestic security matters, Doctor Hallet. Even though your assessment will be duly noted, we have reason to suspect that political motives may be at work here, and those are well within our charter."

"You've learned your rules book well," Hallet said, figuring that smart-ass remark would wind up their increasingly hostile confrontation. He never quite anticipated McCaskey's retort as she paused in his doorway.

"Doctor Hallet, since this is a private conversation, between us only, please allow me to tell you one thing—that you are one of the smuggest and most arrogant little pricks I've ever had the displeasure of meeting."

Usher decided to stretch his legs and find out what the world was saying. He walked along the lakefront to the Drake Hotel, then down Michigan Avenue's "miracle mile" of luxury stores. Across the river, he cut west to the newsstand on State Street that carried out-of-town papers. He picked up the two Chicago dailies, the *Los Angeles Times,* the *New York Times,* and the *Washington Post,* and complained to the vendor about his not carrying the New York *Daily News* when he sold things like *Le Figaro* and *Corriere della Sera* and papers that didn't even use our alphabet. Back on Michigan Avenue, he hailed a cab north and gave an address several doors from his own. The driver pointed to his own newspaper and began a tirade about violence in the streets and the dangers he faced on every corner.

"Lookit," he said, "got a driver shot dead yesterday. Guy's just trying to squeeze out a living, pushin' a hack."

Usher told him flatly to cut the chatter and watch the erratic lane changes, which probably would kill him more surely than all the junkies and stickup men and psychos put together.

Back in the barren white apartment, Usher sat on the parquet floor and spread the newspapers in a semicircle around him. The local papers carried only briefs in their national sections, the *New York Times* had a longer piece but with more quotes from public health authorities than from the cops. The Middle Eastern restaurant on Broadway had been closed; it and its purveyors were undergoing a full investigation and product analysis, though to date no other traces of potassium cyanide had been discovered either in foods stored at the M'rabet or at their place of manufacture. Police had not ruled out an accident but were leaning toward the theory that a disgruntled ex-employee was responsible, though the restaurant had so many angry former workers their inquiries would take more time than Usher knew the public attention span could give it.

Perfect, Usher decided as he carefully restacked the papers. Just what the doctor ordered. For whatever reason the people that Ben stood up for wanted the Arab taken out, they had to be pleased with the result. No big news blast, no Feds other than the FDA involved. Nothing like it was when Usher had shoved that little wop Chuckie Franco into his car trunk, nothing like what went on with the fat man whose last view of planet earth was a putting green in Jamaica. Everything cool, even if the methodology wasn't something he could be proud of. But the Arab didn't drive a car, didn't roam the night streets of the Upper West Side, nor do much of anything except stuff his face full of eggplant and play grab-ass with every chippie on the whole damn Columbia campus.

Usher checked the time: an hour to go before he had to meet Ben. Maybe a bonus for the New York job, or another assignment, which was really the same thing. He'd been in Chicago longer than he'd planned, but until the back-to-back jobs of the last month, his work had been well timed and certainly profitable. Maybe one more contract and, after some cleanup work in Philly he'd promised an old Army buddy, he could hit the West Coast for a while. Almost five years since he'd been in L.A., Usher recalled, since the time he took out that hotshot porn movie producer by sending him and his Lamborghini into orbit with a double dose of Semtex C-4 right in the circular drive of the Century Plaza Hotel—a real message to the Hollywood movie set and its attempts to fund films through the rackets. For the producer that Usher wasted had decided to finance his cum-shot epic by bringing a load of Argentine-made Astra automatic pistols into the local marketplace against the sage counsel of the people who had that business covered.

Usher walked down the corridor, threw the newspapers into the incinerator, thought about giving a knock on Colleen's door. Stupid to walk out on her like he did, but he could say he'd developed a sudden surge of *la turista* or delayed air sickness, or something related to his travels. After all, the warm baths and massage oil were fine after a job, when he really couldn't stand to be with a woman. How did the line go? You meet a better class of people and don't have to make scrambled eggs afterward? But that was no outlet for a man as good as he. He decided to give Colleen a phone call.

He found the scrap of paper with her number. Three rings later, he heard a pair of voices: first one, then the second, finally a duet on their answering machine.

"Hi, this is Colleen."

"And this is Sharon."

A pause, and they spoke in unison.

"We're sorry we're not home right now. So, after the beep, please leave your name and number and a short message. We'll call you when we land."

A muffled giggle came over the line, followed by Colleen speaking softly, not realizing their tape was still rolling.

"Yeah, anybody but Pizza Sal," she said.

112

Usher shook his head in disgust and passed on leaving Colleen any other message than a terminating click.

Usher ran at a slow, limbering gait northbound to the Hamilton statue, then swung toward the lakefront and picked up the pace as he came back south, finally sprinting until he ended up in a decent sweat at the Lincoln Park Conservatory. He cooled down as he walked south to the Farm in the Zoo, saw Ben in his usual black business suit and foulard tie, leaning over the picket fence and looking at a Guernsey calf as if she were a bikini-clad honey on the beach. But there was another black suit, too, off to the side. A huge man, probably six four or five, Usher made him, with a thick head of wavy gray-black hair, a lumpy face like an ex-fighter's, and a set of arms that, even with his loose-fitting suit, looked like tree trunks with size-fourteen hands attached. If Ben and the family had a problem, there were better times and places to solve it than Lincoln Park in the afternoon. Still, Usher knew he was only as good as his reputation for taking shit from no one, so he untaped the Gerber knife from beneath his running sock and slipped it in the waistband of his shorts.

Ben must have sensed Usher's presence. He turned from the fence and offered a beckoning wave.

"Let's walk a little," Ben said. "It's nice and private down by the lagoon."

"That why you had to bring the muscle?"

"He's not muscle," Ben said as if the suggestion were outrageous.

"Then who?"

"My name is Harry," the big man said as he fell in alongside. "And we need to talk together."

Usher had never set foot on English soil, but the accent was unmistakable: The big man was a limey, and he was also a hood trying to sound like a banker.

"It's okay," Ben reassured him. "You'll see why as we walk."

They crossed the wooden bridge by the aviary, walked along the lagoon and under a sprawling sycamore tree. Ben looked at the ducks; Usher and Harry watched each other.

"Harry is a close friend of our family's," Ben said when he was certain no one was within earshot. Compared to the big man, Ben looked mousy and almost delicate with his closely cropped brunette hair, thin face, and gray eyes. "Fact is, your visit to New York was actually on Harry's behalf. He asked for the best, and we delivered it."

Usher kept quiet.

"And we're quite satisfied, indeed."

"You fucking-A should be, *mate*. Nothing was ever cleaner."

"Quite unfortunate about the young woman, however," Harry said. "We'll have to be more careful about harming innocents."

"Who the hell you think you're talking to?" Usher exploded. "She shoulda kept her nose out of his glass." His eyes flashed at Ben, who, sensing an imminent confrontation between the men he'd brought together, spoke to them in quieting tones.

"Gentlemen, please," he began. "You both need to speak calmly, especially since I won't be staying to officiate. So look, Usher, Harry needs your help on some important matters. As I've said, he's a family friend. But you certainly can refuse him if you choose. All I ask is that you hear him out. If you decide to take the work, you deal directly with Harry from now on. You don't, no hard feelings. Sound all right?"

"Consider it a form of lend-lease, hands across the sea, and all," Harry said with a modest sneer in his voice.

"You know," Usher said to Ben, "the past few years I've been watching the family get straighter and straighter. You guys all wearing suits, sounding like something out of Harvard Yard. An occasional problem, somebody has to get iced. That's business. But now you bring along this big lummox who sounds like he wants to start a war."

"No such thing," Harry interrupted. "What we're talking here is big business indeed. Business that may change the world as we know it."

Usher glowered at Harry. "I know you, pal," he said. "You're a big piece of muscle trying to sound like a member of Parliament. But you've pushed a button yourself one or two times. I know it. And you know it. So why don't you just handle things on your own?"

Usher eyed Harry again and saw a thin smile crack his thick jowls as he answered him.

"Because, as Benjamin said, we want the best in the trade. The assignments we have in mind are very delicate ones, indeed. And, what we ask of you will be well worth your while, rest assured of that. There are several missions involved here, and we are not the type of client who'll request a volume discount. Quite the opposite. We pay top dollar, deposited wherever and however you see fit."

"At least listen," Ben insisted.

Usher nodded. "Just so he doesn't call me love, or ducks," he said.

"Fine, Mister Usher," agreed Harry in a conciliatory tone that even Usher knew was artificial.

"Much better," Ben said, as if the final bargain were made. "Then I'll leave you to business."

Usher watched Ben turn and walk back across the bridge to the main roadway. "So let's hear it," he said.

"We'll address matters one at a time," Harry began. "Beginning with a man in Detroit. He's known on the streets as Mike Doran, but his real name is Mahmoud Dahran. And, as soon as possible, we want to see him dramatically dead."

Chapter 9

MaryAgnes McCaskey was still fuming when she returned from the Arbor Institute to her office in the Federal Building, fuming at that bastard Philip Hallet for treating her so shabbily, and at herself for allowing him to see that he'd gotten under her skin. She poured some weak, barely warm coffee from a non-regulation Thermos pitcher she'd brought from home, lighted one of the extra-light menthol cigarettes that stayed in her desk for weeks at a time, longer now that the GAO was blasting anyone who did nicotine outside of designated smoking areas.

She pulled the case jacket on the taxicab killings and decided to summarize for Doc Hermann's benefit what there was of her meeting with Philip Hallet. Hallet, she'd surmised on the way back from the mansion, was either concealing information from her or was truly the most obnoxious human she'd encountered since ex-Detective Tom Massey, a thought she would have wagered was impossible to hold until today. As the golf ball began whirring in her typewriter, Doc Hermann buzzed on the intercom.

"I need to see you."

"Give me five minutes. You'll be interested in my notes, or lack of them, on the good Doctor Hallet."

Doc Hermann's voice sounded as big as the man himself. "Come up *now,*" he insisted. "And whatever you're writing about Doctor Hallet, trash it immediately."

McCaskey crushed out the straw-thin cigarette and fought back the urge to swear aloud: Frank Thorne had always told her, anyone who thinks the intercom is ever shut off shouldn't be working for the Bureau in the first place.

Two minutes later she was on the administrative floor, standing in front of Doc Hermann's horseshoe desk.

"What's so special about Philip Hallet, the arrogant twerp?" she asked before Doc could utter a word. "He literally told me it was beneath him to compromise his academic independence to help us catch the crazy who's blasting away Arab cabdrivers.".

"I'll come to that," Hermann said, his voice less gruff but still tinged with tension. He directed McCaskey to take a seat, shuffled through some printouts on his desktop. "I pulled every possible switch on the murdered drivers," he went on. "Looks like Jack Corrigan knows as much as we do. There's nothing to tie them together, or to any political movements we have an ear to. No third-party connections, plain and simple."

"We tried," McCaskey shrugged, hating to let it go but seeing no other avenue open for Bureau involvement. "I'll give Corrigan a call and let the local constabulary take it from here."

"I would tell you to do that, if you hadn't asked me to run a check on Philip Hallet."

"I'm losing you," McCaskey said.

"Confusion reigns throughout the Bureau on this one. I'm not sure myself what's the sideshow and what's inside the big tent. Maybe you can tell me," Hermann said as he handed McCaskey a single piece of paper. "You're not cleared to read this, by the way. But at least you'll know why we can't push too hard for Jack Corrigan. Go ahead—it's the summary page of Philip Hallet's dossier. And that's all of his file *I* could obtain."

Doc Hermann was right about her clearance, McCaskey saw at once. Sure, every damn bookie and outfit hood had a jacket marked *secret* floating around 919 Pennsylvania Avenue. But McCaskey had only heard about the designation that Hallet's file carried, and never before had she been permitted to read one.

"Doctor Philip Hallet, in some strange, left-handed way, is apparently a member of our team," Doc Hermann said as McCaskey ran through the vague data. "And if not ours, then surely with the other hard guys who labor in the pristine suburbs that surround Washington. That could be the reason he was reluctant to involve himself in our local problem, for any number of reasons I can only guess at."

"I thought something was strange. So Doctor Hallet is really on retainer with the Bureau," McCaskey said, suddenly wondering if that made him seem more or less like swine. "Probably the whole Institute, too."

"Nothing that well defined," Hermann said. "From all I could learn, the Arbor Institute is as straight as they come. Jason Kellaigh, chairman of Arbor Corporation, has spent millions to fund it. Bottom line, there are dozens of legitimate scholars working there—specialists in Islamic and Hebrew cultures, Semitic languages, all of that. That's the part Jason Kellaigh knows about. Then, there is Hallet."

McCaskey took a deep breath and went for the leap of thought. "You think there's a chance that the dead cabdrivers are connected in some way to Hallet and his work?"

"All I could learn is that Hallet's charter has to deal primarily with foreign students and faculty. But I think, no matter what red flags we get from Washington, someone has to figure out if there's a connection between him and whoever's popping those drivers. If only to keep Jack Corrigan and the local bulls from setting off some unpleasant trip wires."

119

"So, we have to find out who Hallet's contacts are, even if he refuses to cooperate," McCaskey said.

"Impossible. The only people who have such access are Hallet and his superior."

"Who is?"

"Someone who could telephone Langley, Fort Meade, and the National Security Council itself and see to it we're both working night stakeout in the projects. Leave it at that."

McCaskey crossed and uncrossed her legs nervously as the reality hit her. "Do you mean to tell me that Philip Hallet is running a private intelligence network inside the Arbor Institute, and that no one but him and his control even knows who their assets are?"

"Something like that. There's a lot more to it that doesn't concern us. But the answer is, basically, yes."

"No wonder he was such a bastard," McCaskey sighed.

"Sorry?"

"Nothing, Doc. I'm just amazed."

"There's something else you should know," Hermann said. "Then I hope you'll overcome your sense of amazement and impart some reason and logic here. While roaming through the files, I came across a special domestic intelligence brief about a Syrian named Mohammed Saami who, along with his girlfriend it seems, got slipped enough cyanide in a New York restaurant to stage a reenactment of Bhopal."

"I saw it in the papers," McCaskey recollected. "Another product tampering, so it said."

"Bullshit. One of the people who received the advisory on how the killing was being purposely downplayed for the media was none other than Doctor Philip Hallet. Which probably means that Mohammed Saami belonged to him."

"Which may give me the entry I need to speak to him on a more collaborative level," McCaskey said.

"I'd say you'd better give it a try. It's going to take a lot of soft treading, you realize. I can cover you with Washington by saying you're acting as special liaison with Hallet on the Saami thing. But if you're to get his help on the other, he'll have to volunteer it. We've got no clout there, other than your making Doctor Hallet a friend."

McCaskey grimaced. "That's asking a lot."

"You want a good case, you have to pay for it. So if you can get Hallet to play ball with you, we may be able to do more than figure out who's wasting our cabdrivers. We may help Doctor Hallet find out who eliminated one of his operatives. And that, my dear Agent McCaskey, moves you into the big time."

"Like I said, Doc. Philip Hallet's not such a tough nut after all."

The whole idea smelled to high heaven, Usher kept repeating to himself as he stripped off his running clothes and, too tense for the ritual of a hot bath, jumped into a shower. The most bloody outrageous job he could possibly dream up, let alone sign on to do. Still, if Ben and the family were backing the big limey, he had little choice but to go along. For a while, anyway. And, with a few hundred thousand in the cooler, on top of what he'd stashed already, he could split Chicago in a wink, get out to that hunting lodge in Montana he'd been dreaming about since the day he'd bagged his first buck in the thick Adirondack forest.

But what in the hell was making Harry come on like Al Capone? Probably, Usher figured, the wogs he wanted taken out were either running guns out of the country, or bringing smack into it. Which in either case, and especially if it undercut the big boys in Motown, was a sure way to get one's ticket canceled. Permanently.

So Harry wanted a big bang. Something no damn newspaper could confuse with an accident. Definitely sending out a message, but to whom and for what reason? None of your damn business, Usher scolded himself, especially when, at twenty-five grand a crack, it would be more than profitable to supply it. Besides, the wogs deserved it anyway. It would be fun.

Usher dried himself and dressed in tan cotton slacks and a yellow golf shirt with some designer's animal on the left breast. He would walk over to Lincoln Avenue, grab a light supper, maybe hit a few taverns or take in a movie to kill the evening. He locked the apartment securely after slipping the two-shot .22 magnum derringer into its custom-welded niche behind his belt buckle.

Colleen and Sharon were dragging their suitcases toward the corner apartment as Usher stepped into the corridor.

"Well, lookit here now. The ghost of Christmas past," Colleen said, her voice cool and eyes distant. "Was it something I said? Or didn't say?"

Usher felt his neck muscles tighten in anger. He hated taking shit from anyone, females especially. But no sense firing some back at the big stew when he had to live so close to her.

"I got sick," he explained. "Must have been the water or something. You were in the bathroom, I needed one. Afterward, I wasn't up to cocktails."

"See, it makes sense," said Sharon as she flashed Usher a toothy smile and a few thousand dollars' worth of caps that still couldn't cover up a major-league overbite. "I told you."

"It happens," Usher said.

"Just once," Colleen responded with a lingering chill.

"I'll make it up to you. Both of you," Usher said. "I doubt you filled up on airline food, so dinner is on me. Okay?"

"We're off four, five days at a time, and you only appear when we're just back from O'Hare. Bad timing," Colleen said. "I'm heading for a hot bath and an early night-night."

Sharon gave her roommate a quizzical look. "There's nothing at all in the apartment, you know. We can handle a quick change, some dinner."

"With a seven o'clock departure tomorrow?" Colleen asked back. "No chance."

Usher watched the big blonde grab her suitcase like a barbell and head toward the apartment. "I guess it's you and me," he told Sharon. "I'll wait in my place while you change."

"No, come over to ours," Sharon said. "Your bottle of rum is still intact. Mostly."

Usher caught Colleen as she gave Sharon a disapproving glance, then shrugged her shoulders in compliance. "What the hell," she said. "But one of us will watch you at all times, make sure you don't pull another disappearing act."

"No chance," Usher parroted back, for a moment forgetting about some Arab in Michigan who called himself Mike Doran.

Lieutenant Jack Corrigan pushed wearily through the kitchen door of his white clapboard bungalow on Chicago's Northwest Side. As was his habit since the kids were small and curious, his first move was to drop his service revolver into an old clay flour canister on top of the refrigerator. The house was still. Corrigan figured his son and daughter were out for the evening, saying no to drugs he hoped, and that Margie was asleep for certain. Fine for tonight. He looked forward to some time alone, to opening the fridge and taking out some of the lean corned beef that the counterman at Bernie's Luncheonette had pressed him into taking home. He'd heat the beef briefly in the microwave that Margie had shown him how to operate just days earlier, then slap it between some sour Jewish rye and smear it good with dark mustard. Perfect. Just the ticket after another rotten day at Eleventh and State, a full day and half a midwatch shift that had yielded nothing more than their sixth taxi driver, and fourth Iranian, executed with another pair of .22-caliber hollow points by the psycho that the tactical cops working the case had begun to call Son of Shah.

Corrigan hung his sports coat on a chair back, pulled the spotted necktie through a damp collar, finally made it to the icebox. There was a stack of Old Style cans on one shelf, some bottles of imported Harp lager, usually reserved for company, on another. Corrigan decided to treat himself, snapped open a Harp, and took a long pull from the amber bottle.

He saw the note Margie had left on the table, tucked securely away from unforeseen breezes beneath a bottle of steak sauce. Three telephone calls that evening, all from the same person. Wouldn't leave a name or return number; said it was urgent, life-and-death. He'll call again at eleven o'clock. What a rude man!

Corrigan had time to create his sandwich, finish the first bottle of Harp and half a second one, and try to figure out what the hell else could go wrong in his working life. Jesus, if it weren't for Margie and the kids, maybe he'd find Frank Thorne and help him sail a cargo of sunburned tourists around Grenada, or St. Wherever-the-Hell, or on whatever seas Thorne was now sailing.

Probably the right idea. It was Thorne's old girlfriend, that damn McCaskey, who was giving Corrigan nearly as many headaches as the wacko who shot cabdrivers. Corrigan had gone to her for help; now all he was getting for it was a cold shoulder sitting atop a stone wall. How do you figure it? She was a good cop once. Corrigan had seen it firsthand when she took down Tom Massey. Or was that just ambition disguised as good police work? Guess I should have known then that she'd want to be the first lady head of the FBI, Corrigan thought. J. Edgar Hoover with tits, and just as ruthless. Hell with her. She wants to serve up the taxi killings on a federal plate, she can damn well have them. It was stretching anyway to make it a Hostage and Terrorism case, and too many favors were getting called in to keep it quiet. Serve her right, too, when the full scope of it hits the papers and the total body count goes public. Doc Hermann may be too long past retirement, but he sure won't stand for the heat of an anti-Arab vendetta on his turf. Especially when the Chicago P.D. had Arab cops volunteering to drive taxis undercover and even consider it good duty to risk their own lives for a crack at the gunman. Yeah, how many Arabs in the WASP Bureau anyway?

Margie long ago had learned to turn down the bell volume on the telephones when she went to bed, but the ring was still sharp enough to give Corrigan a start. He swallowed the clump of sandwich that was doing a fire dance on his tongue (too much of a good thing, that brown mustard) and washed his throat clean with a gulp of Irish lager. He got to the wall phone on its third ring, pulled the long twisting cord back toward the table, and realized he had the inimitable Johnny Roses on the line—straight from the federal penitentiary in Terre Haute, Indiana.

"Hey, Lieutenant, I never figured you for a chaser," Johnny Roses bellowed. "Runnin' around all hours of the night when your lady expects you home for supper."

"I'm out chasing, all right," Corrigan shot back. "See, since we put all the creeps like you away, it's getting tougher to find any sleaze left on the streets."

Corrigan listened impatiently to the wheezing laugh. John Ross was known in the Chicago outfit as Johnny Roses, not for his love of horticulture but for his extraordinary luck in smelling like them no matter how much shit he stepped in. One tough little monkey, Corrigan knew firsthand. So lucky he'd once taken some head shots through a defective silencer and lived to see his would-be executioner, a greaseball thug named Chuckie Franco, find his eternal reward in the trunk of his powder-blue Cutlass. Truth was, though he'd never admit it, Corrigan kind of liked Johnny Roses. As much as any longtime vice cop could like the captain of the Chicago family's gambling-and-girl operations. But tonight, Corrigan decided as Johnny's laughter wound down, his phone call had to be some kind of omen.

"Lookit," Johnny Roses kept sparring, "from all I hear, you got more than enough to keep you busy—all them parties and press conferences you headquarters boys gotta do."

"Hey, shithead, I know life is soft in those federal joints, but I didn't think you had an office and private phone where you can call people day or night just to bust balls. I'm in no mood to play the dozens with you, Johnny. You got something to say, say it."

"Okay, okay. Let's get serious," Johnny Roses said, all the bite gone from his voice. "I got a real problem here, and I need your help."

"The black dudes find you irresistible, right?"

"C'mon, Lieutenant. That's nothing to joke about. But you hear me out, you'll be glad you did. I got something big for you."

"You know I'm not working the family anymore," Corrigan said. "Even if I was, your ass belongs to the Feds. Talk to them."

"The Feds *is* my problem," Johnny Roses whined. "You want to listen?"

Corrigan drained his beer and decided to go along for a while. Who knows? he thought. Johnny Roses walked away from a back-shooter once. Maybe he can spread some luck my way.

"Start talking, Johnny. But I promise nothing up front. And maybe never."

"Sure, Lieutenant. But you know I ain't no snitch, either. I took hard time rather than rat on the family, so you appreciate my situation, too. We don't do business, I never even called you."

"Deal," Corrigan agreed.

"Okay. Now I'm doing six long in this joint. They call it medium security, but you should see the people they let in here. Fuckin' crazies, man. I mean it. Like I'm the only guy in here ain't got something obscene tattooed on his ass. And the guards ain't nothin' but a bunch of rednecked Hooples. Me, I oughta be in one of those camps with the rest of the white-collar people. Oxford or some place. I took a little football action, is all. Nothin' with guns and chain saws."

"Cut the shit, Johnny," Corrigan barked. "First off, I'm not the judge. Second, you ran more bookies than Uncle Sam runs prisons. You drove the new Cadillac, pal. I got a ten-year-old Chevy in a garage that leaks. So don't start crying to me, especially when you'll only end up doing two years and change anyway."

"Doing that much isn't the problem. My family's okay. I got people watching out for my interests. Like that. But this guy I know—"

"Another bookmaker?"

"Nothing that honest. You want the truth," Johnny Roses whispered, "he's with the Feds himself. And he's been telling me that Sid Paris, my old boss and now a star in the witness protection program, has been spilling his guts about some other things. Not gambling, but things I wasn't into, really."

"Sure, Johnny. You're a persecuted saint."

"You got the front part right. What with all them conspiracy things coming down, all the Feds do is hear some people speculating on the telephone, you get nailed even if the thing wasn't done. Imagine that, you get time not for doing a number, but just thinking about it out loud. Nothin' like between you and me. I got paid to take bets, you got paid to stop me. All that's fair."

"Johnny, how about you start making sense? If the Justice Department has Sid Paris strapped to a tape recorder, what do you expect me to do about it?"

"I give you something you both want, something the Feds don't have, and you go to bat for me. You get them to ship me outta here, and leave me alone about things Sid Paris and I did nothing but talk about. That's it."

"Sure thing. I call over to the Dirksen Building, get you sent up to Oxford so you can take a few strokes off your golf game. That's it?"

"Funny thing, you should mention golf," Johnny Roses answered calmly. "That's sorta what I had in mind for you. You heard about this big-time union guy who met his maker with a golf club in his hand? Down Jamaica way?"

Sufferin' Jesus, Corrigan shuddered. The hit was miles away from his jurisdiction. But if Johnny Roses could give him enough on the assassin to get him out from under Jerry De's thumb . . .

"Yeah, I heard something about that," Corrigan said with feigned disinterest. "But what do you know? You got a satellite dish in your cell?"

"Like I said, nothing on the family. But that golf course thing. I might just know who the shooter was."

Corrigan wiped the rim of the mustard jar with his finger, then licked it clean. He'd bet Johnny Roses eight to five that Agent MaryAgnes McCaskey put mayonnaise on her corned beef.

"Terrific, pal. Especially coming from someone on the inside. But Jamaica and union business is a long way out of my territory."

"But Chuckie Franco wasn't. If I remember right, what with all them bandages around my head, you took a lot of flak about Franco getting iced after you cut him loose. Maybe, you get the guy that done that too, and you wrap him for the Feds on the union thing. They'll be grateful about the source, right? And whatever Sid Paris claims—hey, all speculation."

"You telling me the same shooter did Chuckie Franco did the Jamaican thing? You got evidence there, Johnny?" Corrigan fought to keep his tone calm. But taking down a syndicate button-pusher happens less than once in a cop's lifetime. And to date, despite the long years, Corrigan was still batting zero.

"Evidence. *Su gatz,* is evidence. You want any more, you gotta come see me. This ain't telephone talk."

"Yeah, sure I will. But I can't promise anything from the FBI or Justice. Least ways until I got some blue chips."

"Hey, I may be stuck out here in the middle of Soybeania, but I still know what goes on in Chicago. The Feds let aldermen out of jail to vote on election day when the okay comes out of City Hall. And, now that you're big time on the force, right up there with my *paesan',* Jerry De, you gotta be well connected. Am I right or am I right?"

Corrigan didn't bother considering matters further: McCaskey wants to end-run him on the taxi shootings, he'd play out the Franco hit without her. And if he happened to bust open a federal case in the process, maybe he'd have a shot at cutting loose from Jerry De Lorenzo and getting his desk-worn Irish ass back on the street.

"Well, whatta you say?" Johnny Roses asked impatiently.

"I say you tell me when's visiting day, and give me the best way for a civilian to find that Hoosier pen of yours."

Hallet dropped the telephone back into its cradle. You should have called me right away, Macdonald Clelland had told him. By now it's probably too late to stop Agent McCaskey from finding out that the Institute and the Bureau had ties, at least if she's as smart a cop as you say she is.

So, Hallet figured as he dropped his head into open hands, palms pressing against his eyeballs for relief from the headache that had nagged him all day, he'd probably be seeing Agent McCaskey soon again, which wouldn't be all bad if it weren't for the madness that surrounded them—Mohammed Saami poisoned, someone murdering cabdrivers because their names looked or sounded Arabic, the whole damn world going crazy and blaming the people it understood the least for its own insanity.

Hallet knew Stan Bach was back at the Institute and rang his office, knowing exactly what he wanted to do and figuring that, in light of his mood, taking along a chaperon would be prudent.

Stan Bach sounded concerned when Hallet asked if they could meet for a while. "What do you have in mind?"

"Nothing extraordinary," Hallet replied. "Just that the last time I saw you, you had a pistol in your hand."

"I'm still shaking," Bach laughed. "I was in the Army, you know. But my MOS was a chaplain's assistant."

"I need to decompress for a while, talk some things through with you," Hallet said. "Promise I'll get you home to Ruth at a reasonable hour."

"It's not that," said Bach. "I've booked an hour at the flotation center. Let's go together. Perfect peace and silence. Believe it, after a day at this place, some sensory deprivation works a lot better than talk."

"You're joking. You really lay in a tank of warm water with earplugs and a blindfold?"

"It's the best *schvitz* in the world," Bach insisted. "Better than—"

"A saloon?"

"Who's accusing?"

"Okay, then. The parking lot in fifteen minutes."

Stan Bach's accusations came later when Hallet directed him to turn over his car to the parking attendant in front of Fairweather's Rush Street tavern.

"This the last place you should be," he complained, "and the last thing I should be is your accomplice."

"I have a small debt to pay, and an even smaller thirst. Relax."

"I've always guessed you were as much a street person as you were an academic," Bach said when they were inside and he scanned the crowd that filled the bar and booths. "Or is it that you just like being the stranger in a strange land?"

"This isn't strange at all, Stanley. What we do is strange. This is for real."

Val came over and offered his damp hand to both Hallet and Bach.

"Here's the hundred I owe you, and another one to clear up any old tabs," Hallet said.

"You're heavy," Val smiled, "but I'll ride the rest. Except the first one, which is on me."

"Scotch rocks, twist of lemon."

"Perrier with lime," Bach grumbled. "I'm driving."

Maurice cut himself loose from Carmine, his hulking Sicilian bodyguard, and came over to say hello. He did a few minutes of street rap, mostly for Stan Bach's benefit, Hallet guessed, before strolling off to join a group of wheat traders from the commodities exchange who were jointly sweating out a Justice

Department investigation of their practices and procedures.

"Not strange?" Bach repeated. "Your friend Maurice has got a thousand-dollar wardrobe and a twenty-dollar brain."

"That you buy Maurice's act at all is another reason I'm glad I brought you out from behind your dreary studies of Halakhic literature. Maurice, besides being among the richest people in this place, is probably the smartest by far. He does street action, sure. But he also has an investment portfolio that could rival Jason Kellaigh's and endow an institute of his own. What you just saw is what he does for a living he no longer needs to make."

"He just likes hustling honkies?"

"You could say that, if this were still the nineteen-sixties."

Stan Bach watched Hallet take a first sip of his Scotch and shook his head painfully. "I'm beginning to wish Maurice's brainpower was contagious," he said.

Hallet didn't respond. He took another pull on the whisky, enjoyed its stinging sensation and the slight hints of smoke and lemon that tingled his tongue. As Stan watched him silently, Hallet recalled an old Middle East hand he used to drink with in Cairo—a Brit who preferred "Tony" to his proper military title of retired colonel and who, Hallet felt certain, was on the payroll of MI5 in some devious capacity. Tony, when Hallet first began cultivating him, used to add lemon twists to his mug of Teacher's. Later, he moved from twists to squeezes and eventually to lemon slices. Finally, in some aberration of the shandy, a despicable drink in which the British mix equal measures of draught beer and lemonade, Tony consumed huge glasses of what looked to strangers like iced tea. The nourishment of vitamins A and C from the lemons, Tony argued forcibly, enabled him to consume dozens of drinks without any more harmful side effects than indigestion and the occasional incontinence that, in Egypt, simply went with the territory.

"You said only one," Bach protested when Hallet had drained his glass and ordered a second.

"I'm only *buying* one. The first was Val's, remember?" Hallet said as he threw a twenty-dollar bill on the bar.

"You already paid the man."

"That's for another time, whenever I'm short. Besides, I like to see money on the bar. *Az men shmeert, fort men.* The more you grease, the better you ride."

"I knew your Hebrew was serviceable," Bach said, unable to keep the smile from crossing his lips. "But I didn't know Yiddish was among your linguistic abilities."

"I love Hebrew as much as I love Arabic. Too bad what we're fighting is a war among Semites."

"The war's over, Hallet. We won it."

"Israel won it. *We* didn't."

"Which 'we' are you today? Whose side do I get to hear?"

Hallet answered with a shrug and plunged back into his whisky.

"Come on, Philip. Let's get out of this place. Let Ruth cure your blues with some pot roast."

Hallet slumped forward on the bar and stared fixedly at his glass, as if guarding it from removal. "Not yet," he argued. "I need to be here for a while. And you're my friend."

"You know I am."

"I don't share this side of myself with just anyone," said Hallet. "Besides, dear and esteemed colleague, my problems of the past several months had nothing whatsoever to do with alcohol consumption. That was merely a symptom of a greater dilemma."

"Liquor was the dilemma, and you know it. So I'm not going to sit here and watch it resurface."

"You know, Maurice was fascinated that I speak Arabic," Hallet mused. "The language of Islam. Used to ask me to teach him some basics at the bar."

"Terrific. That would make him a real hit with Louis Farrakhan."

"Maurice bought some tapes, then a few texts I recommended. Right now he probably speaks better Arabic than half the people in our Middle East legations. A few more months, he tells me, he'll have mastered the intricacies of Maghribic script and be able to read the Koran in its original. Can you imagine?"

"All right, this place is more fun than the faculty club," Bach said. "But you shouldn't be here and be drinking. You gave me your word you wouldn't, so don't make me feel like a schmuck for tagging along."

"That's the kind of work the Institute should be doing, you know. Really teaching people to understand languages and cultures, ideas and principles. Not shilling for someone like Jason Kellaigh, who sees the Arab world as nothing more than a giant marketplace for his caravans of consumables."

"That's nonsense," Bach argued. "Kellaigh was sponsoring Middle East research before it was either fashionable, or loathsome, or even potentially profitable. I know you don't like many people, but I can't understand why you so despise Jason Kellaigh."

"Sure, he allows us to do our work, our little esoteric studies. But, as Virginia Woolf once wrote, in the middle of our party comes death."

"What are you talking about?" Bach asked.

"Could it be you really don't know?"

"I know you're getting drunk already."

"You don't know shit," Hallet sneered.

Bach grabbed Hallet's wrist as he pushed his glass forward and motioned Val for another refill. But with the glower Hallet threw him in return, he loosened his grasp.

"You son-of-a-bitch, Hallet. Did you just ask me along to have someone around to beat up on with your twisted and inebriated intellect? Why did you do this to me?"

"Only so you'll know who I really am," Hallet answered in the instant before he watched Stan Bach storm out of the bar.

133

Chapter 10

A jumble of days rolled by. How many, Hallet couldn't be certain. Five? Six? A weekend fell somewhere in between, but the days were no different from the others. Not with Hallet spending the long, fruitless hours at the Institute; not with Sandman still in waiting.

So far, nothing worth the time, the effort, the stress. Hallet's people were still digging, but each of them had come up empty. Each one except Mike Doran, who responded with his usual forcefulness that Mohammed Saami's murder and Yousef's poorly transmitted warning might indeed be parts of a whole; that he had, in fact, been working independently on that assumption even before receiving Hallet's cryptic message. As for Yousef, he was somewhere off on his own, among the missing. And Hallet's attempts to find him by locating Nahid had likewise produced zero.

Things were no better in the other half of his life at the Arbor Institute. Stan Bach was still seething about Hallet's drinking spree at Fairweather's and refused to speak with him until Hallet stopped him cold in the Fellows' lounge.

"You really don't get it, do you?" Bach replied scornfully

after Hallet said that he was overreacting to a brief, single interlude of recidivism. "You don't understand that, when you're drinking, you damage people other than yourself. You're dangerous."

Hallet stared dumfounded at his longtime friend, trying to put together the logic behind Stan's words. Bach turned away and headed into the library.

"Think about it," Bach said over his shoulder. "Hard."

Hallet's relations with Isabel Ortega weren't going any better. Especially after his repeated turndowns of dinner invitations and what she termed "opportunities" for them to speak frankly together.

They had a row one of the evenings Hallet stayed late in the vain hope of hearing something from his Prophets. As he waited in the stark, climate-controlled, white and gray computer room for any kind of word, Hallet reviewed with amused disdain the eclectic output of his fellow Fellows—comparisons of calligraphic motifs in the early scrolls of the Torah and Koran; projections of the value of Saudi riyals and Kuwaiti dinars against dollars and sterling; land use and petroleum resource analyses for a more friendly, pro-West Egypt; an updated psychological inventory of Muammar al-Qadhafi which revealed a special dread of stroke and paralysis and related it skillfully, but incorrectly in Hallet's view, to Libyan militarism.

Isabel Ortega had seen Hallet's name in the computer sign-on log and strode into the EDP center determined to make her current feelings known.

"Here I was, taking all your rejections personally," she said. "Thinking the worst, I suppose. That you were drinking again. Why couldn't you tell me you were working late? Is it another one of those special projects that's so proprietary you won't ask me to help with the research? Another job you'd rather not discuss?"

"It's not a research matter," Hallet said flatly, looking up from his terminal at the unsmiling woman who loomed over him in a fashionable pair of wheat-colored jeans and a mauve sweater that brought out the richness of her smooth olive skin.

"A novel, then? Turning your years of roaming the great deserts into an epic? Good idea, Philip, except I can tell you that everyone else around here is trying to do the same thing. I've gotten all the fact-checking requests to prove it."

Hallet punched the exit button and watched the computer screen return to a pale, seasick green.

"What's put you in such a rotten mood?"

"Nothing, except the fact that you've treated me abominably from the day you ran away from the clinic. I've been trying to understand you, the stress of your recovery and all. But I also understand now that you don't give a tinker's damn about me or anyone else but yourself. So I imagine my patience has turned to anger. That's it. I'm damned angry at you."

"You've no reason."

"Don't I?"

"Look, I have a lot to catch up on, a lot—"

"A lot to do," Isabel interrupted. "As always, I'm supposed to wait on the sidelines until you call. Well, that isn't enough, Philip."

"I don't suppose it is," Hallet admitted, wanting to add something more, but not finding the words.

"You are a pompous, selfish son-of-a-bitch," Isabel swore after seeing Hallet wasn't able to take their conversation any further.

"Second time in a week I've heard that," Hallet said as Agent McCaskey's face flashed up from memory.

"Whoever else said it is as right as I am. So if you ever again get the desire to call me, please do me a favor. Don't."

Hallet watched her spin away. He knew that with a little time to calm down, Isabel would be back to normal, and hoped he would be as well. Except that whenever he saw her in the days afterward, she was spending more time than he could ever recall in the company of Bryce Vreeland.

The final oddity, perhaps even more disconcerting than the outbursts from Stan Bach and Isabel Ortega, came about when Hallet received a rare visit from Jason Kellaigh.

Hallet felt somewhat out of sorts that particular morning, what Isabel called *crudo* when she was sufficiently angry at his hangovers to describe them in Spanish. Perhaps it was the final glasses of arak that he'd drunk before bedtime. But despite the unsettled stomach, his hands were steady and his mind focused clearly, a definite indication that he could, after all, take a drink or two now and again and not fall back into the destructive pattern that had led him nowhere but to despair.

He was alone in his office trying to construct a memorandum that would dispel Macdonald Clelland's continuing assumption that the debacle anticipated by the Export file might actually come to pass when he heard Bryce Vreeland's signature knock on his door. Two delicate raps, a pause, then with or without a response, the door creaking open.

"Good to see you hard at it," Vreeland said from the doorway. "Miss Ortega says you have quite a few projects working."

"No more than usual," Hallet replied.

"I see." Vreeland took a deferential step sideways. "Well, there's someone who'd like a minute of your time."

Before Hallet could protest, he saw Jason Kellaigh step into the doorway, give Bryce Vreeland a parting nod, and enter his office.

"Sit still, Philip. I merely dropped by to say hello."

Jason Kellaigh hovered at six-foot-two inches tall, which, after all Hallet's years of dealing with the smaller statures of the Middle East, made him appear giantlike. Kellaigh's sharp features and creeping wrinkles were partially masked by a healthful tan and regally crowned with a full head of white hair that he divided with a precise, eleven-o'clock part.

"So, how are you?" Kellaigh asked as he extended his hand.

Hallet responded with equal firmness of grip and noticed that Kellaigh's gold cufflinks were the filigreed insignia of the Arbor Corporation, an almost Islamic treatment, he decided—the olive branches which constructed the arbor shape of the letter "A" could as easily have been grape leaves.

"Happy to be back at work," Hallet replied.

"Good. Very good. I knew it would be a minor setback only. Tough stuff, too much alcohol. A poison as deadly as any."

"Precisely why I no longer use it."

"Excellent." Kellaigh made an effort at smiling, but Hallet noticed a different look in his eyes, something he had seen often, but never in Jason Kellaigh. It was pain.

"Want to fill me in?" Kellaigh went on.

Hallet ran through his current activities: Besides an overview for the university's business school, there was the forthcoming lecture on Islamic architecture for an Institute-sponsored symposium, plus, of course, his long overdue book, some parts of which the Institute press planned to advance-issue in pamphlet form.

"Have to keep our presses churning," said Kellaigh. "We need all the revenue we can raise, from whatever source. Funding has been getting harder and harder, you see. I'm afraid Islamic culture isn't especially popular these days."

"Was it ever?"

"I suppose not," Kellaigh admitted. "But everyone loves a conundrum. You should know that best of all. It's nothing more than one big puzzle, is it, the Middle East?"

"Which is why there are scholars," Hallet said.

"But scholars with purpose. Whatever we do here possesses no real worth until it is communicated, until it is shared."

"Which is why we keep the presses rolling, as you suggest."

"Partly true," Kellaigh said, "but I've been thinking along other lines. It's something I've wanted to discuss with you for some time now. But with my schedule and your . . . your recovery."

"Which is total," Hallet assured him. "And nothing I'm sensitive about any longer."

Kellaigh seemed relieved with Hallet's casualness. "That pleases all of us," he said. "So I suggest we dine together, say,

139

one evening next week. I'll have my office set up the date, and I can try out some ideas of mine on our best man. Ideas which I dare say will make the Arbor Institute a far more relevant institution in the years to come."

"More relevant?"

"In a strategic sense, yes. Nothing to compromise our charter. But I'd like to discuss ways we can use our extraordinary data base and many talents to assist in the diplomatic and commercial process. Ways that, if not as egalitarian as we're accustomed to, may be considered significant in avoiding further conflicts and confrontations. As Tennyson suggested, perhaps our poet's scrolls can help shape the world."

"You make it sound like you want us to become an intelligence arm," Hallet said. "Which will ultimately mean working against the very people we approach as friends."

"Nothing of the sort," Kellaigh replied with a modest chuckle. "But there is nothing wrong in using our resources—and our many valuable contacts in the region—to anticipate the future a little more carefully. That's what I'm getting at. And that's what will help us recover much of our lost funding. Anticipation, forecasting, proactive thought. But as far as becoming politicized—what would we, a businessman and a scholar, know about intelligence gathering?"

"I'll look forward to our dinner," Hallet said, wanting to duck further discussion of the issue.

"As shall I." Kellaigh rose, smoothed his suit coat and trouser legs, and gave Hallet another handshake. "Until then, keep at it."

"One thing, though," Hallet said instinctively as he eyed the document he'd written for Macdonald Clelland. "According to Tennyson, the poet's scroll *shook* the world. And you should know, too, that some of the best intelligence agents in history have been successful businessmen and humble scholars."

Hallet watched from his window as Jason Kellaigh and Bryce Vreeland emerged from beneath the mansion's main portico and climbed into the waiting limousine. Hallet still couldn't comprehend the purpose of Kellaigh's visit, but the comparison he had made between alcohol and poison, and his curious interest in bringing the Institute into the hard reality of strategic affairs, made Hallet shiver. And as old instincts came back to him, Hallet knew that he had to get away from the Institute immediately, that too many people were closing in on him, that he had to flee.

Macdonald Clelland slammed down the receiver and swore at the silent telephone console as if it were purposely defying him. He was completely out of patience. Hallet had blithely walked out of the Institute without a passing word. He had to be drinking again, for God's sake, Clelland thought as he looked at the paper on his desk. Forget about security; Hallet sent his damn report in the office mail, like it was a requisition for new business cards.

Clelland knew he had to find out what the hell was going on with Hallet, but either no one had any information or they refused to share it with him. Isabel Ortega: he could believe her. She said she hadn't spoken with Hallet in days, and the one time he agreed to visit her for dinner, he'd canceled at the last minute for reasons too weak for her to recall. Stan Bach, Clelland guessed, was probably lying. His response when Clelland inquired if Hallet had gone back on the sauce was evasive and incomplete.

"Something's wrong with him," Bach had said. "But if you're looking for answers as to what, you'd better get hold of him yourself."

Which was exactly what Clelland was trying to do. Which, if it weren't for the shoddy condition and transmission of his data, might mean that Hallet was actually accomplishing something worthwhile with the Prophets.

Clelland went through Hallet's memorandum again, as if there had to be more in it than he'd seen on first reading. But the results were unchanged. Neither Hallet nor the Prophets had any reason to suspect that Mohammed Saami's cover had been penetrated, nor did they have concrete information to support the Export dossier that any "assist teams"—Hallet's euphemism for terrorist death squads—were expected to enter the United States. All of which directly contradicted the information that Clelland was receiving from Washington.

One scenario Clelland pondered was that Hallet's prized intelligence network had become as ineffectual as its control. But the most plausible answer was the one Clelland grumbled aloud in the seconds before he decided to return the phone call from Director Hermann of the FBI.

"That bastard Hallet has to know more than he's letting on. He has to be holding out on me."

The orange sky was lingering on the brink of sunset when the taxi dropped Hallet a half mile from his home. He had done what he had to do to get away from the Institute, and he had done it carefully and securely, using different phones to make the calls to Toronto and Arizona and the other locations where the Prophets operated. It accomplished nothing to disprove that Macdonald Clelland's hunches about the Export file were grounded more in fear than in fact.

Now, Hallet felt the need for fresh air, to walk the side streets westward to his town house, to sort out the lingering questions he had, knowing even as he walked there were no real answers for any of them.

Rush hour had passed; the evening was peacefully still and the air laden with a melange of aromas from the restaurants and food shops that lined Clark Street. Except the smells made Hallet more thirsty than hungry—there was nothing like an iced glass of gin before a meal, no matter what was served. He could almost savor the breathless bite of it. Perhaps, when he reached home, he would have just one to relax and to enable him to attack the scattered, sundry mass of paper that cluttered his desk.

Hallet was a dozen paces from his entrance gate when the car door popped open so suddenly in his path that he had to sidestep it like a halfback and ended up entangled in a low-hanging branch of dogwood. His first instinct was to crouch low, his fists formed into tight mallets, and aim for a groin shot at whoever was coming after him. He hadn't been formally trained to escape kidnappers, but a young French military attaché in Beirut once told him that a quick reaction against the first of the group (four was the normal kidnap team, if anything in Lebanon could be called normal) would give his colleagues enough pause for their target to make a run for it. But Hallet saw no one coming after him, and heard only soft sounds.

"It's important that we talk."

Hallet couldn't place the voice that came from inside the car. "Who's we?"

Agent MaryAgnes McCaskey hit the interior lights, which had been rigged not to illuminate automatically each time the door was opened, something Frank Thorne had wanted back when he was running Operation Clothesline and didn't care to be silhouetted like an easy target whenever entering or exiting his automobile.

"Doctor Hallet. Please," she said.

Hallet let out a deep groan. "I'd have problems talking on a heart-lung machine," he said. "Your kind of an invitation can cause a stroke."

"Of course. And I'm sorry. I didn't think about the stress that comes from living in the Mideast," she said. "Nor did I think you'd be quite so guarded in Lincoln Park."

"Old habits die hard."

"Professional courtesy as well, I take it."

"Agent McCaskey, whatever it is you want from me, I'm not free to provide. I thought you understood that."

"Except you omitted some things that were vital to our original discussion. One in particular."

"Such as?"

McCaskey sounded as if she'd waited outside Hallet's home for hours just to possess this moment. "Such as the network you operate on behalf of the Bureau," she said boldly. "Now, please, can we try it again?"

Hallet slammed the car door and didn't speak until they were inside his house.

"I'm not surprised you know about my activities," he said as he led Agent McCaskey through the vestibule, into the living room. "You're not the type of woman one should underestimate."

"Or the type of federal agent," McCaskey fired back. Hallet threw her an icy glare and, recalling Doc Hermann's advisory to make him a friend, she tried a warmer, more conciliatory tone. "I left word for you at the Institute. I hate disturbing you at home, but you didn't return the call. I said it was urgent."

"I thought it had to do with those taxi driver killings."

"It might," McCaskey said. "Because now we can be straight about what the other is doing."

"You're not cleared to know anything of what I'm doing at the Institute," Hallet said.

"But I'm here anyway."

Hallet turned and eyed McCaskey carefully. She wore a dress of deep green that she'd accented with a black scarf and a bracelet dotted with what appeared to be jade. Her rich raven hair was a perfect crown for a look that was attractive, professional, and revealing enough of her figure to be absolutely sensual.

"You've chosen the perfect colors for our reunion," he said.

For the first time McCaskey lost her look of self-assurance. "How so?"

"Green is the color of Mohammed, the color of peace. It's on the flag of literally every Islamic nation—Jordan, Iraq, Yemen, et cetera. And it's usually accented with black. Some people joke that the black represents oil, but it has a real significance in the Koran."

Hallet watched McCaskey's eyes flare and apologized before she could reply. "Sorry, I suppose I'm lecturing again. I just meant to say that you look nice, and that I hope peace is at hand between us."

"I hope so, too," McCaskey said. "Besides, wearing red, white, and blue can put twenty pounds on a person."

"Touché." He led McCaskey to the sofa and watched her ease onto it gracefully. "So, what do you know about me and my so-called network?"

"As you said, I'm not cleared to know a lot. And I'm not trying to overstep myself either, Doctor Hallet. I'm only here to talk about six dead taxi drivers, and about anything else that might be relevant to a federal investigation of murder and possible terrorist activity. Does that say it all?"

"Indeed, but I think your imagination may be out in front of the facts. It certainly is if you're trying to connect these murders to anything involving terrorism."

"Are you convinced they're not connected? How can you be sure if you won't even attempt to make the inquiries I asked you to make. Look, Doctor Hallet, I have six innocent people killed, and that may mean there is something violent going on inside the Arab community. Now, you have some kind of information-gathering system which my agency is paying for, and I want to use that network to help me find out whether I'm facing some pure crazy acting alone or some local version of an Arab-Iranian jihad."

"Very good," Hallet shrugged. "But I doubt there's a holy war going on among Chicago cabdrivers."

"I'll have to prove that to the police and to my superiors," McCaskey pressed. "I'm still hoping you'll help me."

"If not?"

Screw him, McCaskey thought. The only way to make Hallet a friend was with a hatchet hanging over his head.

"Then I make a call to my director, who will talk with your

director, and helping me will no longer be in the form of a request. But I'd prefer that we operate on a more civil and productive basis."

"Yes, I'm sure you would." Hallet estimated that, should McCaskey make that call, he could pull enough strings to have her taking dictation for the remainder of career with the Bureau, assuming she'd even have one.

But if he could take the chance making such a move, Sandman could not.

He walked into the pantry, dumped a tray of ice into a silver bucket, grabbed a liter of English gin and a split of dry vermouth. McCaskey stared at him with a mixture of rage and surprise as he carried them into the living room.

"Maybe a drink will relax us both," Hallet said. "It's far too late to worry about duty hours, and I make the best martini in the hemisphere."

"No, thank you," she declared flatly.

"Coffee, perhaps. Among Arabs, you know, coffee service is a ritual, a sign of welcome and trust. I have a fine Turkish blend—"

"Damn it," McCaskey snapped. "Cut out the sheik-in-his-tent routine, will you? I think I preferred you when you were just plain rude."

Hallet took a slow, loving sip of his cocktail and sat on a side chair, facing McCaskey directly.

"I suppose I'm just plain tired of it all," he said calmly. "Tired of seeing Arabs and Arab-Americans being treated as a sub-culture of subversives—of seeing them singled out because of events overseas they have nothing to do with. I don't happen to like racism or inquisitions, Agent McCaskey. It's that simple."

"Doctor Hallet, I'm trying to stop someone who's *killing* innocent Arabs."

"But I'm convinced the murders you're trying to solve have nothing to do with Arabs except that they're the victims of the prejudice I've just mentioned. Believe me, you should look outside their so-called 'community' for your motive and your killer.

Everything I know, everyone I know, agrees on that."

"Then you have checked," McCaskey realized.

Hallet nodded. "None of them was involved in anything that would make them an assassin's target."

"They weren't connected with your network, then?"

Hallet made a sound that approached laugher. "You're intent on knowing more about my work than you're supposed to know," he said. "I appreciate your level of persistence and, now that we seem to have become colleagues in a manner of speaking, I'm going to tell you about it. I'm going to tell you because it probably looks better on some classified piece of FBI parchment than it does in reality. This so-called network, you see, is no more than a jumble. I am not an intelligence professional. I'm a scholar who uses his cultural awareness and a few good contacts to make the United States government feel more secure about the Arab and Iranian aliens it has allowed to live and study here. But my network is a jumble because the Arab world itself is a jumble. One guess says that there are about two thousand Arab agents operating inside the United States, in some form or another. They work for governments, for private intelligence services who sell to the top bidder, for factions and groups too countless to name, let alone keep track of. No one is known to the other, not because of some formulated system of compartmentalization but because that is the Arab way of doing things—distrusting even one's allies and neighbors."

"And these agents are all potential terrorists," McCaskey wondered aloud.

"Nonsense. They're students and teachers and laborers and even taxi drivers. They're keeping their sense of allegiance to their homelands, and to their God, by feeding back whatever bits of information they come upon, which in most cases means an amorphous mess that helps no one at all. The people I report to in Washington have problems understanding this. They think the Arab operatives residing here are truly networking, that they're organized and disciplined. They also think that my little unit, which is supposed to keep track of these dangerous foreigners, is itself comprised of duplicitous heathen. So I'm telling you as honestly as I can—all this talk of sleeper agents poised to act against the United States is a joke, because the Arab world is itself asleep when it comes to proactive intelligence."

McCaskey watched Hallet finish his drink and begin fixing a second. "Simply said, then, you have nothing more to tell me than the fact that the dead drivers are neither politically nor personally connected with each other or with any subversive organization."

"That's it exactly."

"That only leaves us one last problem, Doctor Hallet," McCaskey said as she pulled the trump ace from her hand.

"Which is what?"

"How do you explain the murder of Mohammed Saami?"

Usher watched the flat landscape of southern Michigan slide by the window: It was peaceful and prosperous looking, a far cry from his fellow passengers on the bus from Detroit to Chicago. They were, for the most part, black and poor, with two young toughs among them who gave Usher a hard time when he boarded, but who backed off when Usher threw them a look which was at once a dare and a threat.

As for the job, it went perfect, sweet. He had put together the device—explosive and fuse and radio control—from the best of materials, materials he'd gathered over the years before becoming an employee of Ben's family and their strange new colleagues, back when he still had international visions and was going along with the mercenary programs that took him to the Mideast and to Africa and eventually to the Philippines. That was where he had made his biggest mark—taking out a former ambassador right in the heart of Manila with a device that was much like the one he had just used in Detroit, a device put together with components from every left-wing country that made them available, just to confuse the so-called bomb experts when they tried to use the shards as a clue to the origins of its user.

That would be the case again when the local cops or the FBI or whoever the hell else started looking to see who had turned Mike Doran's Cadillac into a ton of human and metallic scrap. They could go ask the Russians and the Frogs and the Cubans, whose Composition C plastique was as good as there was in the world, better than anyone would ever need for clearing sugarcane.

He had seen Mike Doran the Arab ascend into orbit from a rooftop two blocks down range. The car seemed to lift off the street in a flash of white, which turned almost instantly into a ball of orange flame, as if someone had stuck a match into a tank of propane. The sound had shaken Usher's ears before the black smoke began to rise from what was once the Caddie, and he had to fight off the urge to stay on the rooftop and watch the fiasco of attempted rescue. Instead, he quickly disassembled the firing mechanism and threw its parts into trashcans along the side streets that led him to where he could safely grab a taxi for downtown Detroit, near enough to the bus station so he could walk to it in the required ten minutes and catch the Chicago connection with time to spare.

The six hours of driving time were just fine with Usher. Buses gave him a safe and easy exit from any job, especially when he carried nothing to connect him to it. He thought about the money that Ben's limey friend would be coughing up, and that when he finished all that Harry had proposed to him, he'd head somewhere down to the islands to soak up the sunshine and two-dollar-a-fifth rum and some tight tan pussy.

And maybe tonight, he thought, if that dumb bitch Sharon wasn't shoving drinks at passengers, he could get her out for a quick dinner and over to his place for a nightcap. Maybe he could get Colleen, too, and do a double bubble. Probably not their first either, but good enough to make the world right.

By the time the bus was coming across the Skyway into the South Side of Chicago, Usher had the whole event planned in his mind—the quick contact with Ben, the praise for getting it done the way Harry wanted (there'd be no mistaking the motive for this contract, what with all the goodies he'd put into the bomb), then a visit with the stews.

After all the years of scratching, life was good. A long time coming, but never better.

Agent MaryAgnes McCaskey had barely pulled away from Philip Hallet's town house when the beeper signal went off. She pulled in front of a fireplug fifty yards down the street and called Doc Hermann's private number on the cellular car phone. As she waited for Doc to pick up, she cursed the bean-counting bureaucrats for moving so slowly at getting radio communications installed in the vehicle. McCaskey knew that if she ever needed backup fast, the sword she'd fall on would have to be her own.

The voice that finally came over the line sounded like a computer recording. "Communication insecure. Use land lines. Repeat, communication insecure."

Damn, McCaskey thought, as she weighed whether to return to Hallet's house. But she'd had enough of the SOB for one evening. Not a really auspicious beginning for Doc Hermann's order to make him a friend, but not bad enough to force her back to processing surveillance reports on a somnolent old don and his dozing crime family.

She checked the rearview mirror, then rolled her shoulders, stretched her right arm across the seatback, and peered through the rear window. A woman climbed out of an ancient sedan and moved quickly toward Hallet's apartment, darting through the gate, scanning the street cautiously. She was small and dark-haired, McCaskey could see in the eerie amber throw of the streetlamps. Hallet opened the door, leaned forward to embrace her; they both disappeared in an instant.

Well, at least the bastard isn't gay, McCaskey concluded,

already wondering why the subject of Hallet's sexuality held any interest for her at all. She made a note of the woman's license plate number before she dropped the car into low gear and pulled away from the curb. There was a string of saloons that ran for a mile up Clark Street, which would give her access to a "land line," which was Bureau jargon for a pay phone. And there was still half a roll of quarters in the glove compartment, a legacy from Frank Thorne; matter of fact, his only one.

Chapter 11

Nahid clumsily nudged her battered Volare into a tight parking space on a side street west of Paulina, in the far northern part of the city known as the Juneway Jungle—a cluster of rundown apartments and ramshackle houses, its main arteries peppered with electronic games arcades and inexpensive ethnic restaurants, Thai and Mexican mostly, that attract hordes of students from Loyola University, a mile south, and from Northwestern, about the same distance north but over the cultural and economic border that divides a gritty Chicago from the pristine affluence of suburban Evanston.

She led Hallet into an old apartment building, advising him in soft Arabic to be patient with Yousef, who was nervous, upset, and perhaps had been taking things that Mohammed had not sanctioned in the Koran.

"He's certain there's great danger," she said. "He believes someone wants him dead."

Hallet had known that fear himself, far too often and in far too many places. But he gave Nahid no indication he believed her.

"I'm certain Yousef is safe," he said, not entrusting the girl with his real estimation of her larcenous lover—that he was probably doing nothing more than dressing up the window to make another sale.

He followed Nahid down a rubbish-littered flight of interior steps and along a corridor which offered up a curious comingling of smells: the foul ammoniac residue of urine, strong burnt coffee, the unmistakable sweetness of hashish. Though confident that, no matter Yousef's current condition, he would be among friends, Hallet felt reassured by the long-forgotten pressure of the Sauer automatic that rested between his belt and the sweaty curvature of his lower spine.

Nahid motioned him inside a filthy basement room that probably was once the janitor's studio apartment, back when the tenants of the crumbling building could afford one. Plaster wrap from exposed water pipes lay split and strewn across the floor; the room was lighted by a large bare light bulb that came right out of Picasso's Guernica. Behind the metal desk where Yousef and a second man sat was the bathroom, a vision to Hallet that was right out of the Cairo slums.

"Salaam, ya hallet," Yousef said. *"Keef haalak, eh?"* Nahid dutifully and silently closed the door and left her men to their business.

"Nice place you have here, Joe."

Hallet was damned if he was going to speak Arabic when Yousef was in his employ and, judging from his darting eyes, he had been smoking something other than Gauloises. Twenty years of study and fluency in all its dialects weren't sufficient to cope with the complexities of Arabic when the speaker, even a well-educated mathematics instructor such as Yousef had been, was considerably stoned.

"A little down-market for someone with your resources," Hallet went on, "but a good place for interrogation. Is that why I'm here?"

Yousef gave his companion at the table the Arabic equivalent of "get lost." He lit a stale cigarette and, after one drag, appeared instantly to be getting straight.

"I must do the things here that the university forbids," Yousef said. "It's another means for learning. Actually, I prefer it." He reached into the desk and retrieved a fifth of cheap bonded bourbon.

"Ah, yes," Hallet sighed. "The world learns nothing from Americans but their excesses and bad habits."

"Still, you shall have one?"

"I didn't come to this pit for cocktails," Hallet said. "I sent you a signal that you didn't bother to answer. I let your girlfriend drag me here to find out why."

"You know about Mohammed Saami, and you ask for reasons?"

"I know that Saami and one of his innumerable girlfriends accidentally swallowed some cyanide," Hallet said, masking all he felt for his fallen comrade. It had to be that way always: To an Arab, it is not what the heart feels, but that one's suffering is concealed by acceptance and restraint. *Inshallah.*

"Saami was murdered," Yousef said. "Executed."

"If he was, it was no doubt a jealous husband. Or another psychopath getting his rocks off by poisoning food."

"You don't believe a word of that. I see it in your eyes."

"It's your cigarette, Joe. And all the residual hash in here. So if you have something for me that's worth my risking Nahid's dubious driving skills, let's hear it fast."

Yousef sank back in the tattered chair, a false gesture of resignation. "I have no choice but to trust you."

"Trust *me!*" Hallet exploded. "I only put you on the payroll because Mohammed Saami recommended it. But even he warned me, 'Watch out for little Yousef. He thinks only of money.' So tell me what's up for sale, but don't even think of using the word *trust* in my presence."

Yousef now feigned expressions of shock and pain.

"I give you information that helps us keep peace," he protested. "Even if it goes against my own people."

"You sell me interesting tidbits because your scholarship and stipend aren't sufficient to cover whiskey and drugs," Hallet shot back. "Which is the only reason I've put up with you. So before you go back to Tripoli and put your talents to work copying American circuitry onto broken-down Soviet missiles, you'd better earn what you've been paid. Which doesn't mean telling me that half the Libyans in town are tied to Qadhafi's secret police, which we knew even before they had their visas stamped."

Yousef again reached into the desk. This time Hallet went for the Sauer, but when Yousef's hand came out with two water glasses, Hallet left the gun in his belt and found a soft linen handkerchief.

"Now that your sickness has passed, you can drink one," Yousef smirked. "It was the whiskey, yes?"

"It was the gin," Hallet replied. "But I'll pass anyway."

"I have heard things that worry me greatly," Yousef said after downing a double shot. "Bits and pieces, true, but put together, they can mean serious troubles. Perhaps you have heard same things from your other friends. And together we can make sense of what may seem a muddle."

"You and Saami are my *only* friends in these matters," Hallet said, damned if he would give Yousef any sense of community with the rest of his Prophets.

"Such lies." Yousef smirked. "But still, it is better we share our knowledge. And our bread, of course."

"It's only bonus time if you have something worthwhile."

Yousef nodded, apparently satisfied. "I have heard that a mission has been ordered," he began. "A mission to the United States. To bring the struggle here. This is where we start."

Hallet didn't have to fake his disdain. In Arabic he uttered an oath concerning a camel's sphincter, the Bedouin equivalent of "bullshit."

"I am telling you," Yousef insisted. "Remember what happened in England, and how no one believed it would. And such things will soon happen here, in America. In New York and Chicago and other places that only the commandos know."

156

"Joe, I've have been hearing these threats for a decade," Hallet said. "Bring the war to America. Barricade the White House. It's nonsense. No country, not even the fanatics in Teheran or Tripoli, would risk our retaliation and, maybe at last, the condemnation of all the world's irate powers. As for the attack in England, it was done by a handful of suicide-bent zealots that no commando group even bothered taking credit for."

"It was a test," Yousef said unrelentingly. "As you say, a trial balloon."

"It was still suicide, and no country's ready to risk that."

"No country, but an organization."

"No organization in existence has the resources or the power to launch such a mission independent of its government. Each of the movements is beholden to someone—Qadhafi, Assad, whoever. They can't act without an imprimatur. And they'd never get approval to launch an attack in the States."

"I thought you understood us," Yousef moaned. "Perhaps you have been too long back in America. Or you never opened your eyes at all. Suppose there was a unification, a merging of the most dedicated cadre of many organizations? Suppose they created a single military entity that is as strong as any nation itself? Would you consider that?"

Hallet looked longingly at Yousef's glass of bourbon as he tried to organize his thoughts.

"Maybe you should see things with a foreigner's eyes, Joe. You'd know that Arab unity is as dead as Mohammed's vision of it. Borders, like battlefields, are defined by God."

"Allah has always been a battle cry. But now it is one that unites, not divides."

"You're wasting my time, Joe. These arguments have been heard before. And rejected. Look," Hallet tried again, "Syria has the best armed forces in the Arab world, and even they can't control the wild men who are running Beirut. That's because Syrians aren't Syrians; they're Shiites who'll have no truck with Sunnis or Druse or whatever sect you name. No one is ready to form a united front that includes their religious rivals."

"But there is just such a group, Hallet. And it is called Al-Ahzab," Yousef said flatly. "You understand, of course."

"In English it would translate as 'allies' or 'confederacy.' It is the surah of the Koran where Mohammed speaks of seeing the tribes unite," Hallet said, recalling the opening verses exactly— " 'Prophets, have fear of Allah and do not yield to the unbelievers.' "

As did every literate Muslim, Yousef also knew the holy book by rote. " 'Enemies have attacked us from above, and on our land, so that your eyes no longer see and your faith in Allah has been shaken. Nonbelievers thought that the *al-Ahzab* could never lift this siege, but they have little faith and Allah will bring their deeds to nothing.' "

"I know these words," Hallet said. "But this is also the surah where Mohammed talks of a covenant with other prophets in a world of peace, covenants with Abraham and Moses, and with Jesus, son of Mary. It is a verse of peace. Mohammed calls on his tribes to unite under the laws of Islam, not in some task force of destruction."

"You read the Holy Koran like an old mullah, not a man of action. These words have fire in them, Hallet. There can be no peace in the surahs if there is none in life. The people who are Al-Ahzab believe they see the true meanings behind empty words and covenants. It is said in Al-Ahzab, 'Against your enemies we unleash a violent wind and invisible warriors.' *That* is what they read and understand."

Hallet overrode his inner voices and swallowed a good measure of bourbon from Yousef's glass. For an instant, the whiskey seemed to sharpen his thoughts.

"Still rumors and idle threats, Joe," he said. "Unless you have some proof. Unless you're better connected with your secret police than you've led me to believe."

"My fear is my proof," Yousef said. "For not only is Al-Ahzab organized and coming to fight in America, where your people can at last experience our pain and suffering firsthand, but they are coming to purge spies and informants—Arabs like myself who have sold information and secrets to you. Somehow, they know all about us."

"Even *my* government doesn't know that," Hallet insisted. "Sure, I understand that your family sits in Qadhafi's tent at teatime. But if that's what they're telling you, you're only hearing dreams and bluster."

"Saami knew," Yousef insisted. "At least he was beginning to find out. And I swear, it was for that knowing he was executed."

"By poisoning? Impossible," Hallet countered. "That doesn't send much of a message, let alone begin a battle."

"It is said the killer was hired for results, not methods."

"If this group is as powerful as you claim, why would they have to turn to the streets and recruit an assassin?"

"For now, until its commandos are in place. Only when they are ready to strike will you hear too late of them."

"I may be insane here," Hallet said, "but I'm willing to put up enough money for you to find out more. A waste of time and dollars, but maybe you'll at least find out what happened to Saami. Take some trips if you have to, but keep the expenses in line. Probably financing your spring holiday is all I'm buying, but it will be worth it to see if you're up to the job."

"I am not looking for money," Yousef said for the first time in either Hallet's memory or Saami's portents. "And what you ask is very, very dangerous for me."

"How much?" Hallet asked.

"If I find out about Al-Ahzab and its plans, I cannot go home. I will stay in America permanently, and of course receive good work. Can you arrange such a thing?"

Hallet opened his arms in mock supplication.

"Joe, you think I'm some kind of federal prosecutor running a witness relocation program? I work for a foundation that studies Islam for reasons of peace. That I receive a little extra income for gathering news just makes me a government subcontractor of the smallest order. I'm flattered you think I can call Washington and get you a blue passport, but it isn't so."

"I know enough about you, Doctor Hallet, to know that they think you *are* important. You and me and Saami and even Mahmoud Dahran. So you will ask this for me, and I am confident I shall receive what you ask."

Hallet swallowed another whiskey to mask the shudder that ran through him as he heard Mike Doran's Arabic name. Damn, Yousef was better than he'd given him credit for, especially if he and Doran were working the same streets.

"How do you know Mahmoud Dahran?" he asked tentatively.

"I have told you. We're speaking of a confederacy of all Arab brothers, a force greater than any ever organized. That is how I know him, and know that you do as well. So," Yousef said smugly, "you will speak to your superiors on my behalf?"

"I will," Hallet said calmly. "But expect no answers unless you give me something concrete, some proof of what you claim. Remember, Joe, this isn't like selling rugs in some goddamn souk. I need an offering to open the communication."

Yousef faked a mental audit of Hallet's offer.

"Within a week, two at most, I shall give you something undeniable. Only pray to Allah it isn't my head."

"As Allah wills," Hallet said, draining the whiskey and showing Yousef his back. "But your head isn't worth enough to buy me two milking goats and a tent rope."

Hallet decided he'd take no more chances with Nahid's Egyptian-trained driving talents and told her he'd handle the return trip to his town house. They were heading south on a four-lane stretch of Ashland Avenue when he saw the large Buick come up fast behind them, then slide dangerously to the right as if it intended to pass them on the inside track.

"Crazy . . ." Nahid began to shriek.

"Down! Get down!" Hallet commanded her, realizing that

the car wasn't going to pass them at all, but was hanging there and cutting dangerously close to his front fender. Maybe it was being with Yousef, maybe it was thinking there might be some truth to what he'd said about Saami and Dahran. But the only other times Hallet had seen passing cars behave like the one on his flank was when a gunman was trying for a clear shot, or a car was being forced off the road and a kidnapping was in the works.

He swerved left into the oncoming lane, kicked the ancient, sluggish Volare as hard as he could, heard it choke and begin to flood out as the Buick came up faster on his right and began a quick cut in front of him. Hallet slammed on the brakes, watched the Buick sail past. He started a quick U-turn, hoping he could duck down a side street and through an alleyway before their pursuer could recover.

It didn't work.

Whoever was handling the Buick knew all the tricks. The car did a fast power slide after flashing past Hallet's side of the Volare. In another microsecond, it was stopped dead ahead of him, forcing Hallet either to screech to a stop or have a violent encounter with one of the thick old cottonwood trees that lined the avenue.

Hallet hit the brakes, bouncing the rattling Volare and the trembling Nahid, now in silent shock, up over the curb, onto the parkway, stopping dead. He had one choice only: move fast. He reached back, took the Sauer from his belt, and came out of the car low, in a firing position, his left hand wrapped around his right wrist, his aiming point the driver's seat of the Buick. When the interior lights came on, Hallet praised himself for his control in not pulling the trigger. Inside the car, he saw the familiar but definitely enraged face of MaryAgnes McCaskey glowering out at him.

Hallet lowered his weapon instantly, but it was too late. McCaskey had seen it and she seemed to fume even more as she sat motionless inside the Buick.

In the seconds it took Hallet to come around to her door,

however, a quasi-smile replaced McCaskey's icy glare; it was as if she'd finally learned the truth about him.

"What the hell were you trying to do?" Hallet fumed.

"I'd say you overreacted a bit," McCaskey said. "All I wanted you to do was to pull over. I thought you saw it was me."

"You don't have a horn? A goddamn siren in that thing?"

"Actually not. This car was used as an undercover vehicle by an old partner of mine. It's got a phone, but no siren. As for the horn, I thought it would attract more attention than we'd want."

"This didn't?" Hallet asked, making a surveying motion to the Volare hanging off the curb and the passing drivers who eyed them curiously.

"We haven't the time to argue," McCaskey said. "I need you to come with me. Now. It's important enough to warrant our exercise in pursuit and evasion tactics."

"You really want to stick your nose into my business, don't you?" said Hallet. "You're looking for any way you can to use me."

"Just get in the car. My boss is waiting to hear that I've found you. And he wants a meeting immediately."

"What do I care about your boss, whoever it is?"

"I guess I should add that a man named Macdonald Clelland is with him. They're both waiting. Something has happened we have to talk about. All of us. So, please, ask your girlfriend to take the car home, and let's go."

McCaskey watched Hallet walk silently back to the Volare, ease it onto the pavement, and point it north. The girl, who McCaskey could tell even in the dark and the distance was far too young for him, seemed to accept whatever story Hallet told her without emotion; she pulled cautiously into the passing traffic, throwing McCaskey a long, piercing look as she passed by.

Hallet climbed into McCaskey's car and sat rigidly against the door. "This had better be important."

McCaskey waited until they were underway before she told

him. "It's important if you know someone named Mike Doran. Once a resident of Detroit."

Hallet froze for an instant. Mike Doran: twice in one evening, from each of the enemy camps.

"The Mike Doran I know lives in Dearborn," he said.

"Not any longer, I'm afraid. Seems that someone blew him to pieces this afternoon. A car bomb. Very sophisticated and professional job."

"You're sure?"

"We all are. But it wasn't easy putting enough of him together."

"Christ," Hallet sighed.

"So you knew him."

"Yes."

"And he was one of yours," McCaskey said.

It really wasn't a question, but Hallet needed to collect his thoughts, to buy time.

"One of my what?"

"Look, Doctor Hallet, you can tell me all the harmless little tales you want to about keeping track of Arabs visiting our colleges and universities. But don't think I'm naive enough to buy them any longer. Not when you're driving around with an automatic in your pocket, and not when your so-called network is so secret that I can't even get clearance to read about it."

"My rules," Hallet said. "Nothing goes on paper that would either compromise my activity or the loyal Arabs I meet with. You know the Freedom of Information Act, I'm sure. You know how racist it would appear if the Bureau's eavesdropping on them hit the media."

"God, you're smooth," McCaskey said as she swung eastward and headed toward Lake Shore Drive. "A paragon of reason and virtue. Only there's the matter of a second murder to deal with, and this time it's not some visiting Arab who's chasing a sheepskin. So, please, stop with the silk tongue and tell me who Mike Doran really was?"

"His real name was Mahmoud Dahran," Hallet said. "And he was a patriot."

"Which means he worked for you. You were his handler."

"Don't make him sound like one of your petty informants," Hallet railed as he pounded his fists hard on the dashboard, rage and adrenaline coursing through him.

McCaskey, who'd purposefully played it cold and brusque, firing for effect, now regretted pushing Hallet too hard. "I'm sorry about your man," she said. "Honestly. But it's time you and I stopped playing games. Not when people are dying all around us."

"I thought your real concern was with whoever's shooting those cabdrivers."

"It still is," McCaskey said. "But I'm concerned about you as well."

"You mean my network," Hallet said.

"Yes, of course," McCaskey said, her guard back up.

"Mike Doran wasn't doing anything for me that would get him killed," Hallet insisted. "No way."

"He damn well did something."

"Mike had his finger in a lot of pies. Maybe one of them belonged to the kind of people in Detroit who used what you describe as a sophisticated professional to blow up his car."

"Very possible," McCaskey admitted. "That's why we're meeting with Clelland and my boss. Who's first rate, by the way."

"So are you. I'm learning that each time we meet."

"Glad you think so," McCaskey said. "Because, whether you like it or not, we're in this thing together. All the way."

"I suppose we are."

Hallet knew that moment that he'd have to play it out far enough to keep Agent McCaskey, and the Bureau, and anyone else who wanted to stop him, away from Sandman. The way things were shaping up, time was the only weapon he had left, and it was running out. Besides, now he was certain there was a leak to be plugged and an assassin to be found.

Chapter 12

Jack Corrigan got the call at four in the morning and drove to police headquarters with his shoes still untied and his socks unmatched. Cabdriver Number Seven was down, a pair of CCL .22-caliber Stingers entering behind his right ear and turning his cortex into a mound of mush. Exactly the same as the first pair of shootings, Corrigan was told. The driver was an Arab of some as yet unknown nationality, probably an illegal, since the rudimentary paperwork required to obtain a hack license in Chicago was all falsified. The shooter appeared to be his passenger, who had given the cabbie a destination on the near Southwest Side and was taken out in a parking lot off Blue Island Avenue, just north of the Sanitary & Ship Canal.

The disturbing difference, Corrigan found out when he reached his office and got the message to haul his ass pronto up to see Deputy Chief of Investigations Jerry De Lorenzo, was that this time the killing was plastered across the front pages of both the *Tribune* and *Sun-Times*. Even worse, the sidebar stories that accompanied their coverage noted that the latest murder was one in a string of three where the victims had all been Muslims with roots in the Middle East. At least—Corrigan

165

sighed wearily—the papers hadn't picked up on the Son of Shah bullshit that was running rampant throughout the tactical units involved in the case, nor had they come close to the correct body count. Not yet, anyway. But soon. It had to be soon.

He got on the horn to the watch commander who'd been on duty when the crime was discovered and the news broke.

"What the hell happened down there, Terry? We were supposed to avoid the speculations I'm reading in the papers. Like we got us a Beirut in reverse working here."

"We let it slip through the cracks, Jack. I'll admit it. A reporter got ambitious, and we didn't catch it. But you knew, sooner or later, it had to leak."

"I've gotta go upstairs in a minute and watch Jerry De throw a major shit-fit," Corrigan growled. "And I can't get out from under it by explaining enterprise journalism to him. So, Terry, you'd better tell me exactly what slipped through which cracks."

"The Violent Crimes dicks who covered the scene weren't thinking," the watch commander said. "The regular night police reporter was off drying out in some dipso clinic in Oak Park. The kid replacing him didn't know the rules, and the detectives left their goddamn report sitting out in plain sight. The kid sees it and reads what he's not supposed to read. Then he starts checking back files, trying to flesh out his story by seeing how many cabbies have been gunned this year. Right away he finds two more dead Arabs, and bingo."

"You mean to tell me some rookie reporter . . ."

"You got it, Jack. He's looking for a few stats, and the apple cart goes ass over teacup."

Corrigan let the mixed metaphor slide and suppressed his urge to find out the names of the detectives so he could make sure they'd never work days again. Instead, he settled for whatever details he could get from the watch commander that Jerry De wouldn't have read in the morning papers.

There weren't many. The only one that mattered was that the dead cabdriver, unlike his antecedents, had properly filled out

166

his trip sheet and listed the address where he had picked up his final passenger: somewhere along a row of sleazy hillbilly bars and nightclubs in the forty-hundreds of North Broadway, a grim neighborhood between the gay hangouts of Lake View and, farther uptown, the Japanese and Korean groceries that intermingle with cheaters' motels like the Stardust Courts.

As he put together his notes for the surely smoking Jerry De, Corrigan knew they weren't much. The murder clearance rate for the Chicago police ran about 75 percent, not really bad odds for a killer if you have half a brain and consider popping someone.

Of all the homicides in the city that weren't directly gang related, about 85 percent were almost instantly self-solving: Eleven witnesses saw the perp in action, or the killer was the victim's boyfriend or girlfriend, husband or lover. If not on the scene when the body was found, whoever did the deed was probably no farther away than the closest tavern or hiding out next door with a tear-soaked handkerchief in one hand and the murder weapon in the other.

Of the remaining 15 percent, Corrigan knew, about 7 percent were solved within a year. Usually a reticent witness or a snitch came forward with information. Or the killer got nailed for another crime and the facts of the previous venture came out, sometimes because the same weapon was involved, other times, under what the civilian review board often called intense interrogation, the perp just gave up the ghost and swapped his entire life story for a chance to do his time somewhere other than Pontiac, where the hard boys were just waiting for new blood to walk into the block sporting fresh tight denims and an AIDS-negative bill of health.

Six of the remaining 8 percent were the homicides the newspapers loved writing about on the first few anniversaries of their occurrence—the unsolved murders that were beyond the investigatory capabilities of the local cops or the Feds. Mob stuff, most of it; the outfit took care of its own justice with a sure and steady hand. As in the case of Chuckie Franco, which was in the back of Corrigan's mind ever since he'd received that late-night phone call from Johnny Roses.

All of which left a scant 2 percent of the city's gross product of murders that were solved through dogged and determined police work: cases kept alive by the Violent Crimes dicks who keep the files on their desks and reread them before going on shift, looking for ways to tie the pieces together in a way that made sense, then doing it when they get out on the street.

So: Unless the Violent Crimes coppers did some of that hard-nosed police work and got lucky finding out who might have been around North Broadway flashing a long-barrel .22 automatic and boasting about settling some private war with Iran—unless Agent MaryAgnes McCaskey and the wondrous computers at the FBI got the slain drivers connected in some way—the chances were that Jerry De was looking at enough bad publicity to keep him a deputy chief forever, even after the mayor decided that the city of Chicago might again be ready to accept a Caucasian in the role of police commissioner.

Still, Corrigan figured as he headed upstairs to face the De-man, he had one thing going for him—the killer had no reason to stop at seven cabbies dead and was no doubt going to pull his caper again and again.

And that was how, whether he was handcuffed to the Hostage and Terrorism unit or not, Jack Corrigan planned on nailing him.

Jerry De Lorenzo didn't rise from the colonial walnut desk that gave his office a rich, corporate look. When Corrigan entered, he simply peered up at him over a pair of half-lens spectacles; his dark complexion, half from his Italian heritage and half from the sunroom at the Chicago Athletic Association, did not yet reveal any of the crimson that normally characterized his rage.

168

But as soon as he straightened up and looked at Corrigan full faced, the lieutenant knew what awaited him.

"I had Cal Bostic's buns for breakfast this morning," Jerry De began, his voice seemingly calm but the words coming out low and labored. "In fact, I was going to take the entire Violent Crimes Division apart until I found out all I needed to know about dead Arab taxi drivers from an article in this morning's goddamn *newspaper!*"

Corrigan knew it was useless to jump in, to make a preemptive presentation of the facts; nothing ever worked when Jerry De felt his keen sense of media embarrassment.

"Then, to make the day ever worse," De Lorenzo raged on, "I find out the lieutenant in charge of my Hostage and Terrorism unit had told VC to sit on it, to keep the whole thing under wraps. Not just from the press, mind you, but from his own department. His own direct superior. All of which makes the case fester like a boil, a boil that has to pop sooner or later and cover us with pus.

"So you'd better tell me why you did that, Jack. And it had better be better than good."

Corrigan hadn't figured on Cal Bostic being on the carpet ahead of him. But if Cal, as straight as they come, felt compelled to tell Jerry De about the hush-up, it meant that either his pension was on the line or that he was looking at finishing his career on night foot patrol in the bowels of the Cabrini-Green projects.

"No one even noticed the first shooting," Corrigan said. "Some lone Arab gets popped on the West Side and it doesn't even make the papers, let alone the evening news. He wasn't an alderman's cousin, you know."

"Don't smart-mouth me, Jack," Jerry De said as the crimson started to flush his cheeks and forehead.

"When Cabbie Number Two goes down," Corrigan continued, not acknowledging Jerry De's bitch, "there's still no big outcry for fast and certain justice. Another dead Arab, no big

169

deal. But I have to start figuring that either we have some kind of madman out there who likes to off Iranians, or there's some kind of tong war brewing in the Muslim community. And if there's that, then there's a real strong possibility of it being political or terrorist-connected. And that comes under my wing."

"I'm the rooster in this henhouse, pal," De Lorenzo fumed. "Nothing goes under anybody's wing that I don't know about."

"I was waiting until we had something concrete to work with. I figured silence was the best weapon we had. Cal Bostic, who's as good a homicide cop as you have, went along with me. But it was *my* call."

"You call this silence!" Jerry De roared, waving the *Tribune* in Corrigan's face. "This is silence, across the front page!"

"This isn't England," Corrigan argued back. "We can't put out a D-notice like Scotland Yard to force their newspapers to kill stories."

"Watch it, Jack. You got a four-star mouth with nothing but a bar on your collar."

Bag it, Corrigan scolded himself as he calmed down. You get nothing accomplished by squeezing Jerry De's balls. "Sorry, Chief, but I honestly thought we could keep it in check. I also thought we'd have some hard facts to work with by now."

"But *me*, Jack. You didn't bother to brief me on it. I get nothing in the way of a head start that there's some wacko out on the streets shooting Arabs. I get caught with my pants over my ankles when every shit-for-brains reporter in the city is demanding a statement or an interview and I still don't know what's going down."

"I don't either," Corrigan said. "But whatever it is, I can't see rewarding the shooter with reams of publicity. Which may be exactly what he wants."

"You ever think that by keeping this *out* of the papers, you were egging the son-of-a-bitch on? Maybe all he really wanted to do was make the front page just once in his dull, dim life.

Then he'd quit. *Finito!* You think about that, Jack?"

"No one wants to make the front page *once*," Corrigan shot back. "You know that as well as anyone. Besides, that's not the way psychos function. So I'm trying to find some kind of handle on his motive."

"Motive?" Jerry De repeated, in his anger missing Corrigan's crack about publicity-seeking. "What in Christ's name do I care about his motive when I have to go on television and try to explain why the department has been sitting on a serial killer who's waging a vendetta in my city?"

Corrigan wanted to tell Jerry De that he could, of course, let the Commissioner handle the media, or that a key reason for *not* briefing him was because of his propensity for blowing investigations by blabbing them on talk shows. But he figured he was in deep enough already, and should try to calm the De-man by reporting some kind of progress.

"Look, I've got a few things going," Corrigan said. "The FBI is working with me, also on the QT, so don't worry about one side upstaging the other. They're checking out the drivers, their families, like that. There very well may be a political connection to all this, which is why it's stayed within H and T. So far, we've got nothing, but that kind of stuff takes time."

Jerry De slumped back in his chair as if hit by an arrow. "You mean to tell me that you go ahead and single-handedly call in the Feds . . ."

"One Fed. Someone I can trust."

". . . you call the FBI, and I'm not even given the courtesy of a briefing, the opportunity to prepare a contingency statement that would save this department another black eye. I've got to go on television, for Christ's sake."

"As soon as I had something, you'd have gotten it. But if I came up here on every case—"

"This is a homicide case, and you're my Hostage and Terrorism specialist. Remember that, Jack?"

"Let's not worry about where it fits," Corrigan said. "I've

got a plan working. I've got fifty volunteer cops—light-skinned blacks, Latinos, Italians, Serbs, Jews. The key is they're dark enough to pass for Arabs."

"That's terrific. Like a Coca-Cola commercial. We are the fucking world, or something."

"Good cops that all volunteered," Corrigan went on. "They'll be pushing hacks around town with licenses that read like an Arab's book of baby names. Since all we know about our shooter is that he's bound to try again, it's our best shot."

"That's the best you can do? Maybe get a cop killed in the bargain? Where do you come off cutting these orders, Jack? You're a lieutenant of police, not general of the army."

"We've tried everything else," Corrigan said. "One of the shooter's pieces is a twenty-two, and he's using hot-load Stinger rounds in it. We've checked every ammunition sales sheet for the past two years, but nothing yet. We've also checked hundreds of prints from inside the victims' cabs. Again nothing. All we know is that this guy is going to shoot again. When he tries, we'll have radio contact, top cops in place, and a good chance to nail him."

"Textbook detective work, Jack," Jerry De said. "Except for one thing. I didn't put you in charge of Hostage and Terrorism for you to become a one-man crime stopper. I'm paying you for intelligence. I want to show this city that the Chicago Police Department is prepared for the eventuality of terrorism and assassination. I want them to know that we can handle hostage situations better than anyone else because we have good skills that are backed with sound intelligence. Let the Violent Crimes boys deal with this maniac. You get back to what you're being paid to do—get me plans to handle all eventualities in your assigned field. But first, you put together a statement for me, something to get us off the hook with the press. We'll tell the people that we see this as politically motivated, and that our Hostage and Terrorism Unit is cooperating with VC in handling the intelligence end of this investigation. That's what I want from you today."

Corrigan fought to control the Irish temper that Margaret, after all their years of marriage, still found the only thing in Jack's personality she didn't want the children to inherit. But it was getting close.

"I'll give you a statement," Corrigan said. "But it'll have to be as vague as the case itself."

"You write up what I tell you, or I'll get it done over in Public Affairs. And my order still goes. You can go ahead and play footsie with the FBI, but only to get the intelligence data this case will need. I didn't bring you on my staff to see you go back out on the block looking for bad guys."

Corrigan was certain his complexion beat out Jerry De's for redness; he bit his lips again, kept his mouth shut.

"I know what you're doing here, Jack," De Lorenzo went on. "You're using the *possibility* of a terrorist connection to get back on a street case. You've hated working inside from the day you came to headquarters. But that's *my* call, and that's where you're going to stay."

"Chief," Corrigan said as he began a one-eighty turn and stormed out of Jerry De's office, "the day I get paid *not* to get a killer off the streets, that's the day I give you your press statement with my star pinned on it for a paper clip."

The meeting had continued until a fiery sunrise filled Macdonald Clelland's somber, smoky office at the Arbor Institute's mansion. Hallet and Clelland sat together on one side of the conference table, with Director Hermann and Agent McCaskey across from them. Hermann kicked things off by asking McCaskey to "take it all from the top so all of us are on the same footing."

Hallet watched McCaskey carefully as she went through the facts of the past two weeks. She had the habit of crossing and uncrossing her legs nervously between thoughts, he noticed, but had pretty much learned to keep it under control. Still, with the quiet brush of nylon against nylon, and the way her eyes flashed at Hallet as she minimized the extent of his callous brushoff when she first came to him, Hallet suddenly and surprisingly found himself caught up in her allure.

"So, after Lieutenant Corrigan of the local police came to me about the murdered cabdrivers, I visited Doctor Hallet here at the Institute. I had seen him on television, heard him lecture, and thought he might help us find out what, if anything, was going on in the Muslim community that we might relate to the killings."

"And thanks to some idiots in Washington who put a deep-cover intelligence program into the files, Agent McCaskey eventually found out about our activities at the Institute," Clelland said, obviously for Hallet's benefit. "Which is a violation of every agreement I made with Doctor Hallet."

"You forget that domestic security and intelligence are the Bureau's specific charter," Doc Hermann countered. "You do agree with our laws, Doctor Hallet? We are not the enemy here."

"I saw *The House on 92nd Street* too," Hallet scolded back. "But two of my key operatives have been summarily murdered for no reason I can fathom other than that they're part of our program. And a third, whom I have every reason to believe, says they won't be the only ones. That means there's a leak somewhere. Since it's not coming from me or Doctor Clelland, then I think it's not unfair to suggest that someone on *your* side has been lax."

Macdonald Clelland tried maintaining his role as arbitrator. "We're not here to hurl accusations around," he said. "Simply to develop a strategy that will help us get to the bottom of things."

"The issue that remains to be resolved here," McCaskey said properly, "is whether or not the two elements—the cabdrivers and the killings of Doctor Hallet's operatives—are in any way related."

"You've established no connections so far?" Doc Hermann asked for the record.

"Not yet," McCaskey admitted.

"Absolutely none," agreed Hallet.

"And you can shed no light on the murders of the drivers, Doctor Hallet?"

"I don't think they're connected in any way," Macdonald Clelland answered in Hallet's stead as he rolled a lighted pipe in his cool palms. "My real worry is whether some Arab fanatics, as our overseas intelligence sources advise us, have dispatched commandos to the United States, commandos whose missions include the elimination of whatever informers they've uncovered."

"But how would they know who our people are in the first place, unless a leak has opened up in Washington?" Hallet asked. It was a gambit, a weak dodge, he knew, but workable because as yet no one in the room was addressing the real issue. The issue he could not raise. Which was Sandman.

"That is exactly what we intend to determine," Doc Hermann said. "Together. You'll assist us however you're able in both matters, Doctor Hallet. We, in turn, will act only in counsel with you if and when we need access to your operation and the people you employ. Agreed, gentlemen?"

Macdonald Clelland, who could shove more blue chips onto the table if he'd wanted, decided to Hallet's dismay to agree.

So, when the meeting was over, and McCaskey and Hermann were out the door with a newly decided plan of limited assistance to the Chicago police and a cooperative venture to determine what was behind the murders of Mohammed Saami and Mike Doran, Hallet told Macdonald Clelland how he really felt.

"I knew from the first we couldn't keep this contained, Mac. Our program has more leaks in it than the Moscow Embassy. We're in trouble, and our people are in danger."

"Maybe they're in danger because they were doing things they weren't supposed to do," Clelland said.

Hallet knew Clelland was too good an intelligence man to miss it, so he got to Mahmoud Dahran first. "You're talking about Mike Doran."

"You bet your ass I am," Clelland said angrily, before sucking another jowlful of pipe smoke and calming himself. "And I'm wondering if you haven't taken it upon yourself to go beyond the Institute's business. Mike Doran's not what I'd call part of a university-based network."

"Hell he's not. He's got first-rate contacts at Ann Arbor, East Lansing, Toronto. He moves in top circles at all places."

"His circles also include organized crime, say our mentors at the Bureau."

"Maybe that's why he's dead."

"And Saami, too?"

"God knows," Hallet admitted.

"Look, Philip," Clelland said, "I'm not sure this isn't a bunch of nonsense either. But we have to take precautions. The threat of terrorist activity is too real to disregard."

"I don't buy it," Hallet insisted. "Someone is making a concerted effort to make us think that's what's happening."

"Someone has killed two of your people, Hallet. It's our job to find out who it is, why he's doing it, and especially how he knows who they are."

"You're forgetting one other thing," Hallet said.

"What's that?"

"Stopping him. For good."

Jack Corrigan flopped in the frayed chair behind his desk, stacked up the personnel rosters for the volunteer cops who'd act as drivers, decided he had better check in with MaryAgnes McCaskey to see if she'd finally come up with something useful. She was in a meeting, the bitchy voice from the Bureau told him. Could not be reached. Leave a message and she'll return the call. Like that. No matter, Corrigan guessed, if she had anything she'd probably have let him know.

Cal Bostic shook Corrigan's mind clear as he gave the office door a virile slam.

"I've got to talk to you about Jerry De," he began. "I tried to get here earlier—"

"No need, Cal. I know you were under the gun in there."

"I backed you a hundred percent," Bostic said. "But I couldn't *not* tell him how it went together."

Corrigan smiled at the tall black detective with whom he had worked from the very beginning—back when Corrigan had just gotten his sergeant's stripes and Bostic had come out of uniform and into Vice, so young and good-looking that he'd had a hard time busting hookers because some of them just wanted to give away a freebie to see if Bostic was as good as he looked.

"Let it go, Cal. I probably should have gone to see him sooner."

"Well, babe, don't let your pecker hang out on this one," Bostic suggested. "Everything says that this is just some nut with a private war going. Let the regular cops handle it."

"I am a regular cop, damn it. That means I want to see this nailed shut as much as you do. So we'll keep working it together. I'll handle the undercover guys driving the hacks, you keep up the neighborhood and investigative teams. That okay?"

"Working with you's always okay," Bostic said. "But I still think you're blowing smoke. Then again, if I had to sit on my ass all week listening to Jerry De call his press conferences and book his TV appearances, I might want to get my hands dirty too."

"You got that right," Corrigan said. He opened his desk, took out an oversized manila folder. "Here are the operations rosters and their assigned patrol areas. We're working teams of six drivers out of each major garage. That leaves the South Side gypsies out there alone, but that's the only way they would have it."

"My brothers never did appreciate good police work," Bostic laughed. "You gonna come over tomorrow and give these guys their briefing?"

"No, you take it. I have a day of time-due coming and I have to pay a visit to an old friend down in Terre Haute."

"You taking a day off to go to *jail*?"

"Hey, Jerry De may give me grief about getting into cases he doesn't think are on my turf. But he never once told me I couldn't spend some off hours cleaning up business from before."

"I can see it, man. Whatever it takes, you're gonna get your dumb Irish ass back out on the street."

"Compared to this place, it's a picnic." Corrigan sighed as he scanned the sterile chaos of his headquarters. "Besides, you sure do meet a better class of people."

Doc Hermann swung north on Lake Shore Drive while McCaskey, for the first time in weeks, watched sailboats run toward the horizon with a full wind in their sheets without thinking about Frank Thorne.

"I think we've gotten our guidelines established," Hermann said. "At least they know that we're in it for the duration, like it or not."

"I still don't trust Hallet," McCaskey said. "There's something more than he's letting on to us, something deeper."

"He's not quite the minty little professor you made him out to be," Hermann said. "Not when you forget all the dainty mannerisms and pompous language and take a harder look at the man behind them."

It hit McCaskey like a blast of cold arctic air: a goddamn, first-rate epiphany.

"You're a genius, Doc. I was too close to notice at first. But I saw Hallet in action, on the street, when I pulled him over. He moved like a cat, knew as much about protecting his witness as any top field agent we've ever trained. That man's done a lot more than spend his life in a library. And he's got a lot more going than a few college-based Arabs who feed dribs and drabs of rumor back through him to Washington."

"You're doing it again," Hermann said, "taking what I say to extremes, to where the facts don't lead."

"The hell I am," McCaskey insisted. "Our friend Doctor Hallet is not just your genteel academic who's dabbling at intelligence to feed some information fusion center. He's a bloody well-trained professional that's working deep cover. What I'm beginning to wonder is, for which side."

"Come on, McCaskey, you're making this sound like the Walker family spy case. I know you'd like one like that, but—"

"Jesus, Doc, our people *broke* the Walker case. Like you told them at the Institute, that's all within our ken."

"And the possibilities dazzle you. Perhaps too much so."

"Hallet's doing more than he's telling," McCaskey said, oblivious to Doc Hermann's cautions. "And you were right. I have to get close to him. Very close indeed."

"You sound like you're willing to screw him," Hermann said, thinking he was joking until he heard McCaskey's reply.

"Sooner or later, everybody screws someone they don't like," she said. "At least with Hallet, I'd have the line of duty to blame."

Chapter 13

Hallet knew it was reckless to go into the field again, to be seen openly, nakedly. But it was a chance he had to take. Besides, all his instincts told him that if the wrong people were getting close to his Prophets, they might soon get to him and to Sandman, which would only mean catastrophe.

He boarded a half-full shuttle flight out of Midway Airport, flew eastward over a Lake Michigan that was tranquil and beryline, and arrived an hour later—two hours, with the time change—at Detroit Metro. There was no one to meet him, for if he was to learn anything about the assassination of Mahmoud Dahran, the surprise of his visit would have to work in his favor.

He rented a jellybean-shaped automobile with more controls and gauges than he could ever hope to comprehend and headed eastward on the Industrial Expressway. Just before reaching the Detroit city limit, Hallet swung north and drove into the section of Dearborn, Michigan, that juts like a panhandle north from the main part of town into the rib cage of west Detroit, where Dearborn's large Arabic-speaking population—Lebanese Muslims and Maronite Christians; Palestinians and Syrians; Iraqi

181

Shiites—was once as important as emigrating southern blacks to the Ford Motor Company's labor pool.

He turned off Schaefer Highway and onto Warren, an east-west artery lined with Middle Eastern restaurants, grocery stores, furniture and gift shops. The air was rich with the aromas of coffee and olive oil and spices. For the first time in months, Hallet allowed himself to feel homesick for the dry, sunburned lands that offered him asylum and retreat; lands that had created him as surely as they had created Sandman.

He found the small lunchroom just around the corner from the main avenue. Three customers, all men, sat inside—two at a small square table near the front window, the third at the long Formica counter. Behind it, Alex was drying and stacking tea glasses—tall ones for the mint tea drunk in the Berber regions of north Africa, short ones barely larger than shot glasses for the stronger, near-narcotic brew of the Arab states. Alex's wife, Sandy, née Chafik, was in the pass-through kitchen staring down into a pot of what Hallet knew immediately from the aroma were fava beans stewing in tomatoes, garlic, allspice, and cinnamon: a *fuul*.

Hallet walked past both of them. No greetings were offered or acknowledgments made until he came out of the rest room with his necktie removed and the shirt he wore beneath his dark blazer opened two buttons down from the collar, which was now out over the lapels in a style popular in the Mideast. It also signaled to Alex in a private tongue that Hallet was there to talk business (the tie), and that precautions should be taken since they were perhaps being watched (the collar).

Alex went to the table and talked in soft Arabic to the men sitting there. No emotion or reaction showed in their faces as they nodded, rose, and left the restaurant. The man at the counter insisted on another coffee, but Alex told him in English that they had to close for two hours, make some kitchen repairs to be ready for the evening meal. He was sorry, there would be no check for the coffee and honey cake. The man, elderly and

182

stoop-shouldered, took the best offer of his day, drained the small cup as far as he dared, and joined the pair from the table in walking from the restaurant back toward Warren.

Hallet took the last seat at the counter.

"I thought you would come here," Sandy said as she came out of the kitchen. "I told you so," she reminded Alex.

Hallet began in Arabic and greeted the woman first.

"I am well, Hallet. Or so I was," Sandy answered in her pure, university-polished English before praising God in Islamic custom. *"Il'hamdu lillaah."*

"W'inta, Hallet?" Alex asked. And you?

"I am deeply troubled," Hallet said. He nodded his head in Sandy's direction, and Alex knew at once.

"Bring Hallet coffee," he ordered as he took Hallet's arm and led him to a table. *"Mazbhut,* right, Hallet? Not too sweet."

"Shukran," Hallet thanked Sandy in advance.

"Come sit," Alex insisted as he ran his hands nervously through his curly black hair and then along the thighs of his stone-washed jeans. His eyes tried to light up in welcome, but Hallet only saw in them the residual hint of flame that, in a different life, had caused so many to fear him. "And we speak English, okay? We are good Americans, Sandy and me."

Hallet understood. His friend was no longer Ahmed, a contract agent from the old days in Baghdad. He was now Alex, just as Mahmoud Dahran was Mike Doran. Except Alex was alive.

"It's about the bombing."

"It's about who killed Mike Doran and why," said Hallet.

"I don't know," Alex shook his head. "There was no reason. Nothing."

"You saw him a lot."

"Mike? I see almost every day. Three, four times a week, easy."

"And he seemed fine, not worried. No indication he was in trouble."

"Nothing like that," Alex said.

Sandy came by with a cup of thick coffee and a plate of the small honey and sesame cakes she knew Hallet fancied. Alex asked her for a cold Pepsi-Cola with lemon. Hallet saw the look of resignation in the woman's sad, dark eyes: Alex was becoming Ahmed again in a show of Muslim macho for Hallet's benefit, and Sandy, in her grace, was for the moment letting it ride.

"Mike was into a lot of things, you know," Alex volunteered as he sipped his drink. "He had business things going on all the time. Some very good. But you must know there were others. He dealt on many levels, with many kinds of people."

"And you dealt with him," Hallet said.

Alex responded with a look of pain. "What are you saying?"

"I'm wondering if our friend Mike was dealing drugs?"

"No, never!" Alex yelped, hurt by the aspersion on his dead friend's character. "Not for a million dollars."

"I know the rules, Alex. To an Iraqi merchant, everything is for sale."

"Not honor, Hallet. You must know that also."

"All right," Hallet conceded, satisfied that even if Mahmoud Dahran had gotten into the business, Alex knew nothing about it. "But we both know that Mike was doing dangerous things. Weapons, for instance. I know *that* was a part of his import-export operation. And there must have been other deals which, if they went sour, would have provoked reprisals."

"Could be that," Alex admitted. "I have thought it through many times. But I myself know of nothing that would cause him to be killed. Not that kind of stuff."

"Then it could be political," Hallet suggested.

"What politics?" Alex asked back. "Mike Doran moved merchandise, not ideas. He sold, he bought."

"He also listened, and he sold what he heard."

"But there has been nothing. All quiet, Hallet."

"That's not what I've been hearing. In fact, I sent Mike a signal last week. There have been rumors that commandos have been dispatched here. On a mission. Mike didn't reject it out

184

of hand, as he usually does with nonsense. He said he had some checks to make. Maybe those . . ."

Hallet sipped the coffee now that the fine grinds had settled to the bottom. It was as Sandy said. *Mazbhut.*

"Maybe those inquiries . . ." he continued after Alex had time to mull it over.

"Ah, Hallet," Alex protested, though he was already slipping back into Ahmed and pronouncing Hallet's name with the hard Semitic "ch" that sounded much like the Hebrew "*chaim.*"

"Hallet, we hear these things all the time. Everyone who has a cousin back home hears from him that a group of Revolutionary Guards or Hezbollah commandos are heading for the Great Satan of America. This is all true nonsense."

"I had a confirmation out of Canada," Hallet said, not naming the Libyan physician who ran his Toronto network. "And they're often one step closer than my friends here."

"No way," Alex insisted. "Sure thing, we get lots of people coming across from Ontario. But you think the Hezbollah are going to drive through the Windsor Tunnel with a trunkful of plastique and RPGs? We got many more miles together with Canada, and there are other, more easy ways to cross over than here."

"Only no one expects to see Arabs crossing a wheatfield in North Dakota. Here, it's no big thing."

"I'm telling you, we've heard nothing of this kind. And if Mike knew something, I would know, too. And so would you. Immediately."

"Nothing about a group called Al-Ahzab?" asked Hallet. He hated even naming it as he studied Alex's dark eyes carefully for a shade of recognition.

"What, the united front! It's a dream, Hallet. Never could it happen."

"Rumors become realities," Hallet insisted.

"I don't know," he thought aloud. "No, I don't think so."

"Look, if Mike was killed because of some bad business here, that's one thing. But I can't afford to believe that without proof.

For one reason, whoever did the job was well trained in demolitions. And the explosives used on Mike's car were not made here, Alex. They were Russian or Czech, or perhaps Cuban-made from the same recipes. I want to know about that as much as I want to find the man who pushed the detonator."

"I understand. I appreciate this. But I have nothing to give you. I've asked around, sure. But all anyone says to me is that Mike got himself involved with some of the tough people in Detroit, and that they had to settle a score. You know he was like that, always having the tough guys to his club, playing like he was some Italian gangster. Now, you want to look there, go ahead. But I cannot help you. I am finished with those things."

"Too bad," Hallet said. "I was hoping you'd pick up for Mike with me."

"Hallet, we are Americans now. We love America. And we love our people at home. We want no wars between us. You know that."

"I'm guessing that whoever killed Mike is also an American," Hallet said. "Someone who knows about us."

"Look, I'm out of all that. As you should be, too."

"You still worked for Mike. Don't bother telling me a different story. Too many years and too many cover stories, Alex. I know the truth."

"I'm telling you truth. No longer do I get involved. I run a restaurant. Only thing I do on the side is take a few bets on the horses. About your business I know nothing."

"You knew of the plan. The first one."

"I don't even remember," Alex said. "Such plans are dreams."

"It's always a dream to see justice victorious."

Alex dropped his head as he swished the lemon in his glass. "I've done all my killing, Hallet. I can't help you anymore. I love my people, sure, but I can no longer love a cause."

Hallet knew he had to change tack, for Alex as Ahmed had indeed done his share. "I'm still going to look around and talk to some other people," he said. "People Mike told me were as loyal as you. I guess I can do that alone."

"And for me, I keep an open ear. I don't ask too much, but I listen. Anything that comes to me goes to you."

"Good enough," said Hallet. He looked down at Sandy's cakes and wished he could be a good guest and not insult her by leaving them. "Tell Chafik I'm sorry."

"What, you don't like these? Maybe it's too soon, then. You need something first. Sandy," Alex called out. "You bring Hallet some *fuul*. Terrific, Hallet. You try it." Alex's face grew immediately older as he added in a whisper, "Then maybe we go talk to people together. About Mike."

"You're seen with me, our friends will put you back in it whether you wish it or not."

"I know, Hallet. But we've had long times together. And Mike, I loved him like my brother. So, some people I know who worked with him in the old group, maybe they can help you. I'll take you, but one condition first."

"How much?"

"Goddamn, Hallet. Nothing like that. Only if something should happen, if the people who killed Mike . . ." Alex made a surreptitious nod toward the kitchen.

"Nothing will happen," Hallet reassured him. "But if it did, Sandy would be fine."

"No, not that, Hallet. But we find out who did that to Mike, you let me cut the bastard's throat."

Lieutenant Jack Corrigan picked at the plate of cold roast chicken that Margie had set out for him. No matter how dry it looked, it had to be better than the rubber croissant they'd tried to deal him on the Continental flight out of Terre Haute. He ripped three long strips of meat from a breast, slapped them between a kaiser roll, slathered the bread with mayonnaise and droplets of Tabasco, wished there were some cranberry sauce in the house to make the sandwich right.

He also wished he knew whether the bill of goods Johnny

Roses had tried to sell him from across the visitor's table at the Federal Correctional Facility in Terre Haute was worth moving on.

Johnny's trade bait was simple: He'd give Corrigan the name of a major contract buttonman and enough righteous testimony to nail him for taking out that fat outfit weasel Chuckie Franco. And, if the Feds didn't trip over themselves with enthusiasm, they should be able to nail the same bastard for more. What was in it for Johnny Roses was that the Franco hit had been contracted by one Sid Paris, who was at present singing his lungs out to Justice at Maxwell Air Force Base as part of the witness protection program. The new murder rap that they could add to Sid's long list of sins, Johnny Roses figured, would blow off Sid's testimony against him for being the family's key money connection with Vegas and for purchasing a trio of Chicago aldermen to let the dice roll with the good times in certain downtown and South Side precincts. It would, Johnny had told Jack Corrigan, go down as a push.

"Yeah, I get no more indictments with my name on them, and I get outta this godforsaken place," Johnny Roses had said as they sipped coffee in a rank-smelling visitation room. No special privileges or treatment. Jack Corrigan was not there as a detective lieutenant of the Chicago police, but simply another civilian visiting an old pal. That was always the deal. Word gets out fast in the cellblock when a cop comes calling. And when it got back to the Chicago family, as it surely would, Johnny Roses would have more to worry about than dropped soap in the showers.

"Hey, look." Corrigan shrugged. "I didn't fly the dawn patrol down here to hear about the goon who greased Chuckie Franco, who nobody mourned in the first place."

"C'mon, Lieutenant. You guys ain't been able to nail a professional contractor in twenty years."

"That's 'cause the family gets there first," Corrigan said. "So get back to business. On the phone, you mentioned that big noise in Jamaica."

Johnny Roses dropped his voice into a weak whisper. "I can't give you that directly, see, because I'm in this fuckin' rat's nest. That's *family* business and, like I told you, you never get me to go against the old man and my people. But I'm telling you, the guy who did Franco and the guy made the hit in Jamaica—well, like I never seen both in the same place, the same time."

"Johnny, all your worrying about the old man is what got you here in the first place," Corrigan said, giving it one last shot. "If you'd cooperated with me and Thorne, you wouldn't be here at all."

"No, I'd be with the stiffs I'm telling you about, all wrapped up in some car trunk like fresh-slit venison," Johnny said. "So take a good deal when you get it. I can give you this creep for the Franco deal. You and the Feds will find a way to pin the other thing on him. It's there. You won't have to look too hard."

"Okay, okay," Corrigan conceded, "I get the Chicago hits laid out for me, the Feds get the Jamaica blast. I'll have to fight it out with them for first place, but since I'm bringing them the deal, that'll probably work out."

"That's your problem, Lieutenant. Me, I want nothing Sid Paris tries peddling about me to stick. And I want to do the rest of my stretch in some place like Oxford. Minimum security, closer to home, no freaks around. You wouldn't believe the *criminals* in this joint."

"Give me what you promise, and you'll move."

"This guy I'm talking about," Johnny Roses began as he scanned the empty room one last time. "His real name's Bobby Usery. But the family, they call him Usher. That's because he leads people into the dark. Like forever, man. You find Usher, you got the guy who did both numbers."

"How do I find him, Johnny?" Corrigan asked. "I doubt he's got a listed phone number."

"That's your problem, Lieutenant."

"Does he have a record?"

"Never once been busted. Which is one reason the family keeps him on retainer."

"Give me something else, pal. You want too much for too little here."

"Usher moves around a lot, and he's got more names and more papers than you'd believe. But he's a real careful dude, maybe too much so. See, he never gets paid in cash, just has his money credited to a downtown bank. Now, I know that bank and, you know me with numbers. I give you what I think's close to the account number. That's the best I can do, unless I could get outta here for a while, maybe spot him for you when he comes in for cash."

"We're not filming *Forty-eight Hours,* and you're not Eddie Murphy getting a break from jail," Corrigan sneered. "You're staying right here until I get this checked out."

"You got all the chips," Johnny conceded as he handed Corrigan a scrap of yellow paper. "Here's the bank, and here's what I think's all or part of the account number. You find Usher and then, damn it, you keep your deal with me."

Corrigan pushed away from the table and threw Johnny Roses a nod of acceptance. "I'll be in touch," he said. "You take care of yourself."

"Listen, Lieutenant, when it comes to Usher, you're the one'd better take care. This boy ain't goin' down easy. He's a complete psycho, believe me."

"How does he feel about Arabs and Iranians?"

"What the hell you talking about? Arabs?"

"Nothing, Johnny. Nothing at all."

"Just be careful. You get in Usher's cross hairs, you go down, and I'm shit out of luck."

Corrigan had heard him all right, and the bargain still sounded good. But he'd learned long ago, everything sounds better inside a jail, when the cops want to get out as much as the cons.

So now, back in his warm, cozy kitchen, with the salutary effects of Margie's roast chicken and a cold can of Old Style, Corrigan was wondering just how good his bargain with Johnny Roses would actually be.

He realized between bites that the telephone was ringing.

Since Margie and the kids were out at a movie, he walked to it lazily, figuring it was the night watch people giving him an advisory on the volunteer drivers, or maybe Johnny Roses, who never seemed to want for communications access even inside a federal pen. The sound of a female voice surprised him.

"Lieutenant, this is McCaskey."

"So you do return phone calls, even after hours."

"I've had a lot going on," she apologized. "Then I heard you were out of town today."

"Visiting an old friend," Corrigan said. He wouldn't give the FBI anything more for now, and not until they finally showed him some initiative on the taxi shooter. "You have something for me?"

"Thanks to Doc Hermann's clearances and a lot of late hours, we've run every possible make on the slain drivers. None of them are tied to anything political, no known associations with any person or group that we have. In short, zip, zero."

"That's how Thorne would have put it."

"I think that's a compliment, Jack. He was a good teacher."

Corrigan regretted bringing up the past. He'd liked McCaskey from the beginning and was perplexed by the lingering suspicions he'd started harboring about her.

"What you're telling me is, as far as the Bureau can tell, we've got some nut case out there who's taking out his hostilities on innocent Arabs."

"I'm afraid that's how it plays."

"Only I have a problem believing it."

"Sorry, Jack, but I've done what I can. Maybe another time. Okay?"

"Sure thing, kiddo," Corrigan said, angered by what seemed to him a very casual kiss-off. So much for their two-way street. So much for any chance he'd bring McCaskey in on the Johnny Roses deal. He'd take the killing of the union guy to the goddamn National Labor Relations Board before he'd share it with the FBI.

He hung up the phone and went back to his now soggy

chicken sandwich, which he dumped in the trash and replaced with a stiff shot of Crown Royal as an accompaniment to his beer.

By the time Margie and the kids returned home, he was fast asleep on the sofa, dreaming about playing golf with Johnny Roses in a foursome with Sid Paris and the professional hit man that the outfit called Usher.

Ben punched the digits into the automatic gate guard and swung his Mercedes up the long drive, past the glorious flower beds, shrubs, and bushes that the old man had loved to tend in earlier, healthier times.

Vinnie, the old man's bodyguard, driver, nurse, and general gillie, opened the front door. "He's in the kitchen. Cooking."

"Cooking?" Ben asked in surprise. "What can he eat?"

Vinnie shrugged his shoulders, as if acknowledging that the old man was losing it, that the end was near.

"Don't count him out yet," Ben advised him.

"Me? Never."

Ben walked past the living room and the library, until the smells of olive oil, peppers, and fennel seeped out of the kitchen. He found the old man's short, desiccated frame hovering over the large stove; in the pan he tended, a ring of browning sausage surrounded a mound of sweet red peppers. It looked like a target with a bloodshot bull's eye at the cork.

The old man noticed Ben at last and turned away from the skillet. "I can't eat any of this," he said. "But I still can smell it. Even after those."

Ben watched the old man point to the atomizer that was with him everywhere and the portable oxygen system that had become a fixture in each and every room of his home.

"It looks delicious," Ben said, brushing a respectful kiss on the old man's cheek.

"It's the best." The old man tore a chunk of bread from a

round Sicilian loaf, dropped a short length of sausage on it, and covered both with the peppers. "Here, enjoy this for me. And for you, too. What good's your thin body if you have no soul?"

Ben took the open sandwich, lifted it to his lips. "Too hot," he said, blowing over the revoltingly greasy mixture. "I'll let it sit a while."

The old man leaned back over the skillet, took a deep inhale, and began to cough a wet, croupy, painful hack. Ben handed him the atomizer as the old man almost collapsed onto a kitchen chair.

"You're not well," said Ben. "I'll come back another time."

"Sit down," the old man wheezed. "Take off your jacket, the tie. You're with family now."

Ben did as instructed, removed the finely tailored suit coat and the raw silk foulard tie. After the old man pointed longingly to the wine carafe on the table, Ben poured him a modest glass.

"That's better," the old man said, the wine apparently helping clear the dried phlegm from his throat. "We have to talk now."

Ben started to protest, but knew better. The body may be failing, but the head of the family was still the head and, despite the years, Ben knew better than to question the old man's alertness, memory, or resolve.

"What is it we have to speak about?" asked Ben.

"I want to know about Usher. I want to know what he's doing for us. Or, what he's doing for you."

"He did what we asked of him," Ben replied. "What you promised our friend."

"No more than that?"

Ben was certain the old man couldn't know it all, but he wasn't fool enough to duck the question entirely. "I know he's been in touch with our friend's number-one man. The Englishman. Harry."

"In touch with is one thing. Working for is another."

"Whatever Usher's doing," Ben tried explaining, "it doesn't concern us."

The old man pulled himself up in his chair, his clear lucid

eyes looking twenty years younger than the rest of his sagging face. "*Everything* concerns us, Ben. You above all know that. In this town, this country. It concerns us."

"I don't understand what you're driving at."

"Our friends in Detroit are very upset, Ben. They lost a close associate there. Guy we even met once. You remember Mike Doran. They called him Mike the Arab."

"Yes sir. A little."

"Somebody took Mike out this week. Blew up his car with him in it. Our friends liked Mike the Arab. And no one got their blessing to do such a thing. They're upset."

"Jesus," Ben swore.

"Watch it!" the old man admonished him. "You don't take His name in my house."

Ben apologized sincerely, honoring the dying man's dread of blasphemy. "I can understand why they'd be upset," he said. "But not at us."

"Unless we had a hand in it. The word there has it the contract came out of Chicago. That's why I want to know about Usher. If it was him, we have a problem, and a debt to repay."

"I haven't heard a thing," Ben insisted.

"You get paid to hear," the old man barked. "So before I lose patience, you better tell me exactly what Usher is doing for our rich Lake Forest friends."

"I just set him up with Harry," Ben said. "Harry wouldn't say what was going on. I didn't want to push him. Out of respect for your friendship."

"I don't know Harry or care about him. You get him to say what he's doing, and get him to say it straight."

"He won't talk without his boss's approval. Which means, if you want to get answers, we'll have to go higher up. Right to the top."

The old man thought it over for a quick minute. "We've done him many favors," he concluded. "We took care of his problems with that union mess, we've helped his balance sheet look neat and clean. I have a right to know."

"Of course you do," Ben said. "But you'll have to arrange it." '

The old man cleared his throat with a small sip of wine and motioned Ben to hand him the telephone. Ben sat quietly, trying to appear relaxed, in control, as the old man unsteadily punched a number into the telephone.

"Yes, hello. I want to speak with Jason Kellaigh."

Chapter 14

Hallet watched from his office window as daylight eroded and street lamps grew powerful enough to control the sky. The trip to Michigan had been more frenetic and exhausting than he'd anticipated; too bad it had yielded nothing more than speculations, rumors, and shoddy logic. If Mike Doran had known of any imminent danger, if he'd uncovered anything important concerning either Al-Ahzab or Sandman, he'd shared it with no one. All the sources that Hallet visited with Alex—Mike's friends, associates, and probably enemies—were dry; no one had any information to dispel Alex's conclusion that Mike Doran, who was known to cut a hard deck, had perhaps done so to the big boys he played with in Detroit, for which he was punished summarily. Hallet didn't buy that one, but neither could he come up with a scenario that played any better.

Which meant that, like it or not, Yousef was all he had working that could tie the loose ends together. But despite messages out to him through every possible channel, some of them risky, Hallet heard nothing in return.

Then there was the well-intentioned MaryAgnes McCaskey, about whom Hallet found himself thinking continually during the fruitless hours he'd spent waiting for responses to the red signal he'd sent the Prophets. She was a pretty fair cop and had a fine mind, but from all Hallet had learned over the years about its Middle East intelligence capabilities, the FBI was about as effectual in locating an assassin as the INS was in identifying the quarter million illegals working Chicago's fine restaurant kitchens.

He locked his office and was midway up the mansion's wide, elaborate mahogany staircase when he noticed light coming from the slit beneath Bryce Vreeland's door. There were voices, too; one of them belonged to Isabel Ortega.

"That's everything," she said.

"For now," Vreeland agreed.

"Quite a package. All of it irrefutable."

"I'd better secure it until the meeting."

Hallet heard Vreeland spinning the combination lock on his safe, which obviated any need for him to make a later visit.

"You do that, and I'll get the car," Isabel volunteered.

"Yes, dinner. I'd completely forgotten."

"I didn't. We'll stay home tonight. I have some lamb chops soaking in a wonderful mint and ginger marinade."

"Sounds grand."

As Isabel Ortega came through the door, she looked back into Vreeland's office and blew a kiss to him over her long fingers. Vreeland seemed to miss it as he went on gathering a sheaf of papers and tapping them into a neat stack.

"Philip!" Isabel said as she turned to face Hallet. Vreeland looked as if he'd been caught pilfering; his small face contorted from surprise to sneer. Isabel quickly closed the door.

"Looks like you aren't lacking for crash projects and over-time," Hallet said.

"Just an activities update for Mister Kellaigh. He wants them monthly now, though I doubt he ever reads them."

Hallet wasn't about to let Isabel suspect he'd been eaves-dropping. "If you're finished, let me buy dinner. I owe you more than one."

"You don't owe me anything, Philip," Isabel said. "As we say in Spanish, *estamos a mano*. We're even."

"Our friend inside there, is it?"

"Bryce and I *are* friends, if that's what you mean. Good ones."

"Congratulations."

"Don't be spiteful, Philip. And please don't pretend you're interested in whom I see."

"I wouldn't, if it were someone else."

Isabel Ortega's eyes hardened like bits of polished malachite. "Don't you dare criticize me. Especially when it comes to Bryce Vreeland, who's done more to keep this Institute operating than you could begin to comprehend."

"He's a saint," said Hallet. "You know I've always believed that."

"Stop it!" Isabel barked.

"Sorry. I shouldn't be caustic, not if he's what you want."

"I'm not getting married, Philip. Funny how you see everything so black and white."

"It was the only way to survive in the desert."

"Except you're home now. Even if you refuse to admit it."

Isabel reopened the door to Vreeland's office. "I've forgotten something," she said. "Please excuse me."

"What was that about?" Hallet heard Vreeland ask her. Isabel's response summed it up perfectly.

"Nothing worth repeating," she said. "Nothing at all."

Hallet decided to head back to his office and call Stan Bach.

"Is he around, Ruth?" he asked Stan's wife, a tall, slim, athletic-looking sabra whom Bach had met during his tenure at Hebrew University in Jerusalem. Hallet knew that Ruth had never really liked or trusted him, despite all her politeness and the tender looks she emitted while serving up what had to be among the best meals Hallet ever had eaten. Hallet sensed this was not because of his positions on Arab causes, which many thought too sympathetic; for unlike Stan, who took a political hard-line couched in religious history and the direct intercession of God, Ruth had true compassion for the people of Egypt and

Palestine, if not for their leaders. Still, when it came to being around Hallet, she seemed always on edge, tenuous.

"Not now, Philip." said Ruth. "He's gone out."

"I need to speak with him."

"In an hour maybe. He went to the bookstore."

With Stan Bach, Hallet realized an hour was far too soon; Stan attacked bookshops in the type of calculated, precise sweeps that geologists reserve for oil exploration.

"Which one, Ruthie? Did he say which one?"

"You know him. It could be any of them around here, maybe the Hebrew store on Devon. Or in Evanston. Who knows?"

"Okay," Hallet conceded. "But when he returns . . ."

"Are you all right, Philip?" Ruth asked. "Any trouble?"

"I'm fine. I just want to talk with Stan."

"If you need to talk, Philip, come here, please. We can talk together, and when Stan returns, I'll fix a late snack. Okay? You come here."

"This isn't an outreach call," Hallet said. "I'm not staring into a glass of gin, wondering if I should drink it."

"That's not what I meant," Ruth said. "Come over, we'll have tea and sweets."

Hallet always figured Stan Bach for a lucky man, had always envied him Ruth a little, the kind of woman who would serve her husband's friend even if she wasn't all that fond of him. Still, he begged off.

"When he comes back," Hallet said, "tell him to call me."

"It may be later, more than an hour," Ruth said.

"No problem. I'll be home."

"Things are all right, then, Philip?"

"Of course," Hallet replied, until he realized. "Something is troubling you, isn't it?"

"I thought all these times you were together, all these nights. I thought he was helping you."

"Ruthie, don't tell me you're the jealous type. I won't believe it."

"No, not that," she answered with a slight chuckle. "But I

think there is something else. I thought you might know what it was."

"Come on, Ruth. You know how Stan behaves when he's working on something important. He needs his solace. The bookstores, long walks. He's probably off floating blindfolded somewhere in one of those warm tanks, or steaming in the Russian baths you despise so much."

"Terrible, dirty places. *Terefah*," she said, as always choosing Hebrew over Yiddish. "Who wants to see him come home with the herpes?"

"I'll come visit another time, Ruth. *Shalom*."

"*Ma'ha salaama*," she answered back, in the Egyptian Arabic she'd been forced to grow up speaking.

Hallet saw the familiar black automobile parked outside the Institute, Agent MaryAgnes McCaskey behind the wheel, beckoning to him. He climbed inside; even in the suppressing shadows, McCaskey's face looked warm and her eyes glimmered.

"Had a pleasant journey, I trust."

Hallet wasn't surprised by her admission. "So you had me followed."

"Not followed," McCaskey said. "Let's just call it keeping in touch, for your protection."

"And your information."

"Doctor Hallet, however simply you and Macdonald Clelland like to define your operation here, two people involved with it have been summarily eliminated. Hasn't it crossed your mind that you might also be in danger?"

"Not at all, because I can't find anything to link the killings to the Institute. So if they're linked at all, as you suspect they are, it has nothing to do with the work they did for us. Some other matter, perhaps, but nothing that involves me."

"You verified that on your visit to Detroit?"

That told Hallet what he wanted to know: She'd had him

watched only as far as the airport, until he boarded the plane. Otherwise she would have said Dearborn. She was good at it, but not that good. Not yet.

"I simply went to pay my respects to Mike Doran's family," Hallet said. "And to visit an old friend. But I suppose you know that already."

"You weren't being watched in Detroit," McCaskey said. "You don't think I'd jeopardize whatever you're doing by ringing up the Detroit office and having them send a couple of trainees to follow you? We're supposed to be partners, remember? Like it or not."

"Hobson's choice," said Hallet.

"Exactly."

"I think I could get to like it after all."

"I was hoping to hear that," McCaskey said, her smile first keeping pace with Hallet's, then outdistancing it magnificently. "I thought you might like a late supper. How about it?"

"In light of recent events, a very good idea."

"You sound like a man who's been stood up."

"Not really," said Hallet. "She found herself another fellow. Literally."

"You don't seem to mind too much."

"Nothing but good wishes."

"Very courtly of you," McCaskey teased him. "Supper with me, then?"

"What I'd really like is a drink," Hallet said.

"Empty calories, but calories nonetheless." McCaskey hit the ignition and got the Buick's reluctant engine to turn over. "You name the place."

"You know Fairweather's, on Rush Street?"

"Only too well," McCaskey shivered. "But I can't see it as your kind of place."

"That's why I go. And you?"

"I spent a lot of time there. Once."

"Business or pleasure?" asked Hallet.

"Business. Mostly," she replied. "It was an undercover job.

My partner and I infiltrated a syndicate gambling operation, and Fairweather's was one of the places we did it in."

"Sonny Greco." Hallet knew. "I met him. Nice guy."

"Too good for the profession."

"What's he doing now?"

"Running a restaurant in Arizona, last I heard. Phoenix, I think. Scottsdale, maybe."

"And your partner?"

"He quit the Bureau soon afterward."

Hallet guessed that in the process he'd quit McCaskey too, but decided it wasn't time for a question that direct. "We'll skip Fairweather's," he said.

"Let's do. I could use a change of luck."

"Why not come up to my place? Neutral ground, sort of."

McCaskey turned her eyes from the road and threw Hallet a long look. "Your place is neutral?"

"More so than when you came by the first time," Hallet said. "Besides, I saw you admiring some of my prayer rugs, even if you were being too officious to mention it."

McCaskey's glare melted back into a smile. "So you noticed after all. Quite beautiful."

"The one you were looking at most, on the side wall, is Iranian. A marvel of color and intricacy of design, woven so tightly by strong and faithful hands that it's almost impossible to unravel. I bought it in Qum, Iran's holiest city," Hallet said, not volunteering any details about the anti-Shah revolutionary who'd exchanged the rug for a forged Lebanese passport and Hallet's promise to occupy the Savak agents chasing him until he'd time to escape.

"I accept your invitation, Doctor Hallet."

"Once again, let's make it Philip."

"Fine, I think it's about time I got to know more about the scholar in you."

"But a scholar is all I really am," Hallet said.

"Which means exactly what?"

"We decide what's important and what isn't," Hallet said.

"What books are to be kept in libraries, what art is worthy of being saved for posterity, what's to be studied and hopefully understood in the light of history."

"You decide what survives," she added.

"Yes, in a way. I suppose we do."

"A frightful responsibility," McCaskey said, "since the people for whom you're preserving culture have so little say in the process."

"Popular culture survives of its own accord, for as long as the people who consume it want it. We till the rockier soil, to make certain that something wonderful survives even if it isn't popular. We assay and evaluate, and hope to make our appreciation self-generating."

McCaskey's expression hardened again as she turned her face toward Hallet's.

"Still, if what I'm thinking about your other activities is accurate," she said, "deciding what survives may soon become a matter of who."

Usher walked to the edge of the roof and surveyed the street from four stories up. The light was good, the two-foot parapet would provide ample cover, and the tiles atop it were smooth and stable aiming points. He had nothing to do but wait.

Harry had said that waiting would be the hardest part of an easy job, as if he knew anything about it. They had been on the tourist cruiser that departs from the foot of the Wrigley Building for a two-hour spin along the Chicago River and out through its locks into Lake Michigan.

"I'll need a telephone number to give you the go," the big Englishman said. "It will be in Chicago somewhere, but we won't know exactly where until he makes contact. After he surfaces, I'll give you a location, and you'll have to sweat it out."

"I don't sweat these things," Usher replied. "And I don't like working so close to home. This is Ben's territory, pal, not to mention the family's."

"We all have their approval," Harry said. "And we'll keep it if everything falls the way it should."

Usher kept quiet as the tour guide pointed out the architectural landmarks that dot the riverbank. The whole idea of the boat was stupid, and Usher had been chiding himself for agreeing to it. The first rule for any meet was that you had an exit route planned in advance, which was why he liked the zoo and conservatory in Lincoln Park. But being on a damned boat, despite Harry's claims that the engine would override any long-distance microphone, was like being caged.

"I'm still not sold," Usher said. "You're choosing the time, the place, the method. And you want my telephone number to boot. It's not the way I work, and it's sure not the way for me to keep on working after it's done."

"Oh, dear." Harry sighed. "I'd so hoped you wouldn't be difficult."

"Look, pal," Usher shot back, "you're somebody's errand boy. We both know it, so cut out the aristo crap. You want to call all the shots, and you want me to shit where I sleep. Tell me who's being difficult."

The Englishman reached into the breast pocket of his navy suit and retrieved a white business envelope. He opened it and showed Usher the deposit slip. "This amount has already been credited to your La Salle Street bank. It's yours in any event. But you complete this task, and it will be doubled."

And that was it, why Usher now found himself lying prone on the flat, black-tar rooftop waiting for the visitor and a clear silhouette in the lamplit night.

After slipping on surgeon's gloves, Usher pulled the black Heckler & Koch 93 A3 rifle from an olive-drab duffel bag, set the length of its retractable stock to fit his grip, loaded a magazine of .223 Remington cartridges. The only decision he had to make concerned the silencer. It was a half-assed East German model that did okay with sound, but threw a great white muzzle flash in the process. Usher could use it and risk someone spotting his exact location, or he could use the H & K's own flash suppressor and make a noise that would reverberate so loud and long in the street that no one could pinpoint its origin.

Since he wouldn't be hanging around anyway, Usher opted for the silencer. Nothing left but to wait, and to contemplate another bout with Sharon, who'd let her roommate sulk back home while she came to visit. She liked it rough, old Sharon, liked to get tied up with her own panty hose; liked it, too, when Usher penetrated her with the long pearl necklace she'd worn to bed. And her steady moist touch brought him satisfaction in the only way he could enjoy, even if she seemed surprised at his preferences and his disdain for the soft, sucking kisses that all the men she'd ever known craved from her.

He shook away the memories and surveyed the street, wondering if the tall, dark-haired broad was going to spend the night and, because of that, his target wouldn't show. More good luck: Within minutes, he saw her standing in the doorway, giving the guy a good-night kiss that, even from his distance, Usher could tell was shy and coltish. He used her perfect head of raven hair to sight in the H & K's one-inch Q.D. scope, then squeezed the trigger with a professional's smooth, relaxed tension.

The bolt fell softly and smoothly on an empty chamber. Good. Perfect, in fact. He slid the magazine into the weapon, drew back the bolt again, flipped the safety downward until the lever pointed straight at the red firing indicator. Soon, he told himself. If Harry was right at all, it would be soon.

Harry was right.

Philip Hallet heard the doorbell ring not five minutes after MaryAgnes McCaskey's departure, while he still sat looking at the empty martini glasses and the bits of cheeses and olives and pita that had been their supper, while the Guarneri String Quartet finished its magnificent Beethoven cycle on the stereo. If she were coming back, for any reason, on any pretense, Hallet knew that, this time, he would not be so cavalier when she said she'd have to leave. No, this time he would do it right and not camouflage the emotion he felt under his well-trained and carefully maintained facade of disdain.

He reached the doorway before the second set of chimes rang through, threw the switch that activated the outside post lights. But his sense of anticipation changed dramatically when he opened the door. Instead of MaryAgnes McCaskey's beaming smile, Yousef's was greeting him with an insolent smirk.

"*Salaam,* Hallet," Yousef said boldly. "I bring you some very big news."

Usher sighted in as the man at the doorway flapped his arms like some kind of denim-clad street mime. He was Mediterranean looking, dark-complected, probably another Arab. And he fit Harry's description perfectly. That was what mattered.

As the other man grabbed the Arab's shoulder, beckoning him into the house, Usher fired his first shot. It hit between the scapula and the neck, and the Arab lurched forward against the doorjamb. Probably a kill, but the second shot was off before Usher had time to contemplate it. Another hit, dead on the spinal column and tearing every bit of traumatic rigidity from the man's body. The white man threw himself over the Arab in some kind of suicidal shielding motion, and tried to crawl inside with enough strength for both of them. No need for that, Usher thought stoically. If you were meant to get hit, you'd be crossing the Styx already. As for the Arab, you're shielding a dead man.

Usher crept far enough back from the parapet so that he could stand without being seen from the street. He threw the H & K and the two spent shell casings back into the duffel, carried it down the exposed wooden stairs that led from the rear of the four-flat to the alley behind it. Though he hated doing it, he'd dump the rifle some miles away and watch the cops trip over themselves as they tried to figure out who could get their hands on an East German-made silencer, and why they'd want to.

He was ten feet above ground level when he heard the footsteps running toward him. He pitched the duffel bag into a Dumpster filled with garbage, pulled the Walther pistol from his belt. The footsteps came closer. Usher leaped the remaining distance to the tarmac and began to run in the opposite direction from them. The last thing he wanted was to fight a duel in some stinking alleyway, or to pop off at some cop with a parabellum automatic that wasn't silenced.

The man who ran toward him left Usher no choice. The first shot he fired sailed past Usher's right ear; the second ripped through his triceps with enough velocity to send him sprawling forward onto his knees.

The man kept coming. Usher had to act. He got his left leg out in front of him, spun around to face his attacker in a perfect firing position. He was shaking enough to miss his first shot, and the blow-back recoil from the Walther took his second low left. But it hit somewhere, because the man also went down and the gun he carried skidded out of his hand and into the darkness. The desire to finish the bastard then and there was strong, but with lights going on and doorways opening all around, Usher's need to beat a fast exit overrode it. He jumped a waist-high chain-link fence, sped down a darkened gangway between two brick houses, and disappeared seconds before the man he'd dropped in the alley stood up and recovered his weapon.

Someone who refused to identify himself had called the police after the second volley of gunshots echoed up and down the alley. That was it. Just a report of shots fired. A few lights on, then off, and silence. No one had seen or heard anything more.

Four uniformed officers arrived at Hallet's gate almost concurrently, two in each of the patrol cars coming from opposite ends of the street with lights flashing but sirens silent, as if doubting the report that gunfire had shattered the night silence of a peaceful side street. A pair of the uniforms stationed themselves by the entrance to Hallet's front yard, two more approached him in a lumbering quick-step when they saw the fallen body. The larger one wore blue-and-white sergeant's stripes; he leaned over the body as his partner got a quick summary from a shaking Philip Hallet of what had happened.

"Shit," the sergeant swore. "He sure as hell won't need a doctor, unless they can reattach the back of his head."

"I suppose you know the guy," his partner said.

Hallet was numb, bordering on shock. Sure, he had seen death before, and once to save his own life he'd had to kill with a knife. But the carnage the bullets had inflected on Yousef shook him to his soul.

"You know him or not?"

"I knew him from the university," Hallet said. "He was a mathematics instructor working on his doctorate. I was an adviser to the association he belonged to, a foreign students' league."

"So you were just standing there, talking in the doorway?" the officer asked.

The one bending over the body rolled it over. "This guy's an Arab?" he half asked, half decided.

"Yes, his name is Yousef Fakna," Hallet said. "He's from Libya."

The two cops turned their eyes on each other.

"Oh, Christ," the sergeant moaned, "we got another Arab down. Looks like old Son of Shah has given up riding taxicabs."

"I'd better call that lieutenant downtown," his partner said. "What's his name?"

"Corrigan. Least I think so. It's on the duty sheet."

"I'll radio in."

The sergeant stood and hiked his pistol belt underneath his ample belly. "You're okay, then?" he asked Hallet.

Hallet shrugged automatically. "I guess so."

"Why don't you wait inside while my partner calls this in. No reason you gotta stand over this guy."

Hallet looked down at Yousef's shattered body. "I have to make a call myself," he said. "I can do that, can't I?"

"Why? You wanna call a lawyer?"

"No," said Hallet. "I have to call the FBI."

Chapter 15

To the untrained eye, it looked like a model of cooperative law enforcement. The local police snapped pictures, drew chalk lines, got Yousef's body bagged and removed quickly. The two black-suited FBI agents kept to the sidelines, never crossed jurisdictional lines and, in fact, seemed to wonder why they were present at all; they helped the locals when asked, made some notes, finally removed their ominous black sedan from the cordon that had formed in front of Hallet's town house. Inside thirty minutes the prowl cars disappeared too; the street again appeared quiet, normal.

Except Hallet knew better. Another battle was about to be waged inside the house, a tag-team war of wits between him and McCaskey and the tough-looking detective named Jack Corrigan, who was clearly in charge of the police operation and who, Hallet knew the moment he laid eyes on him, could, in his quest for answers, only create new occasions for damage and death.

Hallet saw MaryAgnes McCaskey listening carefully to the two federal agents who stood in the vestibule, saw them nodding in his direction, but couldn't get close enough to overhear them before they shrugged at whatever response she made and departed. Hallet then watched McCaskey and Lieutenant Corrigan, who at first exchanged greetings like old friends, begin to circle each other like wrestlers in a ring.

"The removal's finished, everything out front is secured. So now we talk," Corrigan said brusquely. He took a long sniff at the clear liquid in the pitcher on Hallet's buffet, pulled his head back sharply from the strong gin fumes. "I'll run through everything we know so far. Then it's my turn to hear some answers."

"Whatever we can tell you," McCaskey said from her place next to Hallet on the sofa. "My word on it."

Corrigan gave her a nod, a scowl, both at once. "The shooter was on the rooftop of the four-flat across the street. Definitely a professional. His rifle was a silenced German beauty, a Heckler & Koch. We found it in an old Army duffel bag tossed into a trash bin in the alley, the spent shell casings along with it. Just two, but more than enough. Looks like he planned on taking the gun with him—else why pick up the brass only to toss the whole package at the foot of the stairs?"

"So Yousef was the only one he wanted," Hallet said.

"Be my best guess," Corrigan agreed. "If he wanted you down, he had the time, a full magazine, certainly the skill. Then again," he wondered aloud as he studied Hallet for a reaction.

Hallet froze his expression, said nothing.

"God, Philip," McCaskey said with a shiver. "I said all along you were in danger." There was no scolding, told-you-so tone in her voice; Hallet took her hand and held it softly, a gesture that caused Jack Corrigan to scowl another time.

"It looks like something or somebody interrupted his getaway," Corrigan went on. "Enough so that he had to fire some warning shots, probably from a handgun. We have reports ranging from one to six shots fired. Maybe a dog started chasing him or, more likely, we got what the beat cops call an FCH."

"Which is?" asked McCaskey.

"Yeah, you don't get them in the Bureau," Corrigan said.

212

"Stands for Fucking Civilian Hero. The kind of guy who chases muggers and burglars himself, never stops to call us. We bury a couple of them each year. If it was one, he's either real lucky or the shooter wouldn't bother wasting him without charging an extra fee."

The front door popped open, and a short, dark-haired man with a detective's star pinned on his lapel motioned to Corrigan.

"Give me a minute, will you? And if there's any coffee around . . . ?"

"You got it, Jack," McCaskey said.

Hallet followed her into the kitchen. "After Yousef went down, I counted four more shots," he said.

"You're certain?"

"Two from one handgun, then two from another. Different calibers, different reports. I thought it might be one of your people outside, still looking after me. But I didn't want to mention it to Corrigan until we could talk."

Pretty fair memory for someone who'd just seen a man killed on his doorstep, McCaskey thought. Knows his weapons, too. Which meant Hallet surely had training other than in linguistics.

"Whoever was out there wasn't ours," she said. "I wouldn't have an agent posted when I was with you. Besides, I promised you I'd call off our surveillance. Maybe if I hadn't, you wouldn't have lost a friend."

"Yousef was more than that."

"Why did he come here?"

"Reporting back to me."

"Telling you what?"

"That there was nothing to report," Hallet said. "That's the madness of it. Yousef came here grinning that everything was good news. Only he never had time to tell me exactly why."

"What was he looking for in the first place?" McCaskey asked.

Hallet knew he had no choice but to fill her in a little further, to take her up another plateau. "Can you get your friend

Corrigan to pull back on this, not turn it into the murder of the month?" he asked as the detective stepped back inside the house.

"He'd do it for my boss. Let's see if he's liberated enough to do it for me. Assuming I had good reasons."

"Tell Corrigan whatever you want, but get him to keep this as quiet as possible. Then, believe me," Hallet said, "I'm going to tell you a story. It's about the real work I do at the Institute, about deceit and betrayal. I'll tell you because I need your help, because you were right when you said we're in this mess together, like it or not."

McCaskey nodded her assent as Corrigan got within earshot.

"Looks like whoever did in your Libyan friend got himself involved in a major firefight out in that alley," Corrigan said. "The sweepers found four shell casings, two from a nine-millimeter automatic, two more from a thirty-two. Plus we got a pair of bloodstains that correspond with the location of the shells, which means both shooters were wounded. Not that much blood, so they probably got away on their own. Only one of them lost this."

Hallet and McCaskey looked at the plastic evidence bag Corrigan held out to them.

"My God," McCaskey said, wrinkling her nose. "What is it?"

"About a knuckle's worth of fingertip. Neither pinky nor thumb, I'd guess. But enough, we ever find a full set of prints for the guy who lost it, we'd probably get a match. Any chance you might know who he is?"

"No way, Jack," McCaskey said. "Call him an FCH, and let it go at that for the time being."

The redness deepened in Corrigan's cheeks and, for effect, Hallet guessed, he dropped the severed fingertip onto the glass coffee table.

"Lookit, kiddo, the last time I went and played ball with the Bureau, I just about took it in the ass. And that was only dealing with creeps who made book and dealt coke. Now we got somebody turning my city into a war zone, and you ask me to let it slide until *you're* ready to cooperate?"

"Jack, there's no reason you should even be involved here," McCaskey said. "This doesn't concern the Hostage and Terrorism unit."

"Look, anybody goes around shooting Arabs in this town," Corrigan fumed, "gets to square off with me. Like I said once, when I was dumb enough to think you'd help me out. Shoulda had my head examined for ever calling you."

"This has nothing to do with the crazy who's killing taxi drivers," McCaskey insisted. "That's the absolute truth."

"Probably," Corrigan agreed, knowing it didn't make a bit of sense anyway. "This one looks to me like a mob hit, a contract job. So now I wonder—what's the FBI, some college professor, and a dead Libyan have to do with the mob?"

"The fact that tonight's victim was an Arab is pure coincidence," McCaskey argued. "And whatever else you're wondering concerns a federal investigation that I'm simply not able to discuss. Nor is Doc Hermann, if you're thinking of going over my head."

"What about him?" Corrigan asked, tilting his head toward the silent Hallet. "You just happened to have the FBI over for dinner the same night that kid gets blown away on your doorstep."

"I went to see Doctor Hallet about the cabdriver killings, and we became friends," McCaskey interceded.

"That so, Doctor? Nothing more to it?"

Hallet guessed it was time for him to take a hand in soothing the irate detective and hoped McCaskey would pick up his moves and back him. "I'm far from an expert on murder," he said. "But I think I can clear up some of it for you. As much as I know, anyway. You see, Yousef—"

"Philip, I wouldn't," McCaskey interrupted.

"It's all right," Hallet lied. "It's over now."

"Go on," Corrigan said impatiently.

"Yousef was doing some legwork for me," Hallet said. "It

started when Agent McCaskey came to ask me about the murdered taxi drivers. She thought there might be some of kind of fight going on within our Arab community, something to make sense of the killings. I asked Yousef to check it out, especially with the street gangs he knew. Maybe, in the process, he stepped on some toes, made some enemies."

"That's obvious," Corrigan growled.

"But that's all there was. Yousef came here tonight to tell me that nothing of the kind was happening. No one knew anything about the taxi murders. So, for whatever reason Yousef was killed—gang business, drugs, whatever—it has nothing to do with us."

"Since when do professors help the FBI conduct murder investigations?" said Corrigan.

"Only when they're asked," Hallet replied. "And when they happen to be close with the Arabs in the city and can speak their language."

"That's the righteous truth," McCaskey said.

Corrigan shook his head with an incredulous smile. "Such bullshit. Like I was born yesterday."

"It must have been a gang thing," Hallet persisted. "That's why there was a second shooting out there. Yousef probably got himself caught between two factions, and it caught up with him."

Corrigan pushed his coffee away. "Let me tell both of you, this whole thing stinks to high heaven. Somehow, whether or not it's related to the taxi drivers, you're helping turn this town into a shooting gallery. Which makes me furious."

"That tends to come across, Jack," McCaskey said smugly.

Hallet gave her a slow-it-down look as another of Corrigan's detectives approached and said there were still two reporters hanging around for a statement.

"Jack, let's talk this over in private," McCaskey said as she followed Corrigan to the front door. "Just a street shooting . . ."

Hallet listened until she was out of range, watched as she took hold of Corrigan's arm and said something that seemed to soothe him immensely. Was she doing as Hallet had asked and buying them time, or was she selling him out and making herself a separate bargain with the police? The way it was looking, every person around was using betrayal as their means to an end. And that, Hallet knew, included Sandman.

Minutes later, while Corrigan was outside stalling the reporters, McCaskey came back to Hallet's side. "You can't stay here now," she said. "We'll put you up someplace where no one can find you."

"A safe house?"

"Exactly."

"Where's that?"

"Since we seem to have gotten into a fine mess by ending our evening so early, I was thinking of my place. For tonight, at least."

Hallet's first notion was to refuse, but even if McCaskey had only more questions in store, he was just sick and tired of being alone.

"Give me a minute to grab some things," he said, knowing that two of them would be his Sauer automatic and a fresh bottle of gin.

Usher knew that someday his luck had to run out. In all his years in the business of killing, he'd never once taken a direct hit from a bullet. Sure, in Nam, he caught a little shrapnel here and there, but never any heavier ordnance. Good thing, too. The VC guerrillas used dumdums that tore flesh like paper and hollow points that split into shards when they hit trees or rocks, so, if you caught a splinter in the eye or groin, a miss became as good as a hit. Hell, most of the gooks even dipped their rounds in human feces to make sure infection worsened their wounds. No Geneva Convention for those little monkeys; the slopes played to win, whatever the cost, a lesson for anyone who wasn't too cowardly to learn it.

Usher and the war went south about the same time. During his last liberty in the Philippines, he was mustered out of the service unceremoniously over some incident with a native boy whose name he never even caught. So he signed on as a gun for Ferdinand Marcos and ended up catching a ricochet from some barefoot NPA guerrilla while "advising" a National Guard unit in the stinking rain forests of Mindanao. Luckily, the round only had enough guts left to lodge in his thigh muscle like a burrowing leech; Usher dug it out himself, though he spent a few weeks on his back recovering from the fever that inevitably came with getting popped in the jungle.

This time, he hadn't come off quite so well. The lucky bastard who nailed him put what was probably a low-velocity hardball round through his left triceps. Had it been a larger caliber bullet, it would have ripped the muscle and ligature apart; as it was, the slug passed through his arm cleanly, leaving an exit wound barely larger than the entrance. So, if you had to catch one, Usher decided as he ran through his first-aid procedures methodically, this wasn't the worst the way to do it.

He drenched his still-bleeding arm with hydrogen peroxide, then administered a half ration of Demerol before hitting the wound with a methylate tincture that burned like phosphorus. His compact aid kit was a model of its kind, for over the years Usher had picked up a full supply of emergency chemicals and pharmaceuticals. Infection would be more a problem than tetanus, so he self-prescribed a double dose of oral amoxicillin.

The key things he had left to do were to clear out of the apartment and lay low until he met with Ben or Harry or whoever the hell was running them. With a pressure bandage wrapped tightly around his arm, Usher threw a few clothes into a nylon athletic bag that would go unnoticed in his gentrified neighborhood, where half the people on the street were either coming from or heading to a health club.

He also took his special edition Seecamp LWS automatic through a quick cleaning and loaded three magazines with the Silvertip hollow-points the gun was designed to fire.

When he came out of his bedroom, the Demerol had finally kicked in, and he was barely in pain. What shocked him, however, was to see the stewardess Colleen standing in the living room, staring down at the bloody shirt that Usher had ripped from his back as soon as he'd made it home.

"Hi," she said nervously. "I was, uh, just looking for Sharon and thought she might be over here. The door was open."

"I haven't seen her," Usher said. "And you shouldn't walk unannounced into other people's apartments."

"The door was open," Colleen repeated. "Not just unlocked. I thought, maybe, you were telling me she's here, to come in. You understand?"

Usher cursed himself for not having made sure the door was secured, not dumping the shirt immediately as he had the Walther. Now he faced a dilemma. But taking out Colleen would only add to his problems; her roommate would be worried, they'd find her inside a day, and he needed more time than that to take care of his remaining business in Chicago. Which meant his best weapon was talk.

"Sure, I understand," he said sorrowfully. "Guess I'm a little shaky after my accident."

"Yeah, I can see. What happened?"

"Jogging in the park," he said. "Did seven miles, fast. Maybe too fast. Anyway, I flopped down in the grass without looking, right on top of a broken bottle. Gashed my arm pretty good."

Usher picked up the shirt before Colleen could examine it closely.

"You should see a doctor, all that bleeding," she said. "Want me to look at it for you, make sure it's clean, no glass in there?"

"No problem," Usher said, showing her his well-made bandage. "I went over to Grant Hospital and had them stitch it up in Emergency. Pain in the ass, waiting around there. But I got a good kid, I think. Couple a sutures, a shot. Nothing to worry about."

"That's good," Colleen said, half meaning it. "So you haven't seen Sharon?"

"Not for a week or so. We didn't get on all that well."

Colleen's look told Usher that she knew already, that Sharon had blabbed about their encounter like an adolescent. Christ, if he didn't need the time, he'd like to croak the bitch then and there.

"Look," he said. "I got a lot of things to do. Maybe we could pick this up another time?"

"For sure. Another time," Colleen replied icily. "In the far distant future, make it."

She slammed out the door. Usher poured himself a stiff drink, then decided that with all the painkillers and antibiotics in his system, he'd better take a pass. He waited a few minutes, heard no one in the hall, and left the apartment without ever looking back.

By the time Usher walked to the intersection of Clark Street and Broadway, he'd thought over all the angles and decided that the man who'd shot him wasn't a cop. There was none of that "halt" and "police officer" bullshit that cops have to do. Which meant that either he'd caught one from a passerby who carried an automatic around with him, or someone who knew about his assignment had tried setting him up. The latter was far more likely, especially since Harry had called the shots so closely. So when he met the ape, he'd stick the Seecamp under his nose and find out exactly who was involved, who knew about the hit, and why. Then, he didn't get a good answer, he'd pass on the final assignment and shoot the big limey on the spot.

Whatever came down, Usher knew he couldn't simply walk into a hotel and take a room. The guy who'd tried to pop him wasn't the best, but he'd know enough to check out local hotels. Usher had a few extra driver's licenses and even a spare passport in his bag, but to blow them now with so much uncertainty ahead would be foolish. Besides, his wound needed a little care; semiprofessional would do, and he had a way to get it.

He had found Sherry's by accident, just stopping in one night for a quick beer after walking along Broadway in search of a decent sandwich. The boys at the bar were hostile at first, suspicious of the straight-acting stranger in their midst. Finally the owner, a fat, middle-aged queen named Larry, befriended him, bought him a drink, talked cute enough so that he knew Usher knew where he was. Finally, Larry introduced him around. And among those Usher met, and whom he hoped to see this night, was the one called Brian. He was dark-haired, fragilely thin, yet attractive in a diminutive way. But whatever he lacked in muscle he made up for in knowledge. Brian was a male nurse.

Brian was in attendance at the bar and already half crocked when Usher arrived. Inside a half hour, they were together in the rear booth near the rest rooms, Brian joking that Usher must be looking for real rough trade if he brings his gym bag with him. Usher said he'd had a fight at home, couldn't stand his friend a second longer, was going to grab a room at the Hotel Rienzi or one of the transient joints in the neighborhood.

"You can crash at my place," Brian volunteered at last. "My roommate might be around, but we're hardly speaking these days."

"I don't want to interfere," Usher demurred.

"Dearie, we can all use a little interference once in a while." Brian placed his hand softly on Usher's thigh. Usher touched the delicate fingers; Brian's skin felt like cream cheese. He slid the hand slowly up to his groin.

"I like a soft touch, you understand."

"I certainly do," Brian said, grinning. "And these days, when half the cocks you look at stare back at you with three eyes, it's the only safe way."

Hallet sat back on the overstuffed sofa in MaryAgnes McCaskey's living room and finished what he reckoned was his third double gin. "That's all of it," he said. "Nothing quite as clandestine as you thought. Nothing that would lead to three men being killed."

McCaskey gave Hallet no reproach as he filled his glass another time, nothing like the glares he'd gotten from Isabel Ortega. She was letting him drink excessively, almost wanting him to. Transparent, but so be it.

"Still, there is a lot more to your work with the Bureau than you'd told me before," she said. "The people you call Prophets are full-fledged intelligence agents."

"A few of them are on the roster of foreign intelligence services," Hallet said. "But mostly they're students and professors with high-level political contacts in their home countries, contacts who believe as they do—that exporting terrorism is no way to advance the Arab cause. In fact, the very genesis of the Prophets is counterterrorism, an early warning system, of which my people are only a part."

"Do you honestly believe that will happen, that a terrorist organization is going to strike here?"

"I've never believed it," Hallet replied, "despite the reports we've been getting. It's soured my stock in Washington a bit, but I suppose that's part of the job too."

"Well, you're the expert," McCaskey said. "But people who are willing to kill themselves so readily—"

"Not so 'readily' at all," Hallet interrupted. "That isn't suicide as we define it in the West."

"Driving a truck loaded with explosives into an embassy compound or a Marine barracks isn't suicide?"

"Self-sacrifice is a better term," Hallet said. "Camus understood it best, perhaps because he was born in Algeria and was reared in Islamic as well as French culture. He called such deeds altruistic suicide, said any reason for living is also an excellent reason for dying. I think those were his words, but, in any event, it has nothing to do with the existentialist suicide of despair, of nihilism. The Koran speaks of the despair of the *kafir*, the unbeliever. But for those of faith, despair is an impossibility."

222

"God, and I thought Catholics had it tough," McCaskey said. "But at least suicide is forbidden."

"Not to a soldier who falls on a hand grenade to save his comrades. Altruistic suicide."

"It's just so foreign to our sense of religion, of order."

"Sure it is to us, but not to anyone who follows Islam. Isn't it curious," he wondered aloud, "that Islamic fundamentalism is the most powerful movement in the world today—that at exactly the same time Catholics want to liberalize, want to restructure their church into a modern institution, Muslims around the world are going back to the basics, to strict interpretations of Koranic law."

"Do you follow Islam?" McCaskey asked. "Or is it just a subject for study?"

"I'm a man between," Hallet said. "There is much joy and beauty in Islam, but it's lost when zealots want to substitute fanaticism for fervor, to equate control in a political sense with submission in a religious one. People who murder in God's name are murderers, after all."

"Life in the eighties," McCaskey said, calming Hallet with a smile that showed off her perfect teeth and the warmth in her eyes. Hallet noticed for the first time that she'd changed from her business suit into loose blue jeans and an oversized cotton rag sweater. The down-home girl, the other side of Agent McCaskey, Hallet thought. Why was she so willing to reveal it?

"What about you, Philip? How the devil did you get involved in intelligence work in the first place?"

"It's something I never planned," Hallet said dryly.

"Lots of things happen by default," McCaskey said. "Like my getting recruited by the Bureau when I'd planned a career in prison reform. So how did the big boys on Pennsylvania Avenue recruit their recruiter? Why did you ever become an Arabist in the first place?"

"The second part is easier than the first," Hallet said, relaxing with McCaskey for the first time, letting his mind wander back without the usual pain of recollection. Why not? It was too late to hold back that part of his life. Clelland and her boss knew about most of it. Everything, that is, except the part that included Sandman.

"My father was an investment banker," he began. "In London it's called merchant banking, and I was twelve or so when he was transferred there. Big promotion for Dad, the end of the world for me. I was a small, bookish kid, kind of brooding. At school, the other new boys, the only ones who welcomed me, happened to be Arabs. Perhaps because we were both in a cultural quandary."

"I've never much liked the English myself," McCaskey said. "But there are generations of genes behind that."

"I understand," Hallet said, eyeing McCaskey's Irish profile and the milk-glass skin contrasting with the jet-black hair. "England was never my other Eden, either. Just the only home I really knew until I went to the Middle East."

"It's always tough growing up as an outsider."

"Well, if I was merely an outsider, the Arabs I knew in England were more like outcasts. They were downright persecuted. I'd never seen much racial prejudice in the States—not too many blacks in my parochial neck of the woods. But in England, I saw princes and young kings grouped together as a bunch of wogs. So, to use your word 'default,' I guess that was why I wanted to get to know them, to learn their culture and customs that Westerners seemed to find so loathsome and contemptible."

Hallet paused long enough to finish his drink, to see McCaskey nodding at him sympathetically.

"When I returned to the States for college," he continued, "my fledgling knowledge of Arabic and general interest in their arts got me into a curriculum called Islamic Studies. Then it was back to England, several years at Oxford, finally a few study grants to the Middle East. Bingo, I had become a fully licensed Arabist."

"But not yet a contract agent," McCaskey said.

"No, that came later. I was off to spend two years doing research on Islamic art and architecture, studies that would put me in touch with the finest families in the Mideast, many of whose offspring I'd come to know in my early years in England. Funny how those little wogs grew up to become so important to the Brits before they found their North Sea oil reserves. Anyway, as partial payment for my overseas studies, I made some very special contacts on behalf of the Crown."

"You worked for *British* intelligence?" McCaskey said in disbelief.

"Nothing that clandestine. Not real spy stuff. In fact, it all started so simply, walking across the greens of Oxford and talking to a don about the beautiful illuminations I'd seen in a fourteenth-century Koran in the British Museum. I was soon to head off to the Middle East with my scholar's credentials and the host of contacts that my don and the Oxford sheepskin afforded me. It was to be the most basic of all missions, just some information collection and making good use of where I lived and whom I met—figuring out who saw England as an old friend and who, in the aftermath of Palestine and the Suez, wanted to erase every last trace of British influence from the region. It was a minor project, really, bits and pieces from here and there. Odd lots."

"But, Philip, you were still an American."

"I know you may not like the Brits, but England was as close to a homeland as I had then. It was where I grew up," Hallet said, deciding he would tell her just enough to avoid the more direct questions he could not answer.

"I helped the British because they were so helpless and ineffectual themselves, a five-foot-six nation in a six-foot world, still dancing the Hokey-Pokey in their grimy social clubs. As for intelligence, their services were in a shambles after all the defections and scandals, and all they seemed to know about Arabs was that they're superb horsemen. Amazing after Lawrence, and all the Arab protectorates, but true."

"I can see why Macdonald Clelland tapped you on the shoulder," McCaskey said. "You two have the same skills."

"Macdonald Clelland is himself an Islamic scholar of note," Hallet said. "When I first met him in Washington, he talked to me about working for peace, understanding, all that. And his key to peacekeeping was that the United States needed good advance intelligence. Things like the fall of the Shah, the hostages in Teheran, Libya invading Chad—all of them caught the U.S. napping."

"Intelligence didn't seem to help in Beirut, or at our embassies," McCaskey said, hoping afterward she hadn't sounded harsh or unforgiving.

"All reasons I signed on and came to Chicago," Hallet said. "The only real information we were getting out of the Mideast was through the Israelis, and the Mossad only tells us what they want to tell us, what works to their advantage.

"I was in the Mideast for eight years," he went on, still thinking it was a lifetime ago. "I did my work, published papers and monographs, narrated a couple of documentaries for public broadcasting. All that, on the surface. The rest of the time I was setting up a network, enlisting people I thought would help us, people over there and those I knew would someday be coming to England or the States.

"It was even a bit romantic when I started, roaming the medinas and souks, ferreting out data to feed back to London. All very Graham Greene, you see. But it got old fast. I quit it when I finally realized I wasn't cut out to be a field man."

"That's why you still carry an automatic pistol? Because you're no longer a field man?" McCaskey asked in a way that said she remained unconvinced.

"When a man like Yousef says there's trouble brewing," Hallet said, "you don't take chances."

McCaskey kept tallying all Hallet had told her, and was hell-bent on taking it further.

"We both have to face facts," she said, "someone has uncovered your Prophets and wants them eliminated. We need to know who."

"I need to know why," Hallet insisted.

"The two men who were executed in Baghdad," she pondered aloud. "Could they have given names?"

"Only each other's," Hallet said. "That's why I was so adamant about keeping everything compartmentalized. I'm the only one who knows who and where the Prophets are."

"Not any longer, it looks like."

McCaskey stood, told Hallet she'd fetch him more ice.

"You having another?"

"Sure. After what happened tonight, I could use more than one," she said.

Hallet watched her pour a carefully measured half glass of Chablis, then bring the ice and stand by him mutely as he made another double.

"I think you're more of a field agent than you're willing to admit," McCaskey said. "But you do a good job concealing it. Before I saw you in action, I'd bought your act of the arrogant professor, the intellectual snob. I despised you when we first met."

"You were supposed to. I wanted to keep you out of this."

"It almost worked, but I'm still a cop and you're still a field hand."

"Underneath my skin, maybe. But not the way you think," Hallet said. "All the years of trying to be the proper university gentleman, years of sipping sherry with faculty types and arcanists—well, let's say they took their toll as much as my former activities in the Mideast. So, maybe my leaving the university payroll, signing on with the Institute even when I knew that Clelland wanted me more for my skills at setting up a network than for my scholarship . . . maybe it was my way of getting back to business, after all."

"You needed it."

"I needed something," Hallet said. He finished his drink, spun the cap back on the gin bottle, signaled McCaskey he'd had enough. She came over and touched his face gently, letting a hint of perfume reach his nostrils, allowing her leg to nestle against his.

"I think we both need something tonight," she whispered, bringing her mouth close to Hallet's ear.

MaryAgnes McCaskey wrapped herself in a blue terry-cloth robe and eased quietly out of the bedroom. Three in the morning, she saw on the alarm, but not too late to keep her promise to Jack Corrigan.

Inside the kitchen, she turned on the stove light, which illuminated the room just enough for her to make her way about and find the telephone. Before dialing, she paused and listened: not a sound coming from the bedroom except deep, alcohol-paced breathing; no rustling of sheets and covers, no more tossing, turning, muttering. Hallet was fast asleep.

As she reached for the phone, a shiver—actually a tremor—shook her body, reminding her of the orgasm that had swept her away in spite of herself, confusing her more than a good agent should be.

Philip Hallet was a curious lover, that was for sure. Curious in the way he explored her body, tentatively at first, with gentleness, until the time for gentleness had passed. Had it not been for the excessive amount of gin he'd consumed, enough that she had to postpone her further inquisition of him, he might have been a truly exceptional partner.

Amazing that he could function at all, she thought as she recalled what Rourke and Williams, the two agents at Hallet's house, had told her—that once, when Hallet was off on a bender, they'd been assigned directly by Washington to locate him. Not everyday duty for the Bureau, which underscored her belief that Hallet was looked upon as an asset of considerable merit, perhaps mistakenly.

"He's a drunk," Rourke had said. "And anyone who trusts a drunk is destined to come up a loser."

Sure he is, she'd thought, but after the booze kicks down the defenses, you may also get to hear a little truth in the bargain. Had she heard any tonight? Was the liquor a tip-off that Hallet had something to hide, or merely someone to mourn?

"Jesus, it's about time," Jack Corrigan answered midway through the second ring. "What's with you two?"

"I couldn't get away sooner," McCaskey said, evading Corrigan's allusion to Hallet's presence.

"So, what do you have for me?"

"Still not enough."

"You keep me waiting half the night to say not enough? Come off—"

"Jack, listen for a minute, will you? And calm down. I only played that game at Hallet's to keep him in line. He had to believe I was ready to stiff you."

"I'm ready to believe it, too."

"Well, don't," McCaskey said, catching her voice rising and bringing it down to a bare whisper. "I'm convinced Hallet's working a double game here, and the second shooting proves it to me. I'll fill you in in person, but I think not all of Hallet's loyalties lie with Washington."

"You serious?"

"As serious as you are about what happened tonight, that it was no amateur on that rooftop."

"You haven't been speaking to Johnny Roses, have you?"

"No, should I have?"

"Only if the rifleman is someone I'm looking for on other matters. Guy who uses the same type weapon as the one at Hallet's place." McCaskey didn't react to the probe, which for the moment gave Corrigan a warm glow.

"Look, give me time to get closer to Hallet, and I'll help you get him," she said. "I may not be buying all that he has to sell, but he's wired up high enough in the Bureau to get me pulled off this case anytime he wants. So I'm going to need help, and I'm willing to share."

"What is it you think he's involved in?"

"Not certain. But I know he's more than some academic who can speak Arabic," she said. "His people are getting killed, and the killers are professionals. See, it's not just here, Jack. We have dead men in New York and Detroit, too. That's what I'm in it for, a full interstate and domestic security bust. And that means I'll be glad to swap the Chicago connections for your help."

"This whole thing reeks to me of drugs," Corrigan said. "And I'm not talking about Colombian coke or the crack they sell to kids. I'm thinking the real stuff—grade-A horse, like what they grow in the Middle East. So I'm starting to think that Hallet's at the center of something nasty, and he very well may be one of the bad guys."

"That's exactly what I'm thinking. And that's why I'm staying real close to him," McCaskey said as she suddenly remembered Hallet's drunken mutterings that the only common thread in their puzzle was betrayal.

Chapter 16

According to Nancy Morgan, Lieutenant Jack Corrigan looked overtired, stressed out, downright terrible.

"That's why I hate having a glass wall for an office," Corrigan said back to her. "You can't take a nap, and you can't get away from the well-meaning."

"Whoa, Jack. I come as a friend."

"I'm sorry, Nance," Corrigan apologized as she started to walk away. "Didn't mean to sound so grumpy."

"Maybe it's time we had our talk."

"Would that we could."

Corrigan looked into her kind eyes and wished he were able to unload a little of it. But who could make sense of the things he'd like to tell her? That Johnny Roses had called from the federal slam in Indiana to offer him a professional back-shooter named Bobby Usery just before some goddamn Arab math teacher is gunned down outside the home of Doctor Philip Hallet, renowned Middle East scholar who, if Agent MaryAgnes McCaskey had it right, was either an agent for the Arabs or a drug smuggler, or maybe both—that the wacko who was gunning down cabdrivers was still on the street, despite the battalion of undercover cops who'd volunteered to push hacks around the North Side in the hope of getting him to crawl out from under his rock—that somehow all of the above were connected in a weird, frightening way and Jack Corrigan himself was probably the only one involved who didn't have a firm clue to what the connection was. Which meant that, like it or not, he'd have to continue playing ball with McCaskey and hope she'd honor her promise to share with him whatever she learned, even though his once high opinion of her now contained more than a modicum of distrust.

"If I told you what I was really thinking," Corrigan said to Nancy Morgan, "you'd log me in for the next available straitjacket. That's how sick it is."

"Has to be about old Son of Shah," Nancy said.

"It's like putting on a new shirt, Nance. Just when you think you have it right, there's always one pin left to stick you."

Cal Bostic's rap on Corrigan's door interrupted them; it was a soft knock, incongruous with the black detective's athletic physique. Corrigan, grateful to get away from Nancy Morgan's solicitude, waved Bostic inside.

"Sorry to break in," Bostic said.

"I was leaving anyway," Nancy Morgan said. "Give me a ring, Jack. It's what I'm here for."

"You're a fool if you don't," Bostic said when the door closed behind her. "There's more available with that lady than grief counseling."

"Put it aside, Cal. I'm in no mood."

"Sure, sorry. Joking ain't what I came here for."

"Then what?"

"I need you to put my nose back in joint. See, I don't mind going along with you on the taxi thing. But that shooting last night, that's nothing to do with you. Violent Crimes is supposed to handle that stuff. Except when I go pick up the paperwork, I see that my friend Jack Corrigan has put himself down as chief investigator. Like he doesn't trust me to—"

"No way," Corrigan cut him off. "That's not it at all."

"Then what?"

"That was no ordinary street shooting. It goes way out of that park."

"To where, Jack? Where I can't handle the job?"

"Look, Cal, I should have called you. But I was here until four this morning, and my brain was going soft. Believe me, I never even dreamed of icing you, but this shooting is all wrapped up inside some federal gig, and I'm just along for the ride as FBI liaison."

Bostic let out a deep breath which seemed to take the tension out of his meaty shoulders. "This federal thing's tied into Hostage and Terrorism," he said, at once asking and answering himself.

"This time for real. But there's always room for you."

"So, maybe I have something going for us."

"Jesus, Cal, whatever you got."

"The report says two guys started blasting at each other in the alley after the hit went down. Well, I may have a lead on one of them. Some airline stew, lives Near North. Says her roommate's gone missing."

"You think she was in the alley putting out nine-millimeter rounds?"

"Maybe this guy she's been seeing was. He lives in the same building and, a couple of hours after the shooting, the stew who called us walks into his apartment looking for her roommate. What she sees is the boyfriend's been shot, stabbed, or gotten into one helluva fight. The stew takes off, thinks about it all the time she's flying to Miami. Then, she comes home and her roommate's still a no-show, she dials nine-one-one."

"I don't know. Airline stews aren't known for regular habits and even—"

"Listen up, Jack," Bostic said. "The boyfriend's name is Bobby, and his physicals make him a dead ringer for the family's buttonman you put out the alert for, the one called Usher."

Corrigan was already on his feet and reaching for the crumpled sports coat he'd draped over his chair. "Cal, you're beautiful. Let's hit it," he said, figuring he'd give McCaskey one final chance at teamwork by calling her from Bostic's car.

MaryAgnes McCaskey followed Corrigan and Bostic down the corridor to the suspect's apartment. The way Bostic had eyed her when she'd arrived, McCaskey figured she'd take a step back and let the locals play through. Besides, Colleen, the blond airline hostess, didn't seem too well grounded in facts.

"I knew he was a creep," Colleen said as Corrigan set the pass key in Bobby's door lock. "Like, I mean, I knew it from the first time we met."

"Lady, everybody in Chicago meets a creep and calls the police on him," Bostic said, "how'd we ever have time to write all them parking tickets?"

"Yeah? Well, this particular creep wears a shirt that's dripping with blood and has what looks like a bullet hole in the sleeve," Colleen said. "I was a nurse before I started flying, you know. I spent my share of time in emergency rooms, so I'm not joking about bullet holes."

"Then you should have called us sooner," Corrigan said.

"Hey, look, if Sharon—she's my roommate—if Sharon gets home all right, I don't call you at all. Who am I to get involved with shootings?"

Corrigan eased Colleen and McCaskey out of the way and drew his service revolver. Cal Bostic didn't need directions as he took up his position against the door jamb. Corrigan popped the lock, the two detectives were inside the apartment in an instant—one high, the other low, weapons cocked and ready.

"How did he explain the wound?" McCaskey asked Colleen as Corrigan and Bostic moved through the flat.

"I think I caught him totally by surprise," Colleen began. "I was just looking for my roommate, Sharon."

Not the stuff of a great witness, McCaskey thought. "So you

told us. But that doesn't explain how you saw the shirt."

"All clear. Nobody home," Corrigan yelled out, trying to sound dispassionate as he wrapped a handkerchief around the telephone and called to make certain the search warrant he'd ordered was signed and on the way with the evidence technicians.

"I just walked in on him," Colleen went on as she followed McCaskey inside the apartment. "Bobby had forgotten to close the door, left it open an inch or so. I thought Sharon might be with him, so I walked in. That's when I saw the shirt, right there on that chair. See, a little bloodstain."

"Sounds like Sharon knows Bobby a lot better than you do," McCaskey said.

"She went out with him two, three times. But the guy was a little kinky."

"How so?" McCaskey asked.

Colleen went up and whispered to her softly. "Like they're back at our place. Alone. In the sack. And all the guy wants from Sharon is a hand job. Can you believe it? Like we were back in high school, for God's sake."

"Not Queen of Peace High School, where I went," McCaskey said.

Colleen gave her a blank stare and kept talking. "You should see his eyes, how he looked at me. Like if looks could kill . . . well, with Bobby, you felt his *could*. Never seen anything like it. Real eerie."

"Let's get back to the shirt," Corrigan said as he motioned Cal Bostic to check out the bedroom. "How'd he explain it?"

"He said he flopped down on the grass in Lincoln Park after jogging and cut himself on some broken glass. To me, even from where I was standing, it looked like either a knife or a bullet had done the damage. I checked the papers, saw this little news item about some guy getting shot up near Clark Street. So I called the cops."

"He cleared out pretty fast," Bostic said. "Got a lot of clothing left, personal stuff in the bathroom. Guy must have liked having a massage now and then. There are all kinds of oils and lotions around."

"See," Colleen said, smirking, to McCaskey.

"But check these out," Bostic went on, extending his fists, then opening them. "Found a couple open boxes of shells in the bedroom—two-two-three Remingtons that are right for the H & K we found, plus Winchester Silvertips and nine-millimeter autos, probably the belly gun he used in the alley."

Terrific, McCaskey thought. Only that still doesn't tell us who he used it on. Who the hell else was in that alley?

"Look, Colleen," she said. "We're going to need a full description of this man. If you need us to call someone at the airline, get you taken off flight duty, we'll get a sketch artist up here."

"He's six-foot one-inch tall," Corrigan said. "Fair complexion, sandy haired. And those eyes you were frightened of, let's color them blue. That him?"

"My God, you're right on the money," Colleen exclaimed. "You know him!"

"Question is," Corrigan said diffidently, "how long have you known him? You and your friend Sharon?"

"Six weeks or so. He hasn't been here much longer than that. A professor owns the place, and he rented it out to Bobby when he went off to study Canadian Indians or some crazy thing."

"Since you met Bobby, has he been on any trips? Any vacations? Like to the Caribbean, for instance?" asked Corrigan.

"Jeez, you *do* know him," Colleen said. "When we first got to know each other, like after passing in the hall and all, he'd just gotten back from the islands. A little tan, duty-free liquor, like that."

"Jamaica."

"No, said he was in Puerto Rico," Colleen recalled. "Only, funny thing, he comes over with a bottle of his island booze. A get-acquainted gift. Except it was Jamaican rum. Appleton. Now, I know the last thing they'd sell in Puerto Rico is Jamaican rum, but I figure he had an extra bottle around and was looking for an excuse to get together. So I never mentioned it."

"If you had, you might not be alive to tell us about it," Corrigan said. "Because the man we're talking about, the one you call Bobby, is named Robert Usery, better known around the mob as Usher. And what he does for a living is kill people."

McCaskey took Corrigan's arm and pulled him aside as Colleen stood with her mouth agape; dumbstruck, panicked.

"Jack, I think we'd better get Philip Hallet over here right away. Let's see how he reacts when we lay this on him, see if he's finally frightened enough to open up."

"Wrong way to go," Corrigan shook her off. "I say we don't let him know we're on Usher's tail. Because, if Hallet's tied into this like he seems to be, he might lead us straight to Usher and, with a little luck, to the old man himself."

"You telling me that the old man and the Chicago family are wrapped up in whatever Hallet's doing?"

"Kiddo, that's what I was hoping you'd tell me. All I know about Usher is what Johnny Roses told me."

"Johnny Roses?" McCaskey said. "How does he fit in here?"

"Johnny's not happy serving time where he is, and scared shitless about what Sid Paris is saying about him down at Maxwell AFB. So he offered me something to intervene, and that was Usery. Seems he's a contract killer for the outfit and, Johnny swears, was the one who greased our old friend Chuckie Franco. Usher's involvement with Hallet, I never expected. But however it shakes down, we still work the local angles my way. Right?"

"A deal's a deal," McCaskey agreed, already figuring how she could wrap a federal indictment around the New York and Detroit shootings, and whatever the hell else Hallet was doing. "You call the local shots."

"So, for now, we forget about tipping Hallet," Corrigan said. "I don't want him here screwing up the evidence people. Besides, soon as they arrive, we're both going to the federal building and talk to the U.S. Attorney about getting Johnny Roses cut loose from Terre Haute."

McCaskey turned away and saw Colleen looking at her with troubled eyes and a pouting mouth.

"Hey, I don't want to get involved with—"

"Your name won't even have to come up," McCaskey assured her. "Not with all that Lieutenant Corrigan knows already."

"Wheeew, thanks," Colleen sighed.

"By the way, what do think happened to your roommate?"

"Oh, Sharon. She got around to calling me this morning."

"She's all right, then?"

"Sounds terrific," Colleen laughed. "An *affaire de coeur,* though I'm sure other parts of her anatomy were involved. Just never had a minute to phone in."

"Sure," McCaskey laughed back. "Some girls have all the luck."

Jason Kellaigh stood by the high patio doors of his library and looked past the tables and umbrellas that ringed the swimming pool, out into the night. At the end of the slate-stone pathway that led down from the terrace to the lakeshore, a good fifty yards beyond the tree line, he could see a shimmering of yellow light—a party on the twelve-meter sailboat that was moored to his private dock; a party hosted with Kellaigh's grudging permission by his spoiled-rotten niece and nephew for their beer-guzzling classmates and golf club friends; a party aboard the yacht named *Mickey,* which caused Kellaigh's heart to sink deeper in his already tightened chest.

Harry's knock on the study door was easily recognizable. Kellaigh neither turned from the window nor answered it verbally; a few discreet seconds later, Harry stepped inside the room.

"Your appointment is here, sir."

"Oh, yes," Kellaigh said, his gaze still on the glimmer that the *Mickey*'s running lights reflected off the low, summer heat clouds that massed over the cool waters of Lake Michigan, as if themselves seeking relief from the warmth of the day. "I assume he's alone."

"Yes, sir."

"Then show him in, please. And Harry . . ."

"Yes, sir?"

"I want you with me for this. Quietly, of course, even if that Harvard-boy racketeer starts acting like he's Secretary of State."

"Understood," Harry said, motioning to a rich cordovan leather side chair, "I'll sit on the sidelines, and we'll see how it plays."

A moment later Harry reopened the door. Ben came inside first, in his dark pin-striped suit looking more aptly dressed for a meeting with his bankers than an evening's call at the Kellaigh home.

"Good to see you, Ben." Jason Kellaigh extended his hand. Harry took his chair as the welding of soft, well-manicured flesh went forward. "And your uncle? How is he?"

"About the same. If the doctors can keep his lungs dry, and the heart damage doesn't worsen, he'll probably bury all of us."

"Damn certain he will."

Kellaigh poured himself a decent measure of brandy, knew better than to offer one to Ben: The little bastard acted more like an accountant for the Methodist Church than the *consigliere* the old man had selected to handle money matters for the family. "So, why this sudden need to meet?"

"My uncle is concerned about the turn of recent events," Ben said. "Events which, in his view, were undertaken without his being apprised and which have caused certain problems for our family."

"Be specific, will you? We've done enough business together, you know me well enough. Don't worry about stepping on toes here."

"I'm speaking of Detroit, specifically," Ben replied. "You had Harry send Usher there without the courtesy of a consultation with us. Correct?"

"You know it is," Kellaigh conceded.

"Were you aware that Mike Doran was a close associate of my uncle's equal number in Detroit? And that, should he and his associates discover there is a linkage between us and Mike Doran's death, our family would be in a very embarrassing situation?"

"I had no idea whatsoever about that," Kellaigh said. "And please assure your uncle that, since our business in Detroit is concluded, there will be no further interference in his out-of-town activities."

"What about the recent occurrence here on the North Side? You knew nothing of that? It wasn't Usher again?"

"I know nothing about whatever you're implying," Kellaigh said. "Or whether our mutual employee was involved."

Ben eyed Kellaigh carefully before turning his gaze on Harry. Neither man changed expression, faces frozen in looks that resembled contempt. "I'll take you at your word," he said.

"You've no reason to do otherwise," said Kellaigh.

"Still, since Usher is tied directly to us, and since my family was pivotal in your arrangements with him, my uncle wants to know exactly what happened in Detroit, what you are undertaking at present, and, should he ask it, your commitment that it will be stopped immediately."

"Assure your uncle that my activities in no way will impinge upon his business interests or those of his friends. Mister Doran was an exception, a coincidence that can occur only once."

"The point is, Jason, you are not aware of what our business interests actually are, nor where they lie. That's at the core of the issue."

"I disagree, Ben. What's at issue here is that I don't have to seek your uncle's approval for each decision I make. At least when they don't concern any of our joint ventures."

"That's not what he considers a healthy partnership."

"You know, Ben," Kellaigh said, anger echoing in his voice, "your uncle and I have done much for each other over the years. In fact, I think he's profited handsomely from our association, no matter how oblique circumstances forced that association to

240

be. Our real estate ventures, the acquisitions of companies we desired, and, most important, the financial shelters he's found in my corporation's pension funds—all have benefited your family greatly."

"I'm well aware of that," Ben said. "But don't try to tell me that the street only went one way. When you needed cash to buy back stock and fight a takeover, when certain members of your family found themselves facing substantial gambling losses, my uncle went beyond any profit motive in helping you. And that problem with the union, when the pension funds came under some scrutiny, we solved it for you summarily by sending Usher to Jamaica."

"Your uncle led me to believe that what you just spoke of was a strictly private matter. Between us alone."

"Nothing is private when it involves family unity and security," Ben said.

"Exactly my own view," Kellaigh said. "Because I am now facing problems of a similar nature. Family security is involved. And I plan on solving these problems in whatever manner I see fit. You may have supplied me the means, but your involvement stops there."

"Not when you dispatch Usher to eliminate someone our Detroit colleagues consider part of their organization."

"Organizations be damned. We're speaking of *my* family here," Kellaigh flared. "Your uncle above all should understand about families, about blood."

"Not when you put us at risk," Ben snapped back with equal intensity. "I allowed you to use Usher to conclude a piece of business in New York which you said was personal, and I know he was responsible for the contract in Detroit. I also think he may be active right here in Chicago. Now, Usher is intelligent and a most able professional. But he's also a complete psychopath. Which means that he'll keep on taking assignments until he's eventually and certainly caught. We know how to employ him—how to use his skills in different places, how to time his activities so there's no connecting thread. But you're wading into waters that are dangerous and unfamiliar. So, unless you can give me some reasons why my uncle and I—"

"I said it was family business," Kellaigh insisted.

"My uncle, however, believes it may be otherwise," Ben insisted. "He's especially concerned if any of this involves drugs. You know how he feels about that."

Jason Kellaigh shook with rage, paused to keep himself in check before responding. "That thought is outrageous and contemptible, Ben. For you, or your uncle."

"In any event," Ben pressed on without a sign of remorse or embarrassment, "he has instructed me to tell you to desist from whatever it is you're doing and to tell us where Usher has disappeared to."

Kellaigh froze for an instant, overcame his rage, spoke in carefully measured tones. "You may tell your uncle that my business with Usher is nearly completed. You may tell him also that he is in no jeopardy because of it. And if that's not good enough, you may tell him that we can begin severing all our agreements at the earliest possible opportunity."

"Mister Kellaigh," Ben said, leaning forward in his chair, "please don't equate our relationship with that of your board of directors. We don't accept resignations as they do. I'd strongly advise you to remember that."

Harry came out of his chair in a flash. "Why you little wop bastard! Who do you think you're talking to?"

Jason Kellaigh silenced him with an outstretched palm. "I apologize for Harry's zealous sense of loyalty," he said. "Let's remain calm, please."

Ben sat back and smiled, as if demonstrating to Kellaigh that he felt no threat whatsoever from the big Englishman. "With talent around like Harry," he said, "I've never understood why you came to us for someone like Usher."

"Oh, that's quite simple," Kellaigh said. "Because, when the last of my business is completed, I would never think of having Harry killed to prevent anyone discovering the connection between us—a statement I'm afraid I cannot make for Usher."

Chapter 17

For the sixth night in a row, Joe Rivera pushed the year-old but already rattling cab through the hectic Friday night traffic. Despite the department's advisory that the person being sought could be of any age or gender, he bypassed dozens of young women who waved, yelled, and often flipped him the finger for not honoring their summons. But he did cruise within the boundaries of his assigned route—a North Side triangle that included Clark Street, Belmont, and Broadway; right in the heart of the neighborhood where the last murdered cabdriver, if his trip sheet was correct, had thrown his final flag.

And each night, Joe Rivera and the two dozen other volunteer cops driving hacks around the North Side came up with nothing.

Rivera pulled into a drive-through McDonald's, ordered a large black coffee and apple pie, consumed them in the brightly lighted parking lot while he glanced through the sport pages of a day-old newspaper. The coffee was hot and fresh, but the pie tasted like congealed apple pulp sandwiched between deep-fried cardboard. Another night of crime fighting, he badgered himself, another reason never to volunteer. Just a damn waste of time, a long shot beyond belief.

He dug a Lucky Strike out of the pack he'd stored in the sun visor, smoked it until the coffee ran out, then kicked over the taxi's tired engine. As the interior lights flickered on, Rivera looked at the hack license that hung over the glove box. The boys who'd volunteered for the detail had had a lot of fun making up their Arab names, all except some of the Muslim brothers who'd adopted them already and found the levity insulting. Rivera had chosen the name Qasim Qaddar after much deliberation, mostly because the double use of the letter Q not only sounded but also looked unmistakably Arab. And the photo, with his mustache combed out and slightly curled, his light-brown hair darkened with Grecian Formula, made Detective Joe Rivera look, if not the perfect Arab, definitely sinister and un-American.

Probably nothing but nonsense, Rivera figured as he dropped the cab into drive. But at least it would go down in his personnel file as a volunteer undercover stint—another plus mark that one day might get him transferred out of Vice and having to bust all those sad Latin hookers who were selling the only real asset God had given them to survive.

Rivera heard the voice calling him as he paused by the sidewalk and dumped his bag of trash in the refuse container.

"Hey, you on duty?"

"I am now, sport."

"Then let's go."

Rivera checked out his passenger as the open door lighted the car interior: white male, mid-twenties, brown hair already thinning, wire-rimmed spectacles. He wore jeans—good old straight-legged Levi's, not the stone-washed designer crap common on the North Side—and an Army field jacket that was a little too heavy for the warm evening. Might as well give it a shot, Rivera figured. If the fare wanted to go somewhere inside the covered triangle, Rivera would take him. Anything like the Loop or the gin mills along the Division Street body exchange, he gets dumped immediately. But the passenger got Rivera's attention quickly with an address that was a long way west, out where the city's last, gasping manufacturing plants were dying their unproductive and often arson-inspired deaths.

"What's out there?" Rivera asked.

"Does it matter?"

"You got fare, don't matter to me," Rivera said, hoping his badly feigned accent didn't sound more Mexican than Muslim.

Rivera's meter hadn't clicked twice before the passenger asked where he was from.

"Me? I'm from everywhere. Lived Teheran, Baghdad, Beirut," Rivera said, figuring he'd cover all bets just in case.

"So what are you then? Iranian?"

"Me? Sure thing. Iranian."

Silence. Rivera checked both his mirrors—the rearview and the small fish eye he'd pinned with great care on the fabric liner above the windshield to give him a full view of the rear seat. The fare was slumped back, looking out the side window as if there were any great sights on the ride west.

"My brother died over there, you know that? Your people killed him."

"My people? My people are here. South Side people," Rivera said. He watched the fare sit up straighter, but his hands were in plain sight, empty. Still, Rivera didn't like it. He hit the emergency transmitter that had been wired to the shift lever and slowly moved his Smith & Wesson snub-nose from beneath the seat onto his lap.

"I thought all you people were brothers," the fare said.

"All people brothers. All one world."

"My brother died in Beirut."

"Terrible place today," Rivera said, slowing down to catch a stoplight, buying himself time. "Crazy people there."

"I wish I could go there. I'd get it done."

"Lot of people die in Beirut," Rivera said. He eased away from the green light and said a silent prayer of thanks as the two unmarked police cars that had responded to his signal pulled up ahead of and behind him.

"He never had a chance. Your people never gave him a chance."

"What are you talking, my people? You're crazy, my people."

"What the fuck are *you* talking about!" the fare barked. "How about that Pan Am plane, all those poor kids."

Rivera wasn't interested in provoking an argument with some anti-Arab bigot but figured he had to press hard enough to see if he might cock a psycho's trigger.

"There's American terror, too, my friend," he said. "How about Iran plane Six-six-five?"

Rivera caught him in the mirror, reaching inside the field jacket. Screw it, he yelled at himself. If this ain't probable cause, it's good enough for me. He hit the brakes hard, throwing his passenger forward. As the car skidded to a stop, Rivera reached around with one arm and got the bastard in a full neck lock. His free hand came up with the Smith & Wesson, and he jammed it hard underneath the cursing kid's nose.

"Get your arms straight out, hands open. Try reaching inside that coat and I'll blow your fucking head off."

Within seconds, Rivera's backups were out of their units and ripping open the taxi's rear doors.

"No, no! You can't. Don't stop me!" the kid screamed as the cops pulled him out of the car and spread-eagled him over the hood.

Rivera watched it all through the windshield as he fought to regain his breath. When he recovered enough to climb out from behind the wheel, one of the backup cops threw him a huge smile and held up what was unmistakably a long-barreled .22-caliber automatic.

"Lookee here, Joe," the detective called out. "This young man's got himself a Shah shooter."

By the time Rivera got to him, the suspect's screams and curses had collapsed into an unintelligible jumble of whimpers and sobs.

*　　　*　　　*

Hallet awoke in jerking spasms of awareness. He was at home, that came first; then, as the light grew endurable, he realized he'd never made it upstairs and had collapsed on one of the soft floor pillows in the living room. Finally, as a horrid amalgam of tastes roared in his throat—embalming fluid mixed with rose-water, a residue from the gin that left him dehydrated and parched—he realized he was sporting a hangover as major as the one he'd taken with him into the Oak Park clinic.

He pulled himself to a sitting position, surveyed the night's wreckage strewn around him—the empty bottle and glasses, the brass *ibrik* encrusted with burned-on coffee remains, the Sauer automatic he'd no doubt drunkenly toyed with or perhaps tried to clean. The rest of the evening was even more of a blur. He knew he'd begun drinking at MaryAgnes McCaskey's apart-ment, that he'd somehow managed to flee without her trailing after him, that he had to stay away from her because he could no longer ride out the events that were strangling him.

Hallet got to the kitchen, poured himself a tall glass of water. He finished it, a second, and half a third when the ringing of the telephone nearly shook the glass from his weak grasp.

"Philip, are you all right?"

Hallet tensed. At first he thought the solicitous concern was Isabel Ortega's, until he recognized the harder edge that char-acterized MaryAgnes McCaskey's voice. Hallet said he was well.

"Don't you ever wake up with the woman you take to bed?" she asked, trying to conceal her anger with a jesting probe.

"Never when sleep's an impossibility."

"You shouldn't have left last night," McCaskey said. "Not in the shape you were in. Not just because we quarreled."

"It didn't matter," Hallet said, unable to come up with any substantive memory of the nature and scope of their argument. "I had to be alone, to think."

"I understand that. I only called to tell you I saw Jack Corrigan this morning. They arrested the shooter responsible for the taxi driver killings."

"And he wasn't an Arab," Hallet knew.

"Just some deranged kid who keeps on mumbling about bombs in Beirut and on airplanes. He's a mess, but it appears to be nothing political, just insane."

"All of it is," Hallet said.

"Funny, though, that kid's the one who brought us together," she said, clearly not wanting to pursue Hallet's allusion. "An act of misguided revenge."

"Revenge is always misguided."

"At least that part of it is finished."

Hallet covered the receiver as he let out a foul belch. McCaskey seemed to be waiting for a reply; Hallet decided to let her come up with one on her own as he tried thinking through the day.

"We still have our agenda to keep," she said. "Maybe I should come by so we can figure out our next step?"

"Not today," Hallet said flatly. "I have to visit a sick friend."

"The way you say it, I think either you're making up a story or, more likely, I should go along with you."

"Neither one," Hallet insisted. "I have to see a friend and I don't want the Bureau tailing me, either for company or as protection. This is private, personal."

"I gave you my word, Philip. We'll work this together. Besides," she tried, laughing, "who in the Bureau would believe any of what's going on? This is far too bizarre for them to cope with."

"That's exactly why it's for real," Hallet said, knowing that he'd finally have to interrupt the sanctity of Stan Bach's Sabbath.

Hallet walked in a leisurely, circuitous route from the Illinois Central station to Stan Bach's house on the northernmost fringe of the University of Chicago campus. Aviva, the Bachs' youngest daughter, answered his ring; she was fresh-scrubbed and glowing, ready for bed. Hallet took her hand as she led him happily into the living room, listened to the soft lilt of her Hebrew name as Ruth called to her from the kitchen. Hallet always thought Hebrew names were expressive and beautiful—Chaim is life; Noam is rest; Aviva is springtime—all full of hope and joy and a promise yet to be realized.

"Philip, what a surprise," Ruth said tenuously as she came out to find Aviva bouncing on Hallet's lap. "Is everything all right?"

Hallet assured her it was as he stood to greet her. Ruth violated the stereotype of buxom Israeli womanhood. Her hair flowed in soft, auburn-streaked curls; her face was round and soft, almond eyes gentle; she was tall, slender, elegant—more like a Romanesque madonna than a woman who'd had to sandbag her kibbutz and wield a weighty old Enfield rifle when barely age twelve.

"I must speak with Stan," he said. "Right away, please."

"He's upstairs reading, like always. Wait here and I'll fetch him. Come 'Viva; you come, too. Time for sleep." Ruth turned back toward Hallet from halfway up the staircase. "You like something to drink, Philip? There's wine, sherry on the table."

"Nothing," Hallet replied. "Except I need to talk with Stan alone."

Ruth Bach looked at him sadly, as if she knew why Hallet had come to her home.

Stan Bach came downstairs with his eyeglasses pushed back on his head like an aviator's goggles and a thick book in his left hand. But it was his right hand that Hallet took note of. It was wrapped in thick elastic bandage.

"You don't look well at all," Bach said. "Like you haven't slept—"

"Skip it, Stan. You look a little wounded yourself."

Bach looked automatically at his bandaged hand. "Oh, this. It's nothing. I cut it working in the garden. Dangerous work for a people who've never been farmers, never worked the soil."

"The police found enough of your fingertip to make a match," Hallet said flatly, unemotionally. "If I were to ask them."

"Ah." Bach nodded. He poured himself a small glass of the

thick, red wine that sat on the table, motioned to see if Hallet wanted to join him, shrugged at Hallet's refusal. "Who else knows?" he asked as he flopped wearily on the only chair in the room that would put him face to face with his visitor.

"No one but me," Hallet said. "Which I suppose puts me at risk by telling you."

"If I'd ever wished you harm, God knows you gave me enough opportunities. Drunkenness can lead to all kind of accidents."

"So why were you out there? Why were you watching me?"

"I thought you might be having visitors I should know about. That's it. I was a bystander, literally."

"You carry a pistol to bystand?"

"What do you want of me, Hallet?" Bach asked impatiently. "What do you think I'm going to tell you?"

"First off, did you get a good look at whoever was on the rooftop?"

"I saw a rifle flash, then only his silhouette as he ran down the stairs. But I think I hit him, too."

"You did, but you're one lucky son-of-a-bitch, Stan. He's a professional, the best money can buy. At least that's what the police say."

"I'm a survivor, Hallet. We Jews survive because our journey, like our Talmud itself, is incomplete. You should know that."

"I'm learning," Hallet said. "It's taken longer than it should, but I'm learning." He reached out, deciding after all to help himself to a glass of wine, keeping his eyes all the time fixed on Bach.

"Who's running you, Stan? You working for the Mossad?"

Bach began laughing in a way that made Hallet feel naive, foolish. "Come on, friend, you're more sophisticated than that. Mossad, Mossad. Always the Mossad. Like it's the only operational service Israel runs—credited with everything, blamed for everything. Why not LAKAM, or IMI? Does all American intelligence come from the CIA? Were you working for the famous MI-Six when you started with the British?"

Bach saw that Hallet was unable to mask his surprise, and

interrupted himself. "What, you're startled that we've known about you since then? We'd be a pretty poor service if we hadn't. The surprise was, we thought you were out of the business, had quit it completely."

"So did I," Hallet admitted.

"Until Mac Clelland got to you, brought you back in?"

"And you're at the Institute to find out for what purpose," Hallet said. "You're there to cover me, man to man."

"I was at the Institute first, please remember. I went there because Macdonald Clelland was there. We knew Mac was semiretired, so we also knew he'd be looking for someone to do his fieldwork. Sure, he's been a good friend of Israel's, but there's always more to know. But if you wish to flatter yourself, I stayed at the Institute only because you came. I wasn't sure why, at first."

"Are you now?"

"Not at all. Honestly. But whatever you're doing's not kosher, that's for sure."

"I never figured you to be working a double," Hallet said. "I still can't figure why."

"Why, when I'm born an American? That's what you're asking?" said Bach, growing angry. "You who worked for those anti-Semitic bastards in Whitehall? Why is because I am a Jew *and* an American."

"You sound like Jonathan Pollard," Hallet said, not at all ready to respond to Bach's question, rhetorical or not. "Claiming he's a good Jew by selling secrets to the Israelis because he thinks they should have known them in the first place. You weren't turning him yourself, too, were you, Stan?"

"No, his handlers were elsewhere, the kind that wear uniforms all day long. Can you see me dealing with naval intelligence codes? No chance. I work with attitudes and ideas."

"You trade in them."

"I try to change them," Bach said. "For the benefit of both my countries, and my God."

"I thought we were friends, Stan."

"You are my friend. Dearly and truly, Hallet. But you are arrogant and pompous. You're also deceitful, and only too willing to help your Arab friends in ways detrimental to Israel."

"Nothing I've done, or am doing, is going to harm Israel. I swear that to you."

"You should tell me what it is, then," Bach suggested. "All I can see is that you're handling a network of Arabs who are tied directly to their governments' secret services."

"Is that what you've told your bosses, Stan? Is that why my people are ending up dead? Not only Yousef, but two others."

"I haven't blown your network," Bach insisted. "Because I'm not certain what it's designed to accomplish. Until I do . . . ?"

"Can I depend on your help if I tell you?"

"Talk to me, Hallet. Convince me you aren't helping the Arab cause."

"I'll convince you I'm not harming the Israeli one. That will have to be good enough. Because what I'm doing goes a lot farther than even you suspect."

"Beyond Mac Clelland and the Institute?"

"They don't know about it," Hallet said.

"You sure? That place leaks like the Reagan White House. Bryce Vreeland has seen to that."

"Vreeland?" Hallet said, thinking—Good God, if the leak came from inside the Institute, if Vreeland knows of Sandman, then—"Tell me what you know, Stan. Please."

"First you tell me, Hallet. Tell me what you're planning and why I should help you. But know this up front, I'm free to pass any and all of it back to Tel Aviv."

"A bargain, Stan," Hallet agreed. "Assuming we survive."

Chapter 18

Hallet stacked the computer printouts into a thin, fragile sheaf that summed up the past six years of his life, a metaphor for all he had unwittingly become. He looked over the final, most dangerous pages: details of the Lufthansa flight from Frankfurt to O'Hare, the lading and consignment numbers for its cargo, the exact location of the warehouse where it was shortly due to arrive. All that remained was to find out who would retrieve the information, how they would use it. Then it would be up to Sandman to destroy them, even if it meant destroying himself in the process.

Hallet shut down his computer for what he knew was the last time, but felt no sense of bidding farewell to his past, no sense of transition. For he'd always known this moment had to come, and he'd planned for the eventuality before arriving in Chicago, even while still listening to his control spell out the operation that night in the Georgetown safe house, the night Sandman was reborn and the double-dealing began.

Hallet turned to the telephone and booked a Royal Jordanian flight that ran nonstop from Kennedy to Amman, with a connection on to Damascus. The name he used came from the battered but still valid British escape passport the old don had sworn to him would be left operational by an otherwise stingy Foreign Office. It was another tie to a past no longer his, much like the swirl of names he'd scribbled on his desk blotter, with arrows denoting the connections that bound them—Bryce Vreeland's crisscrossed between Macdonald Clelland and Jason Kellaigh, with a new and disturbing linkage to Isabel Ortega; Clelland's umbrella control of the Institute's Fellows and a dotted but direct line to Washington's intelligence agencies; Stan Bach's, who claimed perhaps too willingly that he would risk his Israeli cover to help—all of it there in front of him, and none of it making sense of the fact that one among them, for whatever twisted reason, was employing a professional killer to destroy his network.

All Hallet could hope was that he had set the table properly with his final computer transmissions and the charade he'd acted out a half hour earlier, when he'd sprinkled himself with gin and stormed into the conference room where Clelland and Vreeland were meeting, had shouted at them in a feigned drunken rage that the Arbor Institute no longer existed as an institution of learning and understanding, but was merely a shill for Langley and a co-conspirator in murder.

It was Bryce Vreeland who seemed most taken aback by Hallet's ravings. All Clelland demanded was Hallet's silence, and he used the threat of a return to the clinic in Oak Park to try to obtain it. But Vreeland pressed harder.

"What plan?" he asked, his voice panicky. "What were these men really doing? Who were they working for?"

"You really don't know?" Hallet yelled back. "You'd no idea what Clelland and I were doing, about our cadre of Prophets? You probably don't even know that Stan Bach is on the Israelis' payroll and feeding them every drop of information coming out of this place. All news to you, Bryce, even that Mohammed Saami was poisoned, Yousef shot, and Mike Doran blown to pieces."

"That's enough!" Clelland exploded as Vreeland's look of confusion turned into one of shock.

Hallet, figuring Clelland was right, that he'd shaken their trees sufficiently to provoke a response, left them in their stunned silence. He weaved back to his office, intercepting Isabel Ortega in the corridor. As she tried to escape him, Hallet grabbed her shoulders, muttered an incomprehensible oath against treachery in her ear, planted a wet and unwelcome farewell kiss on her flushed, overheated cheek.

It took Clelland longer than Hallet had expected to arrive at his office. Hallet stared at the darkened computer monitor as Mac closed the door and calmly lighted his pipe.

"I know you too well," Clelland said. "And I've seen you really drunk and outrageous, which you weren't upstairs and aren't now. So, why the theater? What are you shooting for?"

"Shooting at, Mac. At whoever got my people killed."

"You really think it's someone here, at the Institute?"

"I know exactly who it is. I know where the leak is coming from. I'm just not sure why."

"It doesn't involve me in the least, does it Hallet? Even though we were supposed to be a team?"

Hallet shook his head sadly, knowing Clelland was too smart not to have some of the pieces already put together. "Sorry, Mac, it doesn't."

"And the men who were killed? Those boys in Iraq, the others here. Tell me."

"That's mine to live with."

Clelland mumbled what Hallet took as words of thanksgiving. "I guess I knew all along your loyalties were elsewhere. I even thought it bothered you so much that it caused your drinking to get out of hand."

"No one likes being torn in two."

"You should be used to it," Clelland said.

"I had no choice, Mac. We saw things too differently," Hallet said, which was the most he could tell him.

"But the Export file, Hallet? I have to know."

"I'm sorry, Mac. I can't tell you. Not yet."

"I know they think I'm past it, that I've gotten too old to go operational again. Perhaps I see things only as they used to be, and probably should be still. But if I can help you, if there's anything . . . ?"

"One thing," Hallet said. "I've made arrangements to go home. If I can't keep them, Agent McCaskey of the FBI will receive a message. Make sure she passes it on, because half of it's for you."

"Telling me what, Hallet? Will I ever know who ran you?"

"You'll know it's all been a bloody horrible mistake," Hallet said. He looked at the gin bottle that still sat on his desk, held it as if his hand were a scale. "Now," he said, "before I really drink this."

Clelland nodded in understanding. "I have two security men outside," he said. "I suppose it would look best if they escorted your drunken ass out of the mansion."

"You're still the best,"—Hallet laughed—"even if some people tend to forget it."

"Even when I've lost?" Clelland asked.

"We've both lost, Mac. Just pray that whoever is responsible is about to lose most of all. *Inshallah.*"

Even in his earlier, stronger days, the old man's hands shook when rage consumed him. But as Ben sat at the breakfast table and recounted his conversation with Jason Kellaigh, the old man's tremors rattled the glass he held against his fingernails.

"You were respectful?" he asked.

"But not reverential," Ben replied. "Not after Kellaigh started making noises that he's strong enough to fly on his own."

The old man shook his head, coughed up some phlegm, and looked to the deities above him. "Jason Kellaigh is as greedy as

any of them, those balance-sheet executive types. But I didn't
think he'd get involved with drugs."

"He assured me he isn't. He said it concerned the Institute
and his family. That it was personal business."

"You buy that?"

"Don't you?"

"You're here to answer me, not ask me," the old man shot
back.

"I believe him," Ben replied.

"It's insane. I mean nobody loves Arabs in this damn country.
But we got nothing against them. Nobody's bothered us."

"They will if they're setting up an organization. What else
could it be?"

"I'm tired," the old man sighed. "I'm drinking nothing but
bicarbonate of soda, eating nothing but saltines, and I'm always
tired. That I can handle. What I can't handle is disappointment.
And I'm disappointed in you. My nephew, the one I chose to
handle our affairs."

"I don't understand."

"You're the one says we have to extend our business, work
with the corporate interests, wrap things in linen instead of
newspaper. So, with the pension funds and the unions, we make
a partnership with Jason Kellaigh. We have the capital, and he
has the channels. A clean deal, says you. And look what's happening? First we have to hit a big-mouth from this union; now
we're talking about having Usher take out people we don't even
know, who did us no harm. More people than we had to do
back in the booze wars."

"I can't explain it," Ben said. "Kellaigh has always been a
man of reason, a man of caution. But now . . ."

"It's a vendetta. He feels he's been betrayed by God knows
who, and he's making them pay. I had Sid Paris in my family,
so I know."

"If Kellaigh has a score to settle, whatever it is, Usher's the
one to settle it."

The old man thought harder. "You can't find Usher."

"He's gone. Harry, the limey who's Kellaigh's muscle, says he can't locate him either. Of that, I'm less sure."

"Then we watch Harry, make him our stalking horse. He's got to meet Usher sooner or later to deliver Kellaigh's orders. Get Vinnie, and the both of you stick to him. At least that'll put us a step ahead of the cops."

"What cops? There're no police involved," said Ben.

The old man cracked an icy smile of satisfaction, as if he were still the only one around who knew the full score. "I got word outta Terre Haute," he said. "Seems that Johnny Roses had himself a visitor, that cop lieutenant named Corrigan. He's the one who did us all the damage."

"I know him. Supposed to be straight. Not on anybody's pad."

"Well, it seems Johnny is worrying about what Sid Paris is telling the Feds about their mutual business interests. Johnny can't handle any more time in the joint, so he's willing to make a deal. And his ante is Usher."

"Johnny's going to roll over on the family?"

"Naw, he doesn't know about any of this. He thinks he can get Usher for nailing Chuckie Franco, cut himself a fresh deck with the Feds. I can understand that, even forgive it. But it means that we'd better get to Usher first."

"Usher's bank," Ben said. "He's got to come up sometime for cash. We'll be there."

"None of this should be our thing," the old man said. "But I'm afraid it has to be until we settle it. I'm not letting some damn Arabs bring drugs here, set up their own organization and maybe bring the niggers in with them. Least of all, they're not going to do it through O'Hare. We own that place, and I'm not going to see it turn sour because of Jason Kellaigh or anyone else."

"I can stop it, but you realize that may mean violence from our side."

"No may's about it, Benjamin. Just wrap it up and put it behind us. Do it so I'll rest in peace."

"You're certain?"

The old man's eyes tightened into a fixed squint. "Whatever's happening, we settle it ourselves. *Nostro campo, nostra città.* Our airport, our town. Nobody screws with them."

Since Jerry De Lorenzo's ascension to deputy chief, his appearances on the floors beneath his own were as rare in police headquarters as a decent cup of coffee. Nonetheless, he strode off the elevator and, after a perfunctory rap with his weighty officer's ring, into Jack Corrigan's office.

"Top o' the morning, Jack."

"Likewise, Chief," Corrigan replied, thinking: Jesus, he's in his benevolent Bing Crosby mood, like everyone's going his way, all out of character and saccharine-sweet.

"Well, credit where credit is due. I'll be the first one to say it. You did all right running our guys as cabdrivers. A real long shot, Jack, but you brought it home."

"Joe Rivera brought it home, Chief. Pushed the envelope all the way out."

"That's why I love the department, what makes it the best. Here we got a Mexican cop—"

"Puerto Rican, Chief. Rivera's family is from Ponce."

"Whatever," Jerry De shrugged. "We got this *Hispanic* cop who spends half his career busting hookers but still has the balls to volunteer for most hazardous duty. Out there, one on one with a serial killer."

"All the cabs were wired with distress beepers, and a dozen backup units were working that triangle. Rivera wasn't alone."

"He was inside the taxi, Jack. *Mano a mano.*"

"I sense another hero in the making," Corrigan said.

"Every cop on the street's a hero to me. But Rivera gives me something the press will understand. You agree? Everything about Rivera's legit, right? Family man and all, no major vices?"

"Joe has two kids," Corrigan said. "But he and his wife are separated. Maybe temporary."

"Could be this will reunite the Rivera family unit, seeing Joe on television, getting his well-earned commendation."

Of course, Corrigan realized, noting the hint of face powder that cut the glare on his boss's brow. Jerry De's assuming his most smarmy media persona. Why the hell else would he deign to visit him? "You need some backgrounding for your press conference," he said. It wasn't a question.

De Lorenzo checked the slim Piaget watch he wore upside down on his left wrist. "Whatever you can give me in six minutes flat. Everything you have on the shooter."

"Cal Bostic's people found the second gun in his apartment. It's a match with the one good piece of slug we pulled from the third driver. Same for the twenty-two he had with him."

"Nice and tidy. The way it should be. I'm having a little problem explaining motivation, though. I can't make him sound too pathetic, get too much sympathy."

"Look, Chief," Corrigan said, "his brother got himself blown up with the Marines in Beirut. After that, his mother expresses her grief by tying a clothesline around her neck and jumping off the back porch. Then this kid, who was never a paragon of stability to begin with, goes bonkers and decides to settle the score for America by bumping off Iranian and Arab cabdrivers. Anybody that nuts deserves some sympathy."

"Hey, I don't want to enter his plea in front of the camera. I say all that, he walks on insanity."

"Jesus, he *is* insane."

"Let's leave that to the public defender and the judge. I'll just say it appears to be a matter of revenge. Any questions that go deeper, it's pretrial publicity and I don't want to prejudice the jury. Sound all right?"

"Perfect."

"And next time, Jack, something even approaching this comes up, you make goddamn sure I'm in on it from minute one. This one worked out, but that's only because you're one lucky Irish son-of-a-bitch."

Corrigan decided to keep his own counsel about Hallet and McCaskey as Jerry De Lorenzo backed out of his office to face the bright lights and clicking shutters. Lucky Irishman, indeed. He was just another Harp when he arrived from County Clare, all of thirteen years old; just another city Mick when he took the only option he had after high school and joined the Marines. It was only thanks to Margie's father, a ward superintendent from the old patronage school, that he even got on the cops. Some luck. Hell, maybe he still had a chance to change it. With the kids gone, he could take Margie back to the old house, have her taste the oysters that bred in the cold waters coming down off the Burren, with Michael and Maeve and Aunt Eithne and all his remaining family to pour the stout and poteen. Yeah, maybe. But not until he found himself one more psychopath, the one they called Usher, and uncovered another motive for murder. A motive he was certain Doctor Philip Hallet knew, and probably McCaskey, too, the way she'd sounded when she made her cryptic telephone call:

"Hallet's just left me," she'd said. "By the way he was acting, I'd say he's ready to make his move."

"How was he acting?"

"Like he wanted to say good-bye and couldn't. All that 'I can't be reached for a while, I'm asking you to be patient with me' stuff. Except I'm not going to be patient. I think we can nail him."

"For what?" Corrigan still wondered.

"Get yourself some blank warrants, and let's go find out."

The tavern reeked of stale beer and, in the rear booth where Harry had been instructed to sit, the smell was worsened by a tinge of urine. Two hillbillies were getting steadily hotter at each other as they began their fourth game of nine-ball on the quarter-a-rack pool table; the bartender was a big-bellied Pole whose acne-scarred face was frozen into a perpetual sneer. He noticed Harry's empty schooner and made a feeble wave of inquiry for a refill. Harry checked his watch, figured waiting an hour was more than enough, and declined. He wasn't about to spend another minute in a neighborhood that made Brixton look as fashionable as Chelsea.

"Anyone comes in looking for me, tell him to try again," Harry told the bartender.

"Who's 'you,' pal?"

"I'm the one who was waiting," Harry snarled back. He saw the bartender's fist clench, then relax as Harry's hand came out of his pocket with a double sawbuck instead of a sap, a gun, or whatever else the bartender was expecting.

The street was empty and Harry's car was still outside, seemingly intact, wheel covers and hood ornament in place, tires attached. Why the devil Usher had picked this spot was beyond him. Some kind of paranoid test, maybe, to see if Harry could function as well in the West Side ghetto as he could in the splendor of the north suburbs. Jesus.

He climbed into the car and had just gotten the ignition key set when he felt the gun barrel pressed against the base of his skull.

"One move I don't like, and you're history," Usher said. "So get those hands on the dashboard. Slowly."

"Are you mad?"

"You bet your ass I'm mad. Raging mad. You set me up the other night."

"What are you talking about?"

"Somebody was waiting for me after I made the hit. Somebody who knew where I'd be and when I'd be there. I caught a slug in my wing because of it."

Harry took a deep breath and put his patience to the test, knowing that he'd have to go along with Usher and, when they were through, he'd have to resist taking away his pistol and breaking his arm.

"Okay, you're pissed off," Harry said. "But screw your brain back in for a minute and consider this—if I wanted you taken out, why would I let you finish the contract and then do it? I'd be paying twice, wouldn't I?"

"So who was it? Some guy walking his dog decided to pop off at me with an automatic?"

"You know, your regular employers are a little upset, " Harry said. "Ben came to see my people about it."

"What's his problem?"

"You'd best discuss that with Ben, if you care to take the chance. If you don't, which would be my advice, why don't you put away that pea-shooter and recognize that you're full time on my payroll from now on."

"Forget it," Usher said. "All I want from you is enough cash for me to get out of town and cover expenses until I get my money transferred. If somebody's looking for me, that means they'll be waiting at my bank."

"You don't walk out until we give you the walking papers. And you get nothing from me until we finish what we contracted for up front. Which means one more shot. After that, we'll set you up with cash, papers, whatever you need."

"You think I'm crazy? Somebody was on to me the last time, now you want to try again?"

"This time, I'll be with you."

"I don't work with partners, pal."

"You'll work as I tell you to work. Call me your assistant, if you'd prefer. But if you want Ben and the family off your case, and you want what we owe you, you'd better do it my way. So, I'll need to know how to find you."

"Wherever I am is off limits," Usher insisted, thinking to himself that the big dumb Englishman might enjoy a little piece of Brian himself. "I call you."

"I'll give you a number," Harry agreed. "Check in with me twice daily. Let's say noon and six in the evening." He scribbled on a scrap of notepaper and handed it back to Usher. "Now, where can I drop you?"

"Nowhere, pal," Usher said. "I'm just gone."

Usher ducked out quickly, cut into an alley between the tavern and a pizza takeout. Harry kicked the car into gear and gave only a passing look at the Mercedes SL parked across the street, wondering what it was doing in a neighborhood like this, and not seeing through the tinted glass that Ben and Vinnie were sitting inside it.

Chapter 19

Hallet swung the rented station wagon past the sign that welcomes visitors to O'Hare International Airport. The guard manning the security gate at the cargo terminals barely glanced at the paperwork Hallet held against the rain-splattered window and waved him through with a casual flick of his wrist. And why not, Hallet thought. Anyone stupid enough to try a heist at O'Hare would have to answer to people who, unencumbered by a slowly turning judiciary, play a lot rougher than the local authorities.

He steered down a blacktop roadway, squinted into the floodlights and the heavy rain as if cataracts had fractured his vision. Finally he found the parking lot, drove through the small gate in its chain-link fence, cut his headlights. No other cars in sight, no sounds other than his and Stan Bach's breathing.

The warehouse was a two-story rectangle of cinder blocks capped with a sloping roof of corrugated metal. Certainly not the type of construction one would use for cold storage, but since the shipment had been precleared by cooperative U.S. Customs agents in Frankfurt, the aptness of its final destination mattered not at all to the teamster who'd delivered it from the Lufthansa cargo terminal.

Hallet unlocked the door and let Bach enter first. Except for the single row of freight containers painted as brightly as a circus train, the warehouse was empty.

"Business must be bad for whoever owns this place," Bach said.

"Exactly," Hallet said. "Small freight line that's fighting Chapter Twelve and will take whatever overflow is available without asking questions."

Bach pointed to the iron staircase that led to a trio of small offices that hung like skyboxes from the exposed girders. "I can see every inch of the place from up there," he said.

"Fine," said Hallet. "Want to go through it again?"

"No need. I'll come through for you," Bach said as he un-shouldered the black case containing the carbine, expertly cleared the breech, snapped a magazine in place, chambered a round.

"Just remember, dead men can't tell tales," Hallet said.

"You think I want to shoot this thing?" Bach said as he slung his weapon and headed for the stairs.

Hallet prepared himself for what would be the hardest part: waiting. He walked to the delivered containers. Brought in just a few hours earlier, they already sat in puddles of water from the condensation that dripped from their sidewalls. He looked at their stenciled lettering—Hams of Westphalia. Produce of West Germany.

He unsealed, unlocked one container. The smell of the smoky, cured pork hit him first; then, with its ice shield melting in the steamy warehouse, came the ammoniac smell of rot. He pulled out several soggy boxes of hams, slid them out of his way, extracted the wooden crates that had been concealed behind them. It was a deadly inventory: Czech-manufactured subma-chine guns, rocket-propelled grenades, small blocks of Semtex C-4 explosive that looked as harmless as slabs of cheese. He jimmied the lids off the arms crates and left their contents out in plain sight, like a product display at a weapons trade fair.

Hallet realized he was perspiring heavily by the time he found the other half of his shipment in the third container down the line: two moisture-proof plastic boxes stuck behind the fecund hams, each of them containing five kilos of the finest heroin the growers of Lebanon's Bekáa Valley were able to produce.

He looked upward at the offices in search of Bach but couldn't locate him. Probably better that he's out of sight, Hallet reckoned, as he checked the pistol in his belt and stepped behind the containers to wait for whoever was coming to kill him.

He never even heard their footsteps.

"I suggest you stand exactly where you are."

Hallet knew immediately the voice was English, more from the inflection than any accent. He obeyed it.

"Now, turn around. Slowly, please. Hands in plain sight."

Hallet opened his arms in a wide, supplicating manner. He moved cautiously, as if making his about-face turn in slow motion, and saw there were two of them. Gratefully just two, so that Stan could cover them both when he gave him the signal.

"Very good, Doctor Hallet. I appreciate your being so cooperative," said the Englishman, his huge mitt wrapped around a Beretta 92 automatic. He was the larger of the pair, thickly muscled, perhaps a little overtrained but certainly in shape to handle any eventuality. The other man was sandy blond-haired and a few inches shorter, more wiry of frame. But, when Hallet looked into his cobalt blue eyes, he appeared the far more menacing.

"What's going on here?" asked Hallet. "Are you cops?"

"Call it a citizen's arrest," said the blond. He stepped forward, gave Hallet a thorough, professional frisking, and smirked at the small pistol he removed from Hallet's belt.

"Doctor Hallet, you surprise me. Not what I'd call a tool of scholarship. And all of this, too," said the Englishman, waving his Beretta at the row of containers and exposed weaponry. Hallet wondered what about him made the Englishman seem vaguely familiar.

"If you're not cops, what do you want?" he asked as indignantly as he could in the face of the Englishman's pistol.

"We ask the questions," the blond said. "Like how many of your Arab friends are you expecting tonight?"

Okay, strike one, Hallet thought. They not only knew the place, but also the time. That meant it was his own messages from the Institute that had been compromised, and that no matter who turned out to be the source, Sandman was finished.

"You have it all wrong." Hallet spoke mostly to the Englishman, who seemed to be the easier of the two to work on. "I only came here to meet—"

In an instant, the blond's hand came out of his pocket and the blade of a knife flashed open; in another, he had Hallet by the throat and backed him into the cold, wet metal of a container. "You little fuck," he snarled. "We know what's coming down here. We—"

"Usher!" the Englishman hollered. "Let him go! Now!"

Usher released his grip and threw the Englishman a look that made Hallet shiver as much as had the knife blade.

"Can't you see what he's trying to do?" he asked Usher. "He's trying to draw us out, see how much we know. Which means that, early as we are, he might not be alone. Right, Doctor Hallet? Are there third parties lurking about?"

Usher already had his knife refolded, a pistol replacing it in his hand. He'd leaned back against the cover of some stacked cartons and, with feet apart and arms raised, was in a well-balanced firing position as he scanned the wide horizons of the warehouse.

It was too late.

The first bullet hit Usher squarely in the chest, which appeared to implode under the impact. A large bubble of blood rose from the startled mouth; the last breath Usher would ever take sounded like a hiss.

"No!" Hallet screamed at the muzzle flash he'd seen coming from the catwalk. "Stan, no!"

It didn't matter. By the time Hallet heard the rifle's report, another slug had slammed into Usher's collapsing thorax with enough force to flatten him against the side of the aluminum freight container.

Hallet saw that the Englishman had dropped for cover with the first shot. He looked at Hallet with eyes more sad than enraged. "Why?"

"I didn't . . ." Hallet began. But the sight of the Englishman raising his Beretta precluded further explanation. Hallet tried to dive for cover of his own, but the slippery pool of Usher's blood took away all his traction; he skidded and fell helplessly next to Usher's body.

The Englishman threw Hallet an eerie grin as he sighted in on him. But he had to lift up just a little to make his shot clear Usher's corpse and the cargo dolly. It was a fraction too much. As the Englishman's head rose above the top of the container, it turned into a fireball of gore and bony shrapnel as the single shot that found it tore away a huge section of scalp and a mush of brain.

Hallet, paralyzed, stared at the carnage surrounding him. As the explosions from the rifle fire dimmed in his ears, he heard the footsteps scampering along the catwalk and down the iron staircase. Stan Bach. The bastard. It was Bach all along. For the Israelis? For the company? For himself? Damn him.

Hallet reached over the bloody pile of flesh the Englishman had called Usher, retrieved his deadly little Sauer, and waited for Bach to appear. He wondered whether he could resist shooting him long enough to discover the reason for his treachery. But all he heard in the sudden stillness that hung over the battlefield was the sound of the fire door at the rear of the warehouse slamming shut.

He forced himself to his feet, still skidding uncertainly in Usher's blood. He had finally hit full speed in pursuit when he found Stan Bach's body at the foot of the staircase.

Oh God. No.

Hallet leaned over his friend, rolled him over so he could examine the wound. There was none, and the pulse that Hallet found in Bach's carotid artery was strong and regular.

"Whoa," Bach said as he began to regain consciousness.

"What happened?"

"Somebody cracked me. Felt like a pipe when it hit my neck."

"Did you see him?"

"Nothing, not even stars."

"Damn," Hallet swore, "I'll never catch him."

"What about . . . ?"

"There are two men dead by the cargo," Hallet said. "Whoever slugged you dropped both of them."

Bach's eyes glazed as he stared at Hallet's bloodstained clothing. "You're not hit?"

Hallet shook his head. "Can you get up? Move?"

"I'll be fine," Bach said. "Maybe you can catch sight of him coming around the terminal lot. Go ahead, try it."

"Right. You make your own way out and lay low. I'll be in touch."

Hallet got going, hit the door at full stride. The second he ripped it open, he saw the gun barrel aimed squarely at his gut.

"Freeze it right there!" Jack Corrigan ordered him.

Hallet stepped back inside the warehouse as Corrigan entered, his service revolver still pointed at Hallet's midsection. The next one inside was MaryAgnes McCaskey. Before she could speak, her hand reflexively rose to stifle the sickness in her throat.

"Sufferin' Jesus," Corrigan shuddered when his gaze followed hers to the twisted, grotesque corpses. He spun Hallet around with his free hand and found the handcuffs that dangled from the rear of his belt.

"What are you doing?" Hallet raged. "Don't stop me."

"Consider yourself stopped," Corrigan said. "And under arrest."

*　　　　*　　　　*

270

Vinnie climbed the long carpeted staircase and knocked softly before entering the room. The old man was in his bed, midway between sitting up and lying down; Vinnie heard the soft hiss of oxygen and saw he was wearing a clear plastic mask.

"I thought you'd want to know," he began. The old man nodded and motioned him closer. He made a gurgling sound beneath the mask, which Vinnie took as his sign to proceed.

"Everything's taken care of. I saw to it myself."

"Usher?" the old man wheezed.

"And Kellaigh's man. They're both permanent."

The old man's eyes brightened as he feebly stripped away his mask. "Anyone else?"

"There was no need," Vinnie said. "There were two more of them hanging around. I clobbered one to get into position, took away his rifle. The other one owes me a major favor, like his life."

"Do we know them, these two guys?"

"They weren't Arabs. Or muscle. Clean-cut types—probably Kellaigh's people, too. They had these cases of guns and were waiting for Usher and Harry to pick them up. But I only took care of the two you wanted. No sense adding to our troubles, give the newspapers another Saint Valentine's massacre."

"That's smart. You were thinking," the old man said. "Tomorrow, I send Ben to see Kellaigh. He will conclude our business with him, business we never should have started in the first place. You deal with people who aren't your kind, there's always problems."

"You want me to go along?"

"No, I want you to go down to Terre Haute. You see Johnny Roses and tell him I hold nothing against him. But he never talks to the cops again. Not ever, even if he thinks it's only hurting Sid Paris."

"There were local cops arriving when I split," Vinnie said. "I saw their car."

"Fine, they can clean things up. Maybe that'll get the message on the street—that nobody brings stuff into this city that we don't give a blessing."

"I'll call Detroit, tell them we've finished our end of the Mike Doran thing," Vinnie said.

"Tomorrow, we call together. If God wills I survive this night," the old man said, motioning Vinnie to turn up the oxygen valve. "You did fine, Vincent. With all his colleges and education, Ben can learn a thing or two from you. Now go."

Vinnie nodded and backed out of the room silently, not wanting to disturb the old man's painful repose, happy at his own prospects for a brighter future.

Hallet swirled the cup of cold coffee that Jack Corrigan had delivered before steaming out of the interrogation room to take the call that Hallet knew would come. MaryAgnes McCaskey circled nervously around the marred table like someone playing musical chairs: tense, alert, ready to pounce the instant the music ceased.

"Relax," Hallet advised her. "Everything's going to work out."

McCaskey stopped in her tracks and glowered down at the seated Hallet. "Why couldn't you have been honest with me?" she snarled.

"I don't know all the answers myself," Hallet countered. "As for honesty, you gave me your word you'd keep off my tail. Then you and Bulldog Drummond follow me to the warehouse. That's what you call being partners?"

"So incredible," McCaskey said, as if she hadn't heard a word Hallet had spoken. "I thought you were working for the Arabs. Corrigan thought you were smuggling drugs. Madness."

Hallet drank down the rest of the coffee, wondered how they could make it weak and bitter at the same time. "You're pretty good, though," he said. "I thought I'd double-backed every which way to Sunday. I never saw you once."

"We didn't have to follow you," McCaskey said. "I had some surveillance equipment in my car trunk, left from another case I worked with Corrigan. When he started using beepers to cover the policemen driving cabs, I knew this gear would help me keep track of you. It's what you get for renting your car a day ahead of time."

"I should have guessed."

"No, you shouldn't have. Not if you trusted me," McCaskey railed. "What did you get by going out there alone but a pair of bodies blown to bits by another assassin we can't locate? Maybe we could have stopped it. And besides, damn it, maybe we saved your life."

"You did fine. You'll still get promoted."

"That's not all I care about."

Hallet, wanting to believe her, didn't press the issue. He knew he would finally have to tell her all of it, Sandman included. But not until the last piece was in place, and not until they were a long way from police headquarters.

Corrigan barged back into the room before Hallet could make his offer. He threw a bundle of clothing on the interview table— cotton chino trousers, gold shirt, tan windbreaker. "Better put these on," he told Hallet. "You look like a hunter who's just finished dressing a deer."

"Sounds like I'm free to leave," Hallet said.

Corrigan turned away and spoke to McCaskey. "All the powder and particle tests came up negative. I don't know what the hell he had going on in there, but Hallet sure didn't fire any weapons."

"You made the phone call," Hallet said. It wasn't a question, really. Not if Corrigan was ready to cut him loose.

"And you get to walk out of here," Corrigan said.

"Everything's covered at the warehouse?"

"They got the bodies out. And all the goodies. Whoever the hell your people are, they moved fast. I'm just praying we're all on the same side."

"Believe it," Hallet said.

"You're one smug son-of-a-bitch," Corrigan growled. "Local cops don't have much clout with your kind of Chinamen. But I'm gonna tell you something, pal. I don't care if you've got the Joint Chiefs of Staff, the National Security Council, and the President himself in your corner—you ever pull a trigger in my city, you'll take the fullest fall ever. You got that?"

"It wasn't supposed to be that way, Lieutenant," Hallet said. "I just went to verify that the goods had arrived. Pickup wasn't scheduled for another day. I don't know who did the shooting, or even who was shot."

"I wonder," McCaskey said, simmering.

"We can't pin down the big guy," Corrigan said, "the one you said was English. The other one was someone I've been looking for myself—a syndicate hood named Bobby Usery, known as the Usher and tied directly to the old man and our local crime family."

"The syndicate?" Hallet asked incredulously.

"Well, well." Corrigan grinned. "I finally know something you don't. Unless you can come up with a connection. Like maybe the mob is doing some more of the government's dirty work?"

"I have nothing for you, Lieutenant," said Hallet. "It's something I hadn't even begun to consider."

"Nothing for me?" Corrigan fumed. "How about a warehouse full of smuggled weapons and primo quality smack, not to mention two very shot-up stiffs? How am I gonna explain that to my chief?"

"Probably the outfit got wind of the drug shipment, and they decided to cut themselves in," Hallet said.

"I'd say the old man wanted to interdict delivery," McCaskey said. "Drugs are one thing his family won't deal. So maybe he was trying to do Uncle Sam a favor and keep all that smack off the streets."

"Why don't we take a vote on what I'll report?" Corrigan said.

"You're not reporting anything," Hallet said. "Because, as

you and your superiors will find out shortly, none of this ever happened."

"Philip."

The voice sounded miles away, as if drifting in a windstorm.

"Philip, please."

Hallet came to slowly. He felt the damp chill of his clothing, smelled the warm cottony aroma of the thick quilts that MaryAgnes McCaskey had thrown over him when the tremors began; log cabin quilts, she'd called them, stitched like Islamic scrollwork in an infinite array of right angles, much like the fabric of his life.

"Here," McCaskey said, offering him a tumbler. "Try to drink this."

Hallet sipped the glass tenuously: orange juice, straight. "A little gin would help immensely," he said.

"You drank every drop there was. The cupboard's bare."

"I spilled a lot, too," Hallet said.

"Either way, it's gone," McCaskey said. She wore loose jeans and a sweatshirt so large it fell past her hips. "It won't solve a thing, you know—drinking and brooding, locking me out of your thoughts."

"There's nothing left to think about."

"Yes, there is. I've had a day to think things through, and none of the pieces dovetail. You probably think you've fooled Jack Corrigan, too, but he's letting go only because he knows he's out of his league. I'm not that smart."

"You're very smart. But can you bring back the dead?"

"No, but I can help you."

"All part of the job?" Hallet wondered. "Even into the bedroom?"

"At first, or so I thought," McCaskey admitted. "You never gave me many reasons to like you or trust you."

"I didn't have any to give," Hallet said.

"Doesn't matter now," she shrugged. "I've crossed the thin line between affliction and affection. You see, I do care about you. Believe me."

Hallet pulled himself into a sitting position and tossed off the quilts with trembling hands. It was time to tell her as much as he could.

"The British taught me to do a lot more than read the Koran, things far more devious than I told you before," he began. "Their intelligence people recruited me at Oxford, trained me as an operative, spliced me into their Middle East daisy chain. I ran a counterespionage network for them in Iraq and Syria—a nasty bunch of bandits, actually, who'd sell their sisters for two dinar and their countries for a case of Scotch. Anyway, after one too many people died, one too many bombs exploded, I quit cold, came back to the States, starting teaching."

"Happily?" McCaskey wondered.

"I thought so, for a while. I didn't much like the world then, didn't want to function in it. So I crawled into the cocoon of academia and tried by being obtuse to be humane."

"Until you went to work for Macdonald Clelland and the Institute," McCaskey guessed. "When you and he put together your Prophets."

"Except Clelland never knew what I was really doing. I betrayed him, too, you see, when I took over Sandman."

"Sandman?"

"It was my cipher," Hallet said. "A cryptonym from my old days with the Brits. They thought it rather humorous—my running a network of sleeper agents in the desert. Very old school stuff. The Americans knew about Sandman, too, and we resurrected the name when we put together a plan that transcended what Clelland thought was my work with the Prophets."

"Who's the 'we' this time?"

"Someone in Washington who is very sensitive about covert intelligence operations, especially when they involve shipping weapons and drugs into this country. I mean, if selling arms to Iran causes a scandal . . . well, you can imagine."

Hallet tried the orange juice again, got a swallow down as McCaskey lighted a cigarette. Hallet took it from her hand, had his first drag in years, realized he still relished it.

"What Sandman did," Hallet went on, "was recruit Arab agents who were operating here in the States. I didn't turn them around for Uncle Sam; each one remained loyal to his government, his masters, whatever. But they all had one goal in common—to find out all they could about a group of terrorists that calls itself Al-Ahzab. It's a Koranic reference to uniting all the tribes of Islam. You see, if Al-Ahzab could bring together the most ruthless, the most dedicated terrorists in a single force, without regard to nationality or sect, the destiny of the Middle East would end up in its control. No government wants that to happen, certainly not the U.S. or Israel, and least of all the Arab nations themselves."

"But what does Al-Ahzab have to do with smuggling drugs and weapons?" McCaskey asked.

"It wants to carry its war with the United States to American soil, to attack us here. One way to do that is to dispatch agents, ship them weapons and explosives, and turn them loose. But an easier way would be to arm dissident groups that are already here and spoiling for a fight—all the disenfranchised and dissatisfied, from professional left-wing fanatics like the Japanese who struck in Rome, to urban street gangs who have no great love for the American way. Al-Ahzab would provide them arms and select their targets. The gangs would execute their orders and get paid in the one commodity that never decreases in value on the streets—good old Bekáa Valley heroin."

"Like the El Rukns tried," McCaskey said. "The gang we busted."

"The El Rukns weren't part of anything so formidable," Hallet said. "They were just a bunch of punks who offered to assassinate whatever politicians Qadhafi wanted killed if the Libyans would supply them drugs. A great concept, but poorly executed."

"The way you were operating," McCaskey said, "I actually

thought you'd sold out and were working for the Arabs."

"But I *was* working for the Arabs, at least in part," Hallet said. "That's why I had to have deep cover. I was working for the handful of Arab leaders who want to see terrorism stopped and the massacre of innocents ended—the same people I got to know when I worked for the British. They helped set me up with their agents here, and together we were supposed to penetrate the Al-Ahzab network on both sides of the ocean."

"Al-Ahzab must have found out what you were doing," McCaskey said. "That's why they went out and hired a professional gun to eliminate your agents."

"They had to hire from the mob?" Hallet asked.

"Suppose Usher took their business on his own, without an imprimatur from the old man. That's why the family turned on him at the warehouse. They'd tried it once when he shot Yousef, and they got it right the second time."

Hallet figured he had to keep Stan Bach protected a while longer, so he let McCaskey's supposition pass.

"That still doesn't explain how anyone found out about my people."

"Yes, it does," McCaskey insisted. "It all makes sense. Your man in Detroit, Mike Doran—our records show he was tied into the Detroit crime family. Maybe they found out he was importing weapons and drugs on his own. That's their territory, and Doran was trespassing. So, on a reference from Chicago, they hired Usher to eliminate everyone connected to Doran. When it got too heavy, they knew they had to eliminate their own enforcer to protect themselves. No live assassin, no living witnesses."

"Can't be," Hallet argued. "How did they know who my other people were?"

"From Mike Doran."

"But he didn't know either. The only one who controlled the network was me."

"So you may think," McCaskey went on. "But your people were members of the same tribe—and I mean intelligence services, not just Arabs. Maybe they talked to each other more than you suspected. So, when the mob got ready to take out Doran, they made him talk first, made him name names."

"It's tough to talk when you're sitting on top of a large charge of plastique," Hallet said. "The leak has to be elsewhere."

"Why do academics always want to make everything more oblique than it really is? Unless," McCaskey realized at last, "you think someone at the Institute is involved?"

"I know exactly who it is," Hallet said. "With Usher dead, we've gotten our killer. Now we'd better confront our betrayer."

Chapter 20

Hallet sat motionless on his edge of the bed and watched MaryAgnes McCaskey enjoy the sleep that had eluded him all night. Her breathing was deep and regular, her eyes closed peacefully; she looked almost childlike as she slept. But there had been nothing childlike about their earlier lovemaking. There had been a certain violence to it, in fact—a constant thrashing, roughly switching positions, as if they were both in a rage to discover all the ways to enjoy each other. But joy eluded them, despite Hallet's luxurious exploration of her body and its secret tastes and pleasures, despite McCaskey's loud, quivering orgasms. It was, Hallet knew, the absence of true intimacy, as if too many ghosts were present, watching them like performers in some sordid sex show. It made Hallet feel certain that, when the day was over and their dreadful business concluded, MaryAgnes McCaskey would walk out of his life forever.

He touched her cheek, her breast, her nipple. She made a murmuring sound and buried her head deeper in the pillow; still asleep, still eluding him.

Hallet wrapped himself in McCaskey's terry robe and went quietly to her kitchen. He brewed a double measure of instant

281

coffee, drank a double shot from McCaskey's last bottle of Scotch. It rumbled through his system like paregoric, burning his empty stomach, knotting his guts. A second measure, and he began to calm sufficiently to empty the coffee into a cup and to dial the telephone.

"You're all right, then. Thank God," Stan Bach said. "You got out, too."

"We're both fine," said Hallet.

"I managed to hide. But when I saw the police cars . . ."

"Taken care of," Hallet said, knowing that it still wasn't. "None of it goes public."

"The two men?"

"You don't want to know, Stan. But we're finished. Out of it."

"I'm still shaking, damn it," Bach said. "I was out cold through the whole thing, and I'm still shaking."

"You're not alone."

"Look, Hallet, how finished is it? With the Institute, with Clelland?"

"That, too," Hallet replied. "There'll be no repercussions, no diplomatic breast-beating with your masters in Tel Aviv. But your cover is blown dead away. It's my fault and I'm sorry."

"No need," Bach said through a deep sigh that sounded like relief. "Hitler said conscience was merely a Jewish invention. Besides, I'm leaving. I have a standing offer back at Hebrew University that I'm finally going to take. Ruth has always wanted to go home. Who knows, I might like getting back to the cabala and the more occult elements of our theosophy. I'm a Jew, after all. And the more I see of this planet, the more I realize that Israel's where I belong. You were right—my war's not over yet."

"You mean your peace hasn't yet arrived."

"I suppose so. There's a real need in Israel for a voice that says all Arabs aren't terrorists and murderers, who understands that by treating them only as enemies, we've become the enemy ourselves."

"Do it, Stan. For both of us. Because I'm through."

"Are you, Hallet? Are you going to leave this rotten business once and for all?"

"Would I lie to you?"

"You have all along, damn it. But that's what we're paid to do. I hope it goes well for you."

"You, too, Stan. Be seeing you."

"The Mayer Institute, Hallet. I know people there. You could do good work. Think it over, will you? Next year in Jerusalem?"

Hallet drained the bottle of Scotch and tossed it into the trash.

"Do you have to, Philip? Is it that bad to be sober?" McCaskey asked him. She was standing in the doorway wearing a man's dress shirt that Hallet noticed was several sizes larger than his. All trace of sleep were gone from the onyx eyes that glared at him.

"I have to come down," Hallet said, aware that the liquor was already taking hold of him. "I'm wound up in knots, and I have to come down."

"You have to stay sober," McCaskey insisted.

"When I'm ready. When it's finally over."

"You're feeling guilty, aren't you?"

"Guilt's impossible for me," Hallet said. "You can't feel guilt without a conscience, and I put mine on hold when I started Sandman."

"Perhaps we can resurrect it."

"My part is finished," Hallet said. "It's your case from here on in."

"Then let's close it," McCaskey said, stopping when Hallet's back was turned to make sure the snub-nose Colt revolver was tucked securely in her purse.

Jason Kellaigh himself swung open the huge front door to his mansion. Hallet looked for a glint of surprise in his face, but found only old age and loneliness.

"Ah, Philip. I was expecting you. Come inside, please," Kellaigh said, adding as he eyed MaryAgnes McCaskey, "the both of you."

They followed him to his study; Kellaigh paused by the bar cart and pointed at the cluster of crystal decanters.

"Nothing for me," Hallet said.

"No, I don't suppose so. Very good." Kellaigh poured something from a captain's decanter and carried the glass to his well-appointed desk—probably the most comfortable place for him, Hallet guessed, where whatever control he had left in his life could be administered. McCaskey gave Hallet an impatient look. Was this simply a social call, or shouldn't they proceed immediately? Hallet reassured her with a subtle nod and thin smile.

"This is Special Agent McCaskey," Hallet said.

"Justice Department, FBI," McCaskey said automatically, reaching for her credentials until Kellaigh waved her off.

"I was expecting a different law to be represented today," Kellaigh said. "As I'm certain Doctor Hallet can attest."

"I'm all we need," McCaskey replied.

"I suppose you are," Kellaigh replied, his eyes bordering on mist as he looked at Hallet. "Harry is dead, isn't he?" he asked.

Hallet nodded. "It took me a while to place him, out of uniform, as it were. But when everything else started coming together . . ."

"Harry Dawson loved our family," Kellaigh said. "He was a rough man, but his loyalty never wavered. Not even until death."

"Jason, why?" asked Hallet.

Kellaigh drained his snifter and seemed to gain a second wind and new resolve. "Oh, Philip, you're much too intelligent to look for a simple answer. You'll find my reasons hard to believe, coming from someone who has done so much to promote understanding between ourselves and the East—done so much for peace, and all I've reaped is death."

"I'll allow you to mourn Harry," Hallet said, "but there were three good people murdered by the assassin you hired, the one called Usher."

"Your people were the assassins, Hallet. They were spies and terrorists, all dedicated to waging war against the United States. Don't you dare compare them with Harry Dawson, not in the same breath."

"I thought that's what you believed," said Hallet. "Whoever uncovered my network presented them to you as spies."

"We understood your loyalties all along," Kellaigh said. "From the very day you joined the Institute, Bryce Vreeland warned me that your heart was at one with Islam. That made me admire you, until I discovered you were betraying Macdonald Clelland and using his trust to work against us."

"Clelland only knew half of it," Hallet said. "I suppose when he somehow found out about my other activities, he came and told you. And you started the killings."

"You're wrong. Mac Clelland had no part in this."

"Just you and the mob, then?" McCaskey asked.

"A deal with the devil is always a bad bargain," Kellaigh admitted. "That much you both understand."

"I understand that five people are dead," Hallet said. "Three of mine, one of yours, and a professional killer. They're dead because of you. For some mad reason you've yet to explain."

"What led me from peace to murder? What leads anyone? Grief, and hatred for those who caused it," Kellaigh said, his eyes welling again. "There was an attack in England. Do you remember it?"

"A quartet of commandos attacked an airport terminal," Hallet recalled.

"A seven-year-old boy was killed. His name was Mickey, and he was my grandson—the heir to everything I've worked for, everything generations of my family have created. He was life itself to me."

McCaskey appeared to soften her resolve as she lowered her eyes in deference to Kellaigh's pain.

"I never knew, Jason. I don't think anyone did," Hallet said.

"The point is, no one cared. A few weeks pass, and it's easily, conveniently forgotten. Our government writes off the loss like just another bankrupt savings-and-loan."

"But, Jason, surely *your* grandson," Hallet wondered.

"He was never identified as a Kellaigh. Our family has always worried about kidnapping. We had one, you know, back in the thirties. It didn't end as tragically as the Lindberghs' or Bobby Greenleaf's. My family got the boy back."

"You were the victim," McCaskey knew.

"Yes. A terrifying experience that lives with you forever," Kellaigh said. "So when my grandson went to Europe—he was my daughter's boy, you see, and her husband manages our overseas operations—we created a new, inconspicuous identity for the family, one that masked their relationship to me and the corporation. It didn't matter. He was killed when a hand grenade exploded in his face. Seven years old, Hallet, and blown to pieces. God help us all."

"So you wanted revenge against the people responsible," McCaskey said. "When you found out Doctor Hallet was involved with Arab intelligence agents, you—"

Kellaigh gave her a wave-off that was somewhere between imperious and conciliatory.

"I what?" he said. "Became a terrorist myself? Maybe so, because it was the only thing I could do. How long can we tolerate both injustice *and* inaction?"

Hallet saw it at once. "You wanted to kill these agents for more than simple revenge. You wanted to *start* a war."

"Terrorists kill my grandson. They blow up an airplane full of college kids. Our government does nothing about it. So I saw an opportunity to get both sides off the dime. We start eliminating Arab agents, and we force their leaders to take stronger actions against us. Our side would have to respond, at last, and the final confrontation would begin. For once, public opinion would demand that we fight until we've won. More lives would be lost, people would suffer as I have. But, eventually, we'd defeat terrorism once and for all."

"Except you have no idea what you've really done," Hallet said sorrowfully.

"I know you were collaborating with the enemy. They were using you to help their cause."

"Those agents worked for me," Hallet said. "They were fighting the very terrorism you despise."

"I understand you're well connected in Washington," Kellaigh said. "So they'll believe all the nonsense you'll tell them. You can probably even explain why you reserved airline seats to Damascus in a phony name. Leaving tomorrow, I believe."

"True?" McCaskey asked in a gulp.

"I'm not sure," Hallet said.

"You don't know all you think you do about our devious Doctor Hallet," Kellaigh said to her. "You don't know that the agents he claims to control are part of a terrorist organization called Al-Ahzab."

"You've gone mad," Hallet said. "And in your madness, you've destroyed a plan that could have saved others from suffering your grandson's fate."

"How can you say that so brazenly when I know every detail about you and Al-Ahzab?"

"Through my communications from the Institute," Hallet said. "Who was it, anyway?"

"Don't you know? It was you yourself. You caused us to become suspicious. You came into the Institute drunk and ranting about two students who were hanged in Iraq. You cried that they were doing the Institute's true business—spying."

Hallet slumped back in his chair and tried to shield his eyes from McCaskey's. She breathed his name softly, as if ashamed.

"Bryce Vreeland reported that to me, as he should," Kellaigh continued. "And we decided it would be prudent to monitor everything you did and had done. We were able to, you see, because Vreeland had planted a virus in our computer system long before you came here. I was concerned even then that our work might be put to other than scholarly and peaceful uses. A real irony, because what I wanted to protect us from was exactly what we were destined to do. The point is, Philip, when you went on line, we did also. And those lines led us directly to your agents and to Al-Ahzab."

"So it was Vreeland," Hallet said, thinking that at least Isabel Ortega wasn't part of the disaster.

"Bryce didn't understand the complexities, of course, and I never told him. He was just there to intercept the raw data. As for your codes, Harry and I broke them easily. We found out who your agents were and where they operated. We even learned that you, as their leader, were code-named Sandman."

"Just one tragic mistake." Hallet knew it was finally time to end it. With McCaskey poised to make her move, there was nothing left to salvage.

"Al-Ahzab never existed," Hallet said. "I created it."

Kellaigh appeared to freeze in mid-breath, his jaws trembling. "What are you saying?"

"That Al-Ahzab was a ruse," Hallet said. "A deep-cover operation to penetrate the major terrorist groups in the Middle East, a way to identify their leaders and their overseas agents, and to learn what targets they planned to attack before the bombs went off. Most important, we hoped it would provide the intelligence to locate and free our hostages."

"Al-Ahzab was a cover?" McCaskey said, her look as fierce as Kellaigh's was frightened.

"I knew that the concept of an Al-Ahzab would be irresistible to the terrorist leadership we most want to stop, especially when it included the notion that their Muslim brothers and fellow Maoists in the States would rise up against the great American Satan from inside its borders.

"But Al-Ahzab *never* existed. No one knew that except me and the one person in Washington powerful enough to let me run it. Even the Arab agents you say I collaborated with thought that Al-Ahzab was real, and they were as committed as I was supposed to be in stopping it. I had to deceive them and"— Hallet turned to McCaskey—"everyone else. Only now, it's too late to try."

"But the weapons and drugs smuggled into O'Hare?" Kellaigh

asked, grasping at whatever straws he could to prevent his collapse.

"They were consigned by our defense intelligence people in West Germany," Hallet said. "It was the best bait I could think of to find out who'd blown our operation. I'm just sorry it was you."

"An illusion," Kellaigh realized at last. "A sleight of hand worked by you alone."

"An illusion I had to protect at all costs," Hallet said. "Because it was a plan that should have succeeded."

Kellaigh scanned the high stacks of books in his library, as if they held an answer. As he opened the center drawer of his desk, McCaskey's face tightened and she instinctively reached inside her purse.

"I'm not reaching for a gun," Kellaigh said as he retrieved a small gold frame that Hallet guessed held the photo of a seven-year-old boy. "If I had one, I'd only use it on myself. But I expect the FBI will handle my destruction for me."

Hallet's eyes were downcast as he turned to McCaskey. "He's all yours now."

McCaskey knew nothing would be gained by compromising Hallet's scheme any further, and that it would be pointless to embarrass what she assumed to be the White House just to try to make a very iffy case. Hell, there'd be others. If she could stomach them.

"We have nothing to charge you with," she announced to a startled Jason Kellaigh. "I can't prove you were behind the killings when the killers themselves are dead. And there's no way to link you to anything that the Bureau or Doctor Hallet would want made public."

"You think that matters? You think I'm getting off scot-free?" Kellaigh asked.

"You're in bed with the mob, Mister Kellaigh," McCaskey said. "I'm not sure exactly how yet, or with whom. But I promise you this, I won't quit without finding out."

"It happened so easily," Kellaigh said, as if recalling a wistful time. "We shared a few ventures, some investments. Now, we end up sharing death."

Kellaigh buried his face in his hands and began to weep softly. Hallet took McCaskey's arm, signaled her to leave. She followed him silently out of the study, saw that surprise had replaced sadness in his eyes.

"I thought you'd want the pleasure of making an arrest," Hallet said as they made their way down the corridor.

"If you'd trusted me sooner, maybe we could have saved Sandman," McCaskey said. "All I have now is protecting his master the best way I can."

"Sound politics."

"No," she said, seeing that Hallet's mind was still racing. "It's just caring about you, and knowing when it's finally over."

"Sandman could still work," Hallet thought aloud. "The leaks here are sealed. So, maybe, out of London . . . ?"

McCaskey stopped in her tracks, squared herself to face him. "All the betrayal, all this death, for something that never existed."

"It did for me," Hallet said.

"Good God, Philip. How many people are you? How many hearts do you have?"

Hallet looked over the broad expanse of the Kellaigh estate and surveyed the ancient oaks and willows and sycamores. As McCaskey took his hand, he felt exhausted, drained, defeated.

They were halfway to their car when the black sedan lumbered up the herringbone stonework of Jason Kellaigh's drive. Neither of them was surprised when Jack Corrigan climbed out and stood before them with legs spread and arms akimbo.

"Should've known you'd beat me here," Corrigan said. "Or are you gonna tell me you've saved me a piece of Jason Kellaigh?"

"It's over, Jack. Let it go," McCaskey said.

"I figured Kellaigh was behind this when we made Harry Dawson as his majordomo," Corrigan said. "See, your federal hotshots may have cleaned up the bodies, but I managed to pick up their pistols. Identifying Usher was a cinch from his military records. But Harry had no prints on the big machine. I only found out who he was when Interpol came through."

"But you still don't know who took Harry and Usher down," Hallet said. "Who had the rifle."

"One of the reasons I'm here," Corrigan replied. "A few questions without regard to jurisdiction. Only the Bureau's beaten me to it."

McCaskey stepped up to Corrigan as his voice fell off. "We beat you to nothing, Jack."

"You mean no charges, or no proof?" When McCaskey failed to answer, Corrigan tilted his head back, rolled his eyes skyward. "So the great Jason Kellaigh walks away clean."

"Far from it," Hallet said. He looked over his shoulder at the giant house, and the giant pain that filled it. "Jason Kellaigh is serving his sentence already."

As McCaskey and Corrigan stood by silently, Hallet climbed behind the wheel of his car, found the pack of cigarettes crumpled on the dashboard. He lighted one, stared at it curiously as a thin trail of smoke passed through his lips, then flicked it aimlessly onto Kellaigh's perfectly groomed lawn.

"Why don't you drive back with me?" Corrigan asked. "We can talk it out. Off the record like always."

"No, thanks, Jack," McCaskey said sadly. "I'd better be with Hallet."

"You sure, kiddo?"

"I always go home with the guy what brung me."

"He doesn't have what you need," Corrigan said.

"But he needs *me*, Jack," McCaskey said. "You and me, we're the types who respond to that most."

"You're taking a big chance."

"As Frank Thorne used to say—everything in life is six-to-five against."

291

"Better odds than any of this ever happening," Corrigan said. "Just like that."

"Will I ever know why it did?"

"You'd better hope not, Jack. It would scare you to death."

Corrigan watched her slip inside the car and slide close to the slumping Doctor Philip Hallet. If anyone needed all that McCaskey could offer, he thought, Hallet was the man who did.

He watched silently as they pulled away, then saw McCaskey turn and look back at him with uncertain, hopeful eyes. Corrigan raised his right hand, touched his index finger to his lips in a signal that Hallet, in his mirror, saw for all it was.

A farewell.

A benediction.

A kiss.

Acknowledgments

The author wishes to express his gratitude to the University of Michigan, Ann Arbor, and the Michigan Journalism Fellows, whose generosity contributed greatly to the writing of this book.

R.M.